**Ever[y...]**

"I know whe[...] [...] for a treat."

—Long and Short Reviews

"Carolyn Brown is a master storyteller who never fails to entertain. Her stories make me smile, they make me laugh, and sometimes I cry a few tears."

—Night Owl Reviews

"The most difficult thing about reading a Brown book is putting it down."

—Fresh Fiction

"Hilarious… A high-spirited, romantic page-turner."

—Kirkus Reviews

"Brown's writing holds you spellbound."

—Thoughts in Progress

"If you love small town stories with wonderful characters and witty dialogue… Carolyn Brown will thrill you!"

—The Reading Cafe

"Delightfully fresh and unique… Brown's writing has such a down-home country feel that you will feel like you are right in the heart of Texas."

—Book Reviews and More by Kathy

"Carolyn Brown has magic at her fingertips."

—Wendy's Minding Spot

# Find a Lucky Cowboy of Your Own!

## LUCKY IN LOVE

"Exciting romance…full of wit, wisdom, and love."
　　　　　　　　　　　　　　*—The Romance Studio*

"Delightful humor and sassy dialogue make this true-to-life love story enchanting."
　　　　　　　　　　　　　　*—The Long and Short of It*

"Wickedly funny…lively romance destined to capture your heart."
　　　　　　　　　　　　　　*—Romance Reviews Today*

One Lucky Cowboy
"This is not your mother's Western romance!"
　　　　　　　　　　　　　　*—RT Book Reviews*, 4 stars

"Sheer fun…pure romance."
　　　　　　　　　　　　　　*—Romance Reader at Heart*

"Carolyn Brown takes her audience by storm… I was mesmerized."
　　　　　　　　　　　　　　*—The Romance Studio*

"Wonderful characters, seamless writing, and a firecracker romance has Carolyn Brown at the top of her game."
　　　　　　　　　　　　　　*—Wendy's Minding Spot*

"Compelling from page one... Ms. Brown delivers a great story with scorching passion."

—*The Long and Short of It*

"The Luckadeau men are H-O-T!"

—*Cheryl's Book Nook*

## GETTING LUCKY

"A five-star comfort read! Brown's novel will warm your heart."

—*Love Romance Passion*

"Carolyn Brown has magic at her fingertips."

—*Wendy's Minding Spot*

"Solid romance full of great characters with loads of chemistry...quirky and entertaining."

—*The Romance Studio*

"Delightful... Smart dialogue, strong characters, and red-hot passion."

—*Affaire de Coeur*

"Don't miss these witty, human, and lovable characters."

—*The Long and Short of It*

# Also by Carolyn Brown

# TALK COWBOY *to me*

## CAROLYN BROWN

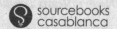

sourcebooks
casablanca

Published by Sourcebooks Casablanca, an imprint of Sourcebooks, Inc.
P.O. Box 4410, Naperville, Illinois 60567-4410
(630) 961-3900
Fax: (630) 961-2168
www.sourcebooks.com

Printed and bound in Canada.
MBP 10 9 8 7 6 5 4 3 2 1

*To Grace Burrowes.*

*Thanks for all the encouragement
and for the friendship!*

# Chapter 1

THE GLEAM IN THE OLD COWBOY'S BLUE EYES AND THE way he rubbed his chin were Adele's first clues that he definitely had something up the sleeve of his faded, old work shirt. He glanced first at her and then over at Remington Luckadeau.

She bit back a groan. The good old boys' club was about to rear its head. They'd argue that ranching took brawn and muscle and that a woman couldn't run the Double Deuce all alone, that women were respected in the ranching business these days, but when it came right down to it, he would feel better selling to a man.

No, sir!

She didn't hold out any hope that the old toot would sell the ranch to her.

"Well, now." Walter Jones gave his freshly shaven chin one more rub. "I expect we've got us one of them dilemma things, don't we?"

That sly smile on Remington's face said he already knew she would be going home empty-handed. With that mop of blond hair that kissed his shirt collar, those steel-blue eyes, and his chiseled face and wide shoulders—Lord have mercy—any woman would roll over and play dead to give him what he wanted.

But not Adele.

She wanted the Double Deuce, and she'd do whatever it took to get it so she could have a place to raise her daughters. Remington Luckadeau could spit on his knuckles and get ready for a fierce battle.

The Double Deuce Ranch was absolutely perfect in every aspect. The two-storied, four-bedroom house couldn't have been better laid out for Adele and her two daughters, Jett and Bella. The acreage was big enough to make a living but small enough that she could manage it on her own, for the most part. And it was close to her family—the O'Donnells over around Ringgold, Texas.

"You both want the ranch, but I can only sell to one of you. I talked to my lady friend, Vivien, about it. I talked to God about it before I went to sleep, and I talked to my old cow dog, Boss, about it this mornin' before y'all got here."

"And?" Adele asked.

"And not a one of them was a bit of help, so I don't know which one of you to sell this place to any more than I did yesterday, after you'd both come and looked over the place and left me to think about it."

Adele had known there was another person interested in the ranch. Walter had been up-front about that, saying he'd talked with Remington Luckadeau that morning and he was ready to meet Walter's asking price.

"We can't both buy it, so I guess you'll have to make a decision," Adele said.

Remington nodded.

———◈———

Remington slid down in the kitchen chair so he could study the red-haired woman sitting in front of him. The hard Texas sunlight flowing through the kitchen window brought out every cute, little freckle sprinkled across Adele's nose. Faded jeans, a chambray shirt worn open over a bright-yellow tank top, and cowboy boots worn at the heels said she was a no-nonsense rancher.

Those two feisty girls out there on the porch with his two nephews were dressed pretty much the same way as their mother. Any other time, he might have tipped his hat and given her the option to buy the Double Deuce, but not today. The ranch was the perfect size for what he had in his bank account. The house would be just right for him and his two nephews, Leo and Nick, the boys he'd inherited when his brother and sister-in-law were killed in a car accident several months ago. And besides, it wasn't far from his Luckadeau relatives in Ringgold and Saint Jo, Texas.

So today, Adele O'Donnell was going to have to walk away disappointed. Too bad, because he'd always been attracted to redheads, and he'd have loved to see how she felt in his arms on the dance floor of the nearest honky-tonk.

"So." Walter cleared his throat. "I've come to a decision."

Remy straightened up in his chair.

"The Luckadeaus are my friends, but so are the O'Donnells. So I can't sell this to either of you on the basis of friendship. Vivien and I have planned a month-long cruise, and we are leaving in one week. We fly out of Dallas on the last day of May and get back home on the last day of June."

"I'll beat your asking price," Remy said quickly.

"It's not got to do with money. Here's what I am willin' to do, though. You both move in here on the morning that me and Vivien leave. Y'all take care of this ranch for me for a month. When I get back, whichever one of you is still here can have it. If you both still want it, we'll draw straws or play poker for it. If you decide you can't work together or that the ranch ain't what you want, you can call Chet to come take over for you. His number is on the front of the refrigerator. Only rule I've got is that you'd best take good care of Boss. He's been a good cow dog, and he likes leftovers from the table, so cook a little extra at each meal. He's not real picky. He'll eat most anything a human will, but he doesn't like pizza. And you have to take real good care of Jerry Lee."

"Who is Jerry Lee?" Adele asked.

"He's my rooster. Pretty little thing, but he never has learned to crow in the morning. He's a late riser, so he crows either in the middle of the day or about dinner-time. I named him Jerry Lee because he's got swagger and he sings real pretty like Jerry Lee Lewis."

"I'll take good care of your dog and your rooster," Adele said, shooting a defiant look right at Remy.

"So will I." Remy nodded coolly. "What about the one who doesn't win the luck of the draw?"

"Then that one gets a decent paycheck," Walter said.

"I don't need to think about it," Adele said quickly. "I'm in."

Remy nodded. "I don't have to think about it either."

Walter pushed back his chair and stood. "Good, then I'll look for you both to be here a week from today. You've seen the place. There'll be hay to cut and haul, fields to plow, and planting to do, as well as the every-day chores with feeding and taking care of the cattle and ranch. I've made a list of what I want done before I get back, and I'll leave it stuck to the refrigerator door."

"I'm not afraid of hard work," Adele said. "One question, though. How does Boss feel about cats?"

"Strange as it seems, he loves them. My wife, God rest her soul"—Walter looked up at the ceiling—"used to have an old barn cat that had kittens real often. Boss thought he was their grandpa."

"Then you don't mind if we bring our cat?" she asked.

"Not a bit. You got a problem with that, Remy?" Walter asked.

Remy shook his head.

"Thank you," Adele said softly.

*Crap!* Remy didn't hate cats, and thank God the boys weren't allergic to them, but that soft, sweet, southern voice could easily distract him from his mission. Remy would have to keep on his toes every day for the entire month of June, and that wouldn't be easy. For years, every woman had been a potential notch on his bedpost. Six months ago, Remy had been the resident bad boy of the Texas Panhandle. He'd spent his weekends in local bars, dancing and sweet-talking the pretty girls into his bed. Then his whole life turned around when his two nephews were tossed into his life. Since he'd started taking care of them, dating had slowed down. Now, he'd be forced to live with a woman he was clearly attracted to.

Walter started toward the door. The meeting was over. "Just bring your personal things. When I sell this place, it goes lock, stock, and barrel—furniture, equipment, everything but my own keepsakes," he said. "Vivien and I are leaving at nine o'clock. If one of y'all ain't here, then the other one will automatically get the place."

Adele pushed her chair back, and in one fluid motion,

she was on her feet. He'd figured she was tall when he sat down across from her and his long legs almost touched hers under the table. But when she stood up, he got the full effect of the way her hips curved out from her small waist, and for a split second, he could feel her in his arms.

Remy shook the image from his head. He had a long, hot month ahead of him, and he needed to think of Adele as an adversary, not a potential date.

"Do we move?" Nick asked when Remy stepped out onto the porch.

"We are moving onto the ranch to take care of it for Mr. Jones for a month. If we do a good job, he might sell to us in time for the Fourth of July party we're planning." Remy told his fourteen-year-old nephew.

"Mama?" asked the smaller of the two girls that Adele had brought along with her.

"Same thing here, girls. We'll be moving here in one week to live for a month. Then Mr. Jones will decide which of us gets to buy the ranch," Adele answered.

"You"—the girl pointed at Leo and wiggled her head like a bobblehead doll—"are going down. You don't know jack squat about a ranch, so you might as well give up before you even start."

"Jett!" Adele chided.

"Well, it's the truth," Jett said. "He don't even want to live on a ranch. He's a city boy who don't even know who Billy Currington is. He'd hate living on this ranch."

"Just because you lived on a ranch don't mean you're that smart," Nick shot back. "Uncle Remy can teach me everything about ranching in one afternoon. I'm a fast learner."

"Me, too." Leo combed his carrot-red hair with his fingertips and tipped up his chin three notches.

"Okay, boys. It's one thing to say something; it's another to do it. Let's get on home and get our things in order so we'll be ready to move next week. There's only four bedrooms, so you'll have to share."

Leo, who had already left the porch, kicked at the dirt. "Uncle Remy, Nick gripes if I even leave a wrinkle in the bed. He's so neat that he shoulda been a girl." He sighed.

"No!" Nick raised his voice. "Leo never picks up anything and—"

"Enough," Remy said. "Into the truck. We've got a lot to do and a short time to get it done."

Leo crawled into the big, black, dual-cab truck. Just before he slammed the door, he caught Jett's eye and stuck out his tongue.

"Young man, you're going to have to live in the same house and work with those girls," Remy said sternly.

Leo rolled his eyes upward. "They are so bossy. Living in the country isn't going to be easy, but living around those two prissy girls…" He sighed. "Do we really have to do this, Uncle Remy?"

"We'll come out stronger men," he said.

A picture of Adele's full, kissable lips flashed through his mind. *Prissy* wasn't a word he'd use to describe any of the O'Donnell women.

Nick groaned. "If we live through it."

"We are Luckadeau men. We'll take the bull by the horns, look him right in the eye, and dare him to charge at us." Even as the words came out, Remy wondered if he was talking to his nephews or himself.

"I'd rather fight a bull," Leo grumbled. "And they ain't bulls. They're girls, and we're Luckadeaus."

"Daddy used to tell us that when a Luckadeau sets his mind, it's set forever," Nick said.

"Your daddy was right." Remy nodded.

Moving the boys from their house in the middle of Denton, Texas, to a ranch would be tough on them, but Remy could not live in town. He'd been fortunate enough to sell his brother's house for enough to pay off the existing mortgage and put a little into savings for the boys' college funds.

Remy had worked for the past fifteen years on a ranch out in the Texas Panhandle. He'd started as a hired hand and worked his way up to foreman. Today, he had enough money in his bank account to buy the Double Deuce, and it was the perfect place for the boys to have a brand-new start. It damn sure wouldn't be easy to live in the same house with a woman like Adele and not flirt, but it was doable with the ranch as a prize at the end of the road.

"So you boys going to help me make those women see that they don't really want our ranch? Or are we going to let them win?" Remy asked.

"Ain't no way I'm going to back down from them two," Nick declared.

Leo chimed right in. "Me either."

---

"Let's look at another ranch. I don't want to live in the same house with those two obnoxious boys," Bella said as they drove away from the Double Deuce.

Adele smiled. "You must really not like those boys to be pulling out your four-dollar words."

"That tells you how much, Mama," Bella said.

"We don't have time to train them," Jett added.

Adele didn't think they'd have to do much training. Not with a cowboy like Remy Luckadeau for an uncle. That man was comfortable in his skin, and there wasn't a doubt in her mind that he'd know the business every bit as well as she did. In any other circumstance, there could be chemistry between them. He was exactly what she'd always been attracted to, with his blond hair, blue eyes, and cowboy swagger, but then he was also what she'd been running away from when she'd married Isaac Levy.

*You see how that turned out*, the smart-ass voice in her head said.

Yes, she did see how it turned out. Isaac was the only son of a family who had dealt in diamonds right in the middle of Dallas, Texas, for more than fifty years. When they'd married, he'd moved Adele into his penthouse apartment, and she'd lived the life she'd thought she wanted.

Right up until Bella was born two years after the wedding. And then she'd started to yearn for her country roots. A child needed fresh air and sunshine, not parties and nannies. Isaac had loved her enough to buy a two-hundred-acre ranch between McKinney and Blue Ridge. The commute wasn't bad because he had a driver, but after Jett was born, he spent more and more weeknights at the penthouse.

"Why do we have to move from our ranch anyway?" Jett folded her small arms over her chest.

"The same reason we had to change our last name to O'Donnell," Bella answered. "Father has a new wife and a son, and we don't matter anymore."

Her daughter's tone created a lump in Adele's throat that she couldn't swallow down. Tears welled in her eyes, but she kept them at bay. Bella had put it into the simplest language possible, but the story was far more complex than that.

"Your father will come to his senses someday," she said softly.

"But it might be too late," Bella declared. "He's mean, making us move off the ranch."

It wasn't the time or the place to tell the girls that part of the marriage problems had been her fault. Isaac thought he was getting a socialite who loved the fast lane, and he never would have asked her to marry him if he'd realized she wasn't ready to break all ties with her country roots.

"We are going to love this new ranch so much that we'll never look back at the old one. Even though they don't have any ranching experience, I just wonder if you two are big and mean enough to show those two boys that nobody can outwork three tough O'Donnell women."

Jett unfolded her arms, leaned up from the backseat of the bright-red, dual-cab truck, and patted her mother on the shoulder. "They ain't got a chance in hell."

"Jett!" Bella scolded.

"Well, Uncle Cash says that, and nobody fusses at him. Besides, I believe it. We're tough and mean, and we can out-ranch any old boy in the state of Texas," Jett said.

"We've got a week to pack all our things, put them in storage, and load up the truck with just what we need for a month," Adele said as she turned east toward Gainesville.

Adele's cell phone rang. She saw a picture of her sister, Cassie, smiling at her. She answered it on the fourth ring and hit the Speaker button.

"We have not bought the ranch yet," she said and went on to tell her sister the deal that Walter had come up with.

Cassie giggled the whole way through the story.

"What's so funny about that?" Adele asked.

"Those boys don't stand a chance. Not any one of them—the grown one or the two kids," Cassie said. "I'll put my money on my sister and my nieces any day of the week."

"Yes!" Bella and Jett squealed at the same time.

"Thank you, Aunt Cassie. We won't let you down," Jett said.

"What are you doing today?" Adele asked her sister.

"Haulin' hay, but I'd rather be doing something else in the hayloft with my boyfriend," Cassie said.

"Cassandra Grace O'Donnell!" Adele raised her voice.

"Don't you double name me. Only Mama gets to do that, and I was talking about kissing my boyfriend. He's really good at kissing." Cassie laughed.

"I miss y'all," Adele said wistfully. "If I get to buy this ranch, I'm having a big Fourth of July party to celebrate. Y'all had better be there."

"Wild horses couldn't keep me away. Is this new cowboy sexy? Maybe I'll visit for a weekend between now and then," Cassie said.

"No!" The girls' loud voices bounced around in the truck cab.

"Why? Don't you want to see me?" Cassie asked.

"We love you," Bella said. "But we don't want Remy Luckadeau in the family at all, and if he sees you, then he'll fall in love with you. Besides, we like Clinton just fine. Go kiss on him in the hayloft, and stay away until the ranch belongs to us."

"If you promise to work hard and show Mr. Jones that you are the right people to sell his ranch to, then I'll stay away until you've run those old boys off your land. But, girls, Clinton and I broke up a while ago," Cassie said seriously. "The new man in my life is Dusty Dillard. We've only been on two dates, but I like him a lot."

"Is he as pretty as Clinton?" Bella asked.

"No, but he's a lot nicer," Cassie said.

"I thought Clinton was nice, and I like his name better than Dusty," Jett said.

"Wait until you meet him. Are you taking Blanche?" Cassie asked.

"Of course," Jett answered quickly. "We wouldn't leave her behind. Mama, please tell me that man didn't say we couldn't bring Blanche."

"I asked about bringing a cat and he said it was fine," Adele said.

Cassie laughed again. "The old hussy would die if you left her. Besides, isn't she about ready to pop out another litter in the next couple of weeks?"

"Yes, she is," Bella said. "And I hope both of them boys hate cats."

"And you, Sister Adele? How do you feel about living with a cowboy?"

"I'm not living with him. I'm sharing a house with him for a month. And don't call me Sister Adele. I'm not a nun," Adele said curtly.

"These past two years you have been. Promise you'll call me often," she said. "Got to go. The hay wagon is here, and it's time to stack bales."

Adele hit the End button, and the screen on the phone went dark. She caught a movement in her peripheral vision and glanced over to see two little boys glaring at her from the windows of a black truck. A whole month with those two smart-ass kids just might make her move all the way to Wyoming or Montana.

She looked in the rearview mirror, and there was Jett, giving the boys the old stink eye. In seconds, they sped on past her, whipped over in front of her truck, and moved on ahead pretty quickly. No doubt about it—this was going to be a long month!

# Chapter 2

ON THE LAST DAY OF MAY, ADELE'S HOUSE WAS EMPTY OF everything but memories. The room with the lilac walls had been the nursery when she'd moved there. Bella had been less than a year old, and with all the pastel colors and lace, it had been a room for a princess. Through the years, it had been transformed from a room with a Cinderella theme to one for a cowgirl. What would it be next? A study or an office?

Across the hall, Jett's room with the pale blue walls was meant for a boy. The ultrasound had said Adele was carrying a son, and Isaac had been so happy. The new nursery had been painted blue and would definitely not have a cowboy theme. No, sir! He was going to grow up to walk in his father's boots and inherit the diamond business. His name would be Jett Levy, after Isaac's grandfather who started the business. Even though the baby was a girl, they'd still named her Jett like they'd planned. Isaac said she could choose whatever middle name she wanted for the baby, so she'd given her the middle name Cassandra, after her sister.

Jett had eyes as blue as the walls. With just a few lacy items here and there, the nursery had become one for a girl. Isaac was so disappointed that he didn't come home for a month after she was born, didn't hold her until she was three months old. Looking back, Adele figured that was when her marriage had really started to fall apart.

"Close one door, open another," Adele whispered as she laid the keys on the kitchen counter, straightened her back, and left with only one stray tear inching its way down her cheek.

Bella rode in the front of the truck with Adele. Jett and the cat carrier with the big, yellow-and-white cat, Blanche, were in the backseat. The sun peeked over the horizon in her rearview mirror, and the gauge inside the truck said it was already warmer than eighty degrees—it was going to be a hot one. Adele was happy it wasn't raining because the bed of the truck was filled with suitcases and boxes.

"How far is it, Mama?" Jett asked.

"Same distance as it was last week."

Bella sighed and did one of her famous eye rolls. "It's ninety-eight miles to the ranch, which means Mama can make it in about an hour and a half if you don't have to stop to go to the bathroom every ten minutes."

"That's right," Adele answered. "And before you ask, if we get to buy the ranch, you will go to school in Nocona, which is a little bigger than the one you've been going to, but we're O'Donnells, and we'll adjust."

"I wish we'd gone to a new school back when Father stopped coming around," Jett said.

"Why?" Adele whipped around a slow-moving vehicle and kicked up the speed to seventy-five miles an hour.

"All the kids wanted to know why we changed our names to O'Donnell, and besides, it took up more room on our school papers than plain old Levy," Jett said. "But the people in Nocona won't know that I was ever anything but an O'Donnell, so I don't have to explain jack shit."

"Jett!" Bella scolded.

"Uncle Cash says that, and no one fusses at him." Jett kicked the back of her sister's seat.

"Stop it," Bella said, her voice raised.

"What? Talking?" Jett asked.

"No, kicking my seat. It makes the words on the page wiggle, and it's annoying me," Bella said through clenched teeth.

"Well, you always get to ride in the front seat."

Bella inhaled deeply. "If you'd grow some in size rather than in attitude, you could sit in the front seat."

"Save your energy for ranching instead of using it for arguments," Adele said. "And, Jett, you do not repeat Uncle Cash. Do you want to get in trouble in front of those boys who are going to share the house with us?"

"Hell—I mean, *heck* no!" Jett answered.

"Then think about your words before you spit them out," Adele said.

"Yes, ma'am. So we'll be there by breakfast time?" Jett asked.

"We will. I hope we have breakfast cooked by the time those cowboys arrive, so we show them up." Adele smiled.

"Only one of them is a cowboy," Bella said. "Those two boys are barely even wannabe cowboys. They didn't even want to live on that ranch, and they were afraid of Boss. I showed them he was friendly, but they wouldn't even pet him."

"They'll come around in a month," Adele said, but the words didn't carry much conviction. Hopefully those boys would be the very reason that Remy Luckadeau threw up his hands and gave up the fight for the ranch.

Blanche settled down and went to sleep in her carrier. Jett clamped on her earphones and sang the words she knew to "The House That Built Me," one of Miranda Lambert's older songs. Bella went back to reading, leaving Adele to her own thoughts as she drove west.

The house that built Adele was sitting smack in the middle of a combination cotton farm and cattle ranch out in western Texas. She should have known that a woman didn't run from her roots, but she'd given it a try. She'd left behind her boots, her jeans, and everything that faintly smelled of ranching when she'd gone to college. When she'd met and fallen in love with Isaac, a city boy with pretty brown eyes and enough confidence to put any swaggering cowboy to shame, she'd thought she'd done the right thing for sure.

When he proposed, she hadn't hesitated for a second before she'd said yes. His father had insisted on a prenup, and she'd signed it without even reading it. After all, they were going to be married forever. She loved Isaac. He loved her. The prenup would grow yellow and curl up on the edges in a safe because it would never come into play.

But it did, while the pages were still very white and legible. And it said that everything in Isaac's name was his and whatever was in her name was hers. That meant all she had was the truck they were riding in and the bank account that she'd squirreled money away in the past eleven years. It had started off as a means to keep her ranching money separate from their joint account, so she could see how well she did each year, and then it grew and grew until she had enough to buy her own place.

If they could make the Double Deuce work as well as

the ranch Isaac had sold out from under her, she would be able to put all the child support he was required to send into college funds for the girls.

She drove through Gainesville, stopped at several red lights, and was on the other side of Lindsay before she realized how much time had lapsed. Bella was still reading. Jett was singing along to an old Wynonna Judd song. That child loved country music; it didn't matter what era it came from.

How could Isaac turn his back on his daughters like he had? Adele relived the moment two years ago when the judge asked if there was opposition to her taking back her maiden name and giving it to her two daughters.

At first, she'd been stunned beyond words. Then, she'd been so angry that she'd wanted to pull the pistol from the side pocket of her purse and leave Isaac bleeding on the courtroom floor. Before she could answer, the judge told her that Isaac was giving her sole custody and he was not asking for any visitation rights. And that he would give her the child support in a lump sum, so he didn't have to be affiliated in any way with her or the children again.

"You don't even want to see them?" she'd asked incredulously.

"I do not," he'd said.

"But they're your daughters." Adele had raised her voice and gotten a dirty look from the judge.

"They're your children now," Isaac said.

Adele looked up at the judge. "I will take the lump sum child support and will put it into a trust fund for each of them to use for their college education. I will raise these kids on my own."

A deer crossed the road in front of her and jerked her back to the present. She braked hard to keep from hitting it, and Bella's book went flying toward the dashboard. Jett squealed, and the cat whined from the backseat.

Adele gasped. "That was close."

"What was it?" Jett looked around.

"A big old buck. Must've had twelve points," Adele answered.

"If we'd have hit it, could we have claimed it for food?" Jett laid her earphones to the side.

"I don't think so." Adele's voice was still shaky. "We're only about fifteen minutes from the Double Deuce. Y'all getting hungry?"

Too many memories. Too much excitement. Her stomach was quivering, and it didn't have a thing to do with hunger.

"Star-ving." Jett said, emphasizing each syllable.

"Then let's get to our new home and make breakfast."

She wanted to kick something when she saw Remy's black truck already parked outside the fence. She pulled in beside it and got a little comfort from the fact that the back was still filled with boxes and suitcases, just like hers.

Walter waved from the porch swing after she got out of the truck. "Glad to see you made it. Vivien is waiting for me to pick her up for breakfast. I've told Boss and Jerry Lee good-bye, and the boys are in the house."

As he nodded toward the cat carrier, Walter eased out of the swing, crossed the porch, and headed toward his truck. "And I talked to Boss. He said he'll be glad to have some cats around the place."

Adele smiled. "Thank you for that."

Remy swung open the door. "The boys and I have breakfast ready to go on the table, so y'all come right on in here and we'll eat before we unload and get things put away. Walter has already taken care of morning chores, so we have until evening to settle in and get things organized. What's that?" He pointed at the cat carrier in Adele's hands.

"Meet Blanche. She's an inside cat. I hope none of you are allergic to cats," Adele said.

Jett pushed ahead of her mother into the house. "Or afraid of them, like you are dogs."

"I'm not afraid of dogs," Leo protested from behind Remy.

"You were afraid of Boss last week. And believe me, if Blanche gets the notion you're afraid of her, then she'll wait until you're asleep and scratch your eyes out." Jett eased around the boy without touching him.

"Jett Cassandra O'Donnell," Adele scolded.

"Looks like we've all got some adjusting to do." The look on his face said he wasn't real happy about sharing the house with a cat. "So that thing will live in the house?" Remy asked.

"Until her kittens are about six weeks old, and then she'll be adapted well enough that I can move her to the barn. But you won't be around then, so you don't have to worry about that," Adele answered.

"Oh, darlin', I will be here long after the dust has settled behind your truck," Remy said with a forced smile. "But that's four weeks away. Right now, let's think about breakfast. I made sausage gravy and biscuits. Nick is scrambling eggs and making sure the blueberry muffins don't burn." He reached out and took the cat carrier from Adele. "I think Blanche will be happy here. There's lots of nooks for her to prowl around. Shall we turn her loose?"

Hot, little shivers danced down Adele's spine when Remy's hands touched hers in the transfer of the cat carrier. *Damn it to hell on a silver poker!* This was no time for hormones to come into play even if it had been two long years since she'd had a man in her bed. Yes, he was handsome and yes, he had sexy eyes and a swagger that would make a holy woman throw away her habit, but this was business, not pleasure, and Adele would damn sure not mix the two.

"Take her to my room and let her get used to that first," Jett said.

"Don't know which room is going to be yours yet," Remy said. "How about we take her to the living room? We can shut the door, and after breakfast, you can see if she's ready for the rest of the house."

Jett nodded. "She's going to have babies pretty soon."

Remy carried the carrier into the huge living room. "Why did you name her Blanche?"

"We didn't. Our neighbor did. He died, and his son was going to put Blanche to sleep so we took her in," Bella answered. "He named her after one of the ladies on that old television show *Golden Girls*. He said she was a hussy, just like the woman on the show."

---

Remy wanted to lick his finger and put a mark in the sky to score one for the guys for getting there early and having breakfast nearly ready. The girls would have to work hard to keep up with them, and by the end of June, they'd be glad to admit defeat.

He brushed past Adele, and sparks bounced around the room. The way his heart threw in that extra beat when his arm brushed hers, she could easily entice him into a situation where he'd be giving her the ranch at the end of the month. And that couldn't happen.

"Okay." He set the carrier down in the middle of the floor. "Do you want to open the door and tell her she's going to love it here?"

Jett gave him a dose of her best stink eye. "I don't know that she's going to love it, and I would never lie to Blanche. I'll let her out, and she can make up her own mind. After we eat, we'll see if she even likes this part of the house. And I bet your sausage gravy ain't as good as Mama's."

"Maybe not, but it's ready. Tomorrow your mama can make her version and we'll compare." Remy nodded. "Feisty one, isn't she?" he whispered as he walked past Adele, careful to keep space between them.

"Which one? Jett or Bella?"

"Both, I imagine," he said.

"No, not both. Jett is the sassy child. Bella is an old soul and has common sense way past her fourteen years," Adele answered.

"Uncle Remy, everything is on the table," Nick yelled from the kitchen.

"I guess that's the breakfast call." Remy didn't offer Adele his arm like he might have if the stakes weren't so high.

The boys were already seated on one side of the table, and the two girls pulled out chairs on the other side, leaving the two ends for Remy and Adele. He was grateful for the space between them. It would make mealtimes a lot easier if there wasn't even the possibility of their hands touching as food was passed or feeling her knee brushing his under the table.

"Since we did the cooking, then y'all have to say grace." Nick lifted his chin a notch as he challenged Bella.

"I'll do it." Jett bowed her head and started before everyone even had their eyes closed. "Father in heaven, we thank you for this food and hope these rotten boys have not poisoned it. If they did, then please let Blanche scratch their eyes out. We thank you for this house and this ranch that we will be buying, and I thank you for a mama who will fight to the death for what she thinks is right for her daughters. Amen."

"Amen," Remy said.

The next four weeks could easily last an eternity if the animosity between the two parties didn't let up.

"And we didn't poison the food, Jett; therefore, we would appreciate it tomorrow morning if you don't add arsenic to our breakfast," he said seriously.

"Good, because I'm real hungry and Blanche isn't in the mood to be mean today." Jett picked up the basket of hot biscuits, put two on her plate, and passed the basket to her sister.

"Your prayers could use some work." Adele took out a large scoop of fluffy, yellow eggs. "But we'll talk about that later. While we eat, I propose that we talk about the division of household chores for the month."

"I second that," Remy said. "I thought we'd each take care of our own rooms upstairs, with a Saturday evening room check of the kids' rooms. If they're spotless, then they can have their allowance for the week."

"Allowance?" Bella cocked her head to one side.

"You don't get an allowance?" Nick asked.

"Never needed one. Mama buys what we need."

He puffed out his chest. "Well, Leo and I have always gotten an allowance."

"Well," Jett piped up, "we don't get paid to keep our room clean. We do it because that's our responsibility, just like it's our job to keep the litter pan cleaned out and help with the house."

"Okay, whether the boys get an allowance is none of our business," Adele said. "We'll take turns cooking. Every other day, the kitchen belongs to us girls. We'll eat what is put on the table without groaning and keep up our other chores as well. I noticed that Walter has a nice garden fenced off right outside the yard, so I intend to keep that going. We'll eat from it as well as either freeze or can anything that is surplus."

"I don't know how to can food," Remy said.

"I'll take care of it on my days in the kitchen, so I won't be in your way." Adele smiled down the table at him. *Well, damn it!* Score one for the girls for knowing how to preserve food. That made them even before breakfast was even finished.

"So tomorrow is our day?" Bella asked. "Does that mean we need to go into Nocona to the grocery store?"

"It means that sometime this evening, after the boys are out of the kitchen, we will take stock of what's here and make a list to take to the store on Sunday afternoon after church," Adele answered. "Walter said we could use whatever is here, and I'm taking him at his word that it means food as well as towels and sheets. Which brings me to laundry duties."

"We don't have to wash their stinky old clothes do we?" Jett moaned.

"No, you do not!" Leo said sternly. "I wouldn't trust y'all to do my laundry."

"We'll each do our own, and that includes bedding and whatever we use in the bathroom," Adele said. "Y'all boys can handle your laundry however you please."

"Sounds fair enough. What about housecleaning, like dusting, vacuuming, and washing windows?" Remy split open two biscuits, laid them on his plate, and covered them with gravy.

"We usually clean on Saturday afternoon. We'll take it this Saturday and trade off each week. That way we'll both have two cleanings to do while we're all here," Adele said.

"You've got to be kiddin' me," Leo moaned again. "We always had a housekeeper who did that. I'm a boy. Boys don't clean and dust."

"Then I hope that Mr. Jones comes home the week after your turn and he can see that you don't deserve this ranch," Jett said.

"Nothing to it, guys. I'll give you a crash course. And remember, unless you want to get married real young, you'll do well to learn to take care of things for yourself." Remy winked at Nick.

"I'll learn to do anything to keep from getting married. Girls are bossy and mean," Leo declared.

Jett flashed a brilliant smile across the table. "And don't you forget it." She accentuated each word by poking her fork at him. "Mama, does Boss get his

breakfast on a plate like us? I think he'd like some biscuits and gravy."

"I bet Boss has a dinner bowl all his own on the back
porch. And I bet that Blanche would like some biscuits
and gravy, too," Adele answered.

Remy took a deep breath and wondered how in the
hell he was going to survive a whole month in the same
house with those four kids. No Saturday night excitement in a bar. No picking out just the right woman to
sweet-talk into going somewhere for the rest of the
night. No fun of the chase and the catch. Instead, he
had kids and a bullheaded, beautiful redhead who was
determined to run him off the ranch of his dreams.

# Chapter 3

THE FIRST LESSON A RANCHER LEARNS IS TO BE FLEXIBLE. The weather cannot be controlled, and rain can put an end to outside jobs. Adele awoke to hard rain hitting the windowpane in her new bedroom, a room that was so strange to her that she'd slept poorly. She slapped a pillow over her head and cussed her ex-husband for taking her old ranch away from her.

The alarm clock, not a foot from her head, buzzed loudly enough to wake Lucifer. She hit the Snooze button and slung her legs over the side of the bed. They would not be painting the picket fence around the yard that day. They would probably be cleaning the hay barn and the tack room, and the kids would all be underfoot, inside instead of out in the fresh air, and that did not bode well for four young'uns who were determined not to like each other.

She crossed the room and pulled the curtains back—gray skies without a single break. It wasn't a shower but a rain, and Lord knew how badly they needed it in Texas, but she still dreaded the day ahead. She tossed her nightshirt on the rocking chair in the corner, pulled up the covers on the bed on her way to the closet, and flipped through the hangers until she found a faded pair of jeans and a T-shirt that she could work in.

When she was dressed, she knocked on her girls' bedroom door to wake them and padded to the bathroom in her socks. One benefit of having to get up extra early to make breakfast was that the bathroom was always empty. She looked at the woman in the mirror. Not much had changed since that day almost two years ago when Isaac came in and said he wanted a divorce. Same red hair. A few more wrinkles around her eyes, but she attributed those to laughter she'd shared with her daughters. She was still near six feet tall and felt like a giant when in a room full of other women. Isaac had said in the beginning that she controlled a room when she walked into it. She wished for a little of that confidence she'd had back then, but Isaac had taken that with him when he'd married his mistress, a short, dark-haired woman with big, brown eyes and a baby-doll face.

"What's done is in the past. Think about today and the future," she said to the woman in the mirror.

Five minutes later, she'd made a stop by her bedroom for her boots and was on her way down the stairs. The aroma of freshly brewed coffee wafted through the kitchen and dining room, down the foyer, and straight to her nose. She hadn't noticed that the pot was one of those newfangled things that had a timer on it, but evidently Remy had set it up the night before. She'd have to remember that on her days for kitchen duty.

"Good mornin'," Remy drawled in a deep morning voice.

Her heart did a flip-flop in her chest, which she quickly attributed to him startling her. She'd grown up around cowboys every bit as good-looking as Remy Luckadeau, and none of them had sent shivers down her spine.

She gasped. "You scared me."

"I slept poorly, but then I usually do when I'm in a

new place, so I got up and started the coffee brewing before I went out to the corral and brought in the milk cow. She was more than willing to follow me into the barn and get out of that downpour. The fresh milk has been strained and is in jars in the fridge already. Don't look like we'll be painting fences today, does it?" He poured a cup of coffee, handed it to her, and refilled his cup.

She took a sip and set it aside before she pulled a pan of cinnamon rolls and a loaf pan full of bread dough from the refrigerator, removed the plastic wrap, and set them on top of the stove to finish rising. Then, she removed a cast iron skillet from the cabinet. This morning they were having bacon, omelets, toast made from the fresh loaf of homemade bread, and cinnamon rolls.

While the oven heated, she went to the pantry and brought out a slow cooker and set it on the cabinet. She chose another cast-iron skillet and set it on the back burner and took two big rump roasts from the refrigerator. Her next step was to brown the roasts and transfer them to the slow cooker, then add a thinly sliced onion, two tablespoons of beef bouillon, two cups of water, and chunks of potatoes and carrots. She would use one roast for dinner with the potatoes and carrots. She would make pulled beef barbecue sandwiches with the other for supper. A pan of yeast rolls was in the refrigerator, so all she'd have to do was take them out, let them warm for a few minutes, and bake them. Bella could cut up a salad, and Jett could set the table.

"You're pretty good at that," Remy said.

"Thank you. Comes from years of practice."

"Your ex-husband was a rancher?"

"My ex-husband deals in diamonds. His family has owned the business for three or four generations." She started frying bacon. "He's a city boy and hates anything with hair, as in cats, dogs, cows, horses, and bunny rabbits."

"I sure can't see you married to that kind of feller," Remy said.

"It does stretch the imagination, but it's the kind of life I thought I wanted until I got it. How about you? Ever been married?"

He shook his head emphatically. "No, ma'am! And don't intend to be."

"Pretty sure about that, aren't you?" She cracked a dozen eggs into a bowl, whipped them until they were light and fluffy, and poured them into a third skillet to scramble.

"I thought you said something about omelets last night," Remy said. "And to answer your question, I'm very sure about not getting married. What woman would want to take on raising the two boys I inherited when my brother died? It would be a nightmare."

"I'm making an oven omelet, and I agree. Taking on a ready-made family isn't something most men or women could or would do."

She turned the bacon over with one hand and stirred the eggs with the other. When the eggs were done, she transferred them to a cake pan, covered them with cheese and diced smoked sausage, then scrambled another dozen to go on top.

"That looks pretty good. Reckon Walter's got any salsa in the fridge?"

Adele shrugged. "Jett eats her omelets with grape

jam. I hope there's some of that in there, or she'll pout all day."

Remy pushed the chair back and stretched, raising his hands over his head and bending from side to side. Adele's blood pressure shot up twenty points.

"I'll see what we've got. My boys like salsa on their omelets and jelly on their toast." He headed for the refrigerator.

Adele stepped to one side. "So does Bella, but Jett likes ketchup on her toast and jam smeared on her omelet."

"You've got a strange kid. But hey, here's some salsa and some grape and strawberry jams. We've got it covered," Remy said.

"Who's to say that we're not the strange ones and she's perfectly normal?" Adele asked.

"Who's strange?" Jett asked as she appeared in the kitchen. "I'll set the table, Mama. Do we have grape jam?"

"Yes, Remy just found some in the refrigerator."

Jett yawned. "Well, at least he's good for something."

<center>~~~</center>

Remy sipped his coffee and wondered if Jett wasn't the very image of her mother at that age. Her hair was blond where Adele's was red, but the eyes were the same, and Remy would bet dollars to cow patties that they shared the same sassy, brassy attitude. That was something a woman was born with, not something she developed.

Bella made her way into the kitchen, taking over the bacon business from her mother with one hand and pouring a cup of coffee with the other. She sipped it as she pulled perfectly browned strips of bacon from the skillet and put them on a paper towel to drain.

"So you drink it black?" Remy asked.

"Is there any other way?" Bella shot back.

"Respect in your tone, young lady," Adele scolded.

"Sorry about that," Bella said.

"R-E-S-P-E-C-T." Jett sang a few lines of the Aretha Franklin song and bumped hips with her sister as she carried the dishes to the table.

Remy tried to hold his laughter, but it didn't work. That was a big voice coming from such a tiny girl.

"What's so funny?" Nick asked as he and his brother entered the kitchen.

"My sister is acting out this morning," Bella said.

"I made y'all laugh, so it worked." Jett did a few dance moves as she set the table.

Leo rubbed his eyes. "Are those cinnamon rolls that I smell cooking?"

"Yes, but you have to eat your omelet, bacon, and toast first," Bella answered. "Mama's rules, and her rules are the law on the days when we run the kitchen."

"I ain't got no problem with that," Nick said. "Since it's rainin', do we get to stay in and watch television or read all day?"

"In your dreams, boy," Jett answered. "I read that list of things Mr. Jones wants done. Between chores, we'll be cleanin' out a hay barn and the tack room. You afraid of rats?"

"No!" Leo said, but the way his shoulders shivered said he was terrified of the very mention of them.

"Did you make enough breakfast for Boss and Blanche?" Bella asked her mother.

"Of course, but they only get scraps. They have dog food and cat food. If Jerry Lee is on the porch, we'll take him a piece of bread." Adele smiled.

—⁓—

Remy drove the boys to the barn through a downpour that the wipers on his truck couldn't keep up with. He parked in the front of the big overhead doors and hit the ground running. The doors squeaked loudly enough that he could hear the noise above the commotion of rain hitting a metal roof, and he made a mental note to oil them on a dry day. He hurried back to the truck and drove inside, leaving enough room for Adele's vehicle behind him.

"Okay, boys, I'm going to show you how to stack that hay, so we can bring more in as soon as we can cut the new crop. No arguing or fighting with the girls. Save your energy to do work."

"But, Uncle Remy, what if they start it?" Leo asked.

Remy lowered his chin and looked up at the boys. "Right now they know more than you do. Fighting with them will only prove it."

"I don't like that," Nick said.

"Then learn to work and don't let them rile you," Remy said.

Fifteen minutes later, the boys were wearing gloves that were a size too big for their small hands and restacking hay. The two girls were shoveling out stalls and getting them ready in case there was a new calf born a little late that would need to be kept inside for a few days. The stall where Remy put the milk cow that morning was particularly messy, but he didn't hear a single word from

Bella and Jett when they shoveled wet hay and manure into the wheelbarrow. He gave credit where it was due, and those two girls worked as hard as any two cowhands he'd ever trained.

Adele stopped so quickly when she opened the door to the tack room that Remy ran smack into her backside.

"Sorry," he said.

"Walter Jones should be shot for letting things go like this. Look at those saddles. I bet they haven't seen a drop of saddle soap in years," she fumed.

"No horses. He's got a couple of four-wheelers in another barn, but he doesn't have horses, so that's probably the reason he's ignored this room."

"But look at the gardening equipment. Only one hoe doesn't have a layer of rust, and the rest of the tools look like crap." Adele folded her arms over her chest. "This is going to take a lot longer than one day."

"Maybe we'll have a few rainy days." Remy rolled up his shirtsleeves.

Before either of them could reach for a dust cloth to clean off the worktable, a scream split the air. They raced through the door and out into the barn, each of them looking toward their own two kids.

Bella and Jett came running from their workstations. Nick had a hand over Leo's mouth, but it wasn't doing much to keep the screams inside the little, red-haired boy. He finally pushed away from his older brother and pointed.

"Rat! Big as a cat."

"I though rats didn't scare you." Jett put her fingers in her mouth and whistled, the shrillness echoing off the barn walls enough that the rat stopped in its tracks and looked at her before it deftly ran down a stud to the lower hay bales.

"I'm not," Leo stammered. "But look at the size of that thing. It's every bit as big as the possum that comes up in our yard at night."

"No, it's not," Jett argued.

Boss ambled through the barn door, and Jett pointed at the rat. "Boss, it's time for you to show us what you're made of. Take care of that, or there will be no more table scraps for you."

As if he understood her, the dog growled and made a lunge toward the rat. Boss grabbed the thing by the neck, turned around, and headed out of the barn. As he did, the rat flopped around, its tail dragging on the floor between the big, yellow dog's front legs.

"Back to work," Remy said. "Boss is a good rat dog as well as cow dog."

"If Blanche had been out here, that rat would have known better than to even show its face in the barn," Bella said. "Rats don't come close to her. When she gets them babies up big enough, she'll come to the barn."

"Until then, Boss will be a good dog and keep them nasty old rats from scaring you boys." Jett turned around and went back to her job.

"Hey," Nick said.

Remy glanced his way. "Remember what I told you?"

"Yes, sir." Nick nodded.

"You boys are doing a great job of getting that hay stacked up neatly," Adele said. "If it's still raining this afternoon, maybe you could come in the tack room and help. There're three saddles in there that need a lot of elbow grease and saddle soap."

"We've got horses?" Nick's eyes widened.

"No, but if we ever do have any, it would be good if the saddles were ready," Remy answered.

———

After a hard day's work, Adele should have been ready for bed, but insomnia crept in and doubts rose up to haunt her. Was she doing the right thing by keeping her girls on a ranch? Could she do better by them if she moved them into town and used her money to buy a feedstore or even get a job as an accountant? That's what she'd been majoring in when she met Isaac and married him. She paced across the neutral-colored carpet in her bedroom until she feared she'd wear holes in it.

Finally, when the walls began to close in, she jammed her feet down into her boots and tiptoed down the stairs to the foyer, opened the front door, and eased out onto the porch. It had stopped raining, and the stars were shining in a bright, pretty clean sky that evening. She loved the primal scent of wet dirt, the gentle drip of water from the rooftop, and the tree frogs serenading in the distance. She sat down on the top step of the porch, and Boss showed up from the shadows on the far end to lie down beside her.

"You were a good boy today," she said softly.

"Yes, he was," a deep voice said over to her left. "You might as well join me on this swing. There's plenty of room."

She had to swallow twice to make her heart go back to where it belonged. "That's the second time today that you've startled me." She twisted her body around to lean against the porch post. No way was she going to sit beside him on that swing. That was entirely too close to the enemy.

"I couldn't sleep. Takes me a while to get used to a strange bed and house," he said. "My last job lasted more than ten years, and I only traded rooms one time. When I first started as a hired hand, I had a bunk out in the main room of the house with the other guys. Then when I was made foreman, I moved into my own little trailer house. It wasn't very big, but it took a week before I could sleep all night."

"I've been sleeping in the same bed for twelve years, except for the few times when my ex needed me to dress up and play trophy wife for him at fancy parties, and then I didn't sleep worth a damn in that penthouse that he keeps in downtown Dallas." She wondered why she'd offered that information. They weren't there to build a friendship or a relationship of any kind. They were there to work the ranch.

"Is he remarried?"

"Six days after the divorce was final," she answered. It felt good to talk about it. Cassie had wanted to put out a hit on Isaac when he didn't care if his daughters had his name. Her mother and father would have done the job themselves if she'd only said the word.

"Does he have any more children?"

"A son born about two months ago. Isaac is an only child and always wanted a son to carry on his name. Now he's got it and a wife that's ten years younger than he is and who looks like a porcelain doll. He's a happy man, and strange as it might seem, I'm happy with my life."

"Would you trust a man again after that?" Remy asked.

"Sure, if I found one who was trustworthy and that my girls liked. A rotten potato in the bag smells bad and can ruin the others if you don't take it out and throw it away. But if you get to it quickly enough, it won't affect the rest of the potatoes."

Remy's chuckle turned into loud laughter that drowned out the tree frogs. "I can't believe you just compared a diamond dealer with a rotten potato."

The giggles that burst out of her sounded more like they came from a little girl on a playground. She'd never been able to laugh graciously, but that night, it didn't matter, and it felt really good.

"Just callin' it like I see it. But FYI, I do not see my girls ever liking anyone enough to bring them into my family, so that pretty well shuts the door whether the potato is rotten or not. And on that note, I'd better turn in for the night." She was glad the porch light wasn't on because her nightshirt was faded and almost threadbare, and the only thing she had on under it was a pair of white cotton, bikini-cut underbritches.

"Don't go," Remy said. "I haven't had adult conversation in weeks."

"I thought you had lots of cousins in this area."

"I do, but I haven't had time to talk to any of them except in short phone calls. But when this ranch is mine, I plan to have a huge Luckadeau family gathering on Independence Day to celebrate."

Adele smiled and brought her knees to her chest, wrapping her arms around them. "Pretty confident there, aren't you, cowboy? I'm planning to have a big party for all the O'Donnells on that same day."

"Guess we'll see who does the best job around here," Remy said.

"I guess so, but that's a month down the road. Tomorrow is what we worry about right now. I think we should work on the tack room and barn some more and let the fence get completely dry before we paint it. If it's got the least bit of moisture in the wood, the paint will peel."

Remy didn't say anything for a full minute, but she could see part of his face by the moonlight. Maybe he didn't take to women telling him what to do. Isaac had had that problem, and she hadn't figured it out until they'd been married several weeks.

"That's a wonderful idea," he finally said.

"What took you so long to answer?"

"I was thinking about the boys and how much they hated that barn," he admitted. "I'm a rancher, and they were left in my care. Neither can be changed, but sometimes I feel sorry for a kid who doesn't like his environment."

"Maybe the boys will change after they figure things out. We've only been here one day," she said.

"I can hope. You got cattle to bring to this operation?" he asked.

"No, since they were on Isaac's land and what belonged to him was his, he sold every single one of them," she answered. "How about you?"

"Not a single one, but Walter has a damn fine herd."

"Yes, he does."

She stood and started walking into the house. "It's really getting late. Good night, Remy."

"Night, Adele," he drawled.

The toe of her boot got tangled up in the welcome

mat, and she grabbed for the door handle. The floor got closer and closer, and then Remy's strong arms wrapped around her and brought her firmly to his chest. Her nearly naked breasts flattened out against muscles hardened from lots of work, not from a personal trainer's instructions in a fancy gym. There was a difference, and she liked the way she felt in his arms for that brief moment before he loosened his hold and took a step backward.

"Close call," he said.

"Thank you for saving me."

"Does that mean you owe me? If so, I'll help you pack and you can leave tomorrow."

"Not in your wildest dreams, cowboy. I might owe you an extra day of cooking if you're dog tired one day, but I don't do laundry for guys, and I'm not leaving this ranch unless I lose the luck of the draw."

He opened the door and stood to one side just as Jerry Lee flew from his end of the porch to the swing and crowed as if his life depended on it.

"Crazy rooster. I'd shoot him if he were mine and make dumplin's out of his sorry carcass," Adele said. "If he wakes up my girls, I may not waste the bullet. I'll just wring his neck."

"Then you really wouldn't get this ranch. Remember what Walter said about taking care of Jerry Lee and Boss. I'm going to warm up one of those leftover cinnamon rolls. Sometimes food helps me sleep. Want one?"

Yes, she did, but there was no way she was going into a well-lit kitchen dressed like she was.

"No, thank you. I'll see you at breakfast."

She hurried up the stairs while he headed down the

foyer toward the kitchen. She kicked off her boots and fell back into her bed, staring up at the ceiling fan's blades making lazy circles in the moonlit room. Could she be friends with Remy and yet still be in competition with him for the ranch? Talking to him out there on the porch had been nice. No, it went beyond nice. An adult to share a few things with at the close of the day—it had been a long time since she'd had that, and she hadn't realized how much she'd missed it.

# Chapter 4

Steam rose up from the wet ground that Friday morning, soaking Remy's shirt before he even got started in the tack room. There's nothing hotter in Texas than the day after a summer rain. The sun comes out, sucks up the moisture from the ground, and creates a statewide steam bath. Remy and Adele opened both barn doors, but there was no breeze, so it did very little good. By noon, the kids were all drenched in sweat, covered in bits of straw, and too tired to argue who got which hamburger and hot dog that the guys made for dinner. They drank more iced sweet tea than they ate food and sprawled out on the porch.

"Hey, guys." Remy poked his head out the front door. "If y'all are willing to ride in the back of the old work truck, I reckon we could all go out to the barn together this afternoon instead of taking two vehicles."

"With the girls?" Leo snarled.

"Long as you boys don't get your sweaty old bodies next to me," Jett said.

"We would never mix our sweat with yours," Nick answered with a sneer.

"The bunch of you can go on around to the back-yard and get into the truck. No touching or fighting," Remy said.

By midafternoon, the barn was spotless, hay stacked perfectly, floor swept free of even a bit of straw, and the tack room was so clean and organized that it could have been featured in a magazine. Remy leaned a shoulder against the doorjamb and thought about a nice, cool swim in the lake.

"What next?" Nick asked.

"I vote swimming," Remy said.

"Yes!" Leo squealed. "Where's the nearest pool?"

"Not pool," Remy said. "My cousins and I went to Nocona Lake to swim, so I thought we'd go there."

"Or we could swim in the pond at the back of the ranch," Adele offered.

Nick's nose twisted into a snarl. "But the pond water is muddy and dirty lookin'."

"Then the lake it is," Remy said. "The wagon train leaves in twenty minutes. We have to be back by dusk to do the evening milking and chores, but that will give us about three hours to swim."

"You girls take a very quick shower and put your bathing suits on," Adele yelled as all four kids found new bursts of energy and sprinted off toward the house.

"You going to run for the house or ride in the truck with me?" Remy asked.

"I'm not running anywhere in this heat." She headed toward the truck, her long legs keeping pace with him.

Remy visualized her in a bikini, and his pulse jacked up. He shook his head, but the picture didn't disappear. God did not like Remington Luckadeau. If the Almighty liked him, he would have never put a woman like Adele in the same house with him and then said that she was off-limits.

The girls were already on the porch, wet hair hanging

in strings, bathing suits on under oversize T-shirts, and a couple of floats ready to blow up in their arms.

"That was fast," Remy said.

"You said twenty minutes," Adele said.

"It hasn't hardly been five."

"What can I say?" She shrugged. "They love to swim. But a word of warning—it makes them hungry."

"Then maybe we'd better plan on stopping by the Dairy Queen for ice cream afterward. Then, after we get the evening chores done, we'll have supper."

"Sounds good to me."

———

Adele was in her room, peeling out of her smelly clothing, when she realized just how easy it would be to start a friendship with Remy Luckadeau. She put it into the back of her mind and pulled her bathing suit from a dresser drawer. When she'd gotten it tugged up over her sweaty thighs, she chose a Texas Longhorns T-shirt to wear over it and slipped her feet into a pair of rubber flip-flops. A quick trip to the bathroom netted four towels—one to sit on so her truck seat wouldn't smell like dirty socks for a week and three to use at the lake.

She had started down the stairs when she heard a door squeak behind her and turned to find Remy on the landing. He wore cutoff jeans, a bright-orange tank top, and sandals. All those muscles, that smile on his face, and the twinkle in his eyes flat out took her breath away. Isaac had never had that effect on her, not even in his three-thousand-dollar suits and handmade wingtip shoes.

"So you didn't take time for a shower either?"

She shook her head.

"Towels! I almost forgot. I'll lead the way to the lake. We'll have to take both trucks, since there's no way those four can all sit in the backseat of one," he said as he made his way toward the bathroom. "You said that your girls love to swim. Are they good at it or do they just love to be in the water?"

"They swim like fish," she managed to say, even though her mouth was dry.

"Nick and Leo were both on the swim team at school. We won't have to worry about them."

She nodded and went on ahead of him, toward the porch. Boys on one end. Girls on the other. Boys talking about water races. Girls discussing how far out they'd float on their rafts. Neither set talking to the other, but at least they weren't arguing.

"You brought towels, Mama. Thank you. We forgot them." Bella tucked a strand of wet hair into the ponytail she'd made on top of her head since Adele had last seen her.

Adele motioned toward her truck. "We're going to follow Remy, since he knows the way, so load up."

"We are wastin' precious time waitin' on boys," Jett mumbled.

"What was that?" Leo asked.

"Nothing. If y'all get us lost and cut down on our swimming time, I'll drown your sorry butts."

Leo strutted across the porch like a banty rooster. "I'm a champion swimmer."

"Good! Then it will be an even bigger victory," Jett said.

"To the truck without another word." Adele pointed.

"Same for you two." Remy slung open the door. "And no scuffling in the water, boys. This is not a pool."

"Mama never let us swim in dirty water," Nick said.

"Well, it's the lake or nothing. Your choice. You can sit on the bank and read a book if you don't want to get in the water," Remy told him.

Adele slammed the door to the truck, quickly turned on the engine and the air-conditioning, and waited for Remy. She didn't have to worry about a friendship or a relationship with or the physical attraction to Remy Luckadeau. Four kids underfoot, fighting all the time, made that damn near impossible.

He drove through backcountry farm roads, making so many turns that she'd have to follow him back to the ranch to ever find her way. Not even Gert, her GPS system, would be able to navigate the roads that Remy took.

The girls wasted no time getting out of the truck, fixing the air pump to their floats, and going to work getting them ready for the water. Adele grabbed three towels, dropped them on the grass under a big scrub oak, kicked off her sandals, and walked out into the cool water until it was waist deep. At that point, she raised her arms above her head and dove out as far as she could, came up for air, and swam straight out for a full five minutes.

When she turned and started back, she found Remy coming toward her not five feet away. He stopped to tread water so close to her that she could see the water droplets dripping from his hair. She resisted the urge to reach out and touch his cheek, but it wasn't easy.

"You are pretty good at this."

"You aren't so bad yourself."

A splash took her attention to the shore. "Guess they got the floats filled. Did your boys bring something?"

"No, they swim for competition, not play."

"Then they have something to learn. Race you back to the shore."

"What does the winner get?" His eyes twinkled.

"Loser buys all the ice cream after we swim." She reached out with one arm and got serious about the race.

She gave it all the steam she had, but it was still a tie, both setting a foot on dry land at the same time. He grabbed a towel, spread it out, and eased down onto his back. She did the same thing a foot away.

"I thought for a minute there you were going to win and the boys would have never let me live it down if a girl beat me at swimming," he said, gasping.

"Same here," she said breathlessly, keeping her eyes away from the lean cowboy's body next to her.

A soft breeze ruffled the leaves in the gnarly scrub oak above her and cooled her wet skin. The water sloshed up onto the shore with regularity. She slung her arm over her eyes, as much to keep from looking over at Remy's wet body as it was to keep the sun out of them. She heard giggles and a cracked voice that told her Nick was talking to someone out there. Leo's high-pitched little-boy's voice wouldn't change for a couple of years. She planned to keep her eyes shut for only a minute, to rest them after a long, hot day's work. But she fell into a deep, relaxed sleep and dreamed of Walter telling her that she had won the ranch because she was the better rancher and had earned the Double Deuce.

Remy had been so busy getting the boys situated that he hadn't seen her in her swimsuit until she came up out of the water at the shoreline, looking like a red-haired goddess in that one-piece bright-blue suit that hugged her body like a glove. It was far sexier than any bikini he'd ever seen on any woman.

He cut his eyes over toward her when he heard the first snore, which was really more like Blanche's purr when he'd rubbed her fur. She'd thrown one arm up over her eyes, and he could almost see the tension flowing out of her body as the sleep deepened. Long legs were crossed at the ankles. Hot-pink toenail polish was chipped in places. She shifted positions, rolling toward him and using her arm for a pillow. Sunrays slipped through the thick tree branches and brought out the freckles across her nose.

The swim had energized Remy and his playboy genes surfaced. It would be so easy to trace Adele's full lips and then wake her with a kiss. It wouldn't be smart, but then a player wasn't trained for intelligence. He had honed his ability to pick up women, have a good time with them, take them home after breakfast, and forget them.

*It would be downright crazy because I have to live in the same house with this woman, work beside her, and I can't take her home and forget her. Besides, she's so feisty, she might blacken both my eyes if I did something like that.*

He was so busy studying her lips that he didn't realize she'd opened her eyes.

"Do I have lake moss hanging in my hair?" Her voice was still husky with sleep and her blue eyes softer than he'd ever seen them.

"No, I was counting the freckles on your face," he lied.

"It's a useless thing to do. The sun brings out more every day. How long did I sleep? Are the kids all right?"

She sat up, giving him a full shot of her bare back. Not a spare bit of fat or a bulge anywhere. Was her ex blind or just blessed with a double dose of stupid to let a woman like Adele get away from him?

"The kids are all having a great time, and you only caught a little power nap that lasted maybe ten minutes," he answered.

"We should talk about tomorrow. On most ranches, the hands only work half a day on Saturday, so they can get their personal chores done, and then they're off on Sunday. Is that what we want to do?"

He sat up and propped his forearms on his drawn-up legs. "I think that would be fair. The boys and I can get our rooms straightened and do our laundry."

"We can do the same. I believe if we all work together, we could get the fence painted tomorrow morning and have that job finished."

"I imagine we can. What's your Sunday plans?"

"We're going to church in Ringgold with my uncle Cash and his family, and then we're going out to his horse ranch for the afternoon. We'll be back to the Double Deuce in time for evening chores," she answered.

"My cousin Slade, who lives over in Ringgold, has asked us to attend church with him and his family, and then we're going to his place for dinner and the afternoon. There's only one church in Ringgold, so I guess we'll be attending the same one. You plannin' on going there all the time?"

"Not if I buy the Double Deuce. If that happens,

we'll go to church in Nocona, where the girls will go to school," she answered.

"And if you don't buy the ranch?" he asked.

"I'll cross that bridge when I get to it."

"Fair enough," Remy said. "So what are you going to do with the ranch if you buy it? Improve it? Keep it right where it is? Run the cattle that's on it, or thin out the herd and get better stock?"

Adele didn't answer, but he could tell that she was mulling the questions over. "First of all," she finally said, "I'll keep it status quo until next year. Get to know every mesquite tree, every cow and cacti on the place. I'll run the cattle that are on it until my first fall sale, which wouldn't be this year but next. Then I'd cull out the cattle that are not up to standard and buy some better stock. But for now, I'd just get used to the place."

"Would you keep making small bales of hay like Walter is doing or invest in the machinery to make the big round bales, so you wouldn't have to go out and feed twice a day in the wintertime?" he asked.

"I've always liked the small bales. It's more work but less waste, and they're easier for me to deal with. Someday I might do the big round or big square ones, but for now, Walter has the equipment for little bales, and besides, kids need to learn to haul hay. It's good for them," she answered.

She was batting two for two so far. Everything she'd said he agreed with and planned to do if he was the winner when Walter came home.

"What if he comes home with a whole new perspective and decides to keep the ranch for himself? He could get out there on that long cruise and get to missing his

cows, or he and his lady friend might get into a hella-
cious argument, and he'll decide that he wants to keep
the ranch." Remy voiced his greatest fear.

"Then I will shoot the son of a bitch and you can help
me bury him," she answered with enough conviction in
her tone that a chill shot up his back. "One of us is going
to own that ranch."

"And if it's me?" he asked, the question hanging in
the air above them.

"Then you will have won it fair and square, and I will
call a real estate agent to find me another one in this
area. And you?"

"Same," he said. "I like this area, so I'm not leaving."

*Fair and square.*

Could he live up to that?

"Uncle Remy, we're starving," Leo yelled as he came
up out of the water. A thin little kid with bony shoulders
and teeth he hadn't quite grown into. With that mop of
red hair, he looked like he belonged to Adele more than
to the Luckadeaus.

"You see a taco stand anywhere around here?" Remy
teased.

"No, but it's only fifteen minutes home, and I might
not starve between here and there," Leo answered.

*Home!* The boy had called the ranch home for the
first time, and Remy's heart doubled in size.

"If you can sweet-talk the rest of the crew into
coming to shore, we might go through Nocona and get
ice cream at the Dairy Queen," Remy said. "But if you'd
rather go home…"

Leo didn't wait to hear any more. He ran back to the
edge of the water and screamed, "Dairy Queen! Come

on in!" The whole time, he waved a thin arm frantically at the others, who were still little more than dots in the water.

They started toward him, and he hurried back to Remy and Adele, picked up a towel, dried off, and jerked his dry T-shirt over his head. "Can I have a banana split?"

"You can have whatever you want. You guys have worked hard, so you deserve it," Remy said. "But this is not an everyday thing, Leo. Tomorrow its right back to work and then cleaning rooms and doing laundry all afternoon."

"I kind of like the lake. There's no boundaries out there, like in a practice pool. I don't like it that I can't see bottom, and I really don't like it when that algae stuff on the bottom touches my feet, but I can learn to live with that," Leo said.

"Ice cream!" Jett squealed as she toted a float from the edge of the lake to her mother. "I want a peanut parfait."

Adele flashed a smile at her youngest child and Remy was reminded of his mother. Not that Adele looked a thing like his dark-haired, brown-eyed mother, who barely came to his shoulder, but the love in that smile was the kind that he'd seen many times growing up right over the border in Louisiana.

Before Jett could dry off enough to throw on her T-shirt and get her float tossed in the back of the truck, Nick and Bella were both there, already talking about what kind of ice-cream sundaes they would order and changing their minds every time they thought of another flavor.

"So y'all had a good time?" Adele asked on the way from the lake back to Nocona.

"Yes," Bella said quickly. "It was wonderful to get in the water. I love that place. Can we go there again real soon?"

"Like tomorrow?" Jett asked.

"Probably not that soon, but we'll go again this month. How about the ranch? Are you starting to feel at home there?"

"Yes, I am, and I really, really want to live there forever. We can't let those boys have it, Mama," Bella said seriously.

The sun was slowly making its way to the horizon twenty minutes later when Remy parked outside the Dairy Queen on Main Street in Nocona. The sign on the door said *No Shirt, No Shoes, No Service*, but it didn't stop Jett from being the first one inside the cool place.

Bella whispered, "Mama, what if there's someone in here that I'll be going to school with and they remember seeing me looking like this?"

"Don't worry about it. They'll never think the Bella with her makeup and pretty jeans on is the same girl as the one with wet hair wearing a Dallas Cowboys T-shirt in the Dairy Queen on the third day of June," Adele answered.

"And you? What if some rich rancher sees you in church next Sunday and remembers seeing you with wet, stringy hair and wearing that Longhorns shirt?" Remy whispered close enough behind her that his warm breath on her neck sent shivers rippling down her spine.

"I don't give a rat's ass," she answered. "I'm not looking for a rich cowboy, a poor one, a sexy one, or an ugly one. I've got bigger plans than finding another man to make my life miserable."

"I thought you plucked that bad potato out and tossed it aside and wasn't judging the other taters in the bag by that one."

"Oh hush, and get up there to the counter with your boys to get your orders in, so we can have our turn," she said shortly. So he had hit a raw nerve and she wasn't totally ready to trust another man yet.

He looked up to see Nick waving at him and hurried forward to order a third banana split and pay for all three.

There was only one empty table in the whole place, and it was one of those big round things with eight chairs around it. Remy and his boys sat on one side, and Adele and her girls took the other, leaving an empty chair between them. Nick and Bella were talking low about how they might be going to ninth grade together, if they all lived in or near Nocona, and Bella finally moved over a chair so they could put their heads together.

*One set down. One to go*, Remy thought as Leo shot dirty looks at his brother.

"They're talking about school and I don't even want to go. Why can't I be homeschooled?" Jett sighed.

Leo's expression said that he'd heard that loud and clear, and he leaned in her direction.

"We've had this conversation before, and the answer is still the same: because you need the social interaction with kids your own age," Adele told her.

"But I'm bored in school. I get my work done, and all I think about is what I could be doing on the ranch," she whined.

"Me, too." Leo shifted down to another chair. "Uncle Remy could teach me at home on the ranch. I bet I could get all my lessons done by noon, and then I could help him. Maybe we could even get a horse and I could learn to round up cattle."

"I thought you hated ranching," Remy said.

"I hated the idea of it, but once I got here and kind of learned that it can be fun, it ain't so bad. And I really hate school, so if we buy the ranch, will you homeschool me?" Leo begged.

"No, and it's not negotiable." Remy shook his head. "You need to be with other kids, and to learn patience and to take orders from your teachers."

"Rats!" Leo sighed.

"Ice cream." The waitress brought a tray filled with three banana splits and three sundaes to their table. "Y'all enjoy."

Adele smiled. "Thank you."

Remy's heart skipped a beat. If Adele ever flashed one of her smiles in a barroom filled with randy cowboys, she could take her pick of which one she'd take home for the night, for a weekend, or even for life. Thinking of another cowboy dancing with her or, worse yet, claiming her forever put a wide jealous streak across his heart.

"You have to be able to interact with people when you go to college," Adele told Jett.

"I'm not going to college. I'm going to be a rancher like you, Mama, so that argument ain't going to work." Jett dug deep into her parfait.

"Then you need to go to school to learn not to say 'ain't.'" Adele's mouth barely turned up at the edges.

Jett might as well stop right there because there was no way Adele was going to lose the argument. *Dammit!*

Remy thought. *And there's probably no way she'll lose the ranch either because when she flutters those baby blues at Walter or has the whole house smelling like fresh-baked bread the day he comes back home, he'll lay down and roll over just like Boss does for her.*

# Chapter 5

ADELE ATE HER HOT CARAMEL SUNDAE SLOWLY. IT WAS A good sign that the kids were starting to talk without constant bickering. The month would go by much smoother if they got along.

"After chores, I thought we might make tacos and a big community platter of nachos and eat in the living room while we watch a movie," Remy suggested.

"Yay!" Leo wiggled in his chair. "What are we going to watch?"

"Whatever Walter has in that library of DVDs I saw under his television," Remy answered.

"Why can't we do a pay-per-view of a new movie?" Nick asked.

"Because Walter does not have cable, a computer, or Wi-Fi," Adele answered.

"Oh. My." Leo clapped his hands onto his round cheeks. "God! You have got to be kiddin' me. No Wi-Fi means I can't play my video games."

"You've been without it since we arrived," Remy told him. "And you haven't missed it until now, so what's the big deal?"

"I didn't want to play my games, but I will, and I won't be able to, and I'll get real cranky," Leo declared.

"So what's new? You are always cranky and whiny," Jett said.

"You are just plain old mean," Leo said.

"So much for them getting along," Adele whispered.

He shrugged and grinned.

It didn't take long for four hungry kids to scarf down their ice cream or to be ready to go home, since tacos and nachos had been mentioned. The ranch was about three miles east of Nocona and a mile north. When Remy made the left-hand turn onto the Double Deuce, he felt like he was home. Even after a dozen years on the ranch in the Panhandle, he'd never had roots as deep as the ones he'd put down on this place in only a few days.

Jett crawled out of her mother's truck and yelled, "I'll milk the cow. Bella can drive the work truck, and you two boys can help her fill up the watering tanks. Surely you're strong enough, Nick, to dump two bags of feed. The cows are on pasture right now, so they don't need much."

"I'll be damned. She is bossy. Is she really going to milk that heifer? She's pretty small to control a cow," Remy said as he followed Adele up the porch steps.

"She's been milking for over a year, and believe me, she can control a cow pretty damn well," Adele answered. "Bella, the keys are in the work truck."

"You really drive?" Nick's eyes cut to Bella.

"Since I was about seven. Mama gave me a pillow to sit on until I could see above the steering wheel. Want me to teach you?" Bella asked.

Nick grinned. "You bet I do."

"Remember, that's Walter's work truck, not ours," Adele cautioned.

"I will, Mama."

Jett pointed at her mother and Remy. "And you two can get the supper ready, so we can watch a movie and eat nachos."

Adele narrowed her eyes. "Jett Cassandra O'Donnell."

"I'm sorry, Mama. Would you and Remy please get supper ready, while us kids do the chores? I'm still hungry and I love nachos."

"That's much better, young lady," Adele said. "Here, you take my cell phone, and if you get into trouble or need us, call. This is your first time to milk that particular cow, and she might not like you as much as old Bessie did."

"Yes, ma'am." Her tone had softened considerably.

"And, Bella, be careful. The brakes are touchier than ours and the clutch is a little loose."

"You drive a stick?" Nick's eyes were as big as silver dollars.

"Sure I do. Let's go get the work done. We might even have time for showers when we get back, so we can watch the movie in our pajamas," Bella said.

Leo slapped his forehead. "Showers! I thought we took a bath in the lake."

"You might need a little soap and shampoo," Remy told him.

The kids looked like sardines piled into the seat of that old, rusted-out truck. Remy waited on the porch until Bella had the engine started and drove toward the barn.

"She didn't grind the gears, not one time," he said softly.

"She's been driving half her life, Remy. I needed someone to drive the hay truck, so we strapped her three-year-old sister into the passenger's seat and she drove for me. We made a good team every summer, and it kept me from having to hire help." Adele opened the door. "How old were you when your dad put you behind the wheel because you were too little to heft a bale of hay?"

"Eight," he said. "But I was a boy."

"Girls can do whatever boys can. Let's get supper started because they'll be back soon. Keeping kids filled up is a never-ending job in the summer." She laughed.

"Good thing we've got a garden. Which reminds me, maybe we'd better do some harvesting tomorrow afternoon, too. I noticed several ripe tomatoes this morning, and the okra needs cutting. Beans are ready to pick, too."

"Good." She nodded. "We'll eat what we bring in for supper tomorrow night. Now, since bossy Jett is out milking the cow, I'm going to dash up stairs, take a shower, and wash my hair while you start supper. Then I'll finish up while you do the same. That way the bathroom will be available for the kids."

Remy chuckled. "I see what DNA pool Jett got that bossiness from."

Adele didn't look back at him. She'd had about all she could endure of looking at him with that semi-wet shirt hugging every muscle on his chest. And that bed of soft hair peeking out called to her to touch it. Adele needed a nice, cool shower and thoughts of something other than a hot cowboy's ripped abs to cool off her hormones.

The cold water helped tremendously, and being in the kitchen alone after that with something to keep her hands busy was even better. She realized the pantry had begun to look bare that evening when she went to look for a bag of corn chips to make nachos. She made a mental note to make a long grocery list. The way things had fallen into place, she was in charge of meals on Tuesday, Thursday, and Saturday. The freezer was full of beef, but maybe she'd buy a ham and a package of chicken for dumplings to switch things up a bit.

"Gettin' a bit on the lean side, isn't it?" Remy said from the doorway.

*Dammit!* How did he keep startling her like that?

"I'll do some shopping Sunday for my three days to cook," she said.

"Me, too. Shall we compare notes so we don't make the same thing two days in a row?" He blocked out the light into the walk-in pantry that had shelves on three sides.

"I'm making ham on Tuesday, chicken and dumplings on Thursday, and meat loaf on Saturday," she said. "We'll have leftovers or sandwiches for suppers."

"Then I'll do lasagna on Monday, pinto beans and garden vegetables on Wednesday with your ham bone to flavor the beans, and grilled steaks on Friday. And we'll do the same thing about supper—sandwiches or else leftovers. We're settling into a routine here."

She nodded and took a step forward, expecting him to step aside, but he didn't. His gaze locked with hers, and she instinctively licked her lips and got ready for the kiss that she read in his expression. That inner voice that kept her on the right track told her in a loud tone to back up, but she wanted the kiss. She wanted to feel his arms around her just one time, and then she wouldn't let it happen again.

"I call first shower." Nick's squeaky voice came from the foyer as four kids made their way into the house.

"I'm second because I don't want to wait on the girls. They take for…ever." Leo's footsteps sounded like an elephant running up the stairs.

"Mama, where are you?" Bella yelled on her way to the kitchen.

Remy hurriedly stepped out of the way, and Adele picked up the last two bags of corn chips from the pantry shelf.

"We need to watch one of the heifers out there in the pasture. She's going to drop that calf, in the next three or four days, and it's so hot, the little critter will need to be kept in the barn until we see if it's healthy. It's the wrong time of year for a calf, and it could die in this heat." Bella sniffed the air. "Tacos smell good. We'll hurry, but I do have to wash my hair. The lake water makes it all yucky and it needs extra conditioner."

Adele nodded. "Did you make a note of the number on the ear tag?"

"Yep, wrote it down right here." Bella held out her hand. "Maybe we ought to bring her on in tomorrow, just in case."

"Might be a good idea. I'll take a look at her in the morning." Adele wrote the cow's ID number on a piece of paper and stuck it to the refrigerator with an electric company's promotional magnet.

"Milk is on the counter," Jett said right behind her sister. "Old girl didn't like me, so we had to have us a come-to-Jesus talk, but I think she'll be all right and let me milk her from now on. Want me to strain it?"

"No, you and Bella get on upstairs and get ready for showers. Don't put those wet bathing suits in the laundry basket or they'll mildew. Drape them over a hanger and put it on your doorknob," Adele said.

"I'll take care of the milk," Remy said. "Soon as y'all get finished, we'll fix plates and take them to the living room."

Jett and Bella chased up the stairs, one behind the

other. Adele kept her eyes away from Remy and made sure that she was at least a foot from him. Talk about saved by the bell; she'd been saved by a bunch of kids still wearing bathing suits and flip-flops.

"I still have trouble believing that Jett could milk a cow, and I'll be hanged if she didn't get the job done faster than I could have." Remy leaned on the counter.

His eyes followed Adele's moves as she dumped two bags of chips into an oversize roaster and set it aside to pour half a gallon of nacho cheese over the top right before serving. It made her nervous as a hooker in church during revival season, but she kept working, chopping lettuce and tomatoes and grating cheese.

"I wonder." She frowned and then stopped.

"About what?"

"I wonder why Walter has all this food in the house. No old bachelor would keep this much cheese and three heads of lettuce in the refrigerator. Granted, the tomatoes are from the garden, but—"

Remy threw back his head and roared with laughter. "That old coot! He planned this from the beginning."

"What?" Adele asked.

"When he found out we were both so interested, he worked us. He wanted cheap labor for a month. He knew we both had to be out of the places where we were living and needed somewhere to go. If he backs out of this deal, I promise I will help you bury the body," Remy said.

"So the player has definitely been played." Adele grinned.

"What did you say?"

"I said the player got played. Maybe not by a woman, but played all the same."

"And what does that mean?" Remy asked.

"It means that I finally remembered where I'd heard your name mentioned. I left the Panhandle fifteen years ago, but my sister is still there. You're the famous Remington Luckadeau who loves the women and leaves them. If they lined up all the women you've seduced, the line would reach all the way around Texas according to my sister, Cassie. I don't know why I didn't remember your name when I first met you."

"Guess it'll take some doing to get past the past," he said.

"It won't happen. That kind of reputation will follow you around like your women do."

He folded his arms across his broad chest. "I'm trying, Adele. That's why I want this ranch. The boys don't need to hear that their role model was a womanizer for more than half his life."

"And does the womanizer wish he were still walking in those boots?" she asked.

He shrugged. "Sometimes. It wasn't a bad life, you know? But we were talking about the food in the pantry. I think that guilt made Walter stock the house with things a bunch of teenage or near-teenage kids would like until we could get to the store."

"Well, we're in it for the month now, so we'll make the best of it." Adele loaded a bowl with chopped lettuce. "But just to be on the safe side, I'm going to spend some Sunday afternoons talking to a few real estate agents about other places for sale in this area."

"I just might do the same thing." Remy picked up the bowl and carried it to the table. "I saw some paper plates in the pantry. Maybe we'll let them build their own tacos and use paper plates tonight. Want me to chop the onions?"

"Not one of us girls eat them, so only chop up what you guys need."

"Leo is the only one who likes them, so it won't take much."

She watched him head toward the pantry again. He wore Dallas Cowboy pajama pants and a red pocket T-shirt. Both were baggy, but there was no doubt in her mind about what was underneath them—a muscled-up cowboy that she had more chemistry with than she'd had with her ex-husband. Madam Fate was a total bitch to do this to her. Why couldn't the old gal have sent Remy into her life when she was twenty-one, instead of thirty-five? Now the timing was all wrong and nothing could work, not with kids and a feud to the death over a ranch.

If Remy had been a man to carve notches in his bedpost, it would have given a totem pole some serious competition. But not one of the women who'd made the bedpost honor roll had ever made him want to hang up his lucky boots like Adele did. It wasn't fair that she'd come into his life now and in this way.

Without a drop of makeup, her wet hair up in a ponytail and wearing Texas Longhorn pajama bottoms with a black tank top, she was absolutely adorable. He'd been ready to kiss her in the pantry—just one time, to prove that it wouldn't be as awesome as he'd imagined. Then he could get on with the business of ranching and stop thinking about her. *Dammit to hell!* He'd known the woman a few days. Of course, they'd met when Walter laid out the rules, but that didn't count. Nothing was black-and-white anymore or straight up and down either, and he didn't like it when his world wasn't in kilter.

The kids came down the stairs like they'd gone up—like a herd of wild animals chasing their dinner. They pushed their way into the kitchen, stopped at the table, and bowed their heads. Since it was really the boys' night to cook, Remy said a quick grace, and they went to work building half a dozen tacos each.

"What are we watching, Uncle Remy? And where's the sweet tea?"

"In the refrigerator. Ice is in a bowl in the freezer," he answered. "And we're watching an old western with Tom Selleck called *Quigley Down Under*. It appears that if we want to watch movies, it's Westerns; Walter is real partial to Westerns."

"Thank God it's not a chick flick with all that kissing crap," Leo said. "I'm taking my food to the living room and claiming the end of the coffee table. I'll be back for my tea."

"About what almost happened in the pantry," Adele whispered as she brought the tea out of the refrigerator. "That cannot happen."

"I agree." Remy nodded. "Bad judgment for both of us."

Adele's head bobbed once and she raised her voice as she set about putting ice in six disposable red plastic cups. "Y'all get settled down around the coffee table and I'll bring in the nachos. I'm calling the recliner."

Halfway through the movie, the tacos were all gone and only a thin layer of nachos was left in the pan. The kids had claimed throw pillows and were stretched out in front of the big-screen television, mesmerized by the story playing out before their eyes.

"Mama, can I ask the dentist to make a split between my front teeth like what crazy Cora has?" Jett asked when they paused the movie for everyone to take a bathroom break and refill their tea glasses.

"No, you can not!" Adele said emphatically.

"But I like her better than any other actress, and I don't think she's really crazy. I think she's just actin' like that. And I'm going to grow up and marry someone who looks like Matthew. He's so handsome." Jett threw the back of her hand over her forehead in a true Scarlett O'Hara gesture. "He just flat-out makes me swoon."

"Good grief, Jett. What do you know about swooning?" Adele giggled.

"It's what girls in the old days did when a sexy man came in the room. Did anyone ever swoon over you, Remy?" She removed her hand and tucked her chin to her chest.

"Not that I know about." He chuckled.

"Well, they should. Not as much as Matthew, but you'd do to swoon over," Jett told him seriously.

"Thank you, Jett." He hadn't blushed in years, but he felt heat crawling up the back of his neck to his cheeks. "So you think I'm handsome, do you?"

"Well, hell yeah! Oops, Mama! I mean heck yes. Sometimes Uncle Cash's words just slip out of my mouth." Jett flashed a wide grin. "But, Remy, don't get your ego all inflated like a Macy's parade balloon. You won't never be the man that Matthew is."

"Guess I won't ever be a movie star then." Remy sighed dramatically.

"Probably not. Here come the boys. Come on, Bella. Give us two minutes and we'll be back. You sure about that split between my teeth, Mama?"

Adele nodded. "Very sure. Positively, absolutely sure."

"Well, rats!" She took off out of the room in a blur.

"She's a charmer. You've got your work cut out with that one," Remy said.

"And Uncle Cash doesn't help a bit." Adele smiled.

"Even when she cusses, she's cute."

Adele nodded. "It's all I can do to correct her."

"Who all wants a glass of cold milk and some chocolate cookies?" Bella asked. "That can be our bedtime snack while we watch the rest of the movie."

They all disappeared to the kitchen, and before long, Adele could hear Jett telling them exactly how many cookies each of them should have so that it would be fair, since there was only half a package left.

"Bossy." Remy yawned.

"It's the O'Donnell in her gene pool. The women in the family have that reputation."

Remy covered another yawn with his hand. Did he even want to take a step beyond a working-type relationship with a woman who was a self-proclaimed bossy gal? He didn't think so. He liked his women feisty and hot, both in bed and out of it, but not bossy.

*And that solves the question of the week*, he thought as he fluffed a pillow and stretched out on the long, buttery-soft leather sofa. *No more wondering about her or dreaming about her either. It's settled. Nothing beyond working together and fighting like hell for this ranch.*

# Chapter 6

THE LITTLE WHITE CHURCH LOCATED ON THE NORTHERN side of Ringgold was full that Sunday morning. Uncle Cash and Aunt Maddie had saved a place on the second pew for Adele and the girls. They slid into their places just before the first congregational hymn and only a few minutes before the squeak of the church door announced there was another late arriver.

Remy and the boys must have sat a bit back behind her somewhere. She couldn't see them, but she could feel his presence in the room by the antsy feeling that he was staring at the back of her head. Keeping her eyes straight ahead as they sang "Abide with Me" wasn't easy. Thinking of how appropriate the song title was that morning didn't help. Then the preacher decided to speak about the beautiful love story of Isaac and Rebecca, talking about how they didn't even know each other, but it was love at first sight.

Adele did not believe in love at first sight. She hardly believed in love after a year's dating, since her marriage with Isaac had fallen apart. She'd done everything right. Dated a year. Engaged six months. Big Texas wedding and reception. Baby the next year, and another one two and a half years later, since the first one wasn't the boy that her husband wanted.

What she could have or should not have done was in the past, and it was time to move forward, get a new start at the Double Deuce, and raise her girls the way she'd always done.

The preacher finally wound down and asked Slade Luckadeau to deliver the benediction. Adele snuck a quick peek at the man who'd stood to his feet to pray. Tall like Remy, with the same build and face shape—a true cowboy with his plaid, pearl-snap shirt and creased jeans. There was no doubt that he and Remy were kin-folks with their chiseled good looks.

Because they were sitting near the back and got out faster than the folks up near the front, she didn't catch sight of Remy or his family again. The girls set up a fuss to ride home with Uncle Cash and Aunt Maddie, so that left her to drive two miles south to the horse ranch alone. Even short times without her daughters' constant chatter reminded Adele that she'd be completely lost without them. She'd always be grateful to Isaac for giving them to her. And she'd always detest the man for tossing them away like a pair of worn-out shoes.

She parked under a shade tree and looked up to see her favorite male cousin, Rye, waving from the porch. Tall, dark haired, and a rancher from head to toe, he was also close to her age. "Hey, Cuz! Been a while since I've seen you. Rachel was so excited when we told her that Jett and Bella would be here today. She's already got them headed toward the corral to see Mama's newest colt."

Adele stopped at the porch to hug Rye and his father, her uncle Cash. "Hopefully, I'll buy the Double Deuce and be closer, so we can see each other more often."

Rye removed his hat and then resettled it on his head. "Got my fingers crossed, but Remy Luckadeau is going

to give you a run for your money. Slade told me that he's
determined that he'll own that place. Old Walter sure
pulled one over on y'all, getting one of you to work for
free in this deal."

"Yes, he did, but if I wind up the winner, then it
won't be such a bad deal and I get a place to live for a
month. If I lose the ranch, he's going to pay me wages
for the month, so it's not a lost cause. Just in case, and
don't you breath a word that I'm asking this, you know
about any other places I might be interested in?"

Cash pulled his dark brows down and nodded slowly.
There was no doubt he was Rye's father; they shared
the same face shape and body build, as well as the same
piercing eyes. "There's a place between us and Henrietta
that you might like. It's not stocked like Walter's place.
You'd have to buy your own cattle and reclaim about
half the land from the mesquite and cactus, but you
could buy it cheaper than what Walter is askin'."

She clapped a hand on her uncle's shoulder. "I'll sure
enough keep that in mind and I'd appreciate it if you'd
keep a watch out for anything else."

"Adele, is that you? We're in the kitchen," Maddie
called out.

"See you guys later," Adele said as she crossed the
porch and went inside.

"Hey, it's good to see you again," Austin said.

Dark-haired, beautiful Austin was her cousin Rye's
wife, and they'd struck up a friendship the first time
she'd met the woman. Austin was one of the few women
who was as tall as Adele and didn't make her feel like a
giant sunflower in a bed of dainty pansies.

Adele plucked a bib apron from a row of hooks and

slipped it over her bright, floral gypsy skirt and turquoise tank top. "Same here. What can I do to help?"

"Cut up the salad," Maddie said.

Her aunt was a force to be reckoned with on most days. On others, she was worse. She ruled the ranch with an iron fist, just like she'd raised her brood of children, and no one ever took her soft-spoken attitude for weakness. At least they didn't after the first time they dealt with her.

"The girls took Eddie Cash with them out to the corral. Can you believe that he'll be in the preschool program this year? I've just been telling Austin that it's time for another baby," Maddie said as she slid a pan of yeast rolls into the oven.

"It's Gemma's turn," Austin grinned. "Holly is five now, and she and Trace need another one to keep her from getting too spoiled."

"It's way too late for that. We've all spoiled Holly from the first day Trace and Gemma brought her to the ranch for a visit." Maddie laughed. "So tell me, how it's going, living with a hot Luckadeau cowboy?"

"I'm not living with him. We're only living in the same house," Adele answered.

"He is a handsome feller. He sat right behind us in church, and I checked him out. If I wasn't married to Rye, I might have winked at him," Austin said.

"Austin O'Donnell!" Adele gasped.

"Well, you aren't married, and he's not married. It might be fun to play house with him for a month." Austin pulled a stack of plates from the cabinet and carried them to the dining room.

"You could bring him to Sunday dinner and we'll see

if he's the kind of man we want our niece to play house with," Maddie whispered.

"Aunt Maddie, I'm not bringing him to meet the family."

"Why not? I really should pass judgment on him. Your mama says I'm supposed to keep an eye on you. She's expecting me to call her this evening and report anything I know about you and that man. She says you been too long without a feller in your life, but this ain't the time or the place. Besides, everyone in Texas knows that Remington Luckadeau is a player."

"Then why would you even want me to bring him to Sunday dinner?" Adele asked.

"Could be that a high-tempered redhead like you is just what he needs to tame him," Austin teased.

Adele shook her head. "Before I could tame him, I'd have to want to do it, and I damn sure do not."

"Then I'll tell my sister-in-law to rest easy. You've tested the horse out and you don't want to buy the old stallion." Maddie laughed.

"Or ride him either?" Austin raised an eyebrow.

Adele's eyes nearly popped out of her head. "Good Lord, Austin."

Jett started talking a mile a minute as soon as she was in the house. "Mama, Aunt Maddie has a new baby horse and it's got a white blaze on its head. And we need some horses on our ranch instead of just four wheelers. Can we buy one from Aunt Maddie? Please, Mama. It don't have to be one of her fancy horses but just one that I can ride to round up the cattle at brandin' time."

"First, we have to live on the ranch a month and see if Mr. Jones is going to sell it to us or to Remy. Then we'll see about a horse in another year or two. You girls get washed up. Dinner will be ready in a few minutes."

"A year is forever," Jett groaned.

"Come on." Seven-year-old Rachel, Austin and Rye's daughter, grabbed Jett's hand. "We can figure out a way to talk her into it while we wash our hands. I'm hungry. Did you make roast, Granny?"

"I did, with potatoes and carrots exactly the way you like them and hot rolls." Maddie hugged the little girl, who was already as tall as Jett. "Now go get cleaned up and don't eat too much because we gathered strawberries from the garden, and we're having shortcake for dessert."

"Yes!" Eddie Cash said with enthusiasm.

Rachel's little brother, the little boy was dark haired like his parents, but something in his eyes reminded Adele of Leo. Were the boys having as much fun as her girls were that Sunday afternoon? Were there other kids for them to play with?

"So are y'all acquainted with Slade Luckadeau?" she asked.

"Sure." Maddie nodded. "He has a ranch on the other side of the highway. Married a wonderful girl a few years back named Jane. His grandmother and her sister both live on the ranch and they're a hoot. Slade and Jane have three—no, four—kids since that last baby was born last Christmas, and she says that she might stop at half a dozen. You and Austin are falling way behind in the baby business, Adele." Maddie shook a serving spoon at them.

"I'm thirty-five years old, Aunt Maddie," Adele said.

"That's the new twenty-five. You could still have half a dozen kids if you'd get on the ball," Maddie said. "And so could you, Austin. I love grandkids, but I really love grandbabies, and it's been a while since we've had one. Besides, Adele, you live the closest to me, and I could spend more time with your babies than with Gemma's or Colleen's, since they are so far away."

"Better get them to move closer," Austin said. "I'm going to start toting things to the table, and, Eddie Cash, if you're all washed up, you can go call your dad and grandpa in for dinner."

Sunday dinner at Uncle Cash and Aunt Maddie's house wasn't all that different from the ones at Adele's folks' ranch out in the Panhandle. It didn't take long after they got home from church until dinner was on the table, grace was said, and food was being passed. Two hours later, they might get up and start the cleanup, but only if they weren't in deep conversation about the ranching business.

That day, it was four o'clock when the kitchen was finally put to rights. The three women poured glasses of sweet tea and joined the men, who'd already claimed two of the half-dozen rocking chairs on the front porch. Bella had begged a quilt from Aunt Maddie, and all the children were sprawled out under a big pecan tree, listening to Bella read a book.

Adele had barely gotten settled in a rocking chair when her phone buzzed. She pulled it from the deep pocket of her flowing skirt, and there was a one-line message from Remy: Come home now!

Her knee-jerk reaction was to call him and let him know that he had no rights to her time nor could he tell her what to do, but before she could position her thumbs to type, she got another message.

Emergency. Please.

"Looks like something is going on at the ranch, so we'll have to go," she said.

"So soon? You haven't even finished your tea."

"Remy says there's an emergency. Probably that cow that Bella said was about to drop her calf, so I'd better go see what I can do to help." Adele took a couple of long gulps of her sweet tea and set the glass back on the table between her and Maddie's chairs. "Thanks for the good company and the dinner and for saving us a spot in church."

"Anytime, darlin'," Cash said.

Bella and Jett didn't argue with her over leaving an hour early, which was a complete surprise. When they heard that the heifer might need help, they quickly folded the quilt, hugged their two younger cousins, and headed for the truck.

"I knew that old girl was about ready. I bet that calf is too big and needs my help pulling it out," Bella said.

"When will I be big enough to pull a calf?" Jett asked.

"It hasn't got a thing to do with size." Adele glanced back at her youngest child, who was small for her age. "When you get enough upper body strength in your arms, then I bet you'll be every bit as good at guiding one out as Bella is."

"Guess I'd better start lifting hay bales so I can get stronger." Jett popped her earphones on her head and started humming something that sounded like a Patsy Cline tune.

Adele was almost to the ranch when she remembered

she hadn't shopped for groceries. She slapped the steering wheel and sighed. At least Mondays were the boys' turn to do meals, and she could make a run to Nocona's small grocery store the next evening to pick up what she needed for the rest of the week. Snack foods were on the top of the list.

She parked beside Remy's truck, ran up on the porch, and slung open the door, intending to chase up the stairs and change into old jeans and a work shirt. But there was Remy, eyes flashing anger, arm propped on the newel post, and jaws working like he was chewing gum.

"What did you do to the air conditioner?" he asked tersely.

"What?" She frowned. "I thought you'd be out there with the heifer."

"What heifer?"

"Isn't that why you made us come home early?" Jett asked.

"No! I called because one of you three broke the air conditioner. You were the last ones out of the house this morning. What did you do? Jack it down too low because your curling iron made you too hot?"

Adele took two steps into his space. Their noses inches apart and a pure old hissy boiling up from her gut, she took a deep breath before she spoke. "We didn't do jack shit to that air conditioner, so don't accuse us."

"I'm not using my money to pay to have it fixed. Not when this isn't my ranch…yet," he said.

"Well, I'm damn sure not putting my money into this place until it belongs to me. I could buy a breeder bull with what it would take to put in a new unit, and I'm not paying for it," she shot right back at him.

"Then I guess it's going to be a long, hot month," he growled.

"I guess it will."

"Oh no! Blanche has a mouse in her mouth!" Leo squealed and climbed up on the third step of the staircase.

The cat carried it right toward him, and he ran to the top of the stairs. "Put her outside, Uncle Remy. Don't let her take that thing to my room."

"It's not a mouse, you stupid boy." Jett raised her voice. "She's had her kittens and she's taking them to our room. She always keeps them under our bed until they get their eyes open."

"I am not stupid!" Leo protested as he watched Blanche carry a gray kitten to the top of the stairs, sniff the air, and go straight for the girls' bedroom.

"If you don't know the difference between a baby kitten and a mouse, you must have cow patties for brains," Jett said.

Bella took the steps two at a time and yelled down when she reached her room, "There're five under the bed, and she's stretched out with them, so I think that's the last one."

Jett started up the stairs to join her sister. "Are all of them gray? I knew that old tomcat next door to our old house would be the daddy."

"No, I see a black one and a yellow one. The rest are gray," Bella said. "We can keep them in the house until they're six weeks old, right, Mama?"

"Depends on whether this ranch is ours or not. Until then, maybe you should open a window. It's getting pretty hot in this place, and Blanche will appreciate any breezes that flow in since *someone* broke the air conditioner," Adele said.

"I'm going out to milk the cow. You boys can help me check the water tanks and feed bins." Remy's voice was so cold that it dripped icicles.

"The girls and I are going to check that heifer. Did you even think to call a repairman for the air conditioner?" she asked, her tone matching his.

"I did, and he said it was too old to put another Band-Aid on it. He told Walter last month that it probably was on its last legs and would have to be replaced before the summer was out."

"Then why did you accuse us of breaking the damn thing?" she asked.

*Men!*

They were all alike. Something goes wrong, it has to be the woman's fault. And just when everything is going smoothly, they'll do something stupid to mess it up.

He stormed across the foyer, slammed the back door, and the boys followed him with Leo mumbling that he wasn't stupid, that kitten did look like a mouse, and he wasn't afraid of mice either.

"Boys," Adele mumbled and headed up to check on the new litter of kittens. By damn, she would own this ranch and those kittens would be her very first barn cats. If Remy Luckadeau couldn't stand the heat, then he could pack up his stuff and get out. Only then would she pony up the money for a new air conditioner.

# Chapter 7

REMY WAS USED TO SWEATING DURING THE DAY, AND IT didn't bother him a bit, but when it came time for sleeping, he liked to be cool. The windows in his bedroom had been opened, but not a single breeze ruffled the thin curtains. The ceiling fan stirred the air, but it felt like it was blown across a blazing campfire, sending nothing but hot air down on him.

The clock beside his bed moved so slowly that he feared the gears inside had been fried in the sweltering bedroom. It was a few minutes past midnight when he finally grabbed his pillow and a sheet and headed down the stairs. Sleeping outside on the porch or under a shade tree couldn't be any hotter than it was in that steam box called a bedroom.

The porch swing was too short for his lanky frame, but he managed to get comfortable. Maybe it was because it kept him moving back and forth that it felt a hell of a lot less hot than his comfortable bed. He finally slept, but it was only to dream of being a small boy again. He was standing in the middle of the kitchen. His mother fussed at him, telling him that a big man would admit it when he was wrong, and if he wanted to grow up to be a real cowboy, he needed to make things right.

Boss cold-nosed his toe not long after he'd gone to sleep, and when he tried to sit up, he rolled right out of the swing to land on the porch with the big dog staring down at him. His tail wagged but only for a second, and then it stopped. Every hair on his back stood straight up, his nose whipped around to the front door, and he growled deep down in his throat.

Remy looked under Boss's belly to see Blanche, every single yellow hair fluffed out and back arched, and heard a menacing hiss coming from the other side of the screen door. He sat up straight, laid a hand on the dog, and was in the process of calming him when Jerry Lee flew over Remy's head. Remy stopped petting Boss and instinctively protected his head with both hands. The rooster lit on the rumpled sheet still on the swing and crowed, but it sounded more like a chuckle. Then he perched on the back of the swing where he promptly left two tiny, black piles on the white sheet.

"So much for sleeping on the porch. Even if you hadn't messed up my sheet, I don't trust you. When I went to sleep, you'd peck both my eyes out." Remy picked up his pillow and went back inside the house.

Blanche was halfway up the stairs when he closed the screen door behind him. A slight breeze flowed through it, so Remy threw his pillow down right there on the relatively cool hardwood floor and went back to sleep. Sometime around daylight, he sneezed and awoke to find Boss curled up at his head, with only the screen separating them. Evidently, the old dog was still shedding his winter coat because Remy had to brush away yellow hairs that had slipped through the screen and landed on his face.

He felt every one of his thirty-five years when he rolled up to a sitting position and sneezed again. He'd never been allergic to dogs, cats, or anything but ragweed. Evidently, it was sending off pollen somewhere in the area.

He heard the back door open and close, bare feet padding across the kitchen, then into the foyer, and wondered if Jett had already gotten up and milked the cow. But it was Adele who stopped dead not a yard from him. She looked so damned cute with her tangled red hair and droopy morning eyes. The nightshirt barely came to her knees and gave him a fine shot of her long, muscular legs.

"Good mornin'," he said. "Guess you couldn't sleep either."

Without a word, she carried her pillow past him and started up the stairs.

"I'm sorry," he said.

She stopped. "What?"

"I was mean yesterday, and I'm sorry. I was so mad about the air conditioner that I had to blame someone, and I knew I didn't turn it down before we left, so I lashed out. It was a dumb thing to do."

"Yes, it was. Apology accepted. What's for breakfast?"

Remy groaned. "Something that does not require the oven, for sure. Where did you sleep?"

"On one of those old chaise longue out in the backyard. Uncomfortable as hell but not as hot as my bedroom," she answered and disappeared up to the landing.

------

Cool water beat down on Adele, showering away hours of sweat and cooling her body. She didn't mind the hard ranch work, even when it was cold enough to freeze the testicles off a brass monkey or hot enough to melt

Lucifer's horns, but when it came time to sleep, she wanted air-conditioning. The only times in her life that she'd slept without it had been when her family went camping, but her father always took them in late spring or early fall, not in the middle of a hot summer.

She'd gladly pay for a new unit if she knew she would own the ranch, or even if Remy would refund her money if he wound up with the Double Deuce. But what if he'd been right about Walter changing his mind? Then she might as well pour water down a rabbit hole because Walter would be within his rights to say that he didn't ask her to finance a new air conditioner so he wasn't giving her a dime.

Renting a room for her and the girls in that budget hotel on the east side of Nocona would be a hell of a lot cheaper than paying for a new air conditioner. But that would show weakness, and she wasn't about to let Remy think she wasn't tough enough to sweat it out.

"Today is the sixth. Five days down. Twenty-five to go. I can do this. I'm an O'Donnell and we're tough." She gave herself a pep talk as she turned off the water and picked up a towel.

She woke the girls on her way down to the kitchen. They'd been raised to be early risers, so they popped right out of bed. That morning, they didn't even need to make a halfhearted gesture at making it because they'd slept on top of the chenille bedspread and had the marks all over their legs to prove it.

"Little hot last night, was it?" she asked.

"It wasn't so bad. The ceiling fan kept things pretty decent, and when we went to sleep, we didn't know if it was hot or cold," Bella said.

Her precious oldest daughter who found the good in everything—most of the time, anyway.

Jett shrugged. "I like it so cold that I have to pull the covers up to my chin, but Leo says he's tougher than me, so I'm not telling him that."

"Good girl." Adele smiled for the first time since she and Remy had had words the evening before. Since they'd been on their own for supper, she'd given the girls permission to eat off paper plates and take their sandwiches up to their rooms. They'd spent the evening writing down potential names for the new kittens.

"I'm going to do the milking this morning. I'll see y'all at breakfast," Adele said.

"I miss having chickens and gathering eggs," Bella said. "If we get the ranch, can we make a henhouse and get some hens?"

"You bet we can." Adele nodded.

Remy looked up from the cabinet when she entered the kitchen. She made sure she didn't touch him as she edged around the counter and went into the pantry. She picked up the galvanized milk bucket, rinsed it out with cold water, and headed out the back door without saying a word to him. Forgiving did not mean kiss and make up in her world.

That he'd accepted the blame was something she'd never experienced with Isaac, so it was a whole new feeling and more than a little bit strange. If anything went wrong, up to and including the divorce, it had always been twisted to be her fault, and Isaac never apologized for anything. He wasn't physically abusive, but even when he was totally wrong, he was right in his mind.

She led the heifer from the corral into the milking stall, put a bucket of feed into the trough for the old girl to munch on, and kicked a three-legged stool into the proper place. She sat down, put the bucket under the cow's udders, and leaned her cheek against the warm flank. The first squirt of milk made a pinging sound in the bucket, and soon the mindless job gave way for her to think about other things.

It wasn't right to compare Isaac to Remy. She'd been married to one for more than a decade; she barely knew the other. Isaac was a diamond dealer who hated to have dust on his handmade shoes; Remy was a full-fledged cowboy who loved the land and tried to remember to wipe the bull shit from his boots before he came in the house for dinner.

Jerry Lee flew up on the top rail of the stall, then hopped down into the feed trough, where he commenced sharing the cow's breakfast. Evidently this wasn't something new, because the heifer ignored him and kept eating until Adele finished milking.

Adele took the bucket of milk out into the barn and set it in a wheelbarrow, then went back to lead the cow to the corral. When she returned, Jerry Lee was helping himself to a few sips of the milk. When she shooed him away, he fussed at her from the overhead rafters.

"You'd do well to be quiet. I can always tell Walter that you disappeared and we think a coyote ate you for supper." She shook her finger at the bird.

He fluffed his pretty feathers, threw back his head, and crowed.

Adele threw back her head and laughed. "So all it takes for you to crow at the right time of the day is to threaten you with coyotes. I'm telling on you when Walter gets home."

Four kids were sitting around the table when she came into the kitchen. The kitchen was a little warmer than when she'd left, but the wonderful aroma of french toast fried in butter made it bearable. She set the milk on the counter, fetched the cheesecloth and two gallon jugs from the pantry, and strained the milk before she put it in the refrigerator.

"I noticed there's a small electric churn on the top shelf in there. I'll skim half the cream off each gallon this week and make a pound or two of sweet cream butter," she said.

"Like we had at home? And we can have it with pancakes and homemade syrup?" Bella asked.

Adele nodded. "Maybe for breakfast on Saturday."

"It's ready. Who's going to say grace?" Remy asked.

"I will." Adele washed her hands and sat down at the end of the table.

Remy set the platter on the table beside another one piled high with sausage patties and took his place. Adele waited until all heads were bowed, and then she said a quick grace.

"Father, thank you for this beautiful day. Help us to appreciate the work that we are capable of doing. Bless this food and the hands that prepared it. Amen."

Jett's head jerked up first. "I can't believe you are blessing Remy after he was a horse's butt to you yesterday."

"Remy apologized and I accepted it. Would you please start the sausage around the table, Jett?" Adele said.

"You apologized?" Nick asked. "We didn't break the air conditioner, so why should you say sorry?"

"Because I accused the girls of breaking it, and they didn't do it either. It wore out and stopped on its own. When a man is right, he needs to stand up and fight to the death for what he believes in. But when he is wrong, he should man up and admit it," Remy said.

"Same goes for a woman." Adele shifted three pieces of toast onto her plate and reached for the syrup pitcher.

"You didn't apologize to him, did you?" Jett moaned.

"She didn't have anything to say sorry for," Remy said. "Now, can we eat our breakfast so we can get on with the day? We've got two tractors and eighty acres of hay that needs to be cut. Plus, the fence on the back forty needs some posts replaced. Walter used wood on that area and some of it has rotted. There's metal posts stored in the back barn. And we didn't finish painting the yard fence."

"Bella and I'll take the job of cutting the hay, and Jett can finish painting the yard fence," Adele said.

Remy nodded. "That leaves the back forty for us guys."

"Why do they get to drive tractors and we have to fix fence?" Nick argued.

"Can you drive a stick-shift tractor?" Jett asked.

Nick glared at her. "I can paint a fence."

"Not as good as I can. You painted too fast and your part had runs on Saturday. I had to come along behind you and fix it."

Adele put up a palm. "Enough bickering. Everyone has to learn and has to be given time to learn. Jett can't drive yet. Neither can you boys, but give Nick a year and he'll be driving as well as Bella. And a year after that, Jett and Leo will make boring rounds in the hay fields. If it doesn't rain next week, we'll be putting hay in the barns and everyone will be learning that job. Even Remy and I are still learning."

All four of the kids' heads popped up and stared at Adele like she had three eyeballs. Remy chuckled, and their gazes shifted to the other end of the table.

"When a person stops learning, they might as well drop over, graveyard dead." He shrugged. "Learning is what makes life fun. Now I'd say we need to finish our breakfast and get on about our jobs. I bought the makings for lasagna for dinner, but now I'm wondering what I should do since it's too hot in here to fire up the oven."

"Rats!" Jett thumped a fist on the table. "That's only my second-favorite meal. Mama, is he really forgiven?"

Adele nodded.

"Then show him how to make it in the slow cooker, and it'll be ready when we come in at noon."

"I can do that," Adele said. "We're burnin' daylight. Go brush your teeth while I show Remy how to make that."

Like always, it was a race from the kitchen to the landing, then an argument over who got to use the bathroom first. Remy and Adele stood up at the same time, loaded their arms with empty plates, and carried them to the dishwasher.

He was damn fine looking in those tight jeans and chambray work shirt, but she'd bet that he didn't kiss a damn bit better than Isaac or any of the other guys she'd dated before Isaac. But suddenly, she couldn't think of anything other than Remy's lips and how the only way she could prove she was right was simply to kiss him.

It didn't mean she would fall into bed with him or that it would be anything other than one simple kiss.

It wouldn't be the first time she'd taken the first step toward kissing a man.

She set the leftover toast on the countertop, waited until he was within reach, and slipped her hand around his bicep. She hadn't expected the sparks to be so hot or the electricity to bounce off the walls, but once she got the kiss over with, that wouldn't happen again. It was like that time she'd wanted to taste a new candy bar so badly, but when she finally bought one, it was a big disappointment.

"What?" Remy asked.

She took a step closer and rolled up onto her toes. His arms went around her waist, pulling her so close that air couldn't find its way between them, and he took control of the most amazing, heat rendering, leg-weakening kiss she'd ever had in her life.

There was not one thing simple or disappointing about it.

"What was that all about?" he asked hoarsely when he released her.

"I wanted to satisfy a question that's been bugging me."

"Which is?"

"How it would feel to kiss you," she answered honestly.

"And?"

One of her shoulders rose ever so slightly. "Better than some. Not as good as others."

She crossed her fingers behind her back like a little girl telling a white lie. She would never admit that her whole body hummed and her hormones whined for more.

He grinned. "We'll have to work on that."

"I don't think so, cowboy. I'm satisfied."

His smile widened. "I'll be damned. It usually takes a hell of a lot more than a kiss to satisfy my women."

# Chapter 8

AFTER TWO MORE NIGHTS OF FIGHTING MOSQUITOES THE size of buzzards, a rotten rooster who wanted to roost in her hair, and trying to get comfortable on a chaise longue, Adele was more than ready to sit down and negotiate a deal with Remy about an air conditioner. The kids were sprawled out all over the living room floor that evening watching another western movie from Walter's collection.

"A word in the kitchen, Remy?" she asked.

A positively wicked grin spread across his face, leaving no doubt he was remembering the kiss from Monday morning. She hoped that the high color in her cheeks could be passed off as the unbearable heat. The outside temperature had topped out that day at a 109 degrees, and the house wasn't cooling down a bit even though the sun had gone down.

She led the way and went straight to the refrigerator for ice, the first cube to rub on her face, the next six to go into a glass for more sweet tea. "We need to talk about this miserable heat."

"Weather-wise or otherwise?" He followed her example and rubbed an ice cube across his forehead.

"The otherwise is done with. I want air-conditioning. Can we come to an understanding about it?" She pulled out a chair and sat down at the table. She wore a pair of cutoff jean shorts and the sweat from the back of her thighs immediately formed a superglue-type bond with the chair.

"Such as?" He leaned on the bar separating the kitchen from the breakfast nook. It wasn't fair that he could look that cool in cotton pajama bottoms and a tank top when she might have to call someone to cut the chair away from her body.

"I propose that we each pay half for a new air conditioner. Then whoever gets the ranch can reimburse the other one. Whichever one of us winds up with it will put a unit in first thing, so we might as well do it now, so we aren't miserable all month. I called that repairman. He says he can bring one out tomorrow and have it operating by bedtime but that it might take until the next day to really cool the whole place down," she said.

"And if Walter doesn't sell us the place? If he comes back and says that he's decided to keep it?" Remy asked.

"Then we simply call the repairman and have him put the old one back in, and we take the one we bought with us. I'd be willing to give you your half at that time and take it with me wherever I go or else sell my half to you, if you're going somewhere that needs a new one," she said.

Remy sipped his tea. "You got things pretty well planned out, don't you?"

"I'm hot," she said.

"I agree," he drawled.

Crimson filled her cheeks again. "As in weather-wise."

"Well, dammit!"

She smiled. "Sorry, cowboy."

"I'm all for your idea. Do we shake on it, or do we have to write something down?" he asked.

She stuck out her hand. "Country agreement is fine with me."

His big hand held on to hers a moment longer than necessary, creating a strange mixture of cold from holding her icy glass of sweet tea to scorching hot from the chemistry between them. Finally, he let go and she picked up her glass to escape the heat.

Remy raised an eyebrow. "What if I'd said no?"

"Then I would have paid for the whole thing and told Walter that I had and he would have sold me the ranch because I took care of it better than you did. The varnish is about to melt off that fancy oak secretary in the living room because of this blistering heat," she said.

"So you were protecting my interests?" Remy asked.

"I was giving us both a fair chance," she said.

"You, Miz Adele O'Donnell, are a force."

"Yes, I am, and don't you forget it. I gave Derrick, that's the air conditioner man, my cell phone number. When he's finished, we'll both come to the house and give him our checks." She smiled.

Jerry Lee perched on a tree limb right outside the open kitchen window and crowed as if the sun were coming up.

"I guess he's sealing the deal," Remy said.

"It wouldn't take much for me to turn that bird into cat food for Blanche," Adele grumbled.

"Then I'd get the ranch for sure. Remember what Walter said about taking care of his dog and rooster."

"Only one more night of fighting him out of my hair...or maybe I'll just do what you've been doing and sleep on the floor in front of the door," she said.

"I'd gladly share my bed with you." He winked.

—∿∿—

Bantering with Adele was more fun than Remy had ever had. The way it had worked before his nephews came to live with him was that he worked hard all week, picking up a woman, most usually at a bar, and spending the night or maybe the weekend with her. They had hot sex and sent out for room service or else they cooked in her apartment/house/condo/trailer, drank a lot, had more hot sex, and then it was over. There was no joking around, no solving problems like air-conditioning or settling fights between kids.

Remy had never hurt for friends, but this was the first time that he'd ever had a woman who he could call his friend, even if it was loosely. He liked it, all of it—breakfast, working on the ranch, getting from daylight to bedtime, all with her by his side.

"You throw off too much heat for me to sleep in the foyer with you," Adele finally answered.

"So you think I'm hot?" he teased.

"I think everyone in this house is hot, including Blanche, who is used to air-conditioning all the time. Poor old hussy has moved her kittens twice trying to find a cooler spot for them. Now they're on a sheet right under the bedroom window."

"Want to go back to the living room and watch the rest of the movie with the kids or stay out here and make out like a couple of teenagers?" he asked.

"Don't forget your tea," she said with a grin as she headed back to the living room.

The movie was over shortly after they returned, and Jett wanted to dye her hair red like her mother's and

Maureen O'Hara's. She argued that she'd give up having a space between her front teeth if she could please have red hair and her mother would teach her how to pile it up on top of her head.

Remy was still laughing about the way Adele had put her foot down when he went up to his room that night. He really did try to sleep in his bedroom, so Adele could have the foyer, but it wasn't possible. He couldn't get comfortable no matter how hard he tried, so he finally picked up his pillow and a sheet and dropped them in the foyer as he went through on his way to the kitchen for an ice cube.

He'd just rubbed the ice on his forehead when he heard a purring sound coming from the utility room. Blanche had moved her kittens again. He should locate them, especially if she'd put them in the washer or the dryer, thinking that they'd be cool in the metal. It wasn't until he was about to step on her that he realized Adele was sleeping on the floor next to the back screen door. The moonlight lit up her red hair and defined the contours of her face and those amazing lips.

Those lips were like nectar to a honey bee, calling to him to steal one more kiss while she slept, but if he woke her, she'd come out of a deep sleep and knock him square on his ass for sure. He braced a shoulder against the doorjamb and watched her sleep for several minutes before he went back to his place in the foyer. Tomorrow night, maybe, with any luck, the house would cool down enough that they could both get a good night's sleep. Adele had black circles under her eyes, and she hadn't been eating enough to keep old Jerry Lee alive.

The sound of pots and pans rattling in the kitchen

awoke him before dawn. He was so glad that he didn't have to make breakfast that morning. Even the stovetop heated the lower level of the house five to ten degrees. The aroma of bacon and coffee wafted through the foyer. He picked up his bedding and took the steps two at a time to beat the kids to the bathroom, where he showered, shaved, and then handed it off to the boys as he went to change into work clothes. They would be hauling hay all day. It had been cut on Monday, raked on Tuesday, and baled on Wednesday. The heat had helped dry it, so the process was a day ahead of schedule. Now it was ready to put in the barn that they'd cleaned the previous week.

"Holy smoke," he murmured. "We've already been here a week. Where has the time gone?"

"You talkin' to me?" Leo peeked through the crack in the door.

"No, to myself. Did you realize that yesterday we had been here a week?"

Leo pushed the door open and sat down in the recliner next to the open window. "I like it here, Uncle Remy. I didn't think I would and I sure thought I'd miss Wi-Fi, but I haven't. Can I change my mind about ranchin' and livin' here?"

"Sure you can, son." Remy tousled Leo's red hair. "Now, we'd better not be late for breakfast."

"I smelled bacon when I woke up. I hope Adele is making fried eggs this morning. She makes them with soft centers so I can dip my toast in them."

The edge of the sun was peeking over the horizon, sending out enough light to define trees into something other than blobs. Through the kitchen window, Remy caught sight of Boss sitting out in the backyard, eyes toward the barn, protecting the house, and Jerry Lee, sitting on a fence post with his head tucked under one wing.

Adele handed him a cup of steaming-hot coffee. "Seems crazy to drink coffee when it's this hot."

"Not any weirder than a rooster that performs in the middle of the afternoon or at dusk rather than dawn," he answered.

"Walter caused it when he named him Jerry Lee. The bird thinks he's a rock star, and they don't get up early." Adele smiled at him.

"What are you going to do with him and Boss if you get the ranch?"

"Keep them, of course. It was their home long before it was mine. We'll make them happy right up until they die, and then we'll have funerals," she answered as she flipped four fried eggs onto a platter and cracked more into the big cast-iron skillet.

"Are you serious?"

"About funerals? Of course I am. Last month, our cow dog died and we buried him under his favorite shade tree. And we had a proper funeral. We put him in a wooden crate and we each said a few words. He'd been with us since Bella wasn't quite two years old," she answered. "What about you? What will you do with Jerry Lee and Boss?"

"The same but maybe without funerals."

"I bet Nick and Leo will insist on them."

Remy shook his head slowly from side to side. "They're boys, not sentimental girls."

"What about girls?" Bella asked as she opened the cabinets to get down the plates.

"Or boys?" Leo smiled when he saw the fried eggs piling up on the platter.

"What would either of you do if, say, five years from now, Jerry Lee and Boss died?" Remy asked.

"Have a funeral for them," Bella said.

"And put stones on their graves, so we could take flowers like we do to Mama's and Daddy's graves," Leo said.

"Score one for me," Adele whispered.

"Mama, can we have a contest today?" Bella asked.

"As in?" Adele put the last of the eggs on the platter.

Jett and Nick finally found their way to the kitchen and, seeing that breakfast was about to be served, sat down in their regular seats.

"Contest about what?" Jett asked.

"Hay hauling." Nick yawned. "Bella says she knows more about it than I do, but I can learn real fast, and we want to see who can bring in the most bales today."

"We can hook up that flatbed trailer to the back of the tractor and Jett can drive it. I've been teaching her to shift gears and steer, and she's pretty good at it," Bella said.

"Oh, you have." Adele cocked her head to one side.

Bella nodded. "I had to put her on a pillow since she's so short, but she's pretty good and hardly ever grinds the gears. We'll throw the bales, and when we get them to the barn, Jett can help us unload and keep track of how many we bring in. The boys can decide who drives Mr. Jones's work truck. As loose as the gears are and as slow as we go, I bet Leo could catch on real quick."

"Whoa! I haven't gotten to drive yet," Nick protested.

"Who do you think can throw bales fastest? You or

Leo?" Bella's finger shot up to point at him. "But hey, it's your call."

"Yes!" Leo's fist shot up into the air.

"You could take turns driving," Remy suggested.

The grin that covered Nick's face said that, by night, he'd be asking if they could stay on the ranch forever, too.

"And what's the prize?" Remy asked, but his eyes were locked with Adele's.

"Ice cream!" Nick said. "We go to town tonight for ice cream and the loser has to buy."

"Y'all girls should give us twenty bales to start with since you already know how to drive," Leo said.

Jett batted her thick lashes at him and threw the back of her hand across her forehead. "But we're just weak little girls and y'all are big, strong boys. You should give us fifty bales to make it fair."

"That ain't happenin'," Nick said.

Jett glared at both boys. "You got it, cowboys. We'll beat your sorry butts without a handicap."

"What do you know about golf?" Leo asked.

"As much as you, probably," Bella said, joining in the fuss. "Can we have the contest, Mama?"

Adele didn't blink or look away from Remy. "Fine with me. I could eat some ice cream tonight."

"Better count your pennies because we intend to win." Remy grinned. "Leo, you should say grace since Adele made fried eggs."

All heads bowed and eyes shut except Remy's and Adele's. Finally, she winked and bowed her head to hear Leo's prayer. Remy took advantage of the situation to stare his fill of her. If and when he did ever settle down to life with one woman, he wanted one like Adele

O'Donnell. Beautiful and yet strong. Someone who loved ranching as much as he did and who could handle kids with a look or a few words.

# Chapter 9

THE BOYS' TEAM WAS AHEAD BY FIVE BALES WHEN THEY quit for dinner at noon. Adele tossed her gloves on top of two smaller pairs on the tack room table and got into the driver's seat of the work truck. The girls were already in the back, plotting against the boys, who were unloading the last of their final load for the morning.

She could see the big, square, two-story house, painted white, with a wide front porch and a small back stoop that led into the mudroom right off the kitchen. It had been built for a family, not a couple, but Walter had told her the first time she looked at the place that he and his late wife hadn't been blessed with children.

"What a shame," she murmured. "It needs the laughter of children."

"What does?" Remy crawled into the passenger seat.

"That house. It would be empty without kids."

"Confession? When I found out that I was going to be raising two boys, I thought my life was over, but now I can't imagine life without Nick and Leo."

"How long ago did you get them?"

"My brother and sister-in-law were killed in a car wreck a couple of days before Thanksgiving last year. My folks went to Denton and kept the boys until I could tie things up at my job, and I moved into the house with them in February. This morning Leo told me that he'd changed his mind about living on a ranch.

It almost brought tears to this rough, old cowboy's eyes," Remy said.

"If he asks for cowboy boots to start to school in, then you'll know you're on the right track." She started the engine and drove toward the house, the trailer bumping along behind the truck and the kids' voices floating inside as they tried to decide who was the hungriest and who worked the hardest and who would win the contest.

"What are we eating?" Remy asked above the din.

"Make-your-own hero sandwiches, with chips and dip, and Popsicles for dessert," she answered.

"Sounds good to me."

"Look! Look! The man is putting in our air conditioner," Jett squealed.

Remy reached across the wide bench seat and patted Adele on the shoulder. "It won't be long until you and Blanche are comfortable again."

"Don't tease me. You know very well you'll be as excited as I am to sleep in the cool comfort of a real bed again," she said.

"Oh, I don't know. I'm kind of getting used to the hardwood floor and the smell of dog on the other side of the screen. And I know Jerry Lee is going to miss that red hair."

"Crazy rooster perched right outside the door and stared at me when I slept in the utility room," she said and laughed.

The week had not gone the way she'd thought it would. She'd planned to divide the chores and only deal with Remy and the boys at mealtimes. She'd certainly never thought about having conversations with Remy or becoming his friend.

*Friend!*

Was that what had happened? She'd had guy friends in high school, but that was a long time ago, and she'd certainly never shared a house with them. Since then, she'd had acquaintances more than friends. Everything had been business with Isaac. Dinners out meant something to do with diamonds or new customers. Parties were all about the same. Even their anniversary celebrations involved his business.

*Well*, she thought as she swung the truck door open and set her feet on the ground, *if I'm going to have a guy friend, I can't think of a better one than Remy. We can talk ranchin', cows, hay, and barns all day, and we like the same music and old movies. Who'd have ever thought that my worst enemy could be a friend? But hey, that does not mean I'll cut him an inch of slack when it comes to this ranch.*

"Penny for your thoughts," Remy said as he fell in beside her.

"It would take more than a penny, but I'll tell you if you'll move off the ranch and let me have it," she said.

"Dream on, pretty lady," he said seriously.

A tall, blond-haired man wearing a shirt with *Thad* embroidered on the pocket rounded the end of the house and yelled at them. "Hey, y'all. I'll have this done in an hour, and then I'll just have to put in the new thermostat. Y'all going to be in the house for a little while?"

"Yes, we are," Remy answered.

"That's good. Then I can give you the bill, collect the payment, and you can start cooling down this house. I told Walter last time I was here that the thing was limping on its last leg. It'll only take fifteen or twenty minutes to get the thermostat installed. That shouldn't slow y'all down by much."

"We can take a long lunch break for cool air," Adele said. "You got plenty of water out there?"

"I got a five-gallon cooler of ice water and a gallon of sweet tea. Already stopped long enough to eat my dinner, so I'm good to go. See you in a little bit." He turned and waved over his shoulder.

Bella was already getting all the makings for hero sandwiches out of the refrigerator when Adele made it to the kitchen. Jett had gotten six plastic cups from the pantry and was filling them with ice cubes.

"Mama, can we take a quilt and our food out under the shade tree and have a picnic?" Bella asked. "At least there's some wind out there."

"That's fine. We've got at least an extra half an hour, so y'all can eat slowly today and maybe even have time for a short power nap."

"I'd rather read as nap," Bella said. "I'll say grace, and then everyone can get their sandwiches made. Nick if you'll carry my tea, I'll get the quilt from the living room."

———∾∾———

Remy stood back and watched four hungry kids slap meat, cheese, and all kinds of different things on long buns. Instead of putting chips on their plates, Jett tucked a bag under her arm and Leo set the container of dip on top of his sandwich. They paraded out into the backyard, and each of them claimed a corner of the quilt Bella had laid out.

"They need a picnic table," he said.

"After today they'll be glad to spend their noon hour

in the cool house." Adele had already set about layering meat and cheese onto her bread.

He really liked that she never mentioned dieting or being too fat and that she enjoyed her food without saying that she shouldn't eat this or that because of calories and fat grams. Seeing her in church Sunday let him know that she cleaned up real good, but he liked her best with her hair pulled up into a ponytail and wearing her faded work jeans and chambray shirt with the sleeves rolled up to the elbows.

"So are we going to the picnic?" he asked.

"Not me. I'm going to sit right at the table, where there're no mosquitoes, ants, or flies and no Jerry Lee eyeing my hair to make a nest or Boss wanting half my sandwich. Besides, they're getting along out there right now. I'm not interfering," she answered.

She opened a bag of chips and set it in the middle of the table and went back to the counter for her tea and sandwich. "Do you ever get bored with ranchin'?"

He prepared his dinner and followed her to the table. "Never have yet and I'm thirty-five years old."

"Me, too. When's your birthday?"

"August eleventh," he answered.

"July fifth. I'm older than you," she said.

"I always did think older women were sexy." He bit into the sandwich.

"Is that one of your pickup lines?"

"Nope, just the truth," he said after he'd swallowed. "So you were almost a firecracker."

"A day late, but Mama said I got the red hair and the temper anyway," she said. "So are you the oldest, the youngest, or an only child?"

"None of the above. I'm the fourth in a family of five boys. Three older than me and one a year younger. Luckadeaus mostly throw boys. My cousins Slade and Griffin have daughters. But for the most part, there's more cowboys than cowgirls," he said.

"Any of those four brothers married?"

"Every one of them, and they've all got kids." He chuckled. "But now there's only four of us, since we lost one brother in the car wreck. My turn. How many are in your family?"

Adele held up two fingers. "I'm five years older than my sister, Cassandra Grace. She's married to her job, which is ranchin'. Jett and Bella are the only two grandchildren. Daddy would love to have a grandson. But my girls know enough about the land and cattle that he doesn't whine too much."

"If I had a couple of girls like them, I wouldn't whine either," Remy said. "Hell, I'd hire both of them."

Adele's mouth curved up in a brilliant smile. "Now that's a compliment."

"It's the gospel truth is what it is. I'm going to go to the living room and stretch out in the recliner for one of those power naps you talked about. Wake me when it's time to write my check," he said.

He had barely gotten still and shut his eyes when Thad knocked on the front door, stuck his head inside, and yelled that he was coming in to work on the thermostat. Then he started talking, and there was no way in hell Remy could sleep, not after Thad's first pickup line.

"So, what's a beautiful redhead like you doin' haulin' hay? You should be modelin' bikinis on a runway in Dallas," he said smoothly.

"And you should be selling used cars," she said with a hint of ice in her voice.

Thad laughed. "You are a feisty one."

Remy had his hand on the handle of the recliner but then thought better of it. Adele could take care of herself, and if he had learned anything, it was that she wouldn't appreciate him coming to her rescue.

"Been told that before. We're burnin' daylight here, so if you could get the job done and we can cool this house down, I'd appreciate it."

Remy heard her footsteps heading back to the kitchen.

"Hey, Red, how about me and you go dancin' Saturday night? I'll take you to dinner first, and then we can two-step until the Lazy Rope closes over near Gainesville." He raised his voice as he spoke.

The footsteps stopped and got louder, then stopped again. Remy eased out of the chair without popping the footrest down and tiptoed across the floor so he could see what was going on.

Adele had a finger right against the kid's nose and the expression on her face was the same one that he'd seen when he'd accused her of breaking the air conditioner. He almost felt sorry for the young man.

"Don't you ever call me 'Red' again," she hissed.

"And if I do?" he asked.

"Then your boss will have to train someone to do your job and you'll be pushin' up daisies on the back side of this ranch."

"Like I said, you're feisty. I've never dated a red-head. Married a brunette and a blond. It might be fun to see just how sassy you can be." The crazy kid had the audacity to smile.

"How old are you?" Adele asked.

He ran his knuckles up her forearm. "Twenty-four."

She picked up his hand and dropped it like it was a piece of trash. "Don't touch me. That and your behavior could get your young ass fired."

"My apologies," he said quickly. "You looked like a fun-loving type of woman. I guess I was wrong."

"Yes, you were. I'll be in the kitchen when you get done," she said.

Remy went back to the chair and popped the footrest down loudly. The way the house was laid out, there was only one way out of the living room, and he had to pass Thad on his way up the stairs to get his checkbook. He met Blanche halfway up. Her tail was twice as big as it should have been, every hair standing on end. Her eyes were glued on Thad. If she could have gotten through the rails, she could have walked out onto his head.

"Hey, old girl," Remy said softly.

Thad looked up to see the big, yellow cat glaring at him and took a step back. "I'm allergic to cats, and they hate me anyway."

"Then I hope you get finished real soon," Remy said.

When Remy returned, Thad was in the kitchen writing up the invoice and signing his name to the bottom. Remy laid his checkbook on the counter and wrote out a check for exactly half of what was on the bill.

"So y'all are babysitting the ranch while Walter is on vacation? I can't believe that old toot is going to sell. Him and his wife, Miz Pansy, have lived here forever. My grandpa used to live down the road and he's the one that Miz Pansy called when she decided to put in air-conditioning. He was already out of the business, but my daddy had stepped in to take care of things." Thad talked too much and his eyes flitted around to everything but Adele.

Poor kid! He had no idea what kind of woman he was flirting with when he'd tried out his pickup line on Adele O'Donnell. Remy almost felt sorry for him.

"So how long has Pansy been gone?" Remy asked.

"Died the year I graduated, which would be six years ago, the year before my grandma and grandpa both passed away, within six months of each other," Thad answered.

Adele finished her check and laid it on top of the invoice. "Thank you for getting this done so quickly. We appreciate it."

"Yes, we do. Kids didn't seem to mind the heat so much, but Adele and I've been sleeping on the hardwood floor to get some relief," Remy said.

Thad's head shot up and his eyes darted from Remy to Adele, and then his thin mouth turned up in a wide grin. "Well, it should be cooler in here tonight. Big as this house is, it might take until sometime tomorrow to get it down to where you like it, but you should be able to sleep in the bed tonight and not on the floor."

Adele heard the door slam and the crunch of gravel under the tires on Thad's truck before she slapped Remy on the arm. "Do you have any idea what that kid thinks and what he will spread all over this area?"

"That we slept together on the hardwood floor. You are welcome."

She met his gaze across the two feet of space separating them. "For what?"

"Now he won't be sending flowers and stalking you.

But I have to admit, when I was twenty-four, I might have tried to make a move on you, too."

"I'm not even going to answer that. Let's shut the windows and get some cool air flowing in this hot house." After abruptly changing the subject, she whipped around to close the kitchen window.

———

The bales of hay weighed somewhere in the neighborhood of eighty pounds, but they felt featherlight to Adele as she tossed them from ground level up to the trailer where Bella manhandled them into stacks. Four across and three high for two rows, and then two high for several rows before she brought in the last ones at only one high. That way they didn't fall off the trailer on the way back to the barn and they were easier to unload.

Take the load back to the barn, unload, and start all over again until the field was cleared, and hopefully, there would be enough rain to bring the grass back up for another cutting or two that summer. But Adele wasn't thinking about the weight of the bales, the rain, or even who would win the contest. She was trying to sort out the roller coaster of emotions that had overwhelmed her since she'd first said she would move to the Double Deuce.

When the day ended, her arms ached even though she was used to hard work, and not one thing was settled other than she'd have to pay for the ice cream that night. The boys had won fair and square, bringing in ten more bales than the ladies. It was just what Nick and Leo needed to give them confidence and what Jett and Bella needed to keep them from getting too cocky.

"We did it." Leo strutted around the barn worse than Jerry Lee did just before he started crowing. "We won, and now y'all have to buy our ice cream."

"This is just round one, boy." Jett glared at him. "Next time we have a contest, we'll bet our summer wages."

"No, you will not," Adele said.

"What summer wages? You get paid? I thought you said you didn't get an allowance." Nick pushed a strand of light-brown hair up under his baseball cap.

"They don't, but if they help me all summer and we don't have to hire an extra hand, then I pay them what I would have paid for part-time help," Adele explained as they walked toward the house.

"Do we get that, Uncle Remy?" Nick asked.

"Not this year because you're still getting an allowance. If you decide to be ranchers, we might work something like that out for next summer," he answered.

"Don't matter. We get ice cream and the girls have to buy it," Leo said.

"I've got an idea. Why don't we be good sports about today, since we all worked so hard? The girls have to buy the ice cream because they have to pay their debt, but why don't we buy supper for them? We could get burgers or tacos or whatever else the Dairy Queen has on the menu and then have ice cream for dessert," Remy said.

It was on the tip of Adele's tongue to say no, but then she realized that Remy was teaching the boys a lesson as valuable as the one her girls had learned that day.

"I could go for a big old greasy cheeseburger basket in an air-conditioned café. Jett and Bella did run us a pretty good race," Nick said.

"Leo?" Remy laid a hand on his nephew's shoulder.

"Long as they buy the ice cream, I'm all in. I like Dairy Queen burgers and tater tots," he answered.

"Cowboys don't go to town all sweaty and dirty, and we will leave in one hour," Remy said.

"Girls get first dibs on the bathroom." Bella took off in an all-out run toward the house, with Jett coming in right behind her, Nick and Leo bringing up the rear.

"Too bad we didn't have another fifty bales in each pasture. With all that energy and the sun not even down yet, we could have gotten more in the barn," Remy said.

"Wouldn't you love to have that much energy at the close of a day? Look at that. Boss is meeting them. I think he's beginning to accept us."

"Looks like it," Remy said. "You ever think you'd be doing this just to buy a ranch?"

"Not one time," Adele said. "But I have to admit, it's going better than I thought it would."

"Me, too. They bicker, but it's like cousins arguing, not like enemies. You should stick around for the Fourth of July party I'm planning when this ranch is mine. I'll show you lots of cousins."

Adele giggled. "You are invited to stick around when this ranch is mine and I have my birthday and Fourth of July celebration combined. You'll see how many O'Donnell cousins I have. I know very well what it's like to argue with cousins, and most of the time I win. O'Donnells are Irish, and they love to argue."

"Luckadeaus come from Cajun background, and they invented arguing." Remy stopped at the gate and opened it for her.

"Then it's a good thing that the Luckadeaus and O'Donnells never mixed their bloodlines."

Remy went through the gate and then shut it. "You got that right. It would be a total disaster."

Adele slipped into the bathroom right after the girls came out all wrapped up in terry robes, with towels around their freshly washed hair. She turned on the shower, adjusted the water to a cool temperature, and peeled out of her sweaty clothing, leaving it in a pile on the floor. It wasn't until she finished cleaning up and washing her hair that she realized how cold it was in the bathroom.

"Hallelujah," she mumbled as she grabbed her robe and shoved her arms into it. "By bedtime it'll be cold enough that I'll sleep like a baby."

"Let's hope not," Remy said from the other side of the door when she opened it. "Babies wake up at all hours and whine and have to be rocked. No one in this house is big enough to rock you but me, and I sure don't want you to wake me up on our first night in a cool house. By the way, that's a real sexy getup you got on."

"Luckadeaus do not flirt with O'Donnells," she said.

He stepped into the bathroom and started singing in a lovely, deep voice. She recognized the old Conway Twitty tune "I See the Want To in Your Eyes." She rushed to her bedroom and leaned across the dresser to look into her eyes. She couldn't see anything there that would make him think of that song, so he was just messing with her mind.

"And doing a fine job of it," she whispered.

⌁⌁⌁

Remy needed to provide an example for his nephews, especially since he'd given them the little speech about cowboys not going to town looking like shit. So he chose a pair of creased jeans and green-and-yellow plaid, pearl-snap shirt from his closet. He splashed on a little shaving lotion, even though he hadn't taken time to shave, and made sure all the dust had been brushed off his boots.

He hummed a Blake Shelton tune as he knocked on his nephews' door. "Wagon train leaves in five minutes."

"We're down here already," Nick yelled. "Adele already left with the girls and said she'd meet us there. She has to stop by the store to get something."

"Then"—Remy started down the stairs—"I guess it's time for us to get it in gear."

It only took about fifteen minutes to go from the ranch to the Dairy Queen, and Adele had just parked on the west side of the café. She got out of the truck and Remy's mouth went totally dry. She wore a bright-blue-and-white-checked sundress that left her shoulders bare and nipped in at her small waist, then flared out and stopped right at knee level. She wore a pair of brown cowboy boots with all kinds of cutouts and designs on them.

It was a good thing Thad hadn't seen her looking like that, or he would have had to nail his chin to his nose to keep his jaw shut. Remy waved and slung his long legs out of the truck.

"Boys," he said hoarsely, "remember your manners."

"Ahh, shucks, Uncle Remy." Leo kicked the gravel. "I wanted to beat them in so I could tease Bella about losing a second time."

"Cowboys respect women," Remy said.

"I'm not sure I want to be a cowboy." Nick looked like a skateboarder in his cargo shorts and sandals, his cap on backward.

"Well, I do, and I'm saving my allowance all summer long so I can have a pair of boots to wear to school this fall. I saw a western-wear store on the way here, and I imagine they'll have some in my size," Leo said stoically. "And if cowboys have to let the girls go in the café first, then I'll do it."

"Maybe I should say it this way, Nick. Men, whether they are cowboys or lawyers, should respect women. Did you ever see your father be disrespectful to a lady?"

Nick's chin dropped to his chest and he shook his head. "Daddy would never do that. Mama would have shot him."

Remy laid a hand on the boy's shoulder. "You got that right. Here they all come. Let's open the door and be gentlemen."

The Dairy Queen in Nocona was made up essentially of three rooms with open spaces between them. The first one had a big, round table and booths. Tables were positioned down the middle, with booths on either side of the room off to the left that used to be the nonsmoking area before the whole place declared it was smoke-free. The soft drink and tea dispensers were in the room to the back, where the smokers used to gather.

Folks surrounded a couple of tables in the back room. No one was in the former nonsmoking area, and a couple of older ladies were having ice cream in a corner booth not far from the counter. There was plenty of room at the counter for the kids to line up across it, like calves bellying up to a feed trough.

Leo sighed and twisted his mouth up to one side. "Would you girls hurry up and order? I'm about to starve plumb to death because I'm being a gentleman."

"A what?" Bella asked.

"Uncle Remy says that girls go first," Leo answered.

"I'll have a bacon cheeseburger basket and a medium drink," Bella said.

"He's crazy if he thinks he can make a cowboy out of you," Jett said. "I'll have the same thing as my sister."

The girl taking their order looked at Nick.

"Chicken strip basket with tater tots and ranch dressing on the salad," he said.

"I want a burger with double tater tots," Leo said. "And FYI, Jett O'Donnell, there's a better chance of Uncle Remy making a cowboy out of me than there is of your mama making a lady out of you."

Remy shook his head at Leo. "That's enough bickering. I'll have the bacon cheeseburger basket with fries and a large drink."

"Make mine the same, no onions," Adele said.

The kids started into the room off to the left, arguing but keeping it quiet enough that the noise didn't knock any of the Coca-Cola trays from the walls.

Remy paid for dinner. The lady said she'd bring it out when it was ready, and he and Adele had already taken a couple of steps in the direction of the kids when he heard someone say his name. He whipped around to find Nellie and Ellen motioning for him to come over and talk to them.

"The gray-haired one is Nellie," he said softly. "The floozy-looking one is her sister, Ellen. Nellie is my cousin, Slade's grandmother. Come on over here and meet them."

Adele suddenly felt overdressed. She should have worn jeans or at the least a pair of shorts and a T-shirt. The sundress left her shoulders bare, and it stopped at her knees, showing entirely too much leg. And she'd applied too much eye shadow. All the insecurities she'd kept buried shot to the top of her thoughts like marshmallows in a cup of hot chocolate.

Damn it! She wanted to slump so she didn't look like an ugly weed in a lovely garden. If only the sun weren't shining so brightly so her hair wouldn't have looked so red and the freckles on her face wouldn't have shone.

She'd bluffed her way through situations before, so she'd manage, but it was taking a toll on her stomach. Double damn it! The last time she'd let herself get twisted up like this was when she met Isaac's parents. At that time, she'd already had a two-carat emerald-cut diamond on her finger, so there had been reason to worry about them liking or not liking her. This was simply meeting shirttail kin of a man she might not ever see again if he won the rights to buy the Double Deuce and she had to go shopping. If she bought that ranch between Ringgold and Henrietta, her girls wouldn't even go to school with Nick and Leo, so that would put a bigger chasm between them.

He made introductions. "Nellie and Ellen, this is Adele O'Donnell, the woman I told y'all about on Sunday."

"I'm a ranchin' woman, too." The taller of the two women held out her hand.

"And I'm the two-bit hussy who drives too fast, so she refuses to let me get behind the wheel. Sit down here beside me, darlin', and we'll talk about sexy men." Ellen scooted over, making room for Adele.

Nellie did the same on the other side and Remy slid right in beside her. When he did, his knees and Adele's had no other place to go except right against each other. Evidently, he didn't feel all the heat and sparks that she did, or he would have moved his legs away.

"So I see y'all decided to come to town to have supper," Nellie said.

"And ice cream." Adele smiled. "We have to buy the ice cream after supper because we lost the battle today."

"What battle?" Ellen asked. "And why would you bet with ice cream when you've got his hot cowboy around? When I was your age, I would have used something a whole lot more fun for the winner."

"Ellen!" Nellie fussed. "Don't mind her, Adele. She's in her second childhood, or maybe I should say her second teenage years. All she thinks about is driving fast, drinking alcohol, and having sex."

"The three best things in life." Ellen sighed. "And I'm too damned old to get to do any of them anymore. Okay, then why did you bet with ice cream, and what was the bet all about?"

"Girls against boys who could bring in the most bales of hay. The boys beat us, but it was close." Adele managed to cut off her blush at neck level. All she needed were clown cheeks to go with her freckles and red hair.

"You have the loveliest red hair," Nellie said. "I've always loved a true redhead, not a strawberry blond or that strange new burgundy color I see girls dying their hair these days, but like Maureen O'Hara's hair when she was young."

"Thank you." Adele smiled.

"It looks like the lady is taking our food to the table,"

Remy said. "It's sure good to see y'all. Tell Slade and Jane hello for me."

"Come on back around any Sunday. We enjoyed the company," Ellen said. "And you can bring Adele and the girls next time."

Remy slid out of the booth, but the heat he'd left behind on Adele's knees didn't disappear so quickly. "Well, thank you, Ellen. Maybe we'll do just that. I'll call if we get a free Sunday between now and the end of the month. But put it on your calendars that all the Luckadeaus are gathering at my ranch for the Fourth of July."

"In your wildest dreams maybe," Adele said. "He won't have the ranch, but I will, and y'all are more than welcome to join the O'Donnells for a bash celebrating Independence Day and my birthday at *my* new ranch."

"Aha, another contest. And this time, it might involve more than ice cream," Ellen said.

Adele was not able to keep the blush from her cheeks that time. She waved good-bye to the ladies and made a hasty retreat to the other room, to sit at the table the kids had claimed. Just like at home, the boys were on one side, the girls on the other, leaving the ends for Adele and Remy.

"Who are those ladies y'all were talkin' to?" Jett asked.

"Remember Slade, our cousin that I told you about, where we went last Sunday for dinner? That's his grandma and his aunt. The grandma is the one with gray hair," Leo explained as he removed the paper from around his burger and bit into it. "OMG, this is the best burger ever in the whole world."

"I guess he's hungry." Remy smiled. "Sorry if Ellen made you uncomfortable. She's a pistol."

"I want to grow up to be just like her." Adele squirted lines of ketchup across her french fries, picked one up, and popped it into her mouth. No way would she admit that Ellen had, indeed, nearly made her blush.

"In all three things?" Remy raised an eyebrow.

Adele sipped at her icy-cold Coke, but it didn't do much to help the crimson filling her cheeks. "I only have two to go. I already drive too fast."

"Yes, she does," Bella said. "Jett and I have to watch the road for cops. They hide in the craziest places and sometimes we barely see them in time."

"Adele O'Donnell!" Remy gasped in mock sur-prise. "Which of the other two things are you going to adopt first?"

"What are they?" Jett asked.

"One has to do with drinking a lot of liquor," Adele answered.

"She don't like anything but a beer once in a while," Bella said. "Father liked martinis, and she made them for him, but she didn't drink."

"How do you know that?" Adele asked.

"Grandmother Levy told us. She said that a sophisti-cated woman should learn to drink something other than low-class beer," Bella answered.

"I told her you didn't drink that brand, that you liked Coors," Jett said seriously.

"Well, thank you, darlin', for setting your grand-mother straight on that issue. I never did like low-class beer." Adele smiled.

"And the last thing?" Nick asked. "What was it? Man, these are good chicken strips. I love fried chicken."

"I can make the best fried chicken in the world,"

Bella said. "Granny O'Donnell taught me how to cut up a chicken and fry it just right."

Adele looked up to see Remy staring at her. "Saved by chicken," he whispered.

It was impossible to keep the smile at bay. Remy was so much fun that she was going to hate seeing him come out the loser. Maybe they should make an ice-cream bet about who Walter would choose when he made up his mind. She'd gladly pay for a dozen banana splits if she could be the one who got the Double Deuce.

She'd taken a big bite of her burger when she realized just what moving in permanently would entail. Two complete trucks full of furniture and belongings, both personal and business, would be delivered to a place that had no room for any of it. Walter had said the ranch was going lock, stock, and barrel, and that meant she'd have to keep everything that was already in the house except what he considered his personal belongings.

"That old toot," she said.

"What?" Remy asked.

"What did you do with all your belongings? Storage?"

Remy nodded.

"How many trucks is it going to take to bring them to the Double Deuce if you're the owner?"

"It took two to take them to the storage unit," Nick answered.

"It'll take a year to sort through Walter's stuff and decide what to use of yours," she said.

"You backin' out?" Remy asked.

"Hell no!" Jett raised her voice and then clamped a hand over her mouth. "Sorry, Mama, but I'm not ready to throw in the towel. I want a rematch with these guys."

"We're not leaving, are we?" Nick whispered.

Remy shook his head. "We're in it for the long haul, even if we have to store our stuff in the equipment barn and have an auction to get rid of what we don't want."

Bella touched her mother on the arm. "That's what we can do, Mama. Don't give up on us."

"Never," Adele said with conviction.

# Chapter 10

ADELE HELD A BOWL OF GREEN BEANS IN HER LAP AND snapped them as she rocked. Remy was busy shucking two bushels of corn and throwing the full ears over into a third basket to be washed and put into the freezer.

"How many do we save out for dinner tomorrow?" he asked.

"Twelve," she said. "That's two each."

"I can eat four," Nick called from under the shade tree.

"So can I," Leo yelled.

"Then sixteen, and we'd better get out the big cooler," Adele said.

"Cooler?"

"It's a fast way to get them ready. We boil two big pans of water in the morning, pour it over the corn that's been put in the cooler, and at dinner, it's ready to eat," she explained.

"If it works, it would save a lot of time." He nodded.

The kids were taking turns at cranking the handle on an old, barrel-type ice-cream maker that Remy found at the back corner of the pantry, hiding behind dozens of plastic bags stuffed inside other bags. Remy had taken the bags to the recycling bin in Nocona that afternoon and gotten the ingredients to make a batch of banana nut ice cream.

"It's my turn now," Jett said.

"You're not strong enough," Nick argued.

"I can kick a bale of hay off the wagon, so if I can't do it with my arm, I'll turn the crank with my toes."

Remy chuckled. "Nothing like a Friday night surrounded by bickering kids."

"Would you rather be at a honky-tonk doin' some two-steppin' with a cute little blond?" Adele asked.

"Not me. I like tall redheads." He grinned.

Adele dug deep into the bowl and let the already-snapped beans fall back in. That left both of her hands full of whole beans that could rest on the top for her to work with. She'd heard that line before about tall, red-haired women, but she'd proven it was bullshit many times. Let a cute, petite blond walk into the room, and every man in the place turned for a second look.

"Earth to Adele."

"What?" she asked sharply.

"You looked like you were a million miles away," Remy said.

"More like a million years."

Her sister, Cassie, was one of those short blonds who turned men's heads. She was the delicate yellow rose; Adele had always been the big, oversize red aster that survived the heat and drought but no one bought when they went looking for flowers.

"Well, float back to this time period," Remy said. "I like sitting on the porch like this. It's nice to have adult conversation after two days of nothing but boys arguing about going faster so we'll beat the girls."

"It's even now. We brought in more than y'all did, thank goodness. I'm not sure Bella could have stood it if we had lost two days in a row." Adele popped a bean and half of it flew across the porch.

Jerry Lee hopped down from his perch on the porch post and snatched it up before she could lean over to retrieve it.

"He needs a chicken house and a flock of hens to keep him busy," Adele said. "When this place is mine, that's going to be my first addition."

"Banty?" Remy asked.

"Of course not. Big old, brown hens that will lay brown eggs and we won't have to go to the store for them. I want to teach my girls to be totally self-sufficient in as many things as I can. I may get some pigs in the spring and raise them, too," she answered.

"It's a great idea, but Jerry Lee needs banty hens to keep him busy. Maybe half a dozen in a separate part of the chicken yard. And I was thinking the same thing about pigs. Nothing like a good home-sugar-cured ham for Thanksgiving and Easter."

Why did he have to agree with everything and want the same things she did? Why couldn't he argue with her like the kids did with each other? He wasn't making it easy to fight with him for the ranch. Maybe that was his strategy—lull her into a lazy complacence and then swoop in and steal the ranch right out from under her.

"How do you think Walter is going to grade us on this contest?" She abruptly changed the subject. "Do you get more points for shucking corn than I do for snapping beans?"

"Or do you get more because Jett really is big enough to crank the ice-cream maker?" he asked. "I have no idea what's in that old coot's mind. I just hope he comes home with the decision made so one of us can settle in and the other can move on."

"It's a perfect place for either of us," she said. "Okay, kids, I can see you're leaning on that handle, which means the ice cream is ready. Throw that towel over the top and get on up here and help with the beans and corn. When the ice cream has set for thirty minutes, we'll call it a night."

"And we can eat it while we watch a movie, right?" Jett asked.

"After showers and all these beans are snapped and the corn is husked."

Nick's hand shot up in the air. "I'll do beans. I hate getting those hairy things in my face."

"Those are called corn silks." Jett laughed. "I'll help shuck corn."

"Me, too," Bella said.

That left Nick and Leo to help Adele. Now wasn't that a switcheroo, as Cassie always said? She had two boys and Remy had her daughters. At least it should cut down on the competition.

She was wrong about that.

"Hey, if we get our beans all broke up, then we get the bathroom first and we get the first ice cream," Leo said.

"No more contests today," Remy said, leaving no room for argument.

Adele raised an eyebrow and he winked. Just that gesture put flutters in the pit of her stomach. Dammit! She'd never given in to physical attractions, but then she'd never had one this damn strong either.

"Oh, okay, then we'll just hurry up and get it done so we can all watch a movie. What're we watching tonight?" Leo said.

"I pulled two out of the cabinet. One is called *The*

*Cowboys* with John Wayne and the other one is *The Sacketts* with Tom Selleck. I never heard of either of them, so y'all can decide and whichever one loses is the one we'll watch tomorrow night," Bella said.

"My grandma showed us how to do this with the beans," Leo said.

"Oh, she did?" Adele kept working, amazed that the boys were really quite good and fast at the job.

"Yep, we got to go to the ranch where she and Poppa live," Nick said. "Daddy and Mama let us go for a week in the summer. We didn't do much but play around. It wasn't like it is here, where we're needed. They had lots of hired help, and mainly we rode the four-wheelers, and sometimes they let us ride the horses, but only in the corral."

"They live over in Louisiana." Leo talked as he worked. "Only a few of the Luckadeaus moved to Texas. There was my daddy and cousin Slade, whose house we went to last Sunday, and cousin Griffin, who don't live too far from here, and then there's cousin Beau, and we're going to his house next Sunday. He's got two daughters who have white streaks in their hair. I wish I'd got that instead of red hair and freckles."

"And then the girls would have flocked around you, right?" Remy teased.

"Yuck!" Leo did his best fake gag. "I'm not ready for all that stuff, Uncle Remy."

"You will be in a few years," Remy said. "He's not talking about my folks. They live out in the Panhandle in a little town called Goodnight, Texas."

"Oh really? I grew up west of Silverton in cotton country," Adele said.

"Small world," Remy said.

"I liked to go visit Nana and Grandpa in Goodnight," Nick said. "We could really make the four-wheelers go fast in that flat country."

Adele nodded, remembering the wind rushing through her hair as she and Cassie had four-wheeler races from the cotton fields back to the barns. "Did they raise cattle?" she asked.

"Oh, yeah, big old longhorns," Leo said. "They scared me. I liked visiting with my grandparents, but I was always glad to go home to where we lived in town. But I like this ranch. It's not scary."

Adele's heart went out to the child. Her girls could adapt to any ranch, move right in, and start all over— after the fit they'd throw about losing. But Leo and Nick—that could be a very different story. They were happy on this place, and they might never find another ranch that would be home to them.

Guilt settled around her shoulders like an icy jacket. Could she really break those little boys' hearts?

---

Remy watched Adele's expressions change from happy to sad to something that he'd never seen before. He wanted to hold her, to tell her that everything would be fine, to kiss her again and feel her melt into his arms. Not that it could happen with four kids on the porch with them, but still, that last look on her face almost brought tears to his eyes. She must have been remembering a dead grandparent or maybe a best friend who died young for such sadness to come through her eyes and sweep across her face.

A few minutes later, the corn and beans were finished, and they hauled them into the house for a thorough washing. The kids darted off upstairs to get their showers and get ready for ice cream and the movie, leaving Remy and Adele in the kitchen together. Remy worked on removing any errant strands of corn silks from between the kernels in one side of the kitchen sinks. Adele washed beans in the other side. When she had a pan full, she covered them with water and set them on the back of the stove to simmer until bedtime.

Then she pulled out two big pots, filled them with water, and set them on the stove to boil. While waiting on that, she filled up two more gallon-sized, zippered plastic bags with clean green beans.

"That's for the first of the week. No sense in cannin' them or freezin' them when we'll use this batch for dinners. I'll throw some of those new potatoes that Walter has in the pantry in with some bacon and beans tonight."

Corn lined the whole cabinet top and Remy looked around for a towel to dry his hands. "Want me to bring out a bowl of potatoes while I'm in the pantry getting the cooler?"

She threw him a hand towel, and he caught it. "Yes, and thank you. And then you can go get the ice cream from the yard."

"No, ma'am. That's the kids' job. They churned it. They can bring it in. It'll teach them teamwork." He grinned.

The smile on her face brightened the whole room. Hell's bells, for a smile like that, he'd bring a ton of potatoes from the pantry plus the cooler, which he thought was a ridiculous idea. No way was corn going to be fit to eat after sitting in a cooler of hot water all that time. But he'd let her fail, and then he'd bring out more ears from the refrigerator and they'd fix them the right way.

He picked up a bowl and carried it into the pantry, which was as big as the kitchen in the house where he and the boys had lived. Setting it on the shelf, he turned around to locate the potatoes and Adele ran smack into him. She threw up her hands to keep from falling, but she'd lost her balance.

He slipped his arms around her and held her close to his chest until her heart stopped thumping so hard that he could feel it against him.

"I told you I'd bring the potatoes," he said.

"I needed"—she gasped for air—"salt for the beans. The shaker is empty."

"I've wanted to do this for hours," he murmured as he tipped up her chin with his fist. The tip of her tongue darted out to moisten her lips. Her big, blue eyes went all dreamy and then closed, leaving eyelashes fanned out on her cheekbones. He didn't even have to bend to kiss her, which was a turn-on in itself. He never had liked small women that made him twist his back in half just to kiss good night.

His lips met hers in a fiery clash of emotion and electricity that put an uncomfortable pressure behind his zipper. He teased the inside edge of her mouth with his tongue, and she opened to allow him inside. Their tongues did a slow mating dance that had him panting by the time he pulled away from her.

"Sweet Jesus," he whispered.

"I did not"—her breath came out in short bursts—"come in here to pray. I came for salt."

His chuckle turned into laughter that echoed off the walls of the pantry. "Well, I'm glad you did because I've wanted to kiss you all evening. I think maybe my prayers were answered, but holy smoke, Adele!"

She leaned back slightly and looked him right in the eye. "This is not smart. We should not fraternize with the enemy."

"This has nothing to do with the ranch. It's this thing between us, lady." His lips closed over hers for another wildly passionate kiss that almost made him go weak-kneed.

Sweet Jesus was right. He'd never lost control with a woman before. He could make out for hours without feeling like he was sinking into the floor. He could have sex for hours, bringing a woman to climax time and time again, before he finally gave in and fulfilled his own desire.

There was definitely something intoxicating and hypnotizing about Adele O'Donnell, and that something could lose him the ranch if he wasn't careful to keep the two things compartmentalized. But right then, the only thing on his mind was never letting her go and making out with her in the pantry like a couple of teenagers until the kids came down the stairs, ready for ice cream.

Adele's arms snaked around his neck, and one hand tangled into his hair. His entire scalp tingled, and her hands, though still cold from washing beans, were like fire against his bare neck.

"Hey, Mama, where are you?" Jett's voice tugged him back into the real world.

Adele's hands were suddenly on his chest, and she pushed him away as she took two steps backward. "I'm in the pantry getting potatoes to go in the beans. You kids go on outside and bring in the ice cream. Bring the towel that's on top to set it on, so we don't get any salt water on the floor."

Remy kissed her on the forehead. "You're very good. I couldn't have thought fast enough to say anything after those kisses."

She smiled up at him and brushed a quick kiss across his lips. "I'm a mother. They think fast, and my mama instincts tell me I'd better avoid this pantry while you are in here."

# Chapter 11

ADELE'S ACUTE MOTHERING INSTINCTS SHOT INTO HIGH GEAR again in the wee hours of Saturday morning when Jett touched her on the arm. She sat up immediately, eyes wide open, and reached for her child.

"I don't feel so good, Mama," Jett said. "My throat is all scratchy. Can I sleep with you?"

Adele touched Jett's forehead to find it only slightly warm. She flipped back the covers and patted the bed. "Of course you can sleep with me, but not before you get a dose of medicine and I spray that throat to make it feel all better."

She knew that Jett really didn't feel well when she opened right up for the liquid medicine and then let Adele spray her throat without a fuss. Then she snuggled down into the pillow, pulled the sheet and quilt up to her chin, and went right to sleep. Adele placed a hand on her child's back and shut her eyes, but it took a long time for her to get back to sleep. She always, always awoke before the alarm but not that morning. The sound jump-started her heart, and with one fluid motion, her feet were on the floor.

Jett didn't even stir, and it took Adele a moment to figure out why her youngest daughter was in bed with her. Then it flooded back in an instant, and she carefully touched the child's forehead. Absolutely cool, so hopefully it was an allergy to something in the air and it would be gone in a couple of days. If not, she'd have to find an urgent care clinic in the area. No use in paying all those new doctor/first patient fees until Walter made a decision about the ranch.

She pulled on a bra, socks, pair of work jeans, and a short-sleeved chambray shirt. She picked up her scuffed-up, down-at-the-heel cowboy boots and carried them down to the foyer, where she set them beside the hall tree. Bella caught her on the way to the kitchen and rolled her eyes.

"Mama, we've got a problem," Bella said.

"I know. Jett isn't feeling too well and she needs to rest, so I'll have to stay in the house with her today," Adele said.

"Not that. There's a strange woman in the kitchen. She's sitting at the table with a cup of coffee and her eyes look weird," Bella whispered. "I don't think she saw me."

"Well, let's go see what's going on," Adele said as a million scenarios ran through her head, most of them having to do with some of Remy's Luckadeau relatives that might have dropped by for a visit.

"Who the hell are you?" the woman asked. "And where is Walter? He knows I like breakfast early when I come to visit. I had to make my own coffee, too, and I didn't know how many scoops to put in for ten cups, and it's probably too strong for him."

"I'm Adele O'Donnell and this is my daughter, Bella. We are living here until the first of July. So are Remy Luckadeau and his two nephews. I also have a daughter, Jett, but she's still sleeping. Walter has gone with his lady friend, Vivien, on a monthlong cruise and we're minding the ranch for him."

"That son of a bitch," she said slowly. "He knows this is my weekend. It's always been the weekend that we go to the cemetery and clean up Mama's and Poppa's graves. Now what am I going to do? My ride dropped me off and won't come and get me until tomorrow evening."

"Good morning," Remy singsonged and then stopped dead in his tracks.

"This is Remy," Adele said. "I didn't catch your name." She turned to the elderly woman with short, kinky, slightly blue hair that didn't look as if it had been combed in a week. She wore a pair of jeans that hung on her skinny frame, big glasses that did indeed make her brown eyes look weird, and a bright-red-and-white-checkered western-cut shirt.

"I'm Dahlia McKay, Walter's sister-in-law. His wife, Pansy, was my sister, and every year we go to the cemetery on the second Sunday in June to put flowers on our parents' graves. We take lawn chairs and a picnic lunch, and when we get done, we have supper at the Dairy Queen and my ride picks me up there."

"I could take you home," Remy offered.

"No, thank you. I'm here for a reason, and if that son of a bitch Walter is disgracing my sister's name by running off with another woman, then I'll take care of it alone, even if I have to walk all the way to the Nocona cemetery and do it myself," she said.

"How long has Pansy been gone?" Adele asked.

"Seven years, but since she died, Walter and I've gone and taken care of things. Now he's forsaken me." Dahlia wiped a tear from her eye.

"I'll take you tomorrow morning after breakfast," Adele said.

Lord, a whole weekend with a sick child, a ranch to run, and an old lady to entertain sure wasn't on her bucket list, but it could be one of Walter's crazy tests. And by golly, she was not losing this battle.

"Thank you," Dahlia said. "You two married?"

Adele shook her head.

"Engaged?"

Remy shook his head.

"Then what in the hell was Walter thinking, letting y'all live together? Has he lost his mind? Seventy-year-old menfolks don't go on cruises with their lady friends. I bet he's gettin' that old-timer's disease. Folks will talk," she huffed. "But oh well, it's done now, so let's get breakfast going. It's been a long time since I sat down to the table with a family. Mostly it's just me since my husband died fifteen years ago. I never learned to drive, so it's a damn good thing I only live a block from my church and three blocks from the grocery store."

"She reminds me of Great-Aunt Rosy," Bella whispered.

Adele nodded. "What would you like for breakfast, Miz Dahlia? It's the girls' day to cook, so I'll make whatever you want."

Dahlia pushed her chair back and headed toward the pantry. "Pansy and I had chocolate chip pancakes on Saturday mornings, and then I'd help her clean the downstairs part of the house. Ain't been able to climb stairs in years. This is our home place. My parents bought this ranch when I was two years old, and Pansy came along seven years later, so this is the only home she ever knew. When she and Walter got married, they

bought it from my mama. Daddy had died, and Mama
had moved in with her sister, my aunt Gloria."

Yes, ma'am, Miz Dahlia talked as much as Aunt
Rosy, who always, always started with the day dirt was
created when she told a story. It was going to be one hell
of a long weekend.

"Girls cookin'? What does that mean?" Dahlia's eyes
went to nothing more than slits as she brought a huge
cast-iron skillet from the pantry.

"It means that the boys cook three days a week and
we cook three days a week, and Sunday we are all on
our own," Remy said.

"That's bullshit," Dahlia said. "Women cook. Men
do outside work."

Exactly what Aunt Rosie would say, including the
swear words. Jett would be cussing even worse than
before if she spent much time around this old girl.

"Well, on this ranch, we all do everything. What
would happen if we didn't have a guy around to do the
outside work, or if the guys get the ranch in the end and
they have to cook? In today's world, we have to be prepared for everything," Bella said. "I'll get the stuff out
of the fridge, Mama, while you bring what we need from
the pantry. Hey, Nick and Leo." She motioned them on
into the kitchen. "This is Miz Dahlia. She's spending
the weekend and we're having chocolate chip pancakes
for breakfast."

"Hello," Nick said. "And after chores it's our day to
clean. Can't we just hire someone to take care of our
Saturdays, Uncle Remy?"

"Like Bella said, we all have to learn everything." In
a few long strides, Remy was right behind Adele at the

door of the pantry. "Do you think this is one of Walter's tests?" he whispered.

"I don't know, but he had to know that she'd show up. Why didn't he at least warn us or let her know he was leaving?" Adele answered softly.

Remy put his hands on her shoulders and turned her around to face him. "We should pack up our things and leave. There's plenty of ranches that we can buy in this area."

"Not me. I'm in this for the long haul," she answered.

He dropped a kiss on her forehead. "You might change your mind before this weekend is done."

If heat brought out more freckles, then that kiss had probably just begat at least a dozen. To get her mind off the warmth of his lips on her forehead, she picked up a plastic container that held five pounds of flour and handed it to him. "I might, but you'll never know it."

His laughter was as sexy as the muscles on his chest and abdomen, which she could see under the tight tank top he wore beneath an unbuttoned chambray work shirt. She wrapped her hands around a canister of sugar and nodded toward the door.

"Don't forget the baking powder, Mama," Bella called out.

She set the small can on top of the sugar canister and followed Remy out of the pantry, watching that tight-hipped swagger and wishing that she could drag him back into the pantry for another make-out session like the night before.

A war between the body and mind was tough, but it wasn't her first time at the rodeo. Hopefully, she'd learned a few lessons that would keep her from falling over backward and pulling Remington Luckadeau down on top of her. It was only two more weeks and four days until Walter came home.

"Mama, I still don't feel good, but I'm hungry," Jett whined as she made her way to the kitchen. She still wore her pajama pants and one of Bella's old, hand-me-down T-shirts, which spoke volumes. Usually she was up and dressed to go milk the cow or bale hay by this time of the morning.

Remy touched her forehead. "Little bit warm there, sister. You'd best stay in where it's cool and watch movies or read a book."

"Is that one yours or Adele's?" Dahlia asked.

Jett cut her eyes around the room until she found the voice. "Hello, I'm Jett O'Donnell."

"And I'm Dahlia McKay. I'm staying here until tomorrow and I'll be sleeping on the sofa, so don't you leave any germs on it for me to catch," Dahlia said.

Jett drew herself up to her full height, which was not even five feet. "Well, don't you leave anything on it for me to catch."

Dahlia giggled. "I like this kid. Y'all can go on and get the work done however you do it. Me and Jett will hold down the fort until you get back."

"We're just feeding and doing some garden work this morning." Remy looked at Adele. "If you want to stay inside and get the vegetables into the freezer, that would free up some refrigerator space for what we'll harvest today. Maybe if we get them in early enough, we could even use some of it for dinner."

"I could do that," she said. "And since I'll be in the house, maybe I'll make some desserts for the next few days. I've got a brownie recipe that freezes well and cookies keep well for months in the freezer."

"If you'll make cookies, I'll do your share of work every day," Leo said. "What can I do to help? I love chocolate chip pancakes with lots of melted butter and warm syrup."

"Set the table," Remy said.

"I thought it was the girls' day," Dahlia said.

"It is. They have to cook but we can help with other things. They help us out, too. Sometimes it's a team effort," Nick explained. "We made homemade ice cream last night and it was so good. Even better than Braum's or the Dairy Queen. We might get to make it again next week, and Uncle Remy said we can make a different kind."

Adele poured two cups of coffee and handed one off to Remy. He deliberately let his hand graze hers and then winked. She felt the chemistry, but he'd better be careful because two people could play that game.

---

After breakfast, Remy suggested that Bella might work in the garden while he milked the cow, and the guys took the old work truck out to check on feed and water for the cows. Bella reminded him to check on the heifer that was due to drop her calf any day now and then picked up a gathering basket and carried it to the garden.

Later, when he carried a bucket of milk into the house, the aroma of cinnamon hit him square in the face. Adele was bent over the oven, her butt filling out those tight jeans so well that it made his mouth feel like he'd just sucked on a lemon.

"Snickerdoodles," she said as she brought a pan of cookies out of the oven. "Don't know how many will make it to the freezer, but it's Jett's favorite and she asked for them."

He set the milk on the counter and wrapped his arms around her waist, drawing her back close to his chest as she put the cookies on the counter.

"We can't keep doing this, Remy," she whispered.

"Why? We're consenting adults."

She wiggled out of his embrace and turned to gaze into his eyes. "Why start something that we can't finish? Better to nip the attraction in the bud than let it get out of hand and cause hard feelings."

"So you admit there's an attraction?" he asked.

"I'm not blind or dead," she said, smarting off.

Remy's smile spread across his face. "Neither am I."

She slid another pan of cookies into the oven and he took the opportunity to scoop a hot one up and take a bite from it. "Hot and delicious."

She straightened up so fast that the oven door slammed with enough force to rattle the salt and pepper shakers on the back of it. "What did you say?" she asked icily.

"The cookies are hot and delicious, just the way I like them. I'm going to take a ten-minute break and eat half a dozen before they cool down. Want to join me? I'll pour two glasses of milk."

She motioned toward the bucket of milk. "Would you let the boys have cookies and milk before they finished their chores?"

He laid the rest of the cookie on a paper napkin he pulled out of a holder on the kitchen table. "Slave driver."

"Yes, but just think about that hot and delicious…"

He put a finger over her lips. "Are we still talking about cookies?"

"Remy!" she gasped. "I'll get the cheesecloth."

Jett's voice floated from the living room to the kitchen. "Mama, are the cookies ready? Me and Miz Dahlia can smell them."

"Almost. I'll bring them to you in a few minutes. Milk or coffee?"

Jett giggled. "Don't make me laugh, Mama. It hurts my throat. I want sweet tea with mine, and Miz Dahlia says she'll have the same."

"That does sound good on a hot day like this. Ice-cold sweet tea and hot cookies," Remy said. "And yes, we're talking about cookies, not the red-haired lady who looks real sexy with a little bit of flour on her nose."

"Remy," she groaned.

"Oh, I like the way you say my name all breathless like that."

"It's been too long since you've been out drinking and carousing. You wouldn't even notice me in a bar full of women ready to jump your bones," she said.

He brushed away the flour. "There, now you aren't sexy anymore," he said as he strained the milk and put it in the refrigerator.

"I may patent that idea. Put a little flour on your nose before you go out with Remy Luckadeau, and it gives you all kind of special powers over him," she said.

"Only if your name is Adele and you have red hair," he said as he removed a half-gallon jar of sweet tea from the top shelf of the fridge. "Four glasses?"

"Five," Bella said from the back door as she toted a basket full of vegetables into the house. "We've got

enough yellow squash to fry for dinner. Plenty of tomatoes to go with it and more beans to snap. Reckon Jett and
Miz Dahlia could do that while they watch television?"

"I bet they can," Adele said.

"Are those snickerdoodles? Man, we usually only get
those at Christmas," Bella said. "Can I have one now
with my tea?"

"Sure, you can. But nothing after ten thirty or else
it will spoil your dinner, and I'm frying chicken,"
Adele answered.

"My favorite," Bella groaned.

"Mine, too," Remy said. "Are we going to fight over
the thighs?"

"No, I'm a leg girl." Bella grabbed a cookie and
headed out of the kitchen. "I'm going to strip the bed in
our room and get the sheets in the washing machine. I
can help with dinner while I do laundry."

"You've trained her well," Remy whispered. "I wish
I had a dozen just like her."

"For real? You'd want a dozen daughters at your age?
You do realize that by the time the first one got through
high school you'd be nearing retirement age?" Adele
told him.

"Luckadeaus live a long time, and kids keep parents
young. So yes, I'd take a dozen like her starting in, say,
about nine months."

"Then, darlin', you'd best start looking for a wife
willing to produce twelve girls at about one a year and
help run a ranch at the same time," she said, laughing.

Remy snatched another cookie and headed out the
back door. "I'll see you at noon. Me and the boys are
going to walk the back fence line and make sure it's all

bull safe until time to come in and eat. I'm going to tell them that I already sampled the cookies."

"You are evil," Adele fussed and shook her finger at him.

Remy left the house with a light heart and an extra spring in his step.

# Chapter 12

THE BRANCHES OF A HUGE PECAN TREE SHADED THE gravestone with both of Dahlia's parents' names engraved on the front. She'd packed lunches that morning in three separate brown paper bags and had found three folding lawn chairs in the tool shed to take with them. There was also a hoe, a rake, and a fistful of hand tools that they hadn't even used, but Dahlia had insisted on bringing them.

Nick and Leo had invited Bella to go with them to church in Saint Jo that morning and then out to their cousin Griffin's place for the afternoon. Bella hadn't hesitated in choosing to go with them rather than spend the afternoon in a cemetery. Jett was better but still not feeling one hundred percent, and besides, she thought it would be cool to go with her new best friend, Dahlia, to the graveyard.

"Peanut butter and jelly sandwich, pickles, a banana, and potato chips. My kind of lunch," Jett said as she dug into the paper bag and laid the food out on her lap. "How'd you know I like dill pickles with my PB and J?"

"Because I do, and we're a lot alike." Dahlia smiled.

"You mean when I get old, I'll be like you? That's awesome." Jett raised a palm and Dahlia slapped it in a high five.

"You know, there's ranches over around Vernon, and since I never had any kids, I'd gladly adopt you and these two girls." Dahlia smiled at Adele.

"Thank you. If we don't wind up with the Double Deuce, we might come over your way and take a peek, but if we do buy Walter's place, why don't we make this a date? Once a year, you come on over to the ranch and we'll take care of graves together," Adele said.

Dahlia wiped a tear away. "I'd like that very much."

"So this lady right here." Jett pointed at the headstone right beside Dahlia's parents. "She was your sister and she was the youngest?"

"That's right. That's Pansy. When Daddy bought the grave plots, he got two extra so that if either of us died young we'd have a place. When she died, I asked Walter to bury her beside Mama and Daddy, and he did."

"Are you going to be in the other space?" Jett asked.

"No, I'm going to be buried in Vernon. That's where my husband is, and our stone is already up and my name is on it."

"So who's going to be here?" Jett asked.

"It might just be an empty space if Walter remarries and doesn't want to be put here when his time is up."

"I think we should put a bench here so when we come out here to see your folks and sister we'd have a place to sit," Jett said.

Dahlia laid a hand on Jett's shoulder. "That's a wonderful idea. We'll have to do that before next year. If we're going to have time to eat an ice-cream cone at the Dairy Queen before my ride arrives, we'd best be going now."

"Do you do Facebook?" Jett asked as she stuffed all the trash into one paper bag.

"It took me a while to learn to work a computer, but I figured I was meaner than a damn machine, so I learned to get email and I'm on Facebook. I don't Twitter or text, though, but I might learn if you'll keep in touch with me." Dahlia wheezed a little when she stood up. "Damned old cigarettes. Should have never started smoking them. Now my lungs aren't what they ought to be even though I quit five years ago. Jett, promise me you'll never smoke."

Jett's nose twitched. "Yuck! Those things stink and make your clothes stink. I will never ever smoke. I promise."

"And you'll bitch at Bella if she does?"

"You better believe it. I'll bitch at Leo and Nick, too. I don't want that stuff on my ranch," Jett said authoritatively.

Adele opened her mouth to fuss at Jett for using bad language, but she snapped it shut. The child and Dahlia were already deep in conversation about the bench and what it should look like. It was one word and she'd let it slide this time, but back on the ranch, now that would be a different story.

Half a dozen vehicles were parked in the lot at the Dairy Queen when they arrived. Adele parked in front, as close to the door as she could. Jett hopped out the moment the truck stopped and held the back door open for Dahlia. The old girl immediately laced her fingers in Jett's and the two of them walked on ahead of Adele. Dahlia would have made a lovely grandmother, even if she could make a sailor blush.

Fate had given her to Jett, and Adele's face broke into a wide smile when she thought about all the instant messages that would heat up both Jett's and Dahlia's laptops. Then she remembered there was no Internet connection at the ranch.

Jett and Dahlia had already ordered three ice-cream cones by the time Adele made it to the cashier's counter. Dahlia paid for them, handed one back to Adele, and nodded toward a booth near the front.

"We'll sit there so I can see my ride when it arrives," she said and led the way over to sit down.

"I need to remind you both that there is no Internet connection at the ranch, so you'll have to depend on the phone," Adele said.

Jett licked her ice-cream cone. "I like that even better. I can hear your voice that way. This makes my throat feel all better."

"Me, too. How about we talk on Sunday afternoon? But you can call me anytime you want to." Dahlia pulled a pen from her big, red purse and wrote her phone number on a napkin. "Now you write yours down, and if something exciting happens in Vernon, I'll call you sometime in the week."

Jett quickly wrote her cell phone number on a napkin and handed it to Dahlia. "Mama, remind me to recharge my phone. I don't think I've used it since we've been on the Double Deuce."

"Now that is truly a good sign." Dahlia giggled. "But remember to get it charged up by next Sunday and be ready to tell me what all you've done. But most of all, I want to hear that you're not sick anymore."

"I'm not sick now. I felt better this morning. I'll be ready to pick beans and work the garden tomorrow morning," Jett said.

"That's the spirit." Dahlia smiled.

"And you'll call me when you get home, so I know you made it all right?" Jett asked.

Dahlia's smile got bigger. "You bet I will. It'll be a couple of hours after I leave. By then, Bella and the boys will be home and you can tell me about her day."

"Is that you, Adele?" a voice said at her elbow.

Adele looked up and then slid out of the booth. "Well, hello, Gemma! It's great to see you."

"I can't believe I'm seeing you right here in Nocona, Texas!" Her cousin hugged her tightly. "I heard you were buying a ranch somewhere east of here."

"Trying to buy the ranch. Meet my new friend Dahlia, and this is Jett," Adele said.

"I wish I would have brought Holly with me, but you'll see her in a couple of weeks," Gemma said. "I hear we're having a big to-do out on your new ranch for the Fourth."

"If I get to buy the ranch, we are. If not, your mama and daddy will have the reunion at their place."

Gemma cocked her head to one side, her dark hair with red highlights floating on her shoulder. Looking at her standing there, it was hard to imagine that she was a world-class bareback bronc rider. "I thought this was Bella."

"I'm eleven years old," Jett said. "Where's Holly?"

"She's home with Mama right now. Don't tell my mother because we're going to announce it on the Fourth, but we're expecting another baby, due about Thanksgiving time," Gemma whispered.

"Hallelujah!" Adele laughed. "Now she'll stop bugging me to have another child."

"And my sister is due at the same time. We're going to spring it on Mama when we're together," Gemma said. "Looks like my nachos are ready. Mama sent me to the store for several bags of ice so we can crank out a couple of freezers of ice cream and I'm sneaking in nachos from Dairy Queen. I've been craving them like crazy! I'd better get going since they're waiting for the ice. It's good to see you and meet you, Dahlia. And Jett, darlin', I can't believe you're already eleven years old. Can't wait to really catch up, Adele."

"Me either, and we'll keep your secret safe." Adele hugged her cousin one more time. "And stay off the broncs since you're pregnant."

Gemma held up both palms. "Trace is an old bear about me doing anything at all. He doesn't even want me to ride a horse, much less break in a rodeo bronc."

"So you have family in the area?" Dahlia asked when Gemma had gotten her order and waved as she left the café.

"Lots of family over around Ringgold and just over the border in Terral, Oklahoma. Gemma and Colleen live out in the Panhandle. They're searching for a ranch out there for me and the girls if Remy winds up being the new owner of the Double Deuce," Adele answered.

"Don't worry." Jett patted Dahlia's shoulder. "It don't matter where we live. We can always come back to Nocona for a weekend to visit the graves. We can stay out at Uncle Cash's place, and he won't care if we bring you with us."

"I might just take you up on that, Jett. See that red car pulling up out there? That is my ride, and I hate good-byes. So I'm going to get my bag out of the truck and you two are going to sit right here. I'm going to hug you both and instead of good-bye, we're going to say 'see you,' and then I'll call you soon as I get home," Dahlia said.

"I'll help you get your bag," Adele said.

"No, my ride will do that. She's young and a good friend, and I get all damned teary-eyed just leaving," Dahlia said hoarsely.

"See you." Jett hugged her tightly. "And in two hours I better hear from you, or you'll be in a hell of a lot of trouble."

Dahlia slapped a hand over her mouth.

Adele shook a finger at Jett.

"Now it's not so sad." Jett giggled.

On the way back to the Double Deuce, Jett sighed and said, "I don't like this business of being an only child. I want you to tell Bella she can't go to college or get married or leave until I'm old enough to go with her."

"You sound like your aunt Cassie," Adele said.

"Well, if she felt lost when you left even for a day, then I feel like her, too," Jett said. "What are we going to do while we wait for the rest of the family to get home?"

"I guess we'd better check on that heifer that Bella's been worried about."

"If the cow needs help, can I pull the calf?"

"We'll see what happens."

Jett had said *the rest of the family* and Adele had been thinking the same thing all afternoon. She missed Bella when she was out of her sight, but she'd missed Nick and Leo and yes, Remy, too, that day. Maybe it was seeing Dahlia reaching out for friendship and comfort, seeing the wistfulness in her eyes when she looked at Jett and knowing that she would have liked to have a big family around her in her old age. Or maybe the empti-ness in Adele's heart was simply because she'd gotten used to having four kids and a man around the house.

When she and Isaac were married, they passed each other sometimes at breakfast and usually went out for dinner. Then Bella was born, and she'd quit her job to stay home and only saw Isaac for thirty minutes in the morning and sometimes not until the next day if she didn't feel like going with him in the evenings. She'd never had a man around all day, and she was finding that she liked it way too much.

---

Remy slouched in a lawn chair under a shade tree on his cousin Griffin's ranch. Bella had a captive audience with Griffin and his wife Julie's two older daughters, Annie and Lizzy. The girls both sported a white shock of hair in their jet-black locks. It was a genetic thing that had been passed down through Griffin's mother, so it wasn't from the Luckadeau gene pool.

What would his and Adele's offspring look like? Would they be redheads, or would they have the normal Luckadeau blond hair? Maybe they'd have her eyes, though. Those deep, penetrating, gorgeous green eyes that reminded him of the water in Panama City, Florida.

"You look like you are taking a time trip into the future or maybe one into the past." Griffin handed him a bottle of cold beer and slumped down into the lawn chair beside him.

"I was doing some woolgathering." Remy brushed a fly from the rim of the bottle and took a long gulp. "Never thought I'd hear myself say this, but I'm a little jealous of you today."

"Got family fever, do you?" Griffin swatted a mosquito from his ear.

"I didn't until I moved the boys to the ranch."

"Got anything to do with Bella's mama?"

Remy shrugged. "Hell if I know."

"She as pretty as her daughter?"

Remy inhaled deeply and let it out slowly. "She's a redhead with freckles. Damn near as tall as I am and built like a runway model. She knows ranchin', maybe even better than I do, and every day I'm more amazed by her. But believe me, Griff, she deserves someone a hell of a lot better than me."

"I thought that about Julie, too, six years ago. And you know what? I still feel the same. After blending our families, adopting Chuck, and now having two more girls of our own, I'm still in awe of her."

"And both of the girls got the white streak, huh?"

"Yes, they did. Chuck wanted to bleach out a section of his hair to match, but we talked him out of it," Griffin said.

"He and Leo sure get along well."

"Two peas in a pod. Bella is really good with the girls, even the five-year-old."

"I've told Adele dozens of times that I'd hire Bella in a minute. Hell, I'd even make her foreman. She's that good on the ranch and in the kitchen. She and Nick get into it sometimes, but it's like a brother-and-sister thing."

Griffin stood up and popped out another folding lawn chair. "Right here, darlin'," he said as Julie walked up.

"Thank you." Julie had braided her red hair into two ropes that hung down her back. It was curly like Adele's and stray hairs kept springing out of the braids. "Remy, can I have Bella for the rest of the summer?

She's really good with kids and the girls love her—even Mandy, who doesn't like either of her older sisters on most days."

"Not a chance." Remy shook his head. "I'm not sure the Double Deuce can run without her. Leo and Jett have tempers. Nick is trying to find himself. She's our balance."

"Our?" Griffin said.

"For now," Remy answered just as his phone rang.

He stood up and fished it out of his hip pocket, answered it, nodded a few times, put it back, and yelled across the yard toward the porch. "Hey, Bella, that heifer you've been watching needs you. You ready to go show Leo and Nick how to pull a calf?"

Bella bounded off the porch and headed toward the truck. "You bet I am. I've been worried about that cow for more than a week."

"I see what you're talking about," Griffin said. "But anytime you get tired of her, just kick her over our way. We'll take her in on a daily or a permanent basis."

"And I'd gladly hire her to babysit some evening so we could go out." Julie nodded.

"Hey, guys, time to go. We've got a heifer in trouble," Bella hollered on her way to the truck.

With her long brown hair flowing behind her, she reminded Remy of a long-legged colt romping around in the pasture. She'd grow into those long legs someday and be every bit as beautiful as her mother. That would be the time he'd have talks with any boys that came sniffing around, for sure.

*Whoa there, hoss!* that niggling voice in his head said quickly. *This is not your daughter, and at the end of this month, one of you is leaving the Double Deuce.*

*Hey!* He drew his eyes down and argued. *She might leave the ranch, but she likes it around these parts, and there're several small spreads for sale not far from here. She'll have her hands full, and I can help out. We're friends, and I'll be around on the day that either Bella or Jett has a boy knocking at the door.*

Good-byes were hurriedly said and the kids loaded up in the truck with Bella and Leo in the backseat and Nick in the front with Remy. Bella stayed on the phone with her mother constantly during the twenty-minute trip to the ranch, and the minute Remy parked the truck, she bailed out and headed for the house. Before he could make it inside, she was already coming down the stairs in a pair of cutoff jeans and a knit shirt that looked as if she'd grabbed it from a ragbag. She wore her work boots and was pulling her hair up in a ponytail as she hurried out the back door.

"I'll drive the old work truck to the pasture. Y'all can come on out there when you get changed if you want to," she yelled.

Remy changed from his Sunday best into work jeans, a faded chambray shirt, and traded his black eel boots for a pair of well-worn ones that he wore every day. Nick and Leo were waiting on the porch when he arrived.

"I want to see this," Leo said. "What if it's already here when we get there and we miss it? It'll be your fault, Uncle Remy, for taking so long."

"I'm not so sure I want to watch." Nick's nose curled.

"Either of you ever watch the birth of anything? Cat? Dog? Maybe on television on the Discovery Channel?" Remy asked as he kept walking toward his truck.

They shook their heads.

"Then this will be a good experience for both of you."

Adele had brought the cow to the barn and put her in a stall. When Remy and the boys arrived, Bella was on the ground behind the heifer, both hands shoved into pink plastic gloves that reached to her elbows.

Adele stayed out of the stall but watched from the gate. Jett had climbed to the second rung of the rough wood wall and propped her elbows on the top railing.

"Y'all boys come on up here and watch this. It's amazing," Jett whispered.

The cow let out a bawling sound, startling Nick so badly that he jumped. He managed to hide it from everyone but Remy, who was careful to not even smile. He took up a place to Adele's side and watched as Bella stuck her gloved hands into a bucket of water.

"It's important to keep things as clean as possible," she said as she eased both hands up inside the heifer. "It's coming right, Mama, but it's too big. I'll need the chains and the puller."

Jett took off for the tack room. "I'll get them. I was the one who cleaned them up and I know right where they are."

In less than two minutes, she was back with the puller and the chain. She handed the chain to Bella first. Remy watched as she expertly took the ends up inside the cow to attach them and then fastened the puller to the chain and set the wide end against the cow's back legs.

"She's pretty good at that," he whispered.

Adele nodded. "She wanted to learn, so I taught her. It's not her first rodeo."

"Okay, guys, now I'll only ratchet this thing when the cow pushes so we don't hurt the calf. Want to make bets on whether it's a bull or not? Size it is, if it's a bull, it might be good breeder stock," Bella said.

"Not me," Leo said. "You sure you ain't goin' to kill that cow?"

The heifer let out a screeching bawl and her side heaved with the contraction. Bella did her part and two hooves appeared. She stopped and patted the cow's flanks. "You're doin' good, little mama. Give me a couple more and we'll have this old boy on the ground."

Another bellow and with some help from Bella, two legs shot out. Nick gagged, but Remy ignored it. Leo's eyes were as big as saucers, and he shivered when the cow let out another bawling noise.

"Here comes the big black head." Bella calmed the cow with gentle rubbing and a soft voice. "One more push, old girl. One more, and I'll get the rest of him out, and you can wash up your new baby."

As if the animal knew what she was saying, she obeyed, and Bella used the ratcheting part of the puller to bring the calf all the way out. She quickly stuck her hands in the bucket of water and stuck her fingers in the new baby's mouth, pulling out a wad of mucus and tossing it to the side. "Breathe! You put your mama through hell and you will breathe, do you hear me?"

The calf's sides heaved with its first breath, and then it made a noise. Not a full-fledged bawl but enough to know that it was alive. The cow raised her head and looked around at the baby lying beside her hind legs. Bella quickly undid the puller and removed the chain from the calf.

"You done good, mama cow, and we've done our

part, so we'll get out of here and let you and nature take care of the rest," Bella said softly.

"That was totally amazing," Leo said. "It don't smell too good but good job, Bella O'Donnell!"

"Nick?" Remy asked.

"Next time, can I give it a try?"

"We'll see what happens." Remy's heart swelled up to twice its normal size.

"Looks like maybe you might have a couple of ranchers here," Adele said.

"Maybe a rancher, but I'm not so sure about a cowboy yet," Nick answered. "What do we do now?"

"The mama will chew the umbilical cord off and wash her baby. It's bonding time and we don't need to be here. Tomorrow, we'll let them out into the corral, and the next day they can go back to the pasture with the herd," Jett informed him. "Let's go get the chores done. I love Miz Dahlia, but I sure missed all y'all, too."

Bella washed the chain and the puller with the water from the bucket. "It's a fine bull calf, Mama, but if we hadn't gotten here when we did, she'd have never had him. His big old head barely made it through the canal and she was tired of pushing."

"You did a fine job," Remy said.

"Thank you." Bella beamed. "Someday I'm going to be a vet, so I need to know all I can about animals. I'll put these things away and me and the kids can go out to do the feeding chores." She pulled the gloves off, tossed the water out of the bucket, and threw the gloves inside it.

"Don't forget to trash the gloves and dry out the bucket," Adele said.

Bella rolled her eyes. "That's ranchin' 101, Mama."

Adele patted her on the shoulder. "And you aced that course, but it never hurts to have a little reminder."

—⁓—

Adele had been acutely aware of Remy beside her during the whole ten-minute process of bringing that gorgeous bull calf into the world. It would belong to one of them, not both, in a couple of weeks.

She turned slightly to tell Remy that, if she stayed on the ranch, she was going to keep the calf for breeder stock. His eyes had gone all dreamy and one of his hands was suddenly on her waist, pulling her closer to him.

Somewhere in the faraway distance, she heard the calf whining and the noise of the new mother licking his fur. Heat engulfed her from the inside out as Remy traced the outline of her jaw with his rough forefinger. She didn't hear anything but a buzzing noise and felt only the warmth that was his breath on her neck when he pushed back the collar of her dirty shirt and nuzzled there, in that very sensitive place between shoulder and neck.

She rolled up on her toes and worked her fingertips into his thick hair, pulling his face to hers for a long, hot, passionate kiss. His hands dropped to cup her hips, and with a little hop, her legs were wrapped around his waist. He carried her to the back stall and kicked the gate open. Then he sat down on a bale of hay without stopping the series of steamy kisses.

There was no doubt he was every bit as aroused as she was. The hard erection pressing against her thigh proved that fact, but did she really want to do this?

She pulled back from him and shook her head.

"I agree. This is not the right place. Not even for a couple of die-hard ranchers," he panted. "You deserve something better than a quickie in a barn stall, darlin'."

She moved from his lap and took a deep breath to clear her mind and ease the ache inside her, but it didn't work. She wanted to have sex with Remy, and if she was totally truthful, she wanted even more than casual sex.

"Mama, Mama, where are you?" Jett yelled.

"I'm right here," Adele said.

"Well, come quick. You'll never believe who just came walkin' out from the backyard. Aunt Cassie is here!"

# Chapter 13

ADELE LEFT REMY SITTING ON THE HAY BALE AND JOGGED out of the barn, across the pasture, and wrapped her baby sister in her arms. The short blond tiptoed to hug her taller sister and then leaned back to look Adele in the face.

"You're happy. I can see it in your face," Cassie said breathlessly.

"Why didn't you call?" Adele asked.

"Didn't know if I'd have time to stop. Barely do. Can't stay but an hour because Daddy wants that bull out there in the trailer home tonight. He paid a fortune for him, and he isn't taking any chances on him dying from heatstroke." Cassie latched on to Adele's arm. "What's for supper? I'm starving."

"Leftovers if you're only staying an hour," Adele said.

Bella braked hard and brought the work truck to a stop and bailed out, leaving the door swinging wide open.

"Aunt Cassie!" she screamed as she raced across the yard and threw her arms around her aunt, talking the whole time. "You should have been here thirty minutes ago. I pulled a big old bull calf and saved him and his mama both. It was beautiful. And it's a gorgeous calf that I think we should keep for a breeder. I bet we could charge big bucks for his sperm, and you've got to meet the boys, and we've got new kittens."

Cassie took a step back and glanced over at the two

young boys who were shyly staring at her. "And this would be Nick and Leo. Hi, you guys. I'm Cassie, Adele's younger sister."

Nick crossed the expanse of grass and stuck out his hand. "Right pleased to meet you, ma'am."

"Likewise," Cassie said. "Where is your uncle that I've heard so much about from my nieces?"

"That would be me. I'm Remy." He was close enough behind Adele that his deep drawl startled her. "I'm glad you could stop by even if it will be a short visit."

Adele waited for his eyes to go all wobbly and his breath to come in short gasps when he looked at her petite, blond, beautiful sister. But it didn't happen. Was he crazy or blind? There stood the prettiest girl in the whole state of Texas, and he didn't show her as much attention as he did the heifer that had just given birth.

Jett grabbed Cassie's hand and tugged her toward the house. "Bella done told you about the kittens, but she's got to drive the truck home, so if we hurry, I'll be the one to get to show them to you. And guess what? I've got a new friend and her name is Dahlia."

"Lead me to the refrigerator so we can put some food in my stomach." Cassie and Jett took off toward the house with Jett rattling on and on about everything she'd done that day.

Adele turned to Remy only to find him grinning down at her.

"What?" she asked.

"So that's Cassie."

"Yes, that is my sister. Beautiful, isn't she?"

He shrugged. "She sure can't measure up to you in that department. She's cute, in a Dallas Cowboys cheerleader way, but beautiful? Not so much. Reckon we'd best go feed the bunch of them, though, so y'all can get as many words in as you can in the next hour or so."

Adele was speechless. Either Remy was shooting her a line or else he had a motive, like manipulating her out of a ranch with those scorching kisses and compliments. Everyone knew that Cassie was the pretty one in the family.

Remy walked beside her all the way to the house. Not a finger even brushed against her, but the sparks between them were as vibrant as the hot June sun hanging in the sky that evening. When they reached the porch, he stepped aside to open the door for her.

Everyone was talking at once while they pulled leftovers from the refrigerator and lined up the containers on the counter. The boys had already lost their shyness and were as noisy as the girls. Adele wasn't a bit surprised, since Cassie, like their mother, had that effect on people. Give her five minutes in a room with a crowd, and everyone would migrate toward her, and when they walked away, they felt like they'd known her forever.

"I'm making a roast beef sandwich with mustard and pickles." Cassie raised her voice above the din. "Want me to make two, Adele?"

"Sounds wonderful," Adele said. "We'll take it to the dining room table, where there's plenty of room for all of us."

"Please stay all night, Aunt Cassie. We've got tons of stuff to show you and tell you about," Bella begged. "You can have our bed, and we'll get out the sleeping bags and take the floor."

"Or we can have a slumber party in the living room, and Nick and Leo can be there, and we can watch movies all night and talk," Jett said.

"I love you, but I can't. Your grandpa says that bull has to be home tonight. One of the reasons I was sent to get him is that we'd be driving home after dark for the most part, and he won't get as hot. You'll have to call me more often and keep me caught up," Cassie answered.

Adele was aware of Remy standing beside her, making a plate of food, and of him carrying it to the dining room right behind her and Cassie. But when he sat down in the chair right beside her and his leg plastered against hers, every sane adult thought left her mind. This flat-out was not fair. She had one hour with her sister, and all she could think about were those hot kisses out in the barn and the way Remy was not besotted with Cassie.

"Sister Adele!" Cassie said sharply.

"Don't call me that," Adele said coldly.

Cassie laughed. "I knew that would get your attention. I asked you a question. When are you coming home for a visit?"

"Not for a while, but I'm having a big O'Donnell reunion on the Fourth right here on this ranch. We're celebrating my birthday and the holiday at the same time. Everyone can come for the day or bring their campers and stay as long as they like," she answered.

Remy's knee pressed harder against hers. "Not if the Luckadeaus have the ranch on the Fourth. We're planning a big party and inviting all of my family, but we would like to invite everyone around this table to our celebration."

Cassie held up a palm, finished chewing the food in her mouth, and took a sip of tea before she spoke. "Looks like a Mexican standoff to me. I'm rootin' for the O'Donnells, but if they don't win and Adele decides to attend your party, I might come along with her. You got any cousins hidin' around these parts that you'd introduce me to?"

"You'll be able to shake any bush on this whole ranch that day and a dozen Luckadeau cowboys will be running out, everyone of them eager to throw their coats on the ground for you to walk upon," Remy said seriously.

Cassie flashed her brightest smile across the table at Remy. "Well, now that does sound interesting."

Adele had no doubt that he would fold now for sure. There wasn't a man in the whole great state of Texas who wouldn't drool for a chance at one of Cassie's smiles. But he laid a hand on Adele's knee and squeezed gently.

"Think you'd ever want to settle around these parts, Cassie? These girls and your sister would sure like to have you closer."

"A woman never knows," Cassie flirted. "It would depend on if there was a reason to do that, now wouldn't it?"

Remy squeezed again. "Your sister and nieces and something besides dirt and sky?"

Cassie turned on all her charm. "It would be tempting."

Remy moved his hand from Adele's leg and draped it around her chair.

The phone rang and Jett jumped up and took off to the kitchen. "This one is for me. I know it is."

"I didn't think she was old enough for a boyfriend," Cassie said.

"She's not. That will be her new best friend, who has to be approaching eighty years old, Miz Dahlia. She promised to call Jett as soon as she got home this evening," Adele said.

"I hate to eat and run, but I've got to go, folks. Daddy will be waiting up, not for me but for his new bull. Walk me to the truck, Adele?" Cassie grabbed two cookies from her plate, wrapped a paper napkin around them, and shoved them in her shirt pocket.

Adele looped her arm in Cassie's and they talked as they walked through the foyer, out onto the porch, where Boss ambled to his feet and followed them to the truck. The bull bellowed a couple of times when he heard voices, and the noise scared Jerry Lee so badly that he flew from the side mirror to the porch railing.

Cassie grabbed the top of her head with both hands. "What was that?"

"That would be the rooster, Jerry Lee. He crows at night instead of in the morning. I'm just grateful that he was too scared to stop. He's been eyeballing my hair for a nest ever since we moved onto the ranch." Adele hugged Cassie.

Cassie crawled into the truck, started the engine, rolled down the window, and motioned for her sister to come closer.

"We don't have time for the Daddy thing." A corner of Adele's mouth turned up in a hint of a smile.

"I know it, darlin'. Lord, I hated it when Daddy rolled down the window. That meant he and whoever was on the other side of the door would talk another half an hour before we could go home."

"Amen," Adele said.

"I don't feel a thing for Remy, but I was testing him,

and I wanted you to know that. I tested Isaac once, and I was ashamed of myself. I never told you because you were still married to him, but he came on to me after I'd flirted with him."

Adele frowned. "What are you talking about?"

"It's in the past, and I put a stop to it before anything happened. But you know that Remy Luckadeau has a reputation out in our part of the world as a big-time player. At least half the women in the Panhandle have had a turn with him. So I deliberately flirted with him today, just to see if what I thought was true."

"I noticed…"

"He's smitten with you, Adele. It's in his eyes when he looks at you. I couldn't even get a rise out of him. My ego is bruised."

"My sister, who is almost as big a player as Remy Luckadeau, has been shot down. But, darlin', you have to remember Remy hasn't been able to go tomcattin' for several months so…" Adele hesitated and frowned.

"Right!" Cassie nodded. "I was giving it my best, and he didn't even notice me because all he can see is you. And it's been months, like you said. Trust me, he really, really likes you. Isaac never looked at you like that. I've got to go, but you might think about proposing a partnership with him. Y'all could buy this place together and see where this attraction leads."

"Why would I do that?" Adele was still trying to wrap her mind around what Cassie had said before.

Cassie kissed her fingertips and then pressed them to her sister's forehead. "Because you are looking at him the same way. Love you, Sister. See you on the Fourth of July, one way or the other."

The window went up slowly and Cassie drove away. When she reached the end of the lane, she honked and then she was gone. Adele stood there in shock. Everything made sense and nothing made sense.

"Hey, I brought you a cold beer. Thought it might taste good after today," Remy called from the porch.

She turned around and started toward him. Remy had no idea the depths of the emotions that had rattled around in her that day. The way that Dahlia and Jett took to each other—a wee bit of jealousy at sharing her daughter with someone else. Bella doing such a good job of bringing that calf into the world—a lot of pride involved there. Cassie arriving so unexpectedly—a jolt of excitement and of fear that she'd take a backseat to her sister's beauty like she'd always done. Then what Cassie had said—pure havoc with all things emotional.

"I stopped by the convenience store in Saint Jo after church so the kids could get a soft drink to hold them over until dinnertime. I picked up two six-packs and a bag of ice. I carry a cooler in the toolbox, so they're cold. You look like you saw a ghost. Is everything all right with your parents and your sister?" Remy sat down on the top step and stretched his long legs out, crossing them at the ankles on the bottom step.

"It's all good." She crossed the yard and sat down beside him. He handed her a cold beer, and she rolled it across her forehead before she took a long drink. "Delicious and my favorite brand."

"You don't go in for the light stuff?" he asked.

"Not me. If I'm going to drink it, I like the real thing, not watered down." She downed a third of the beer and then burped. "Pardon me. I'm so sorry."

"Not bad manners. Just good beer," he said. "Does seeing her drive away make you sad?"

"A little. I try to go out there every other month for a weekend but…"

He laid a hand on her knee. "Ranchin' is hard on the whole family. It's tough on the ones who live on the place because it's a twenty-four seven job. And it's not easy on the ones who live a ways off because you can't drop everything and go long enough for Sunday dinner."

"Cassie reminded me of your reputation out around the canyon," she said, changing the subject abruptly.

Remy nodded very slowly. "It took me a long time to build it. I guess I can't tear it down in a day or even a month, can I?"

"Want to explain?"

"I enjoyed my life, Adele, but I can't live that way and be a role model for those two boys. I need to live halfway across the state so not so many people know me as that wild and rowdy party cowboy."

"And?" she asked.

He was quiet for several seconds before he sipped his beer and went on. "I was never the roots type of guy. I liked my job at the ranch where I had worked up to foreman. Might have stayed there awhile longer if things hadn't worked out the way they did with my brother and his wife. But I've always had wings and not roots. Left that to my brothers. But since I've gotten here, I feel roots going down from my soul into this ranch, Adele. It's a new feeling, and sometimes I'm not comfortable with it."

"I tried the wings, but they were too heavy for me. I fought against the roots, but they took hold after Bella was born. I wanted her to have the life I'd had, not the super-glitzy life of her father. I was talking about the ladies, though," Adele said.

Remy was quiet for a while, sipping his beer as his expression changed from a smile to a frown. "I cultivated that, too. Didn't want any of them to think they could tame me or lead me to the altar. You jealous?"

She couldn't answer honestly and she didn't want to lie, so she turned the subject into a different lane. "Players don't have roots."

"You are so right. I've made up my mind that I want this place. I want roots and I want my boys to have the kind of life I had, like you just said about your girls. The other part, I'm battling with these days. I have to set an example for Nick and Leo. Do I want them to see their male role model as a womanizer and bar hopper or as a solid rancher with morals?"

"You know what they need. Now it's up to you to decide whether you want to sacrifice to give it to them," she said.

"You didn't answer my question. Are you jealous?" he asked pointedly.

"I'm not going to answer it," she said.

Remy finished off his beer and set the empty bottle to the side. By what Adele said, he had his answer. She was jealous, even if it was only a little bit. And that made him happy.

His phone rang and he pulled it out of his pocket. A picture of his mother popped up on the screen, and he hit the icon to answer her call.

"Hello, Mama."

He literally felt the color drain from his face as he listened and fought back the tears in his eyes. "I'll leave in fifteen minutes and be there as soon as I can. Tell him me and the boys are on the way."

He turned to Adele and could tell by her expression that she already knew it was bad news. "It's my father. He's in the hospital in Amarillo. They think it's his heart. I have to go."

"Can I help you get things together?" She stood up. "And don't worry about this ranch. Don't even think about it. The girls and I will take care of it until y'all get back. Come on. You're wasting time."

He stood to his feet. "Thank you."

She wrapped her arms around his neck, hugging him tightly. "I'm here and you have my cell number. If you or the boys need anything, call me. And I'll expect updates all through tonight. Time doesn't matter. Call me every hour."

"We should be there by eleven o'clock, but I'll keep you posted along the way," he said. "And thank you, Adele." He kissed her on the forehead.

In no time, the boys were loaded into the backseat with pillows and their MP3 players and they were all on the way to Amarillo, a good four hours away even if there were no traffic problems. At that time of the evening, he didn't expect anything but clear sailing all the way to Goodnight, where he'd stop and unload the boys to stay with his sister-in-law. She was holding down the fort with all the kids at the home place, and the sons and his mother were at the hospital.

He stopped at a service station in Wichita Falls for

fuel and a potty break. The boys bought a candy bar
and a soft drink each, but they didn't waste time. When
he was back on the road, he wrapped the phone device
around his ear and called his mother. His dad was still
having trouble breathing, but they'd determined it was
not a full-fledged heart attack, but they were talking
about putting in a pacemaker that very night. Then he
called Adele to tell her the news.

"I'm so glad to hear it wasn't a heart attack," she said.
"The girls and I've been playing Scrabble to make the
time go by faster, but it's not working too well."

Just hearing her voice calmed him. "Thanks again,
Adele."

"Hey, that's what friends are for," she said. "I'll
expect the next call when you get out near Quanah or
Acme, and if anything changes with your dad, call me
before that."

"I will," he promised.

"They'll never get it all done without us," Nick said
after Remy had hung up.

"Who?" Leo asked.

"The girls. They need us, Uncle Remy."

"For your information, they've been running a ranch
with no boys around for years, young man," Remy said.

"Maybe we'd never make it without them," Leo said
softly.

"Nah, Leo." Nick yawned. "We're learnin' real fast.
We can run a ranch as long as Uncle Remy is there."

"But it won't be as much fun without them girls there
to pester," Leo said.

By the time they reached Goodnight, the boys were
both sleeping. They stumbled from the truck, barely

opening their eyes enough to get into the house and go right back to sleep on the pull-out sofa that Remy's sister-in-law had ready for them.

"They have him in surgery now, and if this works, he'll be in the ICU tonight, and tomorrow they'll monitor him in a regular room. If all goes well, he'll come home in a couple of days," she whispered. "I'm staying up until he comes out of it and is okay. This scared all of us, Remy. Kind of makes us realize what's important. I'm glad you were able to drop everything and get on out here."

Less than an hour later, Remy walked into the hospital waiting room. His mother met him in the middle of the room and wrapped him in a fierce hug. "He scared me so bad, and now I'm worried he won't come out of the surgery. He's never been sick. Always been as strong as a bull, and I don't know how I'd ever live without him, Son." She wiped at the tears falling down her cheeks.

Floy O'Donnell was a big, rawboned woman with dark hair, nearly black eyes, and a no-nonsense attitude. She was the backbone of the Ted O'Donnell branch of the family and to see her shaken like this broke Remy's heart.

"Maybe this is God's way of telling him it's time to slow down a little and delegate more," Remy said as his brothers gathered around to give him fierce, manly type hugs.

"That's what we've been telling her," his oldest brother, Dallas, said.

"And him for more than a year now," the next in line, Colt, said.

"Well, maybe this will convince him," Remy said.

All four of the brothers bore a strong resemblance to each other, with the angular lines to their faces and tall, muscular bodies. But Remy was the only one with blond hair and blue eyes.

"This going to spoil your chances at buying that ranch?" Wesson, his younger brother, asked.

"Adele says not. She's pretty understanding about things, which reminds me, I've got to call her and give her an update. She's been sitting on the phone all evening," Remy said.

"Aha!" Colt said.

"What's that supposed to mean?" Remy raised an eyebrow as he fished the phone from his pocket.

"Never knew you to care about a woman like that," Colt answered.

"Never did before now." Remy punched in her number and went to the back of the waiting room to talk to Adele.

He gave her a brief update, told her that he wouldn't call again until morning, and said good night. Brief but he felt so much better, again, after hearing her voice. He turned to find all three of his brothers plus his mother staring at him slack-jawed.

"What? She's been good about this. It could have lost me all the rights to buy that ranch and the boys really want it. It's not like I'm in love with her," he said tersely.

"Could have fooled me." Colt grinned.

The doctor came into the room before Remy could pop off a smart answer. "Luckadeau family, I presume?"

Floy nodded. "Is he all right?"

"Yes, ma'am. He's strong as a horse and twice as

stubborn. This should fix him right up. We'll keep him until tomorrow evening for observation. If everything goes well, he can go home then. He'll be in recovery for half an hour, and then we'll take him up to a room. One person can stay with him tonight. Any questions?"

"Does he need to slow down?" Colt asked.

"For a few days, but then he can resume life as normal," the doctor said. "For a seventy-year-old man, he's in remarkable shape."

"I'm staying." Floy's tone left no room for discussion. "You boys can see him when he's awake, but then you are all going home. Remy and the foreman can take care of things at the ranch until I bring him home tomorrow evening. You can all come for supper tomorrow night to show your support. He'll be glad to have you all home."

Just like that, Floy had gone from terrified to picking up the reins and taking control of her family again. Not a single one of her sons argued—not because they didn't want to stay with their father, but because when Mama spoke, it was the law.

*Exactly like Adele*, Remy thought. Maybe that's why he admired her so much—because she had all the qualities of a strong woman like his mother.

*There is that.* He nodded. *But then there's that red hair that feels like silk in my hands and the way she can turn me on just by brushing against me. It's more than her strength. It's the way she makes me feel when I'm with her. Never felt like this before.*

"Hey, Brother, are you asleep?" Wesson asked.

Remy shook himself from the world four hours away to the one right before him. "No, just thinking."

"She must be something else to put that look on your face," Wesson whispered. "I've got to meet this woman."

"Someday, maybe. Right now, we've got to think about Mama and Daddy and getting them through this. They should retire, you know," Remy said.

"They'd both lay down and die if they didn't have a ranch to run. It's in their blood. They love it."

*Just like Adele. Just like me*, Remy thought.

# Chapter 14

ADELE AWOKE TO THE SOUND OF DRIZZLING RAIN HITTING the rooftop that Wednesday morning. She groaned and slammed a pillow over her head. Rain meant that she and the girls would be cooped up in the house. Remy and the boys were coming home that day, and she'd hoped for hard work to make the time pass quicker. One thing was for sure—she was not playing a single board game or watching one of those old western movies.

Remy had said they'd be home by five, so she'd have supper ready then. She tossed the pillow to one side and pushed back the sheet. With purpose, she slung her legs over the edge and put her feet on the floor.

A part of her had enjoyed having the ranch all to herself, but another was downright antsy thinking of Remy coming home. Not just to help out with chores and running the place, but also because she'd missed adult conversation, having a beer on the front porch, and simply exchanging a knowing look across the dinner table.

As she dressed, she decided to let the girls sleep in that morning. She pulled on a pair of work jeans, a button-up plaid shirt, and rubber boots. On the way through the kitchen, she picked up the milk bucket and an umbrella. For the middle of June, the rain was cold, as if it had passed over hail on its way to the ranch. She hunched her shoulders, held the umbrella at the right angle, and hurried out to the barn to take care of the milking for the morning.

She leaned into the cow's flanks and let her mind wander, but it wanted to run in circles. What Cassie had said about Remy's attraction was followed by the way he made her feel with nothing more than a hand on her knee. The way she had fallen in love with those two boys came next, and after that was the guilt she'd feel if she did buy the ranch and the boys' hearts were broken because they had to leave. By the time she got back to the house, nothing was settled and everything was still a total mental mess.

Bella was stirring up a bowl of biscuit dough when Adele pushed her way into the mudroom. She smiled at her mother and turned the dough out onto the counter-top, rolled it out to half an inch thick, and cut a dozen perfect circles with the rim of a water glass.

"What are we doing all day since it's raining again?" Bella asked.

Adele set the milk bucket on the counter and went to the pantry for clean jars to strain it into. "We could play board games or read."

"I miss the boys." Bella sighed.

Jett poured a glass of orange juice and carried it to the table. "Me, too. Mama, you either have to figure out a way for us to keep them or go out and buy us some brothers."

"It's a little more complicated than that," Adele said.

"I hate that word," Jett said.

"What?" Bella lined the biscuits up in a pan and slid it into the oven.

"Complicated!" Jett rolled her eyes.

Adele strained the milk and put the jars into the refrigerator. "Well, then, it's tougher than it sounds. People don't buy brothers off the Walmart shelf, and keeping the boys on the ranch means that we have to leave it, so that's kind of counterproductive."

"Guess we'd best enjoy them while we can, then," Bella said. "Rats! I just made a dozen biscuits for only three people."

"Boss and Jerry Lee are going to love you this morning." Jett grinned.

At five o'clock, she was ready to sell Jett to Dahlia and send Bella off to live with her grandma O'Donnell for the rest of the summer. They almost wore holes in the foyer's hardwood floor running back and forth to the front door to see if Remy and the boys had arrived yet. When they finally did see the truck coming down the lane, they hurried outside and waited on the porch.

Bella grabbed Nick by the arm and hurried him out to the corral to see the calf, which was already filling out and looking more and more like a breeder bull. Jett got a hold on Leo and hauled him to the laundry room, where Blanche had moved her litter of kittens into an old orange crate.

"They've got their eyes open and you can hold them and Blanche don't care." She chattered as she plopped down on the floor and put a squirmy orange one into his hands.

Adele stood in the kitchen doorway as the kids took off in their own directions. Remy looked tired and worried as he carried in two duffel bags. His face was drawn and his shoulders bent against the drizzling rain. He dropped the bags right inside the front door and walked toward her. She had no choice but to open her arms and hug him.

"Rough three days?" she whispered.

"I'm so glad to be home. I was worried about my dad and still am but felt like part of my heart was missing. I wanted to come home, Adele," he answered.

"Remy, Remy, come and see the kittens." Jett tugged at his hand.

"Well, I suppose that I should, darlin'. Did I hear you say their eyes are now open?" Remy let her lead him from the foyer through the dining room and kitchen and into the laundry room.

Adele went back to the kitchen and put the finishing touches on supper, called Bella on her cell phone, and told her and Nick to come back to the house and set the table. The antsy feeling was gone, and things were back to normal on the Double Deuce Ranch that evening.

A few minutes later, the kids and Remy had washed their hands, and everyone was around the table. The boys were talking. The girls were talking. But Remy was staring at her as if he'd seen her for the first time.

"Anyone want to say grace for us?" Adele asked.

"I will," Jett said as she bowed her head and shut her eyes. "Lord, thank you for bringing the boys home safe. Sometimes I want to shoot them, but it was pretty lonely without them these past days. Bless this food that Mama has cooked, even though it was the boys' day to cook. Amen."

"Amen," Remy said with a deep chuckle.

"Amen," Adele whispered.

"To make this fair, I've decided that you should go see your folks for three days." Remy picked up a platter of fried chicken, removed a leg and a wing, and sent it on around the table. "You choose the three days, and the boys and I will hold down the fort for you."

"Not necessary," Adele said. Lord, she'd just gotten them all back in the nest. Why would she want to tear it up again?

"I insist. You should leave Sunday evening and come home on Wednesday, just like we did, to make the whole thing completely fair," Remy said.

Jett clapped her hands. "I'd love to go see Granny and Grandpa. And since we go through Vernon, we could stop and see Dahlia. She would love that so much."

"It's been a long time, Mama, and Sunday is Father's Day," Bella said. "Grandpa would be so happy to see all of us on his special day."

"We'll think about it," Adele said. "Right now, let's eat our supper and then—"

"Watch a movie," Leo said.

Remy winked at Adele from the end of the table. "They're pretty well tired of technology and ready to get back into their rut."

"We're tired of reading. And I never thought I'd hear those words coming out of my mouth," Bella said. "Let's go look at the kittens and maybe play outside since it's stopped raining."

"I'd settle for a cold beer and some time on the front porch to listen to our own brand of coyotes and crickets," Remy said.

"Me, too." Adele passed a bowl of beans cooked with potatoes around the table. "And maybe some adult conversation."

"Mama!" Bella rolled her eyes.

"Bella!" Adele mimicked her.

"And I'd like one-on-one adult conversation rather than a room full of brothers all trying to run my business," Remy said.

"Oh, really? They want you to buy a ranch out near your parents, do they?"

Remy nodded. "But this is home."

A sharp prick jabbed Adele right in the heart. She liked the Double Deuce, and she really liked winning when it came to competition, but was it really home, like Remy said? Or could she be happier somewhere else? She should take a few days to go visit her parents and get some advice, maybe even figure out what she would do if she didn't buy this place. Was fate telling her to let Remy have it, since it was already home to him?

She bit into a piece of chicken and chewed slowly, noisy conversations all around her, and yet she felt alone in her dilemma. Yes, she did need some time away from the forest so she could see the trees, as Granny O'Donnell used to say. But she didn't want to leave the ranch even for one day, much less three. Still, it would be good for the girls, good for her dad, and most of all, it would give her time to think.

"I'll take you up on that offer, Remy. We'll leave Sunday and be back Wednesday, like you did," she said bluntly.

The silence in the room was deafening. A feather floating from the ceiling would have sounded like a freight train running through the room.

Leo finally grabbed his forehead and groaned. "Just when we get it all back to normal this happens. Uncle Remy, why did you suggest such a thing?"

"We want this to be fair, and that's the only way it can be," Remy said. "We'll miss the girls, but I'm sure they missed us."

"Not so much." Bella tipped up her chin and looked at Nick.

"Bull! I know you missed us. Why else would you call me every day? And I'll miss you and call every day, too. I ain't never had a sister, and it's kind of fun," Nick said.

"Can I go with them?" Leo asked. "We took Bella with us to Griff's house, so it would only be fair if they took me with them."

Remy shook his head slowly. "No, son. You're needed here on the ranch. Blanche has to have someone help look after the kittens. And you barely know how to drive the old work truck, so you need practice with that."

"Okay." Leo sighed. "But can they go with us to Ardmore to Beau's place this Sunday before they go away?"

"If they want," Remy answered, but he was looking down the length of the kitchen table at Adele rather than at Leo.

"Thank you for the invitation, but if we're going, I'd like to leave right after breakfast and be there for Sunday dinner, since it's Father's Day," Adele said. "My dad would love it if both his girls could be with him on his special day."

"Aw shucks." Leo pouted.

"But the next Sunday, y'all are invited to go across the river with us to Terral, Oklahoma, for church and dinner with my cousin Rye and his family. Terral is only a couple of miles across the Red River Bridge." Adele slathered an ear of corn with butter and passed the bowl on to Bella.

"You'll love it there. The town is little bitty, but we always have so much fun," Jett told Leo.

"Uncle Remy?" Nick asked.

Remy nodded. "Sounds like a good plan to me. Y'all got the chores done around here?"

"Of course," Bella said. "Chores and then supper, but we've got a whole bushel basket of beans that we have to snap after we get done eating. We can either do them before we have our movie or while we are watching it."

"On the front porch before," Leo piped up quickly.

Everyone whipped around to stare at Leo in his excitement.

"What?" he said with a tilt of his head. "I'm glad we're going to snap beans because I'm not done tellin' the girls about my grandpa's ranch and horses, and I want them to tell me about what all happened while we were gone."

"And we can't talk if we're watching a movie," Nick said.

Adele looked up, and her eyes locked with Remy's, and a whole conversation was exchanged without saying a single word. He was home, and his boys were happy, maybe for the first time in months. She was happy to have them there, and she didn't really want to leave, but she needed to—not only to keep things fair, but also to give her time to think.

"You know, Uncle Remy," Leo said, "things weren't right after Mama and Daddy left us. Granny and Gramps helped keep things going, but my heart hurt. I guess it always will, but since we come here, well, it don't hurt as bad."

Remy patted Leo on the back. "I'm glad, son. Really

glad. My heart hurt too because I lost my brother, but I don't think it hurt as bad as yours and Nick's did. But I agree. It's better since we came here."

Nick swiped at a tear with his napkin. "This is one fine supper, Miz Adele." He smiled through more pain than any fourteen-year-old kid ought to ever experience.

"Thank you." Adele's voice was almost as shaky as her commitment to own the ranch.

———

Adele had just crawled into bed with a thick historical romance book by Grace Burrowes when her phone rang. Expecting it to be Cassie, who'd said she'd call later about a Father's Day gift, she answered on the first ring.

"I've been waiting for your call," she said.

"Adele?"

The voice did not belong to Cassie for sure. It sounded a hell of a lot like her ex-mother-in-law. Adele shook her head and frowned. Why would that woman call her, especially at that time of night?

"Who is this?" she asked.

"It's Priscilla."

A long, pregnant silence hovered in the room. A jumbled rush of thoughts played through Adele's mind, but she couldn't latch on to a single reason why Priscilla would want to talk to her. Especially after their last conversation, when the woman had been so cold that her words came out with icicles attached to them.

"Are you there, Adele?" Priscilla asked.

"I'm here. What do you want?" Adele could feel the chill of her tone, but there was nothing she could do about it.

"Frankly, I'm surprised that you haven't hung up."

"Talk fast. I've got my finger on the button."

"Okay, first of all, thank you for giving me a moment. We were wrong, and we'd like a second chance. Isaac's new wife left him and took the baby. The prenup said that, in the event of a divorce, they would share custody, so he gets generous visitation rights, but there's no provision for grandparents. Of course, we'll see the baby when Isaac has him." She paused.

Adele felt absolutely no pity or sadness for her ex-husband. He'd screwed her to the wall in their divorce, and she'd offered to let him and his parents continue to be a part of the girls' lives, but they'd coldly declined.

"Are you still there? Maybe gloating?" Priscilla's tone had that familiar chill.

"I'm here. Karma can be a bitch, can't it?"

"I deserve that. Okay, I'll lay it on the line. Here's what we want. Isaac's father and I bought the ranch you left behind. We did it to get you totally out of our son's life because his marriage was on the rocks. His wife kept accusing him of sneaking up there to see you and the girls. Regardless, we own it, and we are prepared to give it to you if you will give us visitation rights to our granddaughters, reinstate their last name as Levy, and let us have them two weekends out of every month."

Adele's mind whipped around in circles. Two weekends every single month away from her daughters? To trust those people with her girls in a big-city atmosphere?

Priscilla went on. "They need to have some intellectual upbringing, to know there is more to the world than cows, tractors, and cowboy boots."

"Is there more?"

"We'll put your cattle back on the ranch along with your equipment and have all your things from storage moved back where they belong. And Isaac has asked that he be given visitation on the two weekends when we do not have the girls," Priscilla said.

Adele felt dirtier than after she'd been working out in the hay field on a hot summer day. She'd be selling her girls, sending them into a world of glam and glitter. It made her feel like she was beyond what a shower could wash away. But they were biologically half Levy, so did she owe them the right to refuse or accept this offer before she told the lady to piss off?

"I can hear you breathing, and with your temper, I expect that you are actually breathing fire, Adele. Think about what I've said. Bella and Jett will be much better off than they are living on a ranch with your new boyfriend and his nephews."

Every hair on Adele's neck prickled. "How did you know that?"

"I know every single thing you've done since you left the ranch two weeks ago. If I'd known then what I do today, you would have never needed to move. This is an offer you can't refuse," Priscilla said.

"What makes you think that? What if I brought my new boyfriend and his nephews with me?" Adele was baiting her.

Priscilla's laughter was brittle. "That won't happen. It will be in the small print of the papers you'll sign. And, Adele, Isaac knows he made a mistake. There is hope for you to have a second chance, as well as giving Bella and Jett a father."

Adele could feel the heat from the imaginary smoke

billowing from her heart, straight through her ears, and out into the room. "You got anything else to say?"

"That's basically it. Isaac sends the girls his love," Priscilla said.

Two years.

She'd answered questions, dried tears, hoped that she was doing all she could to keep them from having emotional scars due to knowing their father didn't want them, and now he sends them his love?

"Bullshit," Adele said.

"You think about what I said. Whether or not you and Isaac decide on a second chance is your business. We'll discuss this again when you've had a little time. Good night, Adele."

Adele tossed the phone to the other side of the bed as if it were a rattlesnake poised to strike. She picked up the book that she'd dropped to her lap sometime during the conversation, laid it on the bedside table, and threw back the sheet covering her legs. Her feet hit the floor and the pacing began. From the door to the window, where she peeked out the curtain to see if one of Priscilla's hired people was spying on her even after she'd gone to bed. Back to the door to ease it open and think about going to the kitchen to binge out on cookies and beer. Then to the window again for another peek— was that the glint of binoculars in the distance or just the twinkle of a star?

The walls began to close in on her, and it felt as if the ceiling were falling. In a while, she'd be curled up in the fetal position with no oxygen left. She hurried out of the room, took a deep breath, and went straight for the kitchen. Forget the beer and cookies—she needed a double shot of Jack to get Priscilla's words out of her mind.

The light was on in the kitchen when she arrived, and Remy glanced at her from over the open refrigerator door. He smiled and then his face went serious. He wore a snow-white tank top that hugged his body and red-and-yellow-plaid pajama pants that hung low on his hips.

"My God, Adele, you are as pale as a sheet. What's happened?" He slammed the fridge door and made his way to her, arms wide open.

She walked into them and laid her head on his chest. "I don't want to talk about it. I either need a shot of strong whiskey or someone to hold me."

"We're out of beer, and I haven't run across any whiskey, but I can sure enough hold you for as long as you need it." Remy picked her up and carried her to the living room, where he sat down on the sofa with her in his lap.

# Chapter 15

"Sure you don't want to talk about it?" Remy tipped up her chin with his knuckles.

She shook her head. It was too raw to even say the words.

"It's not a death in the family, is it?" he pushed.

"No, it's just a personal thing I'll have to deal with, but not tonight."

His lips closed on hers, and she gave herself to the feelings she'd been fighting. She needed a man to want her—not for who he wanted her to be, but for herself. She wanted Remy Luckadeau to kiss her, to touch her body, and then maybe she would forget the anger and pent-up hissy inside her. She had to have her normal old heart back before the girls crawled out of bed the next day, and Remy could help her reclaim it.

"I can't do this." She pushed away from him. "I'd be using you, Remy, and that's not fair."

"Then talk to me. You're going to explode if you don't," he whispered.

It all came flowing out like a wild, rushing river in the springtime, and he was right—when the last word had left her body, she felt a lot better.

"Well, that's bigger than a busted fingernail." He planted a kiss on the tip of her nose.

"Slightly," she said.

He palmed the back of her head and gently laid her head on his shoulder. "What are you going to do about it?"

"I'm not sure. What would you do?"

His hands in her hair, massaging her scalp, sent shivers down her spine. She should thank him for listening and get up out of his lap. Tomorrow, things would look better. Her mama always said that daylight shed a whole new light on problems, and so far, she'd been right.

"I'd think about it and cool down for a few days, then talk to my boys about it and maybe my mama to get her take on it. Then I'd tell the woman to take her idea and go to hell with it," he drawled.

"If you were going to do that anyway, why get anyone else's opinion?" She looked up at him.

Moonlight filtering through the window put half his face in shadow, but the part that was visible smiled. "Because it would make me feel better to know that I had the support of my family and kids. You're so beautiful, Adele, and so damn sexy in this light that it sucks the breath right out of my lungs."

She cupped his face in her hands and drew his lips to hers, opening her mouth enough to allow his tongue to enter. His hands found their way up under the back of her nightshirt, massaging the tense muscles.

And then it all stopped.

Her ears suddenly ached from listening so intently past the buzz of hormones that whined for more. Surely he'd heard the kids coming down the stairs, or he wouldn't have quit making out with her.

"Adele, I don't want this if it's going to be a one-night stand to get you over your anger. I don't want it if it's going to make things awkward between us where this ranch is concerned. I want it because I dream about you, think about you, and have wanted to make love with you for days. I miss you when I can't see you, and I can't believe I'm saying all this, but…"

She put her fingers over his lips, stood up, and took his hand in hers. She grabbed a blanket from the back of the sofa in the other hand and led him out into the foyer. Instead of starting up the stairs, she turned left and went all the way to the end, to Walter's bedroom, and opened the door.

"This is Walter's room. You think we should disturb it?" Remy whispered.

"I cheated and peeked inside here while you were gone. There's nothing in here but a rocking chair. The closet is cleaned out, and there's only half a roll of toilet paper in the bathroom. Nothing but a big, empty room— that locks from the inside." She kicked the door shut with her bare foot and turned the lock on the knob.

He took the blanket from her hand and spread it out on the floor, untied the gold velvet cushions from the rocking chair, and tossed them onto the blanket. "A perfect bed, and would you look at the way that big lover's moon is shining through the window."

Adele slipped her hands under his tank top and pulled it up over his head, ran her hands through all that soft hair on his chest, and then laid her cheek close to his racing heart. "What are you thinking right now?" she asked.

"It's been six months. I hope I don't disappoint you," he said hoarsely.

"Two years and I have the same fear." She rolled

up slightly on her toes so that their lips were even and kissed him hard.

"I don't want to rush this."

She sat down on the pallet and then stretched out, her head on a cushion. He did the same and slipped an arm under her shoulders, pulling her close to his side with her head resting on his chest. He shifted his position slightly so he could use his free hand to trace the lines of her face and then the curve of her body, from ribs to hip to thigh, as far as he could reach.

"I love the way we fit together," he murmured into her hair.

"I've never been with a man as tall as you are. It feels right."

That's when the words stopped, and they began to talk with fingertips, slight groans, and long, lingering looks right into each other's souls. It's when Adele learned that there was a major difference between having sex, even good sex, and making love.

He slowly undressed her, his eyes saying things way beyond simple words. She felt as if she were floating two feet off the pallet, weightless, with nothing but the sense of touch. The only noise was Remy's heavy breathing, a coyote way out in the distance, and the whirr of a ceiling fan above them.

That she was tall didn't matter. The way his eyes went all soft and dreamy while he explored every inch of her body said that he thought she was pretty. That she had freckles wasn't important, because he'd kissed every one of them, making them special.

Her fingers circled his erection, and he gasped.

"Your hands are cold and feel so good."

"What I'm holding is hot as hell and is begging for more than steamy kisses and foreplay." She shifted her position until she could wrap her legs around his body.

With a firm thrust, he entered her, and they began to rock together, their bodies glistening with sweat. He took her to the very edge of a climax so big that it sounded like a class five tornado in her already-buzzing ears and then backed off to a slow rhythm. She dug her fingers into his back while he kissed her passionately again and again, building the hunger up until there were no sane thoughts in her mind. She wanted satisfaction, and Remy Luckadeau was the only one that could bring it to her.

"My. God. Remy. I. Am. Going. To," she said between moans.

"Right now?" he drawled.

She didn't have enough air to say another word, but his smile said that he read the answer in her eyes and expression. With a final thrust, he took them both over the edge of the cliff and into the afterglow at the bottom of the long slope. Then he rolled to one side, taking her with him, holding her close enough that their wet bodies stuck to each other.

"So this is the real thing." Her voice sounded as if it were coming from a long distance away.

"I'm not sure. I've never experienced anything like that." He found her lips again and latched on to them, starting another buildup of desire.

"Me either."

"Let's see if it's as good the second time around."

She could feel him getting stiff again next to her belly. "I'm game if you are."

—⁓—

The moon was gone when Remy awoke, and the first rays of sun were dancing through the window in Walter's empty bedroom. Adele was curled up next to him, her red hair in disarray on the gold velvet pillow. He tried to drink his fill of every inch of her but decided after a few minutes of staring at her gorgeous body that it would take a lifetime to ever be full to the brim of Adele O'Donnell.

He touched her on the nose, and it twitched. Then one eye opened lazily. Then the other one popped open, and one hand clapped over her mouth as she tried to sit up.

"What time is it?"

"We've still got ten minutes before the alarms in our bedrooms go off. Good morning, beautiful," he said.

She removed her hand and smiled. "Good morning, sexy cowboy."

"I could spend the whole day right here with you."

"So could I, but there's a cow to milk, a herd to feed, fences to mend, and it's our day to cook, so I have to get up, take a quick shower, and start breakfast. Such is the life of a rancher, you know."

He brushed a quick kiss across her lips. "The next one will be better after I brush my teeth and get some coffee."

"Remy, is this something we should stop now or—"

He laid a finger over mouth. "One day at a time, darlin'. One day at a time."

An hour later, he was setting the milk on the counter like he did on his mornings to take care of that chore. The house smelled like bacon and hot biscuits, and all four kids were busy as ants setting the table and getting things they needed or wanted from the refrigerator. Everything was normal for the Double Deuce, except that he couldn't keep a grin off his face, and he practically had to tie a rock to his heart to keep it from floating right out of his chest.

He had to buy this ranch now. He had to have something in his hands to offer Adele in the future if things worked out.

"Hey, y'all, I called Dahlia this morning," Jett said. "Don't look at me like that, Mama. She said I can call anytime I want, and she even said that she gets up before daylight because she always has. Did you know that she worked as a nurse for more than fifty years right there in Vernon, Texas? And anyway, she's real excited that we might stop by, but I told her we'd be in a hurry on Sunday so we'd stop by on Wednesday and she said for us not to eat lunch that day because she was cooking for us." She stopped to take a deep breath.

Remy winked at Adele as he strained the milk and put it in the fridge. "Looks to me like we should skim the cream off about six gallons of milk and make some more ice cream tonight. Since us cowboys weren't here to help drink this, it's piling up."

"There's room in the freezer for a few gallons," Bella said.

"Friday night could be our ice-cream night," Jett suggested.

Leo seconded the motion by raising his hand. "I like that idea."

"Then I guess that's it," Remy said. "Today we're going to turn over about twenty acres of alfalfa to put some nutrients back in the soil. Then in the fall, we'll plant it in rye grass for spring feeding. So I guess us guys will take old Boss out to the field and move the cattle out of that pasture to another one. When we get that done, then Bella and Adele can fire up the tractors and get it plowed."

Jett raised her hand. "I'll help move the cows and then harvest the garden."

"Looks like our day is planned. Jett, if you would slide that pan of lasagna into the oven at eleven o'clock, it'll be ready at noon," Adele said.

—◊◊◊—

Adele could hardly keep her eyes off Remy. Had last night really happened? There they were, all talking about ranching business and food as if nothing had gone on in that empty bedroom. Suddenly, she felt her eyes go wide and her pulse quicken.

Walter wasn't going to come back with his mind changed. He'd already moved out and either she or Remy was going to own this place. And then something else hit her. Holy smokin' hell! She hadn't taken a birth control pill in eighteen months. Seemed a waste of money to buy them for no reason.

"What?" Remy asked. "You've got that look on your face again."

"Birth control," she said. "I was so upset I didn't even think about it."

"Like I said, one day at a time. We'll be more careful and cross that bridge if and when we get to it. And, Adele, I would never ever leave you to raise a child alone."

"What bridge?" Bella asked.

"Whatever one pops up. We will cross our bridges one day and one bridge at a time," Remy answered.

"You sound like Grandpa. He says that all the time when Mama frets about things." Bella carried a platter of biscuits to the table.

"Grandpa? Well, that knocks the wind right out of my sails," Remy said.

"Sometimes we have to get a little grounding to keep us from lifting off like big old, fluffy clouds," Adele whispered. "And until one of us can get to the store, we'd best stay grounded, Remy."

"This is one time it's tough to agree, but you are so right." He nodded. "But that doesn't mean I can't have a good-night kiss."

"What are y'all talkin' about?" Leo asked. "We can't hear you."

"Boys kissing girls," Remy answered honestly.

"Yuck!" Leo exclaimed.

Nick blushed. "It ain't so bad after that first time."

"You've kissed a girl?" Bella's voice was a high-pitched squeal.

"You haven't?" Nick fired right back.

"Never, or a boy either," Bella said. "I'm saving that for high school and sex for college."

Adele put up a palm. "Too much information, Bella O'Donnell."

"Well, I am," Bella said. "Let's eat breakfast so we can get outside."

---

After a make-out session that left her frustrated and wanting a romp on a blanket in an empty room on

Thursday night, Adele vowed she'd make a trip to town on Friday for a box of condoms. But Friday turned out to be Murphy's day. If it could go wrong, it did. If it couldn't go wrong, it did anyway.

Two cows found a weak spot in the fence and were a mile down the road before someone recognized the brand on their hip and called the Double Deuce to report the problem. While Remy and Leo fixed the fence, the other four took the truck and Boss down the dirt road to bring the cows home.

It sounded easy enough, and Adele had done the job too many times to count. Boss was doing a fine job of keeping them headed in the right direction right up until a mama skunk started across the road with four little black-and-white babies behind her. No cat was going to get in Boss's way, so he charged them. The skunk lifted her tail in self-defense and got the cows right in the face.

That caused them to stampede, bawling loudly and trying to get away from the horrible smell. They frothed at the mouth. Their eyes rolled around worse than Bella's did when she was aggravated. One old girl headed back where she came from; the other took off out into the mesquite underbrush, both of them throwing their heads around spastically.

Boss made a beeline for home, howling worse than any coyote Adele had ever heard. He'd run a few feet, drop to his belly, roll around in the dirt road, get up, and go again, only to repeat the process. Poor old boy didn't realize it was going to take a lot more than dirt to get the smell off him.

Jett and Nick took off after the one trying to hide

from the eau de skunk in the mesquite, and Bella went chasing after the one who was headed to Nocona right down the middle of the road. Adele jumped in the truck and bypassed the one on the road, got ahead of it about a city block, and whipped her truck around sideways to steer the heifer back the other way.

The cow slowed down and whipped around, pawed the ground, and brushed past Bella on the way, leaving her with the rich stench all over her. Bella bent over at the waist and lost her dinner right there beside the road.

"Sorry, Mama," she groaned as she crawled into the bed of the truck and laid flat on her back, gasping for anything but the smell on her body.

"No problem. The cow is headed home. I'll just keep her going that way. Lord, you'll have to use the hose. You can't go in the house like that." Adele gagged a couple of times.

Jett was cussing at her animal as she steered it back toward the house. Nick looked a little green around the gills, but he was doing a fine job of herding. The heifer that Adele was steering home with the truck joined the other one and that seemed to set them in motion. They probably ran off at least five pounds each as they hustled down the road at a pace too fast for Jett and Nick to keep up with, so they hopped up on the truck's running boards and hitched a ride home.

By the time they reached the house, the whole countryside smelled like it had been doused in skunk. Remy opened gates and herded them through the yard, past the corral behind the barn, and into the plowed field where they would be in quarantine until they smelled a lot better.

"Don't go in the house. Get the hose out, and I'll mix up the antidote," he yelled.

"I've got a sick one in the back of the truck," Adele hollered.

"Nick?" Remy whipped around.

"No. Bella."

"I'll be damned," he said and kept moving the cows forward by clapping his hands.

Jett and Nick sprayed themselves down with water hoses and Bella tried hard to stay in an upright position and avoid another bout of dry heaves. Skunks had never affected her like this before, so Adele figured it was the combination of the heat and running after the cattle added to the skunk smell that got to her.

The yard fence didn't break Remy's stride as he ran toward the house. He placed a hand on it and floated over the thing like an acrobat, then kept running straight into the house. When he returned, he held two bottles and a yellow box of baking soda. He set it on the porch, grabbed an old galvanized washtub hanging beside the back door, and carried it out into the middle of the yard.

"You boys all go to the front yard and stay there until Adele calls us. Bella, darlin', since this affected you the most, I want you to take off all your clothes and get into this tub. Your mama is going to give you a bath in what I'm about to mix up here and it will take the smell off you. Wash your hair and everything in it. I'll leave clean towels by the back door, so you can go straight up to the shower when you're done. Soap up at least twice and wash your hair twice, or it will turn an ugly shade of red."

He winked at Adele. "And I don't mean gorgeous red like your mother's hair. Nod if you understand."

Bella barely had enough energy to nod.

"Adele, use that mop bucket and mix this whole bottle of hydrogen peroxide, all of the baking soda, and half of the dish soap with half a bucket of water. It's not as fancy as most soaps you girls like, but it will do the trick. When you finish with Bella, then do Jett and you. Empty the water after each bath. Holler at us boys when you get done and we'll come on around and wash it off us," Remy said.

"Will it work?" Jett asked.

"Always has for my mama. I'm hoping it works in this part of Texas as well as it does out in the Panhandle," Remy said. "I knew what had happened when Boss came home frothing at the mouth. I'll take care of him before I take my dip. See you later."

"I hope he's right." Bella stripped out of her clothing and crawled into the washtub, curling up so that she could get her hair wet.

"I hate this smell worse than pig shit," Jett said.

Adele shot a look her way.

Jett set her mouth in a firm line. "It's the truth, Mama. And pig shit smells worse than pig poop. But right now I'd smear either one on me if it would get this skunk off me."

It took two washings with the mixture and then showers with lots of soap and three shampoo-rinse-repeats before the smell was gone from Adele, but nothing took it out of her nose. Not saline mist or menthol rubbed under her nostrils. She could still smell a faint skunk scent that night when the kids were talking about the horrible day.

The sun put on a lovely show as it sunk below the

mesquite trees, but no one on the Double Deuce even noticed. Bella spent the whole evening in her room with a tray of crackers and several cups of hot tea sweetened with honey. Jett and Leo sprawled out on the living room floor and watched an old John Wayne movie. Nick opted to sit on the floor outside Bella's door and listen to his music—just in case she needed something in a hurry.

"I didn't get to town today," Adele whispered to Remy as she poured another cup of coffee and carried it to the table.

"Neither did I," he said. "But tomorrow is another day."

"And we've got tomorrow."

"We could have lots of tomorrows if we wanted them," Remy said.

"I haven't known you long enough to say yes if that's a proposal," she said.

"God no!" He shivered. "It's not a proposal. I was thinking of something else."

She sipped at the coffee, but neither it nor the camphor-based ointment she'd rubbed beneath her nose completely obliterated the smell of skunk or the taste of that horrendous aroma in her mouth. "And that is?"

"We could do what we did with the air conditioner," he said.

"Have a big argument?"

"No, we could each pay half for this ranch and be partners on it," he said.

She picked up a peanut butter cookie and nibbled on it. "I'm not sure that would work."

"Why?"

"Right now there's an end in sight, Remy. If we did

that, we'd neither one have an outlet and there wouldn't be a light at the end of the tunnel. We'd be stuck with each other, and when the divorce came, it would be devastating to all the kids," she said.

"Divorce?"

"Splitting a partnership is every bit as painful as a divorce, don't you think?"

"Never had one," he said.

"Me neither, as far as a partnership goes, but I did have a divorce. And I would never want to cause you pain or to feel any that you would cause. So the answer is thank you, but no thank you."

# Chapter 16

CASSIE DIDN'T HAVE TO TALK VERY LOUD OR LONG TO convince Adele and the girls to leave on Saturday evening and make it to western Texas by bedtime, so they could spend all of Father's Day with her and Adele's father, Hank O'Donnell. Bags were packed and the guys all helped carry them to the truck.

Hugs were given, and Remy held her tightly a moment longer than necessary, but the kids were so busy with last-minute instructions that no one noticed.

"I'll miss you. Don't go out there and buy a ranch. If I can't have this one, I'm buying nearby so I can be close to you. I hope you'll do the same if I do wind up with the Deuce," he drawled softly.

"I'm not looking to land anywhere but in this area," she said as she got into the truck. "See you on Wednesday. Call me often. Blanche has never been left with boys before."

"We'll take good care of her and the kittens," Remy said.

"Don't get in the way of skunks," Nick teased.

"Don't even mention it." Bella's eyes and head rolled at the same time.

In the rearview mirror, Adele could see the boys and Remy waving from the porch as she drove all the way to the end of the lane. She honked the horn when she turned out onto the road, heading west.

"I got a problem," Bella sighed.

"What?" Adele held her breath.

"I don't want to leave the ranch, Mama. I love it so much. I don't even mind sharing a room with Jett until we see if we are the ones who get to stay there. But I don't want Remy and the boys to leave. I like having brothers around," Bella said.

Adele drove through Nocona and wished she could turn the truck around and go right back to the ranch. But promises had been made and tomorrow was Father's Day. Her phone rang before she'd made it to Ringgold. "Hello, Remy. Did we forget something?"

"No. I have to tell you something that made this old cowboy tear up."

"Blanche okay?"

"She's fine. Leo is in there with her right now, talking all about how he'll be her favorite by the time you get home. When I came back into the house, there was an envelope with my name on it propped up on the dining room table. I thought it might be from you so I took it up to my room to open it."

"I didn't leave anything," she said quickly. *Dammit!* After that amazing night in the empty bedroom, she could have left some kind of sweet little note.

"I know. It was from Jett and Bella. They created a homemade Father's Day card for me. On the outside were drawings of a skunk, a baby calf, an ice-cream cone, what I think might be John Wayne, and a pair of cowboy boots. Inside it said that…" His voice broke. "Give me a minute."

Tears welled up in Adele's eyes, but she wiped them away without either girl noticing.

"Okay, here's the inside. 'You might not be our father, but you are such a wonderful dad to Nick and Leo that we want to say happy Father's Day and that we're a little bit jealous of them but don't tell them. Love…'" He paused again before going on. "They signed it 'Love, Bella and Jett.'"

Adele giggled softly. "That's quite an admission."

"One minute I was trying to swallow down the lump in my throat. The next I was laughing," he said. "Call me when you're halfway there and when you arrive. I just had to share my first-ever Father's Day card with you. Tell them thank you."

"Thanks, Remy," Adele said.

"What was that all about?" Jett asked.

"Remy likes his Father's Day card," she said honestly.

Bella laid her book aside. "I wish we had a dad like that."

Adele took a very deep breath and decided that this was the perfect time to talk to them about their grandmother's proposal. She needed a starting point, and she sure enough had to present it in a noncommittal tone, without her own anger shining through.

"Speaking of fathers…" she started.

"Did we get Grandpa a fishing rod and reel?" Jett asked. "I know that's what he really needs because he talks about fishing a lot, and he and Granny are going camping this fall by some lake, and he says he's going to catch the biggest catfish ever."

"We did get him one. Aunt Cassie picked it out, and we'll give it to him tomorrow," Adele answered. "But this is about your father, Isaac Levy."

"You don't want us to give him a card do you?" Bella scrunched up her nose.

"I don't even know him," Jett said, adding her two cents.

They were so right. Neither had seen him in more than two years. Adele watched the cow tongue cactus, mesquite, cattle, and oil wells fly by her window at seventy-five miles an hour for several minutes before she went on.

"Your grandmother Levy called me. I'm going to tell you what she said, and I don't want you to say a word for at least fifteen minutes. Take the time to process it and get over the initial shock of what it is. Then we'll talk about it all the way to Dimmitt." Adele told the story as calmly as was humanly possible.

Bella sat beside her stone-faced, barely blinking and looking straight ahead. Jett pulled out her phone and checked the time, then laid it in her lap and went back to listening to music. Adele glanced at the clock on the dash. Five thirty. So that meant at five forty-five, she'd open up the topic for discussion.

Her oldest daughter's expression changed as the minutes ticked away. At first she was angry, then sad, then she frowned as if trying to figure out exactly how she felt. Adele knew the stages. She'd lived through every one of them more than once.

She shifted her eyes to the rearview. Jett had made up her mind about the situation in the first ten seconds after Adele finished talking. In that respect, she was exactly like Adele's mother, Myra O'Donnell, who made her decisions based on her gut instinct and never looked back with regrets.

Silence filled the truck as she drove through Henrietta, past the place where the burned-out motel lot still stood empty. Back before the fire, Rye's friend, Wil, met his future wife in that very place. She'd have to be sure to include them in the invitation to come to the party she planned to have on the Fourth of July. She'd lumped Wil and Ace into the O'Donnell family until she was a teenager, when she finally figured out that they weren't related at all but were just friends of her O'Donnell cousins.

That set her to reminiscing about Rhett, Sawyer, and Finn, who'd all wound up in Burnt Boot, Texas. It was only about an hour from the Double Deuce. It would be fun to see them all again. She loved the stories about the family feud they'd landed in when they went to Burnt Boot. These days the feud might be officially over, but Leah, Rhett's wife, said that she didn't look for it to really ever end.

Then there was Raylen and Dewar, who both lived close to Uncle Cash and Aunt Maddie. They'd been off to the Resistol Rodeo when she'd been there for Sunday dinner. Yes, sir, lots and lots of cousins and family in this area, and she full well planned on finding a ranch to raise her girls on. They needed lots of family and cousins around them for support.

"Time's up," Jett said.

Bella laid her book to the side.

"Okay, what's your opinion?" Adele asked.

"I'll go first," Bella said. "Grandma Myra says that sometimes it's too late to do what you should have been doin' all along. That's my stand on this, Mama. I'm not mad at him. I don't hate him. I'm happy where we are, and I do not want to go back to the old ranch. I want a new start in a new school, where nobody knows that at one time my last name was Levy. So that's my opinion. And I hope that when we get the ranch, Remy buys one right down the road and we can all still be friends."

"Jett?" Adele asked.

"Ditto. What Bella said is good enough for me. Only thing I'll add is if Grandmother Levy winds up making us go to the city to see her every month or every other weekend, I will pout and throw fits, and she'll be more miserable that I am for those two days."

"Jett!" Adele's tone chastised.

"Don't fuss at her, Mama. I'll do the same thing. What a miserable weekend it would be to leave the ranch and have to dress up for dinner and be all proper. I'd hate it worse than the skunk," Bella said.

"Then I guess it's decided once and for all. If she calls again, I'll tell her we had a committee meeting and we're declining her offer." Adele passed the Wichita Falls city limits sign. Her daughters continued to amaze Adele. In two weeks, they'd adjusted better than she'd hoped for in a year.

"Anyone ready for a potty break?" Adele asked.

"No, but I see a McDonald's, and I could sure go for a Coke," Bella answered. "And maybe a couple of those fried apple pies."

The McDonald's didn't have many cars at the drive-through, so it didn't take long to get a couple of soft drinks and a latte, half a dozen fried pies, and an order of fries for Jett, who decided she needed them at the last minute. Then they were back on the road with Bella reading and Jett bobbing her head to music. The times when Jett sang along, it sounded like she was really into the Pistol Annies and Taylor Swift on

this trip. Adele caught Highway 70 on the west side
of Vernon after they'd stopped for a potty break at a
convenience store.

While the girls stretched their legs a few minutes by
walking around candy aisles and picking out a Father's
Day card to give to their grandfather, Adele called
Remy. He answered breathlessly on the third ring.

"Hey," he said. "My phone was on the porch railing,
and when I grabbed for it, it fell off. Where are you?"

"Is that Jerry Lee I hear crowing?"

"Stupid bird. I don't think a henhouse full of
pretty ladies to entice him would make him crow at
daybreak."

A pang of nostalgia hit her when she noticed a wind
chime with a rooster at the top hanging on a souvenir
rack right in front of her. "It's the story of our lives,
Remy. A year ago if someone would have told you that
the biggest playboy in Texas would be living on a ranch
with a woman he didn't know and her two daughters,
would you have believed them? And if they'd told you
about Jerry Lee and the skunk episode with old Boss
dog, would you have believed that?"

"Hell no," he laughed. "And I sure wouldn't have
believed that a gorgeous redhead like you would have
spent a night cuddled up with me on a blanket in a big
empty room either. I miss you, Adele, already. And
there's three more days before I see you again."

"Absence either makes the heart grow fonder or else
out of sight, out of mind. You might change your mind,"
she said.

The rooster crowed again and she touched the chimes,
sending a lovely noise through that half of the store. On

impulse, she pulled them off the rack and carried them to the counter as she talked.

"What is that noise? Are you somewhere where there's an organ?" Remy asked.

"No, just wind chimes, and I'm buying them for the front porch," she said.

"You could turn around and bring them back tonight. They might get broken on the way to Dimmitt or Cassie might talk you out of them, and I'm thinking that Jerry Lee is going to love them." Remy's voice lowered to a seductive level.

"You insisted that I take this trip. It's too late to change your mind now. I'll give you a call when we get there. I'm thinking it'll be just before ten."

She could see him with his boots propped on the railing, the ladder-back chair leaned against the house, old Boss near his feet and Jerry Lee tormenting him from his perch somewhere on the porch. And already she was homesick.

"You ever had phone sex?" he asked.

She blushed. "I have not and I'm not having it with you. It would melt my phone."

He laughed loudly and that crazy rooster crowed again. "The boys have driven me crazy this evening. They like having sisters."

"It's my turn to check out. Talk to you later," she said.

"Don't forget to call," he said.

"I won't." She hit the End button and laid her wind chimes on the counter next to a couple of candy bars, a banana, and two small bottles of milk from the girls. When she raised an eyebrow, one of Bella's shoulders popped up.

"It won't be as good as fresh milk, but we already had a soda pop so we thought it would be healthier," she said. "Hey, that looks like Jerry Lee. I bet he'll preen for that shiny thing."

"Won't it be fun to watch him?" Adele paid for the purchases and they loaded into the truck for the final half of the journey.

The last two hours of the trip were done in darkness. Out in western Texas, the towns are few and far between, and most of them are so small that everything except maybe a snow-cone stand or a convenience store shuts down at five o'clock. The constant motion had lulled both girls to sleep, which meant they'd be wired when they got to their grandparents.

Adele kept her eyes on the road, but her mind darted here, there, and yonder, creating scenarios, one after the other. If she and Remy formed a partnership, if they decided that one night of fabulous sex was just a flash in the pan, if they both dated other people—how would all that affect the children? If she bought the ranch and he moved close enough to her that the kids still attended the same school and they did date, what happened then?

Each virtual scene brought on more questions than answers, and every one of them ended with Remy's strong face in her mind, his rough hands making her body come alive in ways it never had, and his voice saying, "One day at a time."

The rolling hills fell behind her, and the land stretched out all the way to the sky. Plowed fields, pastures, cotton coming up well, alfalfa, soy beans—they went on as far as the eye could see and then met up with a bank of twinkling stars out in the distance. She'd been born in this flat country and loved it. Dirt meets sky, and a person could see a tornado coming from twenty miles away.

But the gentle roll of the land between Saint Jo and Nocona was where her soul had found peace. She'd come more often to visit her folks, but she did not want to raise her girls out here. She checked the clock on the dash when she turned off the highway into the lane leading up to the house. Three minutes until ten, so she'd gauged it right.

Her mother must've heard the sound of tires on gravel because the porch light came on and a short, blond figure crossed the porch and was in the yard when Adele came to a stop. Myra O'Donnell and her daughter, Cassie, had been cut from the same bolt of cloth. Both were small women with blond hair, big blue eyes, and curvy figures. Adele had gotten her father's height along with her grandmother's red hair, temper, and green eyes.

Myra grabbed Adele the moment she was out of the truck and hugged her tightly. "It's been too long, my child, and I'm not tolerating this anymore. A visit every other month is the absolute minimum or I'll kidnap my granddaughters and hold them for ransom."

"Yes, Mama." Adele threw an arm around Myra's shoulders. "Where's Daddy and Cassie?"

"Your dad is waiting in the kitchen. I wouldn't let him cut that chocolate cake until y'all got here. Cassie has gone off with some cowboy to some bar to dance. She said to tell you that she'd be home by midnight, and if you're asleep, she'll wake you. And here's my babies. Come here and give your granny hugs and then we'll go see Grandpa." Myra opened up her arms to Bella and Jett.

"Chocolate cake? Yummy," Jett said.

"Good Lord, kid! You had soda pop, milk, fries, and candy on the way," Adele fussed.

"But now she's at Granny's house, and she needs chocolate cake and milk so she'll sleep good tonight." Myra locked her arm in Adele's and they walked up the porch steps together.

There's comfort in things that stay the same. Adele had been raised in the long, low, ranch-style house. Her parents had inherited the place from her maternal grandmother on the day they'd married. Everything that Hank O'Donnell had touched from that day on had turned to pure gold, but he'd never changed the house. The front door led into a big family room with an attached dining room and kitchen all creating a great room. A hallway off to the left held a master bedroom, the ranch office, and her mother's sewing room. One to the right had four bedrooms. At one time, they were all filled with kids: three boys and a girl. But one of Myra's brothers had been killed in a car wreck, another died of leukemia as a child, and the last one had lost his life in Vietnam.

A parent should never have to bury a child. It's an unnatural grief that never has closure, but her grandmother had endured it three times. Maybe that's where Adele got her strength in addition to her red hair and temper.

As she walked into the house and was met halfway across the floor by her dad, she hoped that her strength was never tested by losing either Bella or Jett. She wasn't sure she could endure that kind of pain.

"Come here, my sweethearts," Hank said in a big, booming voice. That he was an O'Donnell was plain as day—black hair, tall, muscled from hard work, and kind eyes. Except for the hair color, he wasn't totally unlike Remy Luckadeau, she thought as she walked right into his arms with her daughters for a four-way hug.

"I'm so glad you're here for Father's Day. It means the world to me," Hank said.

"Grandpa, I've got to tell you about Leo and Nick and my new baby kittens. We haven't named them yet, but Leo is writing down names while I'm gone." Jett grabbed his hand and let him off to the kitchen, chatting all the way.

"And, Granny, you will never believe what Grandmother Levy has done," Bella whispered. "I told Mama what you always say about sometimes it's too late to do what you should have already been doing."

"Well, you come right on in here to the sofa and tell me all about it," Myra said.

Adele used the time alone to go to the truck to get the bags. But she hadn't even cleared the porch when she'd pulled her phone from her pocket and hit the button to call Remy.

# Chapter 17

BEAU LUCKADEAU WAS A COUPLE OF YEARS OLDER THAN Remy and he'd always been lucky in everything he touched—except for women. And then he met Milli and his luck changed for the better. Their oldest daughter, Katy, was eight years old, and they had two sons, Noah and Levi, who were six and four.

The family had barely made it through Sunday dinner when Katy dragged Nick and Leo out to the horse barn. It didn't take much to sweet-talk Buster, the ranch foreman, into saddling up horses for the older kids and ponies for the smaller ones to ride.

Remy propped a boot on the lower rung of the rail fence, a forearm on the top, and watched as Buster hoisted Leo into the saddle. Both of the boys had ridden horses before when they visited his folks' ranch, but they were by no means as accomplished as Katy. She controlled that big mare like she'd been born on a saddle.

Beau leaned both elbows on the top rail and settled his chin into his hands. "What's the news on the ranch you're fightin' for? Seems I heard the name Adele from Nick and Leo about a hundred times over dinner, and it didn't sound to me like they were in a competition with her."

"Good news is that they've fallen in love with her. They've needed a strong female role model since their mother died. Mama did a good job of taking care of them until I could get there, but there's never been a doubt that she was the grandmother. Bad news is that if we do buy the ranch, she'll leave and they'll be devastated."

It was a long time before Beau spoke. "Sounds like you need to apply some of that charm that the good Lord blessed you with and talk her into staying. Form a partnership or marry the woman."

Remy's heart should have stopped beating the moment Beau said the *M* word, but it didn't even slow down. "Offered the partnership. She refused. Can't marry her."

"Why?"

"You know my reputation. She deserves something better than me."

"You've found the one, haven't you, Remy? Never thought any of us Luckadeaus would see the day that a woman captured Remington's heart, but I believe one has."

Remy set his foot on the ground and straightened up. "What makes you say that?"

"It's in your voice when you say her name. You might not want to admit it, but it's there. Look at Leo. He's controlling that horse pretty good, but Nick is still a little afraid."

Remy smiled, glad to talk about something else. "He'll learn. Those two little ones of yours are going to be stuntmen for sure when they grow up."

"Katy is constantly showing off and they think they have to be just like her." Beau laughed. "They've bit the dust many times, but they're tough. Got a proposition for you. If you don't get that ranch down there in Texas, I've got a section of land I'll sell you. We bought Milli's grandparents' place when they retired last year. It's got a nice house and the land is in top-notch shape. I'd be willing to sell off a few acres to you to begin with, and you could always have the option of adding to it as you want more. The boys would have cousins nearby, and I'll make you a good deal."

"I appreciate the offer, but I'd like to stay in that area around Nocona or Saint Jo. We like it there and the school is small. I want the boys to have the kind of experience I did growing up."

"If you change your mind, the land and house are there," Beau said.

---

Adele's mind wandered during church. She'd been gone less than twenty-four hours and already she was home-sick, something she'd never experienced before. She'd left home right out of high school to go to college in Austin, and from there she'd landed the job in Dallas and met Isaac at a party. Not once had she known this antsy feeling that she needed to go home.

When she came to Dimmitt for a visit, she adjusted from city life to country. When she went back to Dallas, she put away her boots and jeans and became a corporate wife and businesswoman again. Even when she moved to the country on her own ranch when Bella was a tod-dler, she still didn't have homesick issues. She simply went from city to country as the situation demanded.

She'd sat on the same pew in this church from the time she was born until she was eighteen years old, and then if she was visiting on Sundays after that. It never really felt like home, not like the little one over in

Ringgold did that week she went to visit her uncle Cash and aunt Maddie. That must mean that fate was telling her that area was supposed to be where she settled forever, amen.

"And now I'll ask Hank O'Donnell to deliver the benediction and wish all you fathers out in the congregation a wonderful day," the preacher said.

The mention of her father's name brought Adele back to the present. She bowed her head and concentrated on her father's short prayer. After all, it was Father's Day, and she should be giving thanks to his influence and love, instead of thinking about Remington Luckadeau so much. The moment he said amen, Jett was on her feet and tugging at Adele's hand.

"Can we go out the back door? I can't wait to get to the lake and fish, and it's thirty minutes from here, and Granny says we have to eat her picnic lunch before we can get out there on the water in the boat and see if they're bitin'," she said before she took a breath.

"Yes, we can," Myra said. "Your grandpa is itchin' to get in his boat, and we did our part by saying the benediction. So let's herd everyone toward the back door."

The girls rode with their grandparents in the truck that pulled the boat behind it. Adele rode with Cassie in her dark-blue truck that carried all the picnic supplies and fishing gear in the backseat. It was only about twenty-five miles to the lake house, which was little more than a one-room cabin, but it did have air-conditioning and a bathroom, and lots of happy memories had been made there.

"You've been watching that phone like it's your lifeline all morning," Cassie said when she turned north.

"It's that cowboy, isn't it? You're falling for him and you don't know what to do about it, right? Karma has come back to bite you on the butt, Sister."

Adele glanced down at the phone again. "And what is that supposed to mean?"

"That you always said you'd never fall for a cowboy, but we all knew that's exactly what you needed. I'm just not sure it should be Remy Luckadeau, darlin'. Sweet Lord, but that man has a reputation. You can kick any bush in the whole Panhandle of Texas and a dozen women will run out who've been to bed with him."

"Have you?" Adele asked.

"Hell no!" Cassie said. "He's not my type."

"Then what makes him mine?" Adele asked.

"I have no idea, but he sure looks at you like he wants to be yours," Cassie told her. "I want you to wind up with the Double Deuce because I'm going to buy out your third of our place when Mama and Daddy retire," she answered.

"Third?"

"Yep, you don't get a full half because you haven't been here and worked your ass off like I have," she said.

"Fair enough. You can have the whole thing, and I'll take Mama and Daddy out to my part of the world when they retire. That way, they can travel when they want to and help me ranch when they get tired of traveling," Adele said.

"Over my dead body. I'm keeping them right here, where their friends are."

"No, you are not. I'm taking them to north central Texas, where tons of relatives are living. Uncle Cash will be so excited to have his brother closer."

They crawled out of the truck at the lake house still arguing. Their mother met them at truck, slung open the back doors, and picked up several grocery bags of food.

"Tell Adele that you are never leaving the Panhandle, not even when you retire," Cassie said.

"I'm never leaving the Panhandle," Myra said.

"Tell Cassie that you might move to north central Texas to be closer to your grandchildren when you retire," Adele said.

"I might move close to Adele when I retire." Myra smiled. "What I do or do not do in another ten or fifteen years has no impact on today, girls. We are here to enjoy the holiday with your father and our family. So stop your bitchin' and help me take this stuff in the house. The kids are starving, and your daddy gets real cranky when he's hungry. Besides all that, he can't wait to take the girls out on the lake to catch supper."

"I'm changing into shorts and a tank top as soon as we get this in the house. And I'm going to sit on the deck and drink a cold beer after dinner," Cassie said.

"Well, la-di-da, the princess has spoken," Adele replied, smarting off.

"I said no more bickerin'." Myra's tone left no room for arguments.

Adele giggled and snorted and then it turned into full-fledged infectious laughter that had Myra and Cassie also holding their sides before any of them could catch their breath. Adele got it under control first.

"All this crap that's landed in my lap isn't Cassie's fault, but I had to have someone to argue with and it felt so good." Adele wiped at the tears streaming down her face. "Thank you, Sis."

Cassie hugged Adele. "Anytime. I'm always up for a good argument but, honey, if you hook up with Remy Luckadeau, you might do well to keep him over there in the country where his reputation might be excused as rumor. In this part of the world, it's the gospel truth."

"I will keep that in mind. Now let's get all this food into the house, turn on the AC, and have Sunday dinner," Adele answered.

The lake house hadn't changed any more than the ranch house had. Bunk beds, where Adele and Cassie slept, were still covered with pink chenille bedspreads. A Mason jar was in the middle of the yellow-topped chrome table with four chairs around it. Adele always picked wildflowers for the jar when they stayed for more than an afternoon. A small kitchen took up the east wall, and two doorways opened off toward the west. One led into her parents' bedroom and one into a bathroom with an old claw-foot tub, a wall-hung sink, and a potty.

The whole place was less than four hundred square feet, but it bulged with happy memories. Adele had gotten her first kiss from a boy at the lake house. She'd wept when she broke up with that same boy at the end of a summer of awkward kisses. She'd almost lost her virginity out there on the deck, but her parents had come home early from fishing.

"Everything changes and yet nothing does," she murmured.

"You got that right," Cassie said.

Adele's phone vibrated in the pocket of her flowing gauze skirt. She pulled it out and found a text message from Remy saying that he missed her and he was an idiot for insisting that she take three days and go visit her folks.

She wrote back as she went to the truck to bring in a duffel bag with clothes for her and the girls to change into. And immediately she got an answer: *Meet me and the boys at that Mexican place on the west side of Nocona at five on Wednesday for supper? My treat to welcome you home.*

She sent one word back and then turned her phone off: *Yes!*

And just so she wouldn't be tempted to turn it back on, she left it in her purse on the passenger's seat of the truck.

# Chapter 18

THE DAYS WENT BY IN A BLUR, EVEN IF THE NIGHTS SEEMED to take forever for Adele. When Wednesday morning finally arrived, she was more nervous than she'd been on her first date. She was going home. She was going to see Remy again. Even a vision of that silly Jerry Lee brought a smile to her face. And Blanche would be so glad to see the girls.

Jett bounced into her bedroom with Bella right behind. They dove onto the bed, one on each side of her, both talking at once about how they couldn't wait to get home and see the boys and Blanche.

"And we get to see Dahlia on the way, and she said that she's taking us to dinner because she doesn't want to cook, but we're supposed to come to her house," Jett said. "Get up, Mama. We're burnin' daylight, and we've got lots of miles to go today."

"I'm so glad we're going home." Bella sighed. "I love being here, but it's not home and the Double Deuce is."

Adele pushed back the sheet. "Even more than our old ranch? You lived there most of your life."

Without hesitation, Bella's head bobbed up and down. "Yes, Mama, it is. Aunt Cassie says that she likes to go places, but when she comes back out to this flat country, her soul is at peace. Well, that's what the Double Deuce is to me. I knew it the first time we went there."

Adele fought back the tears threatening to spill down

her cheek. If that's the way her child felt, there was only one option for guaranteeing without a doubt that she could stay on the Double Deuce. She'd have to give it a lot of thought on the way home that day and talk at length with Remy about it before she put it up for the girls to vote on.

"Are you both packed and ready to go?" Adele's voice only cracked slightly.

"Our bags are sitting on the porch. Hey, do you think Jerry Lee missed us? I can't wait to see what he thinks of the new wind chime." Jett bounded out of bed.

"Help me strip these sheets off," Bella said. "We can take them to Granny with ours while Mama is getting dressed. We need to be on the road at eight if we're going to be in Vernon at noon. I checked the maps on my phone. It's pretty neat having Wi-Fi again. Maybe we can get it at the ranch when we buy it, Mama."

"Yes, we will before the end of summer, but the old rules will apply," Adele said as she dressed in jeans and a dark-green tank top. She brushed her hair and braided it into a single rope above her right ear, letting it hang over her shoulder.

Breakfast was hurried because Bella kept a watch on the clock. "I know you and Granny will stand by the truck and remember all the last-minute stuff, so we need to be in it at fifteen minutes until eight."

Myra smiled. "She knows us too well."

"And she's more like her super-organized Granny than anyone I knew." Hank chuckled.

"Jett might look like her, but you're right." Cassie nodded. "Bella got all Mama's good qualities."

"Thank you," Bella said. "I'll take all those compliments."

"And I love that I look like Granny and Aunt Cassie." Jett grinned.

At exactly eight o'clock, Adele honked at the end of the lane, stuck her arm out the window, and waved at her folks one more time. Peace settled around her like a familiar, old, warm sweater on a brisk fall morning.

How could she have put down such deep roots in only three weeks? She'd lived on the previous ranch over twelve years and thought she was planted firmly, but it hadn't grieved her at all to leave it behind.

*That place never belonged to you*, the voice in her head said loudly. *From the beginning, you could make a living on it. The profit that you made on your calf crop each year was yours. The money you saved from your budget by having a garden was yours. But the land was never yours, and that's why you couldn't put down roots.*

Adele nodded as if she had a third person in the truck with her. The sun was straight up above her when she saw the sign welcoming them to Chillicothe, Texas, population 707. "Okay, ladies, next stop for this wagon train is Vernon, which is nineteen miles away. At seventy-five miles an hour, Miss Bella, how many minutes is it?"

"Sixteen and a few seconds," Bella said quickly.

"I'm calling Dahlia to tell her to be ready, we're almost there."

"I need her address so Bella can plug it into the GPS and we won't waste time trying to find her place," Adele said.

"I already got that." She rattled off the street name and house number. "Dahlia wanted a real picture of me and her to put in a frame, so she sent me her address. We need to pick one out from the ones you took at the cemetery, Mama, and get it fixed for her next week."

Dahlia was waiting on the porch, purse in hand, ready to go. When they stopped the truck, she was already heading toward them, a big smile covering her face. She slung open the back door and crawled in beside Jett, who slid over and hugged her tightly.

"I thought we'd never get here," Jett sighed. "I'm so glad to see you again."

Dahlia patted Jett on the leg. "Not as glad as I am to see you and Bella and your mama. It's been a long morning waiting for you. Take the next left, Adele. We're having dinner at a little home-grown café that makes the best chicken fried steak in the whole state. And they do a bang-up job of a double bacon cheeseburger, too."

"Man alive, a cheeseburger sounds good. Do they make their own fries, or are they frozen?" Bella asked.

"Honey, their claim to fame is that nothing in their café has ever seen the inside of a freezer," Dahlia answered. "Now I want to know all about your vacation and the fishing trip. Get out your phone, Jett, and show me the fish you caught."

"It's not a big one like what Grandpa snagged." Jett flipped through the pictures on her telephone.

"Who cares? It's a fish and you caught it," Dahlia said. "Me and my husband used to love to go fishin', and sometimes we'd build a fire and panfry our catch right there on the beach."

Dinner took two hours, and then Dahlia insisted they have dessert and coffee at her house. She served miniature cheesecake bites with several toppings in the dining room on a lace-covered table. Her house had all the signs of being built at least fifty years ago. A living room opened into a dining nook, which had a bar separating it from the U-shaped kitchen. A long hallway led to two bedrooms and a bathroom with a couple of extra doors that probably housed a coat closet and a place for linens. It had been well maintained, and the yard was worthy of being the main feature in a magazine.

Dahlia handed Jett a small bowl of glazed strawberries. "Try this on top of your next little cheesecake. I have a little strawberry bed out in the backyard."

"You made all this just for us?" Bella asked.

"I could either use my energy to make fancy things or cook dinner. I chose to make the fancy," Dahlia explained. "Adele, I noticed you were admiring my yard. It's been my pride and joy since I retired from nursing and lost my husband the same year."

"It's gorgeous. Someday I hope to have flowers and roses at the ranch."

"Pansy had lovely flower beds, but they were too much for Walter to take care of after she passed away. I'd love to see the yard brought back to the beauty it was when she was there."

"We'll make it happen," Jett said seriously. "Then when you come to visit next year, you can see it and we'll take pictures to send to you."

Dahlia smiled, but it didn't reach her eyes. "I'll look forward to that. Now, Bella, you have to try this caramel on top of that little cheesecake. If you like it, I'll send you the recipe and you can make it for the boys sometime."

Bella's eyes lit up. "I'd love that. Could I have the recipe for these little cheesecakes, too?"

"Sure you can. I'll write them up and put them in the mail in the morning." Dahlia beamed and this time her eyes twinkled.

Bella kept a watch on the time and said it was time to go at three o'clock. They made their way out to the truck with Dahlia right behind them, everyone still talking at once, telling each other important last-minute things. After the girls were in the truck, Dahlia wrapped her fingers around Adele's upper arm.

"I want to give you something, but don't open it for a while. You'll know when the time is right." She slipped an envelope into Adele's purse and hugged her tightly. "You don't know what it means to me to know that you and these girls are going to take care of Pansy's home. It's like having family living there. Jett could be the great-granddaughter that neither of us ever got to have. I know that if Pansy is able to look down from heaven, it makes her real happy to have those two sisters living in her home. Now I want your promise you won't open this until the time is right."

A cold chill shot down Adele's spine. "I promise, but please tell me it's not something that will make me cry."

"I can't do that, darlin', but know that you and the girls have made me very happy." Dahlia hugged her one more time. "Now get on out of here before I cry. I hate good-byes."

Dahlia waved and blew kisses from the porch until they were out of sight. She had a smile on her face the whole time, but it was one that held sadness. Adele glanced back at Jett, who was wiping away a tear.

Bella sniffled.

"We'll see her at our Fourth of July celebration, and that's only two weeks and three days away," Adele said.

"I hate good-byes. They suck." Bella swiped at her eyes with the back of her hand. "And today we had to do it two times."

"And before long, we have to do it again and that's going to be really hard," Jett said. "Because that's when we have to tell Remy and the boys good-bye."

"It's a no-win situation," Bella said. "No matter who stays, we still have to say good-bye. I thought I'd hate those guys in the beginning, and sometimes I don't like them very much, but now I can't imagine living on the ranch without them around."

They'd barely gotten out of town and back on the highway when Adele's phone rang. Bella picked up her mom's purse from the console, fished it out, and rolled her eyes toward the ceiling. "It's Grandmother Levy. Let's not answer it, Mama, okay?"

"Bella O'Donnell," Adele scolded, but her tone didn't carry much weight. "Answer it and tell her that I can't talk and drive."

Bella sucked in a lungful of air and let it out very slowly. "Hello," she said cautiously, and then she gasped, hit the Speaker button, and laid the phone on the console.

Isaac's voice filled the cab of the truck. "Bella, is that you? Are you still there? This is your father."

"And this is Adele. What do you want?" she asked bluntly.

"Actually, I want to talk to you," Isaac said.

"Bad time. It'll have to wait until later."

"Then give me a time and I'll put it on my calendar."

"July Fourth, twenty years from now," she said.

"Don't be a smart aleck. I'm free at eight tonight. Does that work for you?"

Adele figured she might as well get it over with so she nodded. "That works for me."

"Good, I'll call back then," Isaac said and the call ended.

The silence was so heavy that it sucked all the oxygen out of the truck. It felt like Adele's lungs were collapsing when she finally remembered to inhale. At that point, she pulled off the side of the road and put her forehead on the steering wheel. Hands shaking, heart thumping, and cold sweat beading up on her forehead, the whole world did a couple of spins before it settled down.

Isaac and his mother had deeper pockets than anyone in the state of Texas, and they got their way when they wanted something. She'd heard them talk about making and breaking deals in their business. They were ruthless, and that was with strangers. This was personal, so they'd be even more cold-blooded.

She should back out of the ranch deal, buy a small trailer, and go to work for her uncle Cash over in Ringgold. He'd told her repeatedly that she would always have a place on his ranch if she ever needed a job. The girls could still go to school in Nocona and see Leo and Nick in classes, and maybe she and Remy would be better off with some distance between them.

"What are we going to do, Mama?" Jett whimpered.

"I'll tell you what we're not going to do." Adele straightened up and pulled back out on the highway. "We are not going to let that phone call ruin the rest of our day. I'll talk to him tonight and see what's going on before we jump to any conclusions. Let's go eat Mexican food with the guys and then get on home to see how Blanche and the kittens are doing. I bet they've doubled in size since Sunday."

Bella laid a hand on Adele's shoulder. "Thank you, Mama."

"For what?" Adele asked as she set the cruise control to the speed limit. She would rather push the gas pedal to the floor and watch the speedometer whip around to 120 miles an hour—maybe the speed would blow all the worry out of her mind—but she couldn't endanger her girls like that.

"For everything that you do and are about to do," Bella answered. "We don't want to go back to that life we had. We like this one better, and we know you're going to fight for us."

"Yes, I will." Adele nodded.

"And win," Jett said. "Now, let's think about baby kittens. That other stuff scares the shit out of me."

"Jett!" Adele raised her voice.

"Just sayin', Mama. Just sayin'."

———※———

Remy and the boys arrived at the Mexican restaurant on the west end of Nocona fifteen minutes early. The place was empty, so the waitress told them to choose their own table. Remy looked at the booths and the tables for four and then noticed a big table that would seat eight toward the back of the room. The chairs were heavy and painted in bright colors.

"That one okay?" he asked.

"Just fine. You must have more joining you."

"Three more. They should be here soon."

The waitress picked up six menus and followed them

to the table. "I can go ahead and take your drink order. Maybe you'd like an appetizer while you wait? You look so familiar. Are you related to Slade Luckadeau?"

Remy smiled. "He's my cousin. Folks have thought that we were brothers before."

"Love him and his family. We go to church with them. I thought I saw you and these guys in church a couple of weeks ago. You are welcome anytime you'd like to come over that way. I'm Brenda and I'll be your waitress."

"Maybe we'll have this bottomless chips and dip appetizer. And a big bowl of queso to go with it." Remy pointed to the picture inside the menu. "And thanks for the invitation to attend your church. We'll wait until we get settled permanently to make a decision, but we appreciate your offer. And I'll have sweet tea. Boys?"

"Dr Pepper," they said in unison.

"Got it. Be back right soon," Brenda said.

Remy was glad that the chairs were lined up four to a side with none at the ends. If he played his cards right, he could maneuver things so that he could sit beside Adele. Nick and Leo had chosen the left side, with a chair between them. Remy had settled into a chair in the middle of the right side, where he could keep an eye on the door and the window facing the road.

His chest tightened up when Bella and Jett came through the door, their eyes scanning the long, narrow room until they found Nick and Leo. Then it was smiles and waves as they made a beeline toward the table. There was an awkward moment when the guys stood up and didn't know what to do other than stand there with grins covering their faces, and then Jett grabbed them in a big hug.

"I missed you, but that don't mean you can let it give you an ego trip. I can live without you, but I don't want to." Jett pulled out the chair between them and sat down.

Bella patted Nick on the shoulder and Leo on the top of his freshly combed red hair. "We're glad to be home."

"And we're glad you're home, but don't let that put you on an ego trip, neither." Nick blushed.

Remy listened, but he didn't take his eyes off the door. "Where is your mama?"

"She got a phone call about the time that we pulled up. She'll be here in a minute," Jett explained. "You've had time to study this menu. What looks good, Leo?"

Remy heard the kids discussing food and their trip and the kittens. But it was nothing more than buzzing in his ears for the next five minutes. No matter how many times he checked his phone for the time, it wouldn't go faster. When Adele finally walked inside the restaurant, he remembered to get up to pull out her chair.

"Thank you." She smiled.

Something was terribly wrong. It was written on her face and veiled her eyes. He could feel her pain as his knee touched hers under the table. That morning, he'd talked to her and she'd been so excited about coming home and meeting them for supper. She'd sent him a text when they left Dahlia's, saying that in two hours, they'd be home or at least back in Montague County and that was close enough.

She picked up the menu and barely looked at it before closing it again. She opened her mouth to say something and the waitress appeared with appetizers and drinks.

"And what can I get you ladies?" she asked.

"What kind of beer do you have?"

The waitress rattled off a whole list.

"Coors in the bottle," Adele said.

"Make that two." Remy laid a hand on Adele's knee and found she was trembling.

"Milk," Jett said.

"Same." Bella nodded.

"Are y'all ready to order, or do the ladies need a few more minutes?"

"I want the chicken enchilada dinner," Adele said.

The waitress wrote that on her pad and then went around the table for the rest of the orders. As soon as she had collected the menus and disappeared, the kids started talking again.

Remy could feel Adele's whole body humming in anger. "What can I do to help?"

"Girls, this is mainly for you, but I think it needs to be said right now. I need to say it and you need to know that we've gotten a reprieve." Her tone was edged with ice.

"That was our father, wasn't it? I thought I saw Grandmother's picture when the phone rang," Bella said.

"It was your grandmother. He didn't have the nerve to call, evidently. But things have changed. His wife came home with their son and everything is off concerning you having to spend every weekend in Dallas."

Jett's whole face lit up in a brilliant smile. "Then this is a celebration dinner."

"However, your grandmother said to tell you both that if you ever get tired of living like tomboys and want to visit them, their door will be open. And your father sent a message that his is also."

"If"—Bella's eyes twinkled—"we ever get tired of

our lives, we will remember that. But I don't reckon that day will ever dawn. We love our ranchin' lives."

Jett poked Leo in the arm. "So tell me what you've come up with for names for our kittens."

Nick nudged Bella's shoulder. "I'm glad you said that because me and Leo love it, too."

"Oh, to be a kid again." Remy squeezed her knee gently.

She laid her hand on his. "It's not over. Daddy says that he's hiring a lawyer to go over every single word in the divorce papers. If the language needs to be revised, now is the time to take care of it, not when they get another burr up their butts. I didn't mean to ruin supper."

Remy laced his fingers with hers. "You haven't ruined a thing. I'm glad you feel close enough to us to let us share in your sorrow as well as your joy. That's what friends are for, Adele."

"Is that what we are, Remy? Friends?"

"It depends on what you want us to be," he answered.

"Right now." She smiled at the waitress, who brought two beers and two more drinks to the table, plus two baskets of chips, a couple bowls of salsa, and a big bowl of queso.

"Be back shortly with your orders," she said. "Can I get you anything else?"

"Not right now," Remy said.

"Right now," Adele said again, raised her beer bottle, and tilted it slightly toward his.

He picked his up and touched hers with it.

She went on. "Right now, we are going to live for the moment, share good beers and good food, and be grateful that we don't have to sweat the big stuff this day."

"Fair enough," he said.

The kids followed their example. Milk glasses rattled against those containing Dr Pepper. "To being home and getting to go out to supper," Jett said.

"Hear, hear." Nick grinned.

"And just like that, they have moved on," Adele said softly.

"Like I said, wouldn't it be great to be a kid?" Remy winked.

She smiled, and that time, her eyes twinkled. "Tomorrow I want some time with you alone."

He leaned over and whispered in her ear, "Anytime, darlin'."

She shivered. "It's serious, Remy."

"Oh no! Are you breaking up with me?" he teased.

She slapped him on the leg. "No, but I'm not proposing to you either."

He ran a palm over his forehead in a mock dramatic gesture. "I'm sure glad on both issues."

"Oh?" She raised an eyebrow as she sipped her beer.

"I don't want to break up, but my daddy always says the guy is the one to do the proposing," he said.

Jett held up a hand. "What are y'all talkin' about over there?"

"We were thinking that maybe tomorrow night you kids might like to go swimming at the Nocona public pool for a couple of hours," Remy said smoothly.

"Yes!" Nick held up his glass for another toast, and the other three touched theirs with his.

"Are you responsible enough that we could let you

238          CAROLYN BROWN

stay there alone?" Remy asked. "We need to buy groceries and thought we'd do it together, so we wouldn't
duplicate anything."

"We've been left at the pool before," Leo said. "We'll
mind our manners."

"Good, then it's a done deal. We'll get our work done,
have supper, and then take y'all to the pool," Adele said.

"Too bad we don't have a van, so we could all go
together," Bella said.

Now that a new idea had been introduced, they were
suddenly talking about swimming and how many laps
they could do and how many different dives they could
each execute from whichever height.

"You covered that well," Adele whispered.

"It isn't my first rodeo." He grinned. "Will that give
us enough alone time?"

"Maybe, if we don't spend too much time in the grocery store," she said.

Her body had stopped trembling and her face had
relaxed. His Adele had finally come home. Remy wanted
to dance a jig right there on the long table. Instead, he
raised his beer bottle and gave her a brief nod.

The boys must have forgotten that they'd parked a
van in a storage unit along with the rest of their belongings when they'd left Denton. It had belonged to Remy's
sister-in-law, and he hadn't wanted to take it with them
to the new ranch. He'd wanted to start all over with as
clean a slate as possible, but maybe he should talk to
them about bringing it to the ranch for times when they
did want to go somewhere all together.

*Whoa!* his conscience shouted at him. *You have one
week and one day until this month ends. Today is the*

*twenty-second day of June, and Walter will either be*
*home on the thirtieth or the first day of July, and a*
*decision will be made. At that time, you might not even*
*need a van. Don't get all excited and make a rash deci-*
*sion here.*

He couldn't argue with logic, even if he didn't
like it. Besides, they'd managed without a vehicle big
enough for everyone for all this time. They'd make do
for another week and see what happened. Maybe at that
time, he'd be ready to sell the thing, put the money into
an account for the boys, and be completely done with
the past.

---

Remy parked beside Adele's truck and helped carry in
bags, since the kids all made a run for the house to see
about Blanche and the kittens. Boss met them at the yard
gate, wagging his tail, and Jett paused for a minute to
kiss him right on the nose. The old boy followed the
kids up onto the porch and lay down next to the house
as if his world was complete now that the family was
home. Jerry Lee hopped on the porch railing, threw his
head back, and crowed like dawn was on the way rather
than dusk.

"Hey, I bought something for Jerry Lee." Adele
reached into a paper bag and brought out the long wind
chime with the brightly painted rooster at the top. "Let's
hang it up as soon as we get this baggage in the house
and see what he does with it."

"It'll probably scare that stupid bird into a cardiac
arrest." Remy chuckled. "I'll get my toolbox from the
utility room and you pick out a good place to hang it."

He dropped the bags at the foot of the stairs, and within a few minutes, he was back on the porch. Boss opened one eye and his tail thumped against the porch. Jerry Lee was still singing his sad tale of woe, trying to wake up the folks who worked the midnight shift at a factory.

"Okay, my lady, where do you want this thing?"

Adele pointed above the rail at the end of the porch. "Right here. It'll catch the wind better than if we put it on the front."

Remy deftly put a screw in place and hung her wind chime on it. "Now you can be the first one to rattle the chain and we'll see what he does."

Jerry Lee flew down to that end of the porch and cocked his head to one side and then the other as the last rays of sunlight caught the bright colors of the ten-inch rooster above the metal chimes. He fluffed his feathers and preened right up until Adele rattled the chain holding the metal disk in the center. Then he flew back to his original perch and crowed his loudest.

Remy closed his big hand around Adele's and led her to the other end of the porch. "Sit with me, just the two of us for a little while, and we'll see what he does. I missed you, Adele. It's not the same without you around here."

He pulled her down to sit close enough that he could wrap an arm around her shoulders. "I was afraid you'd find a place out there after all. When you walked into the café, my heart almost stopped. The look on your face said that you had decided to move across the state and didn't know how to tell me and the boys."

She laid her head on his shoulder. "The trip convinced

me that I didn't want to live in that part of the state. Would you look at that?"

"What?" he asked.

"Jerry Lee. Look at what he's doing."

The rooster had hopped down the rail until he was right under the chimes, and when they stopped making noise, he flew up and hit the chain with his feet, then settled back on the rail a couple of feet away and crowed the whole time it was jingling.

"I'd say he likes his new prize, but not as much as I like what you just said," Remy told her.

"I'm scared, Remy. Not about living here, but about this thing with Isaac and his family. They are very wealthy and they have dozens of lawyers at their fingertips."

"We'll face it a day at a time. Dammit!" He stomped his boot on the bottom step. "I meant to drop by the drugstore or a convenience store bathroom and flat out forgot."

"Then I guess we won't be visiting the empty bedroom tonight. But we are going to town tomorrow evening, so we can go to the drugstore." She grinned.

"Thank God. I love waking up to find you beside me. You want to give me a hint about what it is you want to talk about tomorrow? Are you pregnant?"

"It has nothing to do with babies, and I want to sleep on it before we talk about it. So be patient with me, Remy," she said.

"That patience stuff is not one of my strong suits, but I'll give it my best." He cupped her face in his hands and kissed her like he'd wanted to do all evening...long, hard, and with lots of heat.

# Chapter 19

WORK MAKES THE TIME GO BY FASTER, BUT THAT THURSDAY, the old adage didn't apply. The whole family spent the day on the far south side of the property making sure the fences were bull tight and cleaning them up with hoes and shovels. It was slow going, since the weeds had grown up all spring and trash had blown in to add to the ugly mess, but it had to be done at least once a year.

At noon, they stopped long enough to rest under a shade tree and have a picnic lunch: sandwiches, chips, cookies, and bananas and apples. Then it was back at the job until four that afternoon, when they'd finished about a fourth of the job. They'd be back on Friday and Saturday if it didn't rain. Hopefully the job would be done when Walter arrived next week.

Of all ranching business, cleaning out fence lines was the one that Adele did not like. That's probably why time stood still, and it took forever for the afternoon to pass. Not even a wink or two from Remy or a quick peck on the cheek when no one was looking helped a whole lot.

She'd pondered the idea of a partnership all day, and when the kids were finally loaded up in the back of the truck, she still hadn't decided whether she should really approach the subject with Remy or not. From the time she moved onto the small ranch that Isaac had bought, she'd taken care of things without much help. Having to ask a partner about buying a bull or which cows to breed to that bull, how much land to turn over for hay, and how much to plant in wheat or soy beans for a cash crop didn't sound like something she'd want to do.

The meat sauce for spaghetti had been simmering all day in the slow cooker, so all she had to do for supper was cook the noodles, slice up a loaf of Italian bread, and toss a salad. In thirty minutes, it was on the table. The girls still had the dust and grime of the day on their jeans, but their hands and faces had been washed. The boys had used the time to take showers, so they came to the table smelling clean and with their wet hair parted on the side and combed.

"We'll take care of cleanup after supper," Nick said after grace. "That way you girls can get your showers and we can get to the pool faster."

"Don't forget to pack towels and rubber shoes in your bag," Leo advised as he scooped a big portion of spaghetti onto his plate and passed the bowl to Nick.

"Little hungry are you?" Remy teased.

"Starving nigh unto death," Leo laughed. "That's what Gramps says when Granny takes too long with supper."

"That fence-cleaning business is some hard work," Bella said. "It could make a person plumb cranky."

"You mean that there is something about ranchin' that you don't like?" Remy asked.

Bella nodded. "Fence cleaning and painting yard fences. Must be something to do with fences altogether. I don't mind stretching barbed wire or mending fence. But cleaning and painting go so slow. It's enough to drive a girl into a bad mood, right, Mama?"

"You got it," Adele said.

"Not me. I loved it," Leo piped up. "Lookin' back, I could see how much better it looked than it used to, and looking ahead, I could see how much needed to be done and having someone to talk to and work along beside me sure made things go better. That don't mean you know more than me, Bella."

"Of course I do, but I'm willing to teach you," Bella retorted quickly.

*Out of the mouths of babes*, Adele's conscience whispered.

A partnership might not be all rainbows and unicorns, but it was right, and she was fighting it because it meant giving up a little control. Joining forces with Remy would mean that she'd have capital to work with, that neither set of kids would have to leave their new homes, and that poor old Walter wouldn't have to make a decision. Plus, as an added bonus, it would make Dahlia very happy because it was a guarantee that the girls would be there every year when she came to clean the grave sites.

———

Adele left her truck in the parking lot at the public pool and crawled into Remy's after they'd paid for admission for four kids and given them their last-minute orders.

"First order of business is a trip to the drugstore. Then we'll make a run through the grocery store, get a six-pack of beer or a bottle of wine at the convenience store, and take it to the park to have our alone time," Remy said.

"Beer, please. I never learned to like wine."

"My kind of girl." Remy kissed her on the cheek. "I'm glad that you thought of this. We should do it all summer, no matter who gets the ranch. We'll take the kids and meet at the pool on Thursday nights, and you and I can have a couple of hours to ourselves."

"Why, Remy Luckadeau, are you asking me out on a weekly date?" She batted her long lashes in a mock flirting gesture.

"I am." He nodded.

"Let's see how today goes before I hold you to that. And I'll go into the drugstore with you. I need a bottle of those allergy pills."

"I also want to see if they carry Stetson aftershave. I need a new bottle and it's not easy to find. Most of the time you can get the cologne but not the aftershave." He backed the truck out and headed to the downtown section of Nocona.

Isaac wore some kind of imported cologne from France, and the scent suited everything about him. She'd liked it, but she'd never wanted to put it on her pillow at night like she did Stetson. That should have told her she was wandering down the wrong path in the beginning of their relationship, but she was naive and young in those days. She thought she wanted to change everything about her life. Little did she know that the heart had to be in agreement with such a drastic adjustment, and hers had not been.

"You're doing that again," he said.

"What?"

"Going to wherever you were visiting at the supper table. One minute you're here with me; the next you're either in the past or the future because you sure aren't in the present." He laid a hand on her shoulder.

She topped his with hers and squeezed. "I'm not such

a good Thursday night date, am I? I was visiting the future at supper, and just now, I'd slipped back into the past. I guess I need to be sure of both before I face the present this evening."

"Are we going to talk now?"

"No, at the park." Just a few more minutes to get her thoughts in a row, so she could present the idea to him intelligently with all the pros and cons. He and Cassie had both brought it up, but now she was ready to embrace it, and yet, maybe he'd changed his mind or forgotten all about it.

He snagged a parking place right in front of the drugstore, and once inside, he headed straight for the men's toiletries counter and Adele went in search of the allergy shelves. They reached the check-out counter at the same time. Remy set the biggest box of condoms Adele had ever seen on the counter beside two bottles of Stetson. He paid with a credit card and stepped aside to let Adele pay for her allergy pills and a bottle of pain pills.

She fought the blush turning her cheeks crimson and fumbled with a piece of paper from her purse. "I just need a few things from the store, since us girls only have four more days to cook before Walter gets home. I was expecting this month to drag by."

"I was expecting more fights between the kids and for sure more between us," Remy said as he made a right-hand turn out onto the highway that ran right though Nocona.

"Me, too," she said.

It took ten minutes for them to each fill a cart and another ten to check out at the small grocery store. They were in the truck, and he was about to turn left to go back toward the Dairy Queen when she held up a finger and pointed the other way.

"I'll forgo the ice-cream cone. It might take the rest of our time to get all this settled, and I want it done before I tell the girls, so can we please just go to the park now?"

He nodded and drove a couple of blocks to the right, made a left, and at the end of the road, he parked in front of a little park with a pavilion, tennis court, benches scattered around under shade trees, and lots of playground equipment. "Now what?" he asked.

Adele opened her door. Hot air flowed inside. Cold air rushed right out into the evening. Before she could turn around, a fine bead of sweat had already formed under her nose. "I'd like to sit on the bench over there."

"Your wish and all that." He grinned.

When they were on the bench, he closed his hand around hers and said, "Okay, Adele, you called this meeting, so you've got the gavel, the stand, and a captive audience of one rugged old cowboy."

His hand on hers gave her courage. "You remember what you said about a partnership, so neither set of kids would have to uproot what they've found at the ranch?"

He nodded. "Yes, ma'am, I remember very well."

"I've been thinking about that, Remy, and it's beginning to make sense to me. So if you are willing—"

He scooped her up like a bride and turned around half a dozen times right there in the middle of a public park. "I am willing, Adele. I am so, so willing."

"Don't you want to hear the rest of my speech?" she asked.

"No, ma'am, I'm willing and ready to enter into a

partnership for the ranch. We already own an air-conditioning unit together. The rest is a piece of cake." He set her down on the ground, drew her close to his chest, and kissed her with so much emotion that it brought tears to her eyes.

"We haven't even had a big fight yet, Remy. What if we hate each other after a month and we've already signed papers?" she said breathlessly when the kiss ended.

"We'll cross that bridge when we get to it."

His phone rang, and he slipped it from his hip pocket. "It's Nick. Better take this and make sure no one is hurt."

"Hello, what's going on? Y'all ready to leave yet?" Remy asked and listened for a few seconds before he glanced at Adele.

"They want to know if they can stay until closing instead of eight o'clock. They've met some kids they'll be going to school with," Remy said.

Adele nodded. "That's fine with me."

"Sure. We'll pick you up at closing, right beside the gates," Remy said, then hung up. "And now, Miz Adele, we have about three hours on our hands, and I have a wonderful idea about what to do with it."

"We might get into trouble doing that right here," she giggled.

"It's too hot and too public. I've got another idea." He slipped an arm around her shoulders and one under her knees and carried her back to the truck. "Darlin', I can't tell you how happy you have made me tonight. This is the perfect plan."

"You might not think so the first time we disagree on how to run the place," she said.

"Like I said, we'll worry about that bridge when it's in front of us, not when it's not even built yet." He managed to open the door and slide her into the passenger's seat, then whistled as he jogged around the front of the truck and got inside.

"And where are we going?" she asked.

"Not far." He grinned.

When he parked in front of the office at the motel on the east end of Nocona, Adele gasped. "You sure this is a good idea?"

"Best I've had in ages. I'll get the six-pack of beer, and we'll have almost three hours in a room with a bed," he answered.

"Don't forget the condoms."

"Yes, ma'am." He nodded.

In less than five minutes, he was back with a key for a room at the very back of the U-shaped motel. He tossed it in her lap with a wicked grin, drove around to the room, parked, and picked up two sacks from the backseat. "Give me a minute to get these inside and I'll carry you inside."

Adele didn't need to be carried into the motel room. She bailed out of the truck and was right behind him when he opened the door. He set the packages on the table, kicked the door shut with his boot, and caged her against it with a hand on each side of her body.

"No kids. No pallet on the floor. A bed. Even if it's not in a luxury suite, it's a real bed with real pillows," he whispered softly in her ear.

Her hands snaked up around his neck, fingers tangling up in his blond hair, eyes staring into his, and then his lips were on hers. With a little hop, her legs were around his waist and he carried her to the bed. The springs squeaked in protest, and the headboard rattled against the wall as they tumbled onto it.

Adele didn't hear either one. The whine of her hormones begging for a bout of pure, hot sex obliterated every other noise from the room. She untangled her legs and he propped his head up on an elbow and ran the backside of his hand down her cheek.

"I love every one of these freckles," he said.

"That's a horrible pickup line."

"It's not a line, Adele. I was never going to settle down. No, sir. That life was not for me, but here lately, my heart has had very different ideas than my mind. And now I'm beginning to think that I should have listened to it years ago. I know you don't believe me. Why should you? And I sure don't deserve even the moments we have but—"

She put her finger over his lips. "I do believe you, Remy. It's all in the eyes, and they're saying that you are telling the absolute truth. I'll be the judge of what I believe and what I deserve. Right this moment, though, I want sex—plain old sex in a bed that bounces instead of an unforgiving floor. Then I want the afterglow stuff again."

"Your wish," he said softly as he began to unbutton her bright-blue, sleeveless shirt, taking time to kiss the bare skin revealed with each undone button.

Lord, she thought her skin would combust, leaving nothing but a hole in the mattress by the time her shirt was on the floor. She wiggled out of his embrace, and in a few seconds, every piece of her clothing plus her sandals were in a pile in the corner of the room.

With a wide grin splitting his face, he rolled off the

bed and kicked off his boots. She tugged at the pearl snap on the top of his shirt and a loud popping noise echoed off the thin walls as every snap let go. In a few swift movements, she'd pushed it from his shoulders and it was tumbled in with her clothing. She undid his belt and slipped his jeans down over his thighs, gasping only slightly when she realized he wasn't wearing underwear and that he was very ready to oblige her need to forgo foreplay.

"I want you, Remy," she said, panting between words. "I love it when you touch me, but I want you. It even goes beyond *want* and has become *need* right now. My whole body is humming."

"Me, too," he said hoarsely as he picked her up again and laid her on the bed, her head on the pillow.

She guided him inside her and they began to rock together in perfect unison, their bodies melding together as if they'd been made for each other. The kisses grew hotter and hotter, and the bedsprings made squeaky music while the headboard provided the bass drum for the concert going on in the room.

Time stood still in the vacuum that held only Remy Luckadeau and Adele O'Donnell that evening as the sun set in the window above the headboard. It was light, then it was twilight, and then it was dark, all in the matter of a split second. Or was it an hour or two hours? It didn't matter because Adele was on her way to the apex of a cliff higher than anything she'd ever known.

Sex was never like this before.

Never!

Then Remy rose up on his elbows and looked deeply into her eyes. Without saying a word, she knew that they were going to explode at the same time. His lips turned up slightly and she felt hers do the same.

"My. God. Adele," he said.

"I know," she whispered and the beauty of perfect sex washed over them both.

He collapsed on top of her, and she sucked her first hickey ever onto his shoulder without even realizing what she was doing. If she never had another night of sex again, she would die a content woman, knowing that she'd had the best in a little budget motel in Nocona, Texas, one hot June night.

"Thirty minutes." She looked at the clock on the bedside table. "How could only thirty minutes have passed?"

"It wasn't my personal best when it comes to time." He rolled to one side and gathered her into his arms.

The air conditioner kicked on and she shivered.

He wrapped the edge of the floral bedspread over them both, sealing them inside like they were in a cocoon. "All better?"

She nodded. "If it had lasted any longer, I might have gone up in flames. So tell me, Remy, is this going to be a partnership with benefits? Are we going to date other people?"

"That, darlin', is totally up to you," he whispered.

---

Sucking on a lemon couldn't have wiped the contented smile from Adele's face on the way home that evening. The girls were talking nonstop about the kids they'd met, thank goodness. She and Remy had agreed that they would tell the kids about the new partnership at breakfast the next morning. If they told them that night, they'd never get to sleep, especially with all the excitement of having found new friends at the swimming pool.

"Mama, are you listening to a word I'm saying?" Bella asked.

"Yes, you made new friends. I'm happy for you," Adele said.

"And the two girls I met are both in Future Farmers of America, and they show cattle and sheep at the fair, and they wanted to know if I was going to show anything this year."

"It will depend on whether we've got time to get a steer trained to the halter and to stand, won't it? Have you got one in mind?" Adele asked.

"Yes, I do, and I'll have to go to work soon as we know if the ranch and cattle are ours because the county fair is in September, and that will only give me a couple of months to get him ready." Bella bounced around in her seat as much as the seat belt would allow.

"What about you, Jett? Tell me about your new friends." Adele turned slightly to catch a glimpse of her younger daughter.

"I was talking to a boy named Creek, and he'll be in my and Leo's class. He's kind of geeky, but I like him. He knows a lot about computers, and his daddy is a teacher at the school but not computers. He's the science teacher up in high school, so me and Creek won't have him this year, but I bet Bella does, and Creek says he's real tough on the kids in his class."

That set off a conversation between Bella and Jett. The girls barely let the truck come to a standstill when they reached home before their feet were on the ground and they were rushing to get inside the house to talk to the boys about all the new people they'd gotten acquainted with.

Remy sat on the top step, his feet stretched out and crossed at the ankle. The remnants of Stetson still clung to him, even though he and Adele had shared a shower before they'd left the motel room. He patted the place next to him and she sat down.

Boss wormed his way past her and stretched out between their feet. Jerry Lee was busy flying against the rooster wind chime and making it sing. He joined in with his evening crowing, happy as if he had a whole pen full of hens to keep him company.

"It takes on a whole new look, doesn't it?" he said.

"What? The wind chimes?"

"No, the ranch. Knowing that neither of us has to leave. I wanted this place, Adele. I'll admit it. But guilt was already setting in for the day when the girls would cry because they had to leave it," he answered.

"I have to admit that when we drove up, it seemed like I could feel my roots going even deeper and it did have a new aura around it," she said.

"Kind of like afterglow, only in a different way?"

"Good Lord, Remy! You are a romantic."

"All playboys are romantics. How do you think we sweet-talk the ladies?"

A slight twinge of anger rose up. "And what happens to our partnership when you want to go find a woman to do some sweet-talkin' to?"

"I told you earlier that it's up to you how far this partnership goes," he said.

"And that means?"

"Mama, Mama, come quick. The kittens have gotten out, and we can't find the black one," Jett yelled from the foyer.

He jumped up and extended a hand toward her. "Guess we'd better go herd cats."

"This conversation is not over." She put her hand in his.

"Knock on my door anytime of the night and we can take it to the empty room." He grinned. "We can talk or forget about words and do something more important. It's up to you, darlin'."

Bella was frantic when they got to the foyer. "It's black and could be hiding anywhere, so be careful where you step. A boot could break the little thing's back. Jett!" she yelled. "Turn on all the lights in the downstairs."

"What about upstairs?" Nick yelled back.

"I don't think he's big enough to climb," Bella said as she dropped down on all fours and looked behind the credenza and the hall tree.

"I propose that we go get a glass of sweet tea and sit down in the livin' room. Looks like there's enough huntin' going on," Remy said.

"I second that. I imagine he'll come out from wherever he's hiding when he hears all the yelling and commotion," she said.

That reminded her of the bedsprings and the headboard in the motel room and dotted her cheeks with two circles of crimson. Sweet Jesus! She was thirty-five years old, and it wasn't the first time she'd been to a hotel room with a man.

*But it was the best time, wasn't it?* a wicked little voice in her head said with a giggle.

"You're doing that again. Past or future?" Remy asked as he filled two glasses with ice cubes.

"Very much the present," she said honestly and quickly changed the subject. "What about July Fourth?"

"Why can't we have a combination of all our relatives? The Luckadeaus and the O'Donnells? There's lots of land here, and if anyone wants to come a day before and bring their tents or campers, we can manage. If they want to come for the day and bring their potluck dishes, we'll be happy to have that, too."

"Now, that sounds like fun." She carried her glass of tea to the living room and settled onto the end of the sofa.

"Shh." Remy pointed toward a navy-blue throw that one of the kids had left on the floor the night before. There was a little black kitten curled up on it, sound asleep.

"Are you going to tell them, or should I?" she asked.

"You can, and then they can take themselves up to bed. It's after ten, and tomorrow we've got more fence line to clear out," he said.

"Hey, kids, we found it!" she yelled over her shoulder.

They came running from the four corners of the house. Bella picked up the tiny thing, scolded him, and then carried him to the basket in the utility room where his mother and siblings waited, most likely unaware that one of them was even gone.

"And now it's bedtime," Adele said.

"But, Mama, we haven't had a snack, and we're starving after three hours of swimming. Y'all didn't do anything but sit in a truck and wait for us, so you don't have any idea much of an appetite we worked up," Jett argued.

"Oh yeah," Remy said inside a cough that he covered with his hand.

Adele blushed again. "Go on and have some cookies and milk or ice cream if you want it. Then it's off to bed, and no reading before you go to sleep tonight since it's gotten this late."

"Yes, ma'am," Nick said. "I'm just glad we're getting to eat. My stomach would have never survived until morning. I'm having a chunk of that peanut butter pie you whipped up for supper. Man, that's good."

They left in the same way they arrived, in a blur of running kids. Remy pushed Adele's curly red hair back and kissed the soft spot between neck and shoulder. "And you, darlin'? Did sitting in a truck work up an appetite for you?"

"No, but what we did in that motel room did. I'm thinking maybe some cookies and one of those beers we forgot to drink would be good," she said.

"Sounds good to me." He helped her up. "And I've changed my mind about you knocking on my door. I would much rather you just ease on into my room and crawl into bed with me. I sleep so much better with you curled up beside me."

"Be careful what you open up, Remy. You might want to close it and find it impossible to do," she said.

He shook his head slowly. "I don't think I'd ever want to close the door to you, Adele."

# Chapter 20

ON FRIDAY MORNING, THE SMELL OF COFFEE AND BACON filled the house when Adele awoke. Her first thought after opening her eyes was that they needed to bolt the headboard to the wall, and then she realized that she was in her bed at the ranch house and not in the motel.

A rap brought her to a sitting position, and then a sliver of light from the landing flooded the room as Jett swung the door fully open. "Hey, Mama, breakfast is nearly ready. Didn't your alarm go off this morning?"

Adele checked the clock. "I forgot to set it. I'll be down in five minutes."

She bailed out of bed, grabbed the first work jeans and chambray shirt she came across in her closet, and hurriedly got dressed. A quick trip through the bathroom took an extra couple of minutes, so she twisted her springy curls up into a ponytail that morning without even running a brush through them. Her boots were beside the hall tree in the foyer, socks inside them from the night before, so she padded into the kitchen in her bare feet.

"Barefoot and..." One of Remy's eyes slid shut in a seductive wink.

"Bite your tongue," Adele whispered as she poured a cup of coffee and headed toward the table.

"This is when we put the idea on the table. Are you ready?" Remy asked.

"Idea? What idea?" Leo asked. "I thought we were

putting bacon and scrambled eggs on the table. We need to build a henhouse, Uncle Remy, so we can have fresh eggs."

Jett removed three kinds of jams and jelly from the refrigerator and took them to the table. "You want to stick your hand up under a big old hen with mean eyes and steal her eggs in the morning?" she asked.

"No, you can have that job. I clean out fencerows," Leo said.

"We should have chickens for sure, Mama," Bella said. "And maybe even a hog lot, so we can cure our own ham for Thanksgiving. It could be way down on the back side of the barn, so the smell wouldn't reach the house."

"What idea?" Nick eyed his uncle cautiously. "You mentioned an idea, and I don't think it's got a thing to do with eggs or ham."

"*Green Eggs and Ham*. Remember when you used to read that story to me?" Bella laughed.

"Bella!" Jett rolled her eyes toward the ceiling.

Adele's long, slender finger shot up to point right at her youngest daughter. "Hey, girl, you can't roll your eyes like that. It's Bella's gesture. You have to find one of your own."

"Mama!" Bella raised her voice.

Remy set the hot biscuits in the middle of the table and took his place at the end opposite from Adele. "Nick, you can say grace this morning."

Other than a couple of kittens fussing in the background, the whole room went silent when everyone bowed their heads.

"Dear Lord, thank you for this day and this food, and

please let the idea that we're about to hear be a good one. Amen."

"That was short," Jett said. "But I'm not complaining one bit. I'm hungry."

"The idea?" Nick looked at Remy.

Adele's eyes locked with his and she couldn't blink. For just a few more days, she wished that it could be their secret and they didn't have to share it with anyone, not even the kids. But counting that day, there were only seven more until Walter came home, and things had to be settled and set in stone by then.

"You presented it to me last night, so you tell them," Remy said.

"You came up with it days ago, so it's yours to tell."

"Somebody speak up," Nick said in exasperation.

"Okay, guys, you've both said that you don't want to leave this ranch. Think about it for a few minutes and be sure you are still feeling that way before I go on," Remy said.

"Mama?" Jett gasped.

Adele laid a hand on Jett's arm. "Don't panic."

"I don't have to think about it. I want to live here forever," Leo said quickly.

Nick tucked his chin to his chest and narrowed his eyes. "I cannot think of a place that I'd rather be than right here, Uncle Remy. Please don't ask me why, because I'm not sure I could tell you. I just know it in my heart, and that sounds kind of sissy, doesn't it?"

"Not at all," Remy said. "Your turn, Adele."

"Same question for you girls. Think before you speak, because it will have a bearing on what comes next," Adele said.

Adele was more than a little surprised when Bella spoke up first. "I'm with Nick. I don't know that I could give a five-minute speech about why I feel this way, but I don't want to leave. But…" She paused and sipped milk before she went on. "I'm going to feel real guilty when we get to stay, and I have to tell Nick and Leo good-bye, Mama."

"Jett?" Adele asked.

"I'll cry and wilt away to nothing if I have to leave this ranch. I won't be able to eat or sleep, and Leo and Nick will be so sad when they have to attend my funeral. I will haunt their dreams forever because they didn't talk Remy into leaving so I could stay on the ranch and live," she said dramatically. "Now someone pass that bacon before it gets as cold as my dead body if I have to move off the Double Deuce."

"I'd say that was pretty definite," Remy said with a chuckle.

"Here's what Remy and I talked about last night while y'all were meeting new friends at the swimming pool. We'd like to form a partnership, and all of us continue to live right here at the ranch. It would mean living together in this house, not for another week but permanently," Adele said.

Four kids whipped their heads around to stare at her as if she had a third eye right in the middle of her forehead.

"That would mean I'd have to share a room with Leo forever?" Nick said.

"Do those boys get a full say in the decisions? I mean, after all, we know more than they do," Bella asked.

"Yes," Jett said and dipped deeply into the bowl of scrambled eggs that had been passed to her.

"Yes, what?" Adele asked.

"Yes, I'd rather share a room with Bella than be buried in the cemetery in Nocona beside Dahlia's sister, Pansy," she said.

Bella shivered. "Jett, that is morbid."

"Maybe so, but if it makes Leo and Nick let us have the ranch, it's worth it." She grinned.

"Adele and I will make the decisions together concerning the ranch. I will make decisions concerning Nick and Leo, and she'll make the ones that concern Bella and Jett. If there's something that a whole family needs to discuss, then we'll sit around this table and talk about it," Remy said.

"Like we are real brothers and sisters?" Leo asked.

"Kind of like that," Adele answered. "Now, we're going to eat our breakfast, and then we'll take a vote. That will give you four time to consider the idea, but remember, once you raise your hand, there's no going back, so be sure which way you're going to vote."

"If it's a tie?" Nick asked.

Remy sent a smile down the length of the table toward Adele. "We'll cross that bridge when we get to it."

"After breakfast and after the vote is in, Mama, are we all going back to the fence-cleaning business today?" Bella asked.

Adele nodded. "Yes, we are. It's the last thing on Walter's list, and we want it to be finished when he gets back next week."

"But if we're going to be in a partnership and no one has to leave, then why does it matter?" Bella asked.

"What if that fence line is what would make him

change his mind and say that he doesn't want to sell the Double Deuce after all? It might be a test to see if we'll take care of this place and love it as much as he does," Adele answered.

"Well, then I'll take the bad with the good. I'm just glad it's not a weekly job and only has to be done once a year."

"Tell you what. Next year, you take care of the garden, and I'll do your share of cleaning the fencerow. I hate garden work," Nick said.

"Is that okay in a partnership, Mama?" Jett asked.

"We'll see about that when the time gets here," Adele said smoothly.

At the end of breakfast, Bella announced that it was time for the vote, and all four hands shot up without hesitation. The vote was four in favor of a partnership, none against it, and they couldn't wait to get outside in the heat to show Walter that they were serious about taking care of the ranch.

They talked nonstop about starting school with their new buddies and when they could go back to the pool all the time, working like little work mules as they hoed the weeds from the fence line and removed any trash that had blown up from the section line road.

Remy leaned on the hoe he'd been using and took a long draw from a bottle of water that he'd set on a wooden fence post. "Happy kids work faster. I believe we'll have this fence cleaned up by nightfall."

Adele leaned an elbow on the post next to him. "Probably so. I was thinking that if they get it all done, maybe tomorrow we could drive over to Wichita Falls and let them pick out the fireworks for July Fourth. We'll need a pretty big display since we're inviting both sides of the family."

"I hear there's a big waterslide park over there. We could get the fireworks and then let them spend the afternoon at the park. You own a bathing suit?" he asked.

"I do."

"A tiny little string bikini?" He tipped his straw hat back on his head and wiped the sweat from his forehead with a big red bandana.

"No, sir! It's a tankini and you've already seen it," she said. "Do you wear a Speedo?"

He shook his head. "Not this old, ugly cowboy. I do have one though, and I'll wear it for you if you wear a bikini for me some night."

"I'd rather go naked."

"Now you're talkin' my language."

"Changing the subject here, Remy. Please tell me we can make this work. The kids would be devastated if all we do is fight and argue and call it quits before the end of the year," she said.

"We can make this work, Adele. I know we can because we've been doing a fine job of it. We can expect arguments. We can expect the kids to hate each other sometimes and to fight for each other the very next hour. It might not be easy, but it is doable. I just hope and pray that, now that we've found a solution, Walter doesn't change his mind."

"If he does, I'm sending Jett in to talk to him," Adele giggled.

"That would be our best bet. Now it's my turn to

change the subject. I really hoped that you would knock on my door last night."

She took a sip from her water bottle and set it back on the ground beside the fence post. "I wanted to, but I was afraid one of the girls might need me in the night. We took a big chance when we used the empty room downstairs, you know?"

"But it was so worth it." Remy, the playboy of all time, couldn't believe he was falling in love with a tall redhead.

*Love!* his conscience yelled so loud that he looked around to see if someone had said the word out loud. *You cannot be in love. This is just the by-product of a couple of wild bouts of sex after a long dry spell. Sit back and think about that word and what it means. You are a player, Remington Luckadeau. You are not a man to settle down with one woman when there are still millions out there who have sweet treats you have not tasted yet.*

Remy picked up the hoe and went back to work without looking at Adele again. Holy smokin' hell! What had happened in the last three weeks? And what was he going to do about it? He'd never been in love before. Could a man fall out of it as easily as he fell into it?

At noon, he still didn't have a single answer to his questions. They had dinner and went back to the fence, finished the last of it at five thirty because the kids didn't want to look at it another day, and went to the house again for supper.

---

Adele could tell something was wrong with Remy. It had started when they were teasing each other about bikinis out there in the pasture, and he'd been quiet ever since. Maybe he was remembering all those beautiful women he had been with, those who wore skimpy bikinis and did not have baggage to bring to a relationship.

*Relationship? Hell!* the voice in her head said. *He's never had a relationship. What he had were one-night and weekend stands. Are you sure you even want a partnership with a man like him? Maybe he just thinks he wants something permanent and he'll wind up breaking you heart like Isaac did.*

The day ended finally, and they all trudged home to a beef roast that Remy had cooked in the slow cooker. Using a couple of forks, he tore it apart, creating a whole cooker full of barbecued pulled beef to put on sandwiches. He removed cabbage slaw and a bowl of cold baked beans from the refrigerator, set out pickles and sliced tomatoes from the garden, and gave the kids a choice of water, fresh-squeezed lemonade, or sweet tea.

"You kids came close to working me to death today," he moaned as he sat down at the end of the table.

"But we've got it done." Leo's voice was full of well-earned pride.

"And Walter won't change his mind, will he, Mama?" Jett asked.

"Let's hope not. We've all done our best and that's all anyone can ask for from you kids," Remy answered. "Who's going to grace this food?"

"I will." Jett bowed her head. "Father up in heaven, thank you for this food, but most of all, thank you for a decent day to get that rotten old fencerow cleaned out. Talk to Walter and don't let him change his mind. If he does, hit him between the eyes with a lightning bolt to get his attention and then remind him of how hard we've all worked. Amen."

Adele clamped her mouth shut to keep from laughing, but when she looked up and saw the expression on Remy's face, she couldn't hold it in.

"What is so funny?" Bella asked in a tired voice.

"It's a grown-up thing," Nick said. "Only they know and they don't share."

Adele wiped tears from her cheeks with a paper napkin. "That's right. Eat your supper. We've got a surprise for tomorrow, since y'all worked so hard. After we get the housecleaning done, we're going to go to Wichita Falls and buy the fireworks for the Fourth of July. It will take a lot, since we're inviting all the family on both sides to our party, and you kids will need to help us pick them all out."

"Do I get to help set them off?" Nick asked.

"Not this year. There'll be too many grown Luckadeau and O'Donnell men here to do that job," Remy answered. "There is more to the surprise. I heard there's a water park over in that area, and we thought maybe we'd spend a few hours there at the end of the day. Does that sound good to all y'all?"

If catcalls and squeals were any indication of how much they liked the idea, then it went over quite well. Remy cupped his hands over his ears, but the smile on his face and the way he locked eyes with her said he was enjoying every single moment.

Adele and Remy were tidying up the kitchen, and the kids were arguing over which movie they would watch that evening. The little black kitten crept into the kitchen, and Adele picked him up and loved on him a bit before putting him back into the basket with his siblings.

"You going to keep that whole litter in the house?" Remy asked.

"No, we have a system. We bring Blanche inside a few days before she gives birth, and then we take them to the barn when they're six weeks old and big enough to get around. Blanche comes in and out as she pleases and is happy to be inside, but she likes chasing around in the barn, too. Do you think she'll be all right with Boss?"

"He seems like a pretty laid-back old boy to me. Now Jerry Lee might be a different matter. She might have him for dinner one evening, so it's probably a good thing if we keep her inside until after we buy this place," Remy said.

Adele's phone rang before she could agree. She picked it up from the cabinet, didn't recognize the number, and started to ignore it, but then cautiously said, "Hello?"

She felt the color leave her face and the room take a couple of spins, so she sat down at the table. Remy pulled a chair up right beside her and held her hand.

"Thank you for calling," Adele said, but her voice sounded like she was in a tunnel. She laid the phone down, tears rolling down her cheeks and her hands shaking. "Oh, Remy, Jett is going to be devastated. Dahlia died."

# Chapter 21

REMY WRAPPED HIS ARMS AROUND ADELE, HOLDING HER so close that she could feel his heart beat against her cheek. "Funeral?" he asked.

Adele shook her head. "The lady who called said that Dahlia hated funerals, so they are going to bury her beside her husband tomorrow. She didn't even want to be embalmed. She'd made all the arrangements."

"Did she seem that sick when you saw her a couple of days ago?"

"She mentioned having lung problems once, but the lady said she had a heart attack and that it was a godsend because she had lung cancer and had only six months to live and the last months would be painful. Dahlia didn't even mention it to me, Remy."

He kissed the top of her head. "Let's wait until morning to tell Jett and the others. That way they'll have all day to process it, and we'll be off on a family trip, so that might help her. I liked that old girl and was looking forward to seeing her again at our party."

"Me, too, but she and Jett had a special bond." Adele sighed. "And this will be the first time Jett has lost a dear friend."

"She's a tough girl, like her mama, Adele. She'll grieve, and she'll always remember the good times she's had with Dahlia, but it will prepare her for greater losses on down the road."

"You're probably right, but that doesn't make telling her any easier. We'll do it at the breakfast table then, and after the morning chores, we'll go to Wichita Falls. Let's plan on getting there right about noon so we can eat out. Maybe a pizza bar?"

He kissed the tip of her nose. "Sounds like something they would like."

The sound of the door slamming combined with someone running on hardwood floors and weeping made Remy stand and Adele sit up straight in her chair. Jett flew through the door in a rush and threw herself into her mother's lap, crying as if her heart was shattered.

"Dahlia is dead." One word at a time came through the raw sobs. "I called to tell her about us all being partners, and a lady answered and said she died this afternoon."

Remy laid a hand on Jett's back. "I'm so sorry, darlin'. We all loved her even though we only knew her for a little while."

"It hurts now, but before long, you won't remember this hurt and you'll only remember the happy times that she had with you." Adele hugged her closer and kissed her on the forehead.

"But, Mama, why did she have to die?"

"That's a question no one can answer, but think of it like this, sweetheart," Adele said softly. "Dahlia had very bad lungs, and she would have been in a lot of pain if she had lived. Maybe she was taken so that she wouldn't hurt so much later."

The other three kids filed into the room and sat down at the table. Tears dripped from Bella's cheeks onto her shirt, leaving big wet splotches in their wake. Nick's chin quivered but he kept it together, but Leo wept openly.

A vision of Dahlia slipping that letter into her hand came back to Adele. Was that what Dahlia meant when she said that Adele would know when to open it and read it to Jett? And if so, shouldn't she read it privately first?

"If I could have just talked to her one more time," Jett sniffled.

"Bella, would you please bring my purse from the credenza in the foyer?" Adele said. If that letter had an ounce of anything in it that would help Jett, then she should have it right now.

Without asking why, her older daughter retrieved Adele's big, hobo-style leather purse and brought it to the table. Adele fished around inside until she found the business envelope.

"Before we left on Wednesday, Miz Dahlia gave me this to read to you, Jett. She said that I'd know when the time was right. I don't think either of us would have thought it would only be in two days, but I'm going to read it to you. Do you want it just to be the two of us, or are you comfortable with everyone being here?" Adele asked.

"We're all family now, so just read it," Jett said.

Adele carefully opened the envelope and removed the letter. A check fell out into her lap, and she gasped at the amount, but she deftly put it back into the envelope before anyone saw it.

"'My dear children,'" she started to read. "'If Adele is reading this, Jett, then you will know that I've passed over from life into eternity. Don't weep for me, because the sooner the better so I don't have to go through the suffering that comes from this disease in the end days. If

I could, I would go on Wednesday night after you leave. I already know it's going to be a perfect afternoon that we get to spend together.

"'I've known for a while that this would be my last year on this earth. That's why I wanted to visit the cemetery in Nocona again, and you, Jett, made it such a fun day. I felt like a kid that afternoon at the cemetery. I had the same feeling in my heart that I did when Pansy and I went to take care of the graves. I loved staying at the old home place over that weekend and getting to know the children. Don't pout, Adele and Remy. I liked being a part of your lives, too.'"

Nick managed a weak smile.

Leo cried harder.

Bella sniffled.

"Go on," Remy said hoarsely.

Adele swallowed three times, but the lump in her throat wouldn't disappear in spite of the humor Dahlia had tried to put into the letter.

"'I'm so glad that there are children on the ranch again. It needs laughter and arguments and good old-fashioned living there, like it was when my sister, Pansy, and I were a part of the place. Knowing all you children has brought so much joy into my life. In this short time at the end of my life, I feel like God has blessed me with grandchildren. So if I leave after Wednesday night, that is fine. If I live for the six months the doctor has given me, that means I get more conversations with Jett.

"'Jett, I want you to think of it like this. I've gone away to see my dear husband, my precious sister, and my parents. Think what a glorious day that will be for me and them, and don't be sad. You can still tell me everything that happens, and I'll listen even though I won't be able to talk back. But I bet if you listen real hard, you'll know what I would say anyway. That's the way of good friends.

"'I think I've said everything. I'm putting a little check in this envelope. It is to be deposited and used to buy a van, so you can all go places together, or if you've already figured that out and gotten one, I want you to use the money for a family vacation. Maybe next year at spring break, you can go on a cruise together. I always thought I'd like to cruise to some of those fancy islands in the Caribbean. Or maybe a week at Disney World. Whatever you decide as a family, I'm sure you will enjoy whatever you do with the money, but you have to do it all together, no matter who gets control of the ranch. I wanted to do something for all you kids.

"'My body is gone, but my heart will be with you forever on the Double Deuce. Love you all, Dahlia.'"

Jett sniffled one more time. "Dahlia doesn't want me to be sad. She wants me to be happy, but it's sure not easy, Mama."

"Uncle Remy, we have a van in Denton. We don't need to buy another one," Nick said.

"It was your mother's van. Will it make you sad to have it around?" Remy asked.

Leo wiped his wet cheeks on his shirtsleeve. "Not me. I think Mama would like for us to use it so we could all go places together."

"Why don't you and Adele go down there and get it right now? It's only an hour from here, and y'all would be back by dark. We can put a movie in, and that will take Jett's mind off all this," Nick suggested.

"And if we have it by tomorrow, we can all go to Wichita Falls together. I call the very backseat." Leo managed a weak smile.

"Jett?" Adele asked.

"Dahlia might not have known about the partner thing, but she wanted us to be able to go places together. I'll be fine, Mama. Bella and Nick and Leo are here."

Adele turned to Remy. "What do you think?"

"That's up to you. I'm willing to go get it if you'll drive me down there in your truck or if you'll let me drive it there. Like Leo said, it's only an hour. We could be back long before bedtime if we go right there and back."

"Where is this van?" Bella asked.

"Sitting in a storage unit about a mile off the highway. It was full of gas when we parked it there the first of the month. I'll just have to get in it and drive it up here," Remy said. "But I want you boys to be sure about this."

"I think Mama would like the idea of us being here and having…" Nick stumbled.

"Friends, sisters, family," Leo finished for him.

"Whatever we are, I think she would like it," Nick said, "because it makes us less sad. We still miss her and Daddy, but we aren't as sad as we were before we came here."

"That gives me hope," Jett said dramatically. "The sadness will get better, like you said, Mama, because Nick and Leo are telling me the same thing."

"Then are you ready, Adele?" Remy asked.

"Ready as I'll ever be. You kids keep your cell phones close. Don't let a stranger in the house," Adele said.

"Mama!" Bella's eyes went toward the ceiling. "I've

babysat for people before. I know the drill. We'll watch a movie, and then if you aren't home, we'll go on and get our showers, and then if you still aren't home, we'll watch another movie. We'll be fine. Go get the van so we can all go to Wichita Falls together tomorrow. And about that cruise—if we have a van, maybe we could do a road trip instead."

"That's on down the road, and we'll vote on it when the time comes," Adele said. "But you kids are free to talk about it all you want between now and then."

"It might help Jett to think about what Dahlia wanted us to do," Leo said.

"It might at that." Remy smiled. "We'll be back in a couple of hours. Call us if anything at all happens."

"Other than that black kitten getting lost. If that happens, you are on your own," Adele said.

—◆◆◆—

Remy laced his fingers in Adele's, bringing her hand up to rest on the console separating them in her truck. "It makes me a little nervous to leave them there alone. Is that normal?"

Even after working and being dog-tired that evening, the electricity was there between them. Simply touching her hand made him want to hold her, to kiss her, to take away all the pain of having an unhappy child, to sleep with her and wake up with her in his arms every morning.

"Very much so." She squeezed his hand. "It's never easy to leave them with a sitter or, like right now, alone, even though the two oldest are fourteen. Being a parent is tough business."

"I'm finding that out one hard step at a time. And just

think, in a couple of years, we'll have to face the dating scene. Oh. My. God!" Remy slapped the steering wheel.

"What?" Adele quickly scanned the area they were traveling through for stray deer or maybe a drunk staggering down the side of the road.

"Dating!" he groaned.

"You're getting hit with everything at once, but be thankful you've got boys. I'm dealing with girls."

"No!" He hit the steering wheel again. "Not that. Not simple dating and first kisses, but what if they turn out like me? I don't want that kind of lifestyle for them. I want them to be—"

"Shh," Adele shushed him. "A wise old cowboy told me once that you cross that bridge when you get to it. Besides, you're in a new area, where few people know about your past, so you can start all over just like the boys are doing."

"And you?" Remy asked.

"And all of us."

Remy caught Interstate 35 at Gainesville and then it was just a short thirty-minute drive to Denton. The place where he'd stored the furniture and the van was located on the north side of town and only a mile from the highway.

"Something I had not thought of before right now—this partnership is going to involve more than paperwork, Adele. There's already a house full of furniture because Walter is selling the place 'lock, stock, and barrel,' as he said. There are two units down here that are full of stuff, and you've got things in storage. How are we ever going to get it all sorted?"

"One day at a time. It's all just material things, and

we won't sweat the small stuff." She smiled. "There's not much in the way of big things I care about bringing into the house. They'll just remind us of the past. But we'll all have one of those 'round-the-table discussions and see what we want to do with what we don't use."

Beautiful and smart. Quite a catch for any man with something to offer a woman. Remy wished right then that he could be that cowboy because she was surely everything that he'd ever thought about—those few times that settling down entered his mind.

He cleared his throat. "If you ever did think about a permanent-type relationship again, what would you look for in a man?"

She cut her eyes at him. "Someone who would accept me—tall, gangly me with all my flaws, freckles, and red hair—who wouldn't want to change me. Who'd love me just like I am, in my faded jeans and chambray work shirts and boots. And they'd have to get along with my girls so well that someday they would call him Dad or Daddy and not Father because anyone can be a father, but it takes someone special to be a daddy. Why?"

"I just wondered," he said.

"And you, Remy? What would you look for other than hot sex?"

He chuckled, more out of nervousness than actual humor. "You. But I'm smart enough to know that in the long haul, you deserve something so much better than this old rough cowboy."

Afraid to look at her, he kept his eyes glued on the road ahead.

"Why don't you let me be the judge of that?" she whispered.

He turned slightly to find her smiling and the last sunrays of the day lighting up her eyes. "Really?"

"Really. But that's something we'll talk about later. Tonight, we've got a van to take home so our children will be happy campers tomorrow. We've got a partnership to take to the lawyers and figure out once Walter is home. And we'll have to figure out more than what *we* want because other people are depending on us. And we need to give this a lot of thought before we dive into it."

Remy was ready to take the leap, whether it meant saying those three magic words right then or vowing to love her forever, but if she needed more time, that was fine, too. What she had said was enough for Remy for that moment. Enough to give him hope that something other than friends with benefits would come out of the arrangement they'd made. More than enough to make him forget all about chasing other women, about one-night stands and living the life of a player.

# Chapter 22

THE CONVERSATION FROM GAINESVILLE TO DENTON THE night before kept replaying in Adele's mind on a continuous loop. Was Remy shooting her a line of bullshit, or was he serious? Could someone as sexy as Remington Luckadeau really want a plain Jane redhead like Adele on a permanent basis? Or was he saying *if* he ever settled down, he might like to have someone like her? That word was tiny, with its two letters, but it packed quite a wallop.

Four Saturdays ago, Adele would never have thought she'd see the day that the kids would work together to get the house cleaned. But there they were, running the vacuum and dusting the high places where Bella and Jett couldn't reach while she cleaned the bathroom upstairs. She also slipped into the one in the empty room and gave it a quick tidying up.

And during the whole process, she kept thinking about the night before and how close she and Remy had come to saying words that carried so much weight they should only be said out loud after lots of careful consideration.

The kids loaded into the bright-red van, with Leo and Jett claiming the backseat and Bella and Nick settling into the bucket seats behind the driver and front passenger. As they were driving through Henrietta, Jett and Leo got into a heated discussion that went from disagreement to yelling in less than a minute. According to Leo, Jett was a spoiled brat, and just because she was the youngest of the whole bunch of them, she shouldn't always get her way. According to Jett, Leo was a brat and he didn't know shit from chocolate.

"Whoa! You two put a foot between you and don't say another word to each other until we get to the pizza place," Remy yelled over the top of their voices.

It was a crazy thing to get mad about and Adele knew it, but anger boiled up from the soles of her sandals all the way to her head, sending waves of blistering-hot steam out her ears. Jett was her baby, and she'd suffered a horrible loss the day before. Remy had no business correcting her. If he wanted to scream at his kid, that was fine. The little brat needed it. But to holler at her child was a different matter altogether. If Jett needed correction, Adele would deliver it. If this was what happened when they all went together, then by damn, she'd take her truck and her girls from now on and Remy could travel however he wanted—by van, by truck, by four-wheeler, or by an old, stubborn mule. It didn't matter as long as he didn't take it upon himself to yell at either of her children.

Leo moved so close to the side of the van that light couldn't get between his lanky body and the metal. Jett did the same on the other side and stuck her tongue out at Leo. He made a face at her, and then they both got tickled. Just like that, their argument was over and they were making bets about who would go down the longest slide at the water park. If Leo did, then Jett had to dust on his day to clean next week. If Jett did, then Leo had to take on her vacuuming chores.

"Kids," Remy said.

"Men," Adele mumbled.

"What was that?"

"Nothing that won't wait until later," she said.

She'd barely gotten the words out of her mouth when Nick kicked the back of her seat and then stomped the floorboard of the van right behind her.

"There won't be a boy in high school that will even look at you if you keep doing that," Nick said hatefully.

Adele's first thought was that he was talking to her, and then Bella tied into him. "I can snort when I laugh anytime I want, and besides, at least I'm reading something to make me laugh and not one of those nasty, old, vampire, crappy things like you read. Girls don't like boys who are all dark and goth."

"I'm not goth," he said vehemently with another kick to Adele's seat.

"Young man, if you kick my back again, you are going to walk all the way to Wichita Falls," she said.

*Oh. My. Sweet. Lord*, she thought immediately. She'd just done the same thing Remy had. She quickly glanced over to see a wide grin splitting his sexy face.

In for a lamb, might as well go on and get hung for the sheep. "And, Bella, that was uncalled for. Both of you are too young to be thinking about girls and boys other than for friendship. And it's none of your business what he reads, just like it's none of his if you snort when you laugh."

"Uncle Remy?" Nick asked.

"I'm in agreement with Adele, and right now, I don't know why she and I took more than two hours of our time and worried about you kids the whole way to Denton and back just to get this van. You four are the ones who wanted to start going places in one vehicle. You're the ones who wanted a van. And first rattle out of the bucket, you act like this? I'm thinking that tomorrow, we'll put this vehicle up for sale and go back to our trucks," he said.

"Nooo," the four whined in unison.

"Then straighten your butts up."

Adele glanced over at Remy and he nodded. "Made you mad, didn't I?"

"You had the same reaction, didn't you?"

He nodded. "Guess we've got some adjusting and talking to do. You don't want me correcting your kids, right?"

"And you don't want me to discipline yours?"

He tapped the brakes. "I see a fireworks sign up ahead. Looks like one of those really big stands where we could get everything we need."

She pointed to the sign. "Two for one is a good thing. And, Remy, we'll each pay for half. That's partnership."

"You'll get no gripe from me on that," he said.

"And we can talk about the correction thing later?"

"We can do that. Just don't puff up and be mad at me all day."

"You should know me well enough by now to know that I speak my mind and put it all out on the table."

Remy brought the van to a stop. "Good! Because pouting women should be shot."

"The same for men who leave the house and run off to work or the barn before things get settled," she shot right back at him as she got out of the van and headed toward the fireworks stand.

It didn't take long to decide that maybe they should have brought the two trucks when they started trying to fit the fireworks into the back of the van. Adele had spent a lot of money, but she wanted their first holiday on the ranch to be something really huge. Even if worse came to worst and Walter came home refusing to sell the property, she intended to tell him that he owed the whole bunch of them the right to have their party before they turned the ranch back over to him.

"It's like playing Tetris," Leo said as they carefully worked one box after another into the space.

"Or a jigsaw puzzle. We should do one of those on the dining room table instead of watching movies." Bella worked a small box of sparklers into a tiny little hole off to one side.

"I like puzzles, but Nick hates them," Leo said.

Jett laid the last box of bottle rockets on top of the stack. "So do I. Me and Nick will watch our western movies, and y'all can put a puzzle together. Bella has tons of them in storage. When we unpack, y'all can have your pick of dogs, horses, birds, or cats, and she's got the Eiffel Tower and the Statue of Liberty, too. We'll have the biggest fireworks show in the whole country, Mama."

"Looks like it." Adele smiled. "Now, who's hungry for pizza?"

"I'd rather have Dairy Queen!" Bella said.

"McDonald's!" Leo shouted.

"We can't go to both, so y'all decide without shouting, and no nasty little remarks after the decision is made. That's what partnership is all about," Remy said.

"Can I borrow your pocketknife, Uncle Remy?" Nick asked.

"What are you going to do with it?"

"I'm thinking if I'm going to be a rancher, maybe I'd better ask for one for Christmas."

Remy worked the knife out of his pocket and handed it to Nick. "What Daddy used to do when me and Leo had two different minds about things. Leo, get me a straw from the glove compartment," Nick said seriously.

Leo disappeared from the back of the van and brought back a plastic straw wrapped in paper. He tore open the end, removed the paper, and stuffed it into his pocket before handing the straw to Nick.

"Don't go thinkin' you're all grown up because you get to do Daddy's job," Leo grumbled.

"Uncle Remy can do it if you don't think I'll be fair." Nick opened the knife, cut the straw into two pieces—one a little longer than the other—closed the knife, and handed it back to Remy.

"I didn't say you wouldn't be fair."

"Then what were you saying?" Remy asked.

"He gets to cut the straw like Daddy did. And I'm big enough to know how to use a knife, so I should get to cut the straw some of the time," Leo said, pouting.

"Then next time you can do just that." Remy nodded.

"What I want to know is how you knew there would be one in the glove compartment?" Jett asked.

"Mama never used straws, but she wouldn't throw them away. She put them in the glove compartment, and if Nick and I had an argument like McDonald's or Burger King, then we drew straws to settle the fight," Leo explained.

Nick put his hands behind his back and then brought out a fist. The straws looked exactly the same. He held them out to Bella first and she chose one. Then Leo chose the other and they measured them.

"Leo has the long straw, so he gets to choose where we eat," Nick said seriously.

"I thought we were going to have pizza at the all-you-can-eat bar," Adele said.

"I think we should agree on pizza," Leo said without hesitation. "It sounds good, and we should have it because Jett really likes it and she lost her good friend yesterday. We all liked Dahlia, but Jett really loved her."

"Kids," Remy said again but with a great deal of pride.

"We should learn from them," Adele agreed.

"Then pizza it is." Nick stuffed the pieces of straw into his pocket. "And I'm glad, because I'm really hungry and it's all you can eat at the pizza place."

They piled into the car, talking about how many pieces of pizza they could eat and what their favorite toppings were. Remy buckled his seat belt and glanced over at Adele. "Where did you eat the best pizza you've ever had?"

"From a street vendor in New York City," she answered as she snapped her belt into place. "In Times Square, not far from the Marriott hotel. And you?"

"My kitchen out in the canyon. I make a mean hand-tossed crust and I make my own sauce. Not too sweet, not too spicy, so it doesn't overpower the cheese," he said. "I'll make it sometime this winter when we have to stay in all day, and you can decide if it's as good as your fancy big-city pizza."

"I look forward to it," she said.

Remy was just full of surprises. Would she ever figure them all out, or when they were as old as Walter and getting ready to sell the ranch, would he still be able to surprise her? If they really got to buy the ranch, she vowed that she would never sell it. She would die right there on the place, and they could even bury her under one of the pecan trees on the north forty acres.

———〜〜〜———

It took a while to find the water park after they'd had their fill of pizza, but after stopping to ask for directions twice, Remy finally drove the van into the parking lot and got a "hip hip hooray" from the backseats.

Remy removed his wallet when they reached the ticket gate and paid for six tickets. "Don't fuss at me. You can buy supper, and just think about how hungry they're going to be after swimming. I may wind up owing you money if we get out the pen and paper."

Adele didn't argue, which amazed him. Partnership was one thing. A date was another, and this should be considered a date, since he planned full well on courting Adele once she got into her bathing suit. Give a bunch of kids a choice of a dozen water-park attractions, and they'd be happy for the whole afternoon, giving him and Adele lots of time alone—if a whole park full of squealing kids and people could be considered alone time. But then, when he was with Adele, it was as if everyone else faded into the background and they were the only two people in the world.

He and the boys changed into swimming trunks, tossed all their clothing into the duffel bag, and shoved it into a locker. There was still plenty of room inside, so they waited for the girls to toss their tote bag inside, too.

Remy caught sight of the girls before the boys did, and he was damn glad he was wearing sunglasses, so

Adele couldn't see his eyes. As it was, he had a hard time controlling the grin. There she was, in a cute little tie-dyed bathing suit, hair braided in two ropes, long, long, well-muscled legs that went on forever, and a waist that nipped in from well-rounded hips. Taking long strides across the pavement with the girls right behind her, she reminded him of a beer commercial set on the beach that he'd seen on television.

Bella didn't ask questions but jammed their tote bag into the locker. "Where do y'all want to start? I looked at the brochure they gave us and I don't mind going down the slide, but I'd rather go to the Shipwreck Beach because they have tidal waves and that sounds like fun."

"Then lead the way," Leo said.

"And you?" Remy raised an eyebrow toward Adele.

"Might as well follow them. I'd love to get wet and then lay on a chaise longue and just watch from a distance," she answered.

"Do you have sunblock in that little bag you're carrying?"

"Oh, yes, I surely do. Bella and Jett both have enough of their father's DNA to tan beautifully. I burn, peel, freckle, and never turn brown." She fell in beside him as the kids went on ahead, with Bella telling them how to get to the right place.

"So your ex tanned well?" he asked.

"Isaac had a lovely, light-tan color to his skin even in the winter. He'll be one of those older gray-haired men who turn women's heads even when he's eighty," she said.

A bolt of pure green envy shot through Remy. When he was eighty, he'd look like his grandfather—little if any hair left on his head, wrinkled like a pair of old leather boots that hadn't been shined in a decade, and not a woman in the state of Texas would even give him a first look, much less a second one.

"But looks are not the be-all and end-all of a man. Isaac is controlling, has a touch of OCD, and if he can't manipulate a woman into giving him what he wants—and that includes everything, not just sex—then he pouts. And that is enough about my ex. Matter of fact, that is too much about my ex. Let's go enjoy an afternoon of pretend beaches," she said.

"Pretend?"

"I'd rather have the real thing. Maybe that's where we'll go with our vacation inheritance. Want to go to Panama City Beach at Christmas?"

"Sure. You make the arrangements for the trip, and I'll talk one of my cousins into coming to the Double Deuce and taking care of things for us," he said. "But I suppose we should have a vote with the kids first."

"The way they're diving into that water"—she pointed at all four of them jumping into the pool—"I would expect that the idea of leaving behind cold weather and spending a week on a beach would be a wonderful idea. Cassie and her friends have gone to a little place on the west end of the beach that's pretty private. We'd have to make arrangements soon if we really want to go there."

She laid her bag and towel on a chaise longue and slipped into the pool. Remy did the same, gliding in close enough to her that her slick, wet legs were right next to his. He'd long since ceased to be surprised at the reaction he had to her bare skin on his, but there was something different about a pool compared to the showers they'd shared. The sensation jacked up his pulse until he could hear it in his ears.

Cool water against his skin. Hot vibes shooting through his body. A brand-new sensation that a player like Remy should have experienced before. He let his mind drift back to long summer weekends at a lake or in a pool out in someone's backyard, the women of those days, skinny-dipping with them, having sex with them in the water. None of them had ever brought on the heat that he knew sitting there with his elbows on the edge of the pool and his legs plastered against Adele's.

"Look at them," Adele said. "They work hard and they play hard."

"I can't," Remy whispered.

Her neck twisted around so she could look into his eyes. "Why?"

"Because I can't take my eyes off you," he drawled.

"If that's a pickup line, it's a damn good one. If it's not, then I'm flattered all to hell." She smiled.

"It's not a line, darlin'. It's the truth."

"Then I wish we were back at the ranch and all these rowdy kids were asleep," she murmured just loud enough for his ears.

"So do I. Can we write that in stone for later tonight? I've got the rock if you're up for some chiseling."

She ran her toes down his calf and shot a smile toward him that paled the hot sun shining down on them. "Always. Now let's get out, and I'm going to ask you to put sunblock on all the places I can't reach."

"Oh, honey, with pleasure," he said.

# Chapter 23

ADELE AWOKE SUNDAY MORNING WISHING THAT SHE HAD not agreed to spend the day in Terral, Oklahoma, with Rye and Austin. She would have much rather driven into Nocona for church services and then spent a lazy afternoon at home. But there would be no going back now, not since Jett and Bella found out that Rye raised rodeo stock and that he and Remy were planning to ride a couple of broncs that afternoon.

That's all they could talk about on the way home from the water park the day before, and according to all four of the kids and Remy, it was absolutely going to be the coolest weekend ever. She dressed in a bright floral sundress with lots of blue and greens, a matching necklace that Bella and Jett had bought for her Mother's Day gift, and a pair of comfortable sandals. After she applied makeup, so she wouldn't hear her mother's voice in her head all day about Sunday being the day that women were women and men were men, she packed a pair of jeans, comfortable cowgirl boots, and a long-sleeved chambray shirt into a tote bag.

If Remy thought he was the only one from the Double Deuce who was going to enjoy the unbridled excitement of riding a wild bronc that day, he had cow chips for brains. Adele hadn't ridden since before Jett was born, but if she couldn't have a lazy Sunday, then she would have all the bells and whistles of a wild ride. Just before she walked out the door, she picked up a pair of leather gloves and her hat. A cowgirl didn't ride anything without her hat.

Remembering the wild ride she'd had the night before—and without a hat—put a smile on her face and two faint spots of crimson in her cheeks as she made her way down the stairs, where Remy waited.

"Well, don't you look absolutely stunning this morning," he whispered.

"You, darlin', don't look too shabby yourself." The smile widened.

"I can clean up when I'm going to meet the girlfriend's family," he said.

"Girlfriend? Is that what I am now?"

He offered her his arm. "Kids are waiting on the porch, bags packed for ranch fun after church, and, honey, you are anything you want to be in my eyes. 'Girlfriend' sounds more like high school than people our age."

"After all the notches on your bedpost?"

He kissed her on the forehead and then opened the door, stood to one side, and laid a hand on her lower back to usher her out onto the porch. "You make me forget every one of those."

"Time to load 'em up and move 'em out?" Leo asked.

Remy was about to tousle Leo's hair but realized the kid had taken great pains to get it swept back without a part that morning.

"New hairstyle?" he asked.

"Me and Nick both decided that if we're going to be cowboys, we need to look more like them and not so much like preppy kids." Leo jumped off the porch and ran toward the van.

"He's stealing my heart," Adele whispered.

Remy's breath was warm on her neck. "He's had mine for a long time."

———

Remy met Rye and Austin on the church lawn. Remy liked Rye from the moment they had shaken hands the Sunday they all attended church together in Ringgold, and he looked forward to spending the afternoon with another rancher. But truth be told, he would have just as soon stayed home that afternoon and had a lazy afternoon with Adele.

Bella and Jett latched on to seven-year-old Rachel's hands and asked if she could sit with them during services. Austin said that since everyone would be sitting in the same area, that was fine with her. Bella offered to take Eddie Cash, too, but the five-year-old little boy shook his head and grabbed his daddy's hand.

"A couple of weeks ago he was in love with Jett," Austin said.

"But that was on his grandpa's ranch, and there weren't two strange boys in the wings," Adele said. "He'll get used to them by the time the day is over."

Folks were every bit as friendly at the church in Terral as they'd been at the one in Ringgold, inviting Adele and Remy to come back, to make it their home church, to come to the church social the next week. Remy figured they might visit on occasion, and he'd have to call a partnership meeting, but twenty miles seemed a bit far to travel every Sunday. However, this one and the one in Ringgold were little country churches, and they'd both probably appreciate the membership more than a bigger place over in Nocona. Besides, there was enough family on both the Luckadeau and the O'Donnell sides that they would always have an invitation for dinner, or they could take their relatives home with them, either one.

When the last introduction was made and the last hand shook, Remy headed toward a black truck parked across the street from the church.

Adele grabbed him by the arm and pointed to the van. "You are no longer a big, sexy, stud cowboy who drives a black truck. You are now a father figure who drives a van. Is this going to be a problem?"

"Not at all. My heart is getting the idea. I just have to work on the mind thing." He slung an arm around her shoulders, and they followed the kids to the van.

Dinner was served out in the yard under a big shade tree. Austin had set up two tables. One held the food, served buffet style; the other one was already set up with napkins and silverware, so all they had to do once Rye said grace was load up their plates and get on with the business of eating.

"I decided to go simple, with tacos and a pan of enchiladas, rather than making the usual pot roast today," Austin explained. "And Rachel wanted a picnic with her cousins." She lowered her voice to a whisper. "And truth is, I have trouble telling her no."

"I know the feeling." Adele smiled. "And this is amazing, Austin, but I hope you didn't plan on leftovers for supper, because my kids are big eaters."

"So are mine. Dessert will be served in the house because it's too hot to have ice-cream sundaes out here in the yard. So who's in the lead to buy that ranch?"

Adele explained the situation as they carried their plates to the end of the table and sat down. "It seemed like the best way to do things so my girls and his boys didn't have to leave."

"Sounds like a pretty good plan to me. But I do believe I see sparks between you and Remy. Anything going to come of that?"

"Right now, we're going to iron out a partnership, and then we'll see what happens afterward." Adele kept her eyes on her plate, but she could feel the vibes every time Remy glanced her way.

"Just between me and you, I think that cowboy is love drunk." Austin giggled.

"And that means?"

"Drunk on love. Rye was like that when we first met, and it didn't take me long to catch up either. I thought I loved that cowboy at the first, but what we have now eight years later is so much deeper. I'm going to hope for the same for you."

"Thanks, but I'm not sure I trust myself anymore, and he's been a playboy his whole adult life. I couldn't hold on to a man who was a hell of a lot less than Remington Luckadeau. It scares me to even think of anything permanent," Adele said.

Austin tucked a strand of dark hair behind her ear. "Fear will ruin the future quicker than anything."

"Mama, can I ride the broncs today? I want to be like Aunt Gemma, and she said she was riding at my age," Rachel asked from her place beside Rye.

"No!" Austin answered emphatically. "You are not getting on a bronc today."

"When I'm a teenager?" Rachel asked.

"We'll talk about it when you're a teenager and not every day from now until then."

"It's okay, Rachel." Jett patted her on the shoulder. "Mama won't let me and Bella ride anything other than tame old horses that are so old they won't even trot, much less run. But someday we're going to grow up and ride broncs and maybe even bulls."

"Yes, we are, and we're going to be like Aunt Gemma," Rachel said.

Rye got in on the last of the conversation. He hugged Rachel and kissed her on the top of her black hair. "You're going to give me gray hair just thinking about that day when I have to sit in the stands and watch you come out of the chute on a big old, mean bronc."

"But, Daddy," she said sweetly, "you'll still be handsome with gray hair."

"She's a charmer for sure." Remy chuckled as he joined them.

Rye nodded. "Just like her mama."

Remy's breath caught in his throat when a vision appeared in his head of his delicate Jett, so tiny and so frail looking, with her blond hair and tiny features, on the back of a one of the meanest horses in the world. In the picture, he could see her with one hand in the air and the other around the rope. Then, suddenly, she was flying through the air and hitting the dirt with a thud.

He wasn't sure he could endure that moment if it ever happened in reality. He'd probably have a heart attack right there in the stands or on the edge of the stall where they'd turned her loose. Lord, raising girls was going to be even more difficult than he'd imagined.

He finished his dinner and then had a chocolate

ice-cream sundae for dessert before Rye asked if he was ready to take on a couple of broncs that afternoon.

Rye carried his ice-cream bowl to the sink and kissed Austin on the cheek. "Great dinner, darlin', and dessert was perfect. I told you not to fret about these folks. They're ranchers, too."

"Yes, ma'am, it was great. And yes, Rye, I'm ready to see if I can still stay on a bronc for eight seconds. Who's going to time us?"

Austin raised her hand. "I've got a timer and an old-school bell that you can't miss hearing."

Rye clapped a hand on Remy's shoulder. "We'll ride the middle-class boys, not the demons, but they'll give us a little workout."

"Lookin' forward to it. You been runnin' rodeo stock long?" Remy asked Rye.

"Ever since before we got married," Austin answered for him. "He and his family are big rodeo fans. Y'all will have to go with us one weekend down to the one below Dallas."

"Yes!" Rachel squealed loudly. "I'll show you all around. It's a lot of fun, and we take our travel trailer, and I bet you can borrow one from Grandpa because he's got an extra one."

"Sounds like something we'd enjoy," Remy said. "But first we've got to finish planning our Fourth of July party, which you are coming to, right?"

"Yes, we are! And Mama says that we're having fireworks on the ranch and that we can stay the whole day, and Jett and I are going to play with her kittens," Rachel said. "But right now we're going out to the corrals and watch you and Daddy ride."

"Adele, let's take the girls all into the office and change clothes. I don't expect that you want to ride in that pretty dress do you?"

"It could make for more problems than I want to face, especially since it's been several years since me and a bareback bronc have come to an understanding."

Remy's heart stopped. Flat. Out. Quit. Beating. No way was he letting Adele get onto a wild horse and attempt to stay on its back for eight seconds. What if something happened to her? What if he lost her, and he'd never even told her that he was in love with her? What would he do if her ex-husband came and took the girls away from the ranch, and there wasn't one thing he could do about it because they weren't his?

He changed from his Sunday best into work clothes in a bathroom and tried to calm down, but nothing worked. Not taking deep breaths. Not staring at his face in the mirror while he gave himself a lecture about Adele being a grown woman.

Finally, he opened the door to find her right in front of him in the hallway. She wore a chambray shirt that she'd tied up in a knot at her waist, tight jeans, and an old, beat-up straw hat that put her right at his height.

"I don't think this is a wise idea," he said.

"What? Riding isn't like swimming. You don't have to wait thirty minutes before you hit the water."

"You riding a bronc. Think of all that could happen," he said.

"The same could happen to you," she said. "And, Remy, I don't take orders too well, so don't think you can tell me not to ride this afternoon."

She turned and walked away before he could say

anything else. Anger worked its way up from his boots to his dusty, old hat. Was the woman totally insane? She had two daughters who'd told her that they didn't want to even visit their father, and if she died out there today, their biological grandmother could sweep in, and they wouldn't have a choice.

"Dammit to hell!" he mumbled.

Rye had already caught and corralled two broncs before church that morning. He and Remy saddled up a couple of horses to get those two into the chutes and to use as pick-up horses after they'd ridden. The kids all climbed up to the top of the rail fence and lined up across it like six little birds sitting on a wire. Remy hoped that, when the day was done, none of them were weeping over a hurt or dead mother. A chill ran down the length of his spine at even thinking such a thing, but there wasn't a thing he could do about it. He truly knew at that moment what it was like to between a rock and a hard spot.

"Ladies first," Rye said when they'd gotten the first big, black horse into the chute. "Get comfortable, Adele. How long has it been since you've done this?"

"More than ten years," she answered.

Remy's breath caught in his chest and ached for several seconds before he remembered to inhale again. Ten years since she'd tried to stay on a bronc for eight seconds. She was rusty at best, out of sync with the whole thing at the worst.

Rye got the rope around the horse, and Adele slid off the top rail onto the horse's back, took a minute to get the feel of the animal beneath her, and tightened up on the rope. She tucked it into one gloved hand, held the other one up, and then shook her head.

Remy almost jumped for joy. She was calling it quits. "Halle-damn-lujah," he mumbled.

"I haven't quite got the feel for this old bruiser yet. You didn't give me the meanest devil in your stock, did you, Rye? It would be like you to do that just to see me get bucked off," she said.

"No, ma'am. This is Blister. He's mean, but he wouldn't get the points that Demon would in a real rodeo. I saved Demon for Remy." He chuckled.

She clamped her legs to the horse's side and pulled up on the rope again, getting a firmer grip. She blew a kiss to the kids, adjusted her hat, and then nodded at Rye. He jerked the door open, and Blister came out of the chute with all four feet off the ground. Remy inhaled deeply and held it. The first second lasted an hour. The second one, a year, and the third one, only three days past eternity.

Kids screamed in the background, but all he could hear was the whooshing noise in his ears as his heart tried to plow its way out of his chest. If she got off that bronc in one piece, she was never riding again. They might fight about it, but it probably wouldn't be their last one.

Finally, Austin rang the bell, and Remy spurred his horse to get out there in the ring to pick her up. He sidled up to the side of the bronc, reached out an arm, and swept Adele over onto his horse.

"I did it, Remy! I stayed on that brute for eight seconds," she squealed.

---

Heart pounding and pulse doing double time, Adele climbed the rails of the chute fence and grabbed the rope, holding the handle of the gate. In that moment, she understood why Remy had been so worried. He eased down onto the horse that was already rolling his eyes wildly, got the rope situated, and nodded to Adele to open the gate. Her hands froze. She couldn't let him go out there and break his fool cowboy neck. If that happened, the boys couldn't live at the ranch. It wasn't that Adele couldn't or wouldn't go right on living if Remy died, but part of her soul and her heart would wither up and die, and she needed both for a very long time.

He winked at her and nodded again, this time more emphatically. She jerked the rope and the chute opened. The big roan horse came out with his back arched so high that Remy's butt barely had a place to sit as it bounced up and down. The horse whipped around to the left and then to the right like a contortionist. Time stood still as the dust rolled up in waves to fill her nose. She could taste the red dirt and feel the heat bearing down on her body and her chest caving in from lack of oxygen.

The bell sounded, and on a downward movement, Remy simply stepped off the horse like a pro, ran to the nearest fence with the animal right behind him like a charging bull, and hopped over it. Then, and only then, was Adele able to refill her aching lungs with oxygen.

Remy was not getting on a bronc or a bull again. If he did, she was going to dissolve the partnership. He ran around the edge of the corral fence, pulled her down from her perch, and kissed her with so much heat that she felt as if her insides would explode. Thank God the place they were standing was shielded from everyone's eyes at the moment or she'd be explaining to Austin, to the kids, and then to everyone in the whole family about her relationship with Remy. Jett O'Donnell, bless her heart, would have pulled out her cell phone and called her aunt Cassie first and her granny next.

"Sweet Lord, I'd forgotten what a thrill that is," he said when the kiss ended.

"What? The ride or the kiss?" she asked.

"Both, darlin'." His sexy face broke into a grin. "Now, it's Rye's turn, and then we're going to saddle up some horses and let all the kids ride for an hour before we start home."

Rye opened the door into the tiny area beside the chute and climbed up the rails. "Haven't ever seen what this old boy can do, but when I know he's a hunk of pure, hot devil, so I don't expect to stay on the full eight seconds. Remy, I'd like for you to score him for twists and turns." Rye handed Remy a small notebook and a pen. "This will help me build a page for him on my website."

Remy parked his fanny on the top of the fence in a good spot. Austin swung her body up into the saddle of the horse that Rye had dismounted. Adele took the timer and the bell from Austin, circled the fence on the outside, and sat on it beside Bella. When Rye gave the nod, Austin opened the gate and then got out of the way.

Rye had been right when he said the horse was pure evil. He'd also been right about not staying on the critter for eight seconds. He made it all the way to six, and then he went flying in the air. He came down on a shoulder and his side, rolled several times to get away from the hooves of the still-bucking horse, and then ran to the fence.

Austin rode around the circle to where Adele was sitting. "How'd he do?"

"Six," Adele said.

"That's really good for that mean-spirited devil. He's going to do very well financially with it, but to be honest, it scared the shit out of me when he said he was going to ride it today," Austin said. "I knew what he did for a living when I married him, but it still terrifies me."

"Today, I believe you," Adele said.

"We can't tell them they can't do what they love, but we can't control the way we feel. God has a real crazy sense of humor to put all this in a woman's heart."

Adele nodded. "Amen, sister!"

The sun was starting to fall toward the west when they crossed the Red River Bridge south of Terral, drove a few miles, and turned east on Highway 82. The kids were chatting about how much fun they'd had, how they wanted to go back to Rye and Austin's again, and when could they have horses on their ranch, and on and on until Adele's ears ached.

Then, out of the clear blue, Jett yelled from the backseat, "Mama, would you please take me to the cemetery where Dahlia's sister and her mama and daddy are buried? I need to see those graves."

Remy glanced up in the rearview. "Of course we can."

"I think she asked me, not you," Adele said tersely.

"If you could see what I see in that mirror, you wouldn't be able to tell her no either," Remy said. "The sunrays are hitting it just right to put a halo right above that blond ponytail, making her look like an angel."

"I didn't like it when you rode that horse today. It scared the hell out of me. I want to ask you not to ever ride again, but that's not fair. The excitement, the energy, the kiss told me that you aren't one to stand on the sidelines. I'm still a little on edge, though, and I don't mean to be cranky about you answering Jett," Adele said.

"I hear you loud and clear. The moments you were on that animal were the longest eight seconds of my life. I thought I'd have a long, gray beard by the time they were over. I was determined to demand that you never ride again, but I can't do that."

"Kind of like letting something go and if it comes back to you, then you know it's yours?" she asked.

"I will ride horses. I might even ride them very fast, but, Adele, I would never want you to go through the fear I had today, so you have my promise right now that I won't ride a bronc again. Besides, I'm going to be sore in places I didn't even know I had tomorrow," he said.

It took a while before she could talk around the lump in her throat. "It's a Danny Glover situation, isn't it?"

"And that means?" Remy frowned.

"In the *Lethal Weapon* movies, he made a statement. Remember what he said?"

"Oh." Remy grinned. "He said that he was getting too old for this shit."

"That's the way I feel," Adele said. "It was exciting today, but I know a room with a pallet in it that I can get even more excited about. And if I break a leg or an arm or, worse yet, my neck, I might not get to visit that room for a long time. So I'm not riding a bronc again either."

"I love you, Adele," Remy said.

Had she heard him right? Had he said the magic words right there in a van full of kids? But yet, what better place to say them?

"Because I said I wasn't going to take such big risks again?"

"No, darlin', because you are you, and I'd never change a thing about you. If you want to take risks, I'll just suck it up and learn to hold my breath for eight seconds. If you aren't going to ride again, I'll thank God for that every day. But I wouldn't change you because it's everything you are that made me fall in love with you."

Tears welled up in Adele's eyes. "That may be the most romantic thing I've ever heard."

"It's the simple truth, darlin'," he drawled.

"There's the turn to the cemetery, Remy." Jett pointed. "Mama, you do remember how to get to that big tree where we sat in our lawn chairs, don't you?"

"Turn right when you go through the gates and you'll see a huge pecan tree. That's where the graves are," Adele said, wanting to talk more about what he'd said as opposed to visit the cemetery.

Jett had already crawled up to the second seats when the van came to a stop. She pushed a button, and the wide door slowly opened. She jumped out and went straight toward Pansy's grave, where she dropped to her knees, pulled a small gardening spade from her back pocket, and started digging a hole.

The three other kids gathered around her.

"What are you doing?" Bella asked.

"Something that needs done so I can stop thinking about Dahlia dying," Jett said.

"Is she okay?" Remy asked as he slipped an arm around Adele's waist and helped her from the van.

Adele stopped walking when she reached the shade. "Just stay back here and let her do what she needs to do."

"Pansy, I only have one thing to share with you today that was your sister's. It's this paper napkin that she wrote her name and phone number on for me, but I want you to have it. It's kind of like giving you flowers because your sister has died. I know that you are already aware of it and that you are probably having your first good talk in a long time." Jett laid the paper napkin she'd brought in the shallow hole she'd dug. "I'm jealous because I can talk to her, but she can't talk back to me, and you get to have it both ways. But I know you're both happy because Dahlia told me so in her letter. So you take this napkin, and I'll keep my memory of when we came here to clean up your grave."

Adele sniffled.

Remy stuck a finger behind his sunglasses and wiped away a tear. "I told you I saw an angel. She's a whole lot like her mother."

"And you need new sunglasses, cowboy. This hot weather is affecting your eyesight," Adele told him.

# Chapter 24

ADELE WANTED TO SAY THE WORDS IN HER HEART, BUT they would not come out of her mouth. Not Sunday evening when they got home, or when they were in the heated moments of really hot sex later that night.

The next four days went by in such a blur of activity— getting ready for the party, doing normal ranch chores, and trying to analyze just when she had fallen in love with Remy—that looking back that Thursday evening, she wondered where they'd gone and if she'd really lived through them or dreamed them.

Dusk settled around them as they sat on the porch the last day of June. The kids were all stretched out over the living room floor. Bella and Nick were playing a game of Chinese checkers. Jett was reading a book, and Leo was lying on the sofa listening to music through his earbuds.

Adele tucked a red curl behind her ear and started petting Boss, who laid on the steps beside her on the left. Remy sat beside her on the right, one hand massaging her neck and the other on her knee. Jerry Lee had taken up his evening post beside the wind chime and was crowing his delight about the setting sun.

It wasn't so different from any of the other evenings in the week until every hair on Boss's back stuck straight up and he growled down deep in his throat. About that time, a raccoon peeked around the end of the porch. Boss took off like a blast and scared Jerry Lee, who flew toward the ground to land on the raccoon. The poor old thing didn't even know what hit him, what with a bird on his back and a dog rolling him in the dirt like a soccer ball.

Adele bent over at the waist, her nose practically touching her knee, in laughter. It echoed over the ranch and circled back around, so infectious that Remy was soon laughing, too.

The coon finally got enough traction that he tore away and hid in a nearby mesquite thicket. Jerry Lee went back to preening and singing to his wind chime, and Boss took off after the coon, pawing at the brush in vain.

Adele swiped the back of her hand across her eyes. "I love this ranch. I love these crazy animals, even Jerry Lee, almost as much as I love you, Remington Luckadeau."

Remy stopped laughing and everything went silent. Not even the crickets chirped, and Jerry Lee was even stiller than the chimes.

"What did you say?" he asked.

"I said I love you, cowboy. I've tried to say it all week, but the words wouldn't come out of my mouth because I'm more afraid to say them than I was when you got on that bronc last Sunday. I'm terrified, Remy. We're up to one of those bridges you talk about and I'm ready to cross it with you, but it doesn't stop me from being afraid."

Remy pulled her to a standing position in the yard, right below the steps. Then he dropped down on one knee, her hand still in his. "I think I loved you the first time I laid eyes on you, even if you are a redhead and

I was determined not to like you at all. But it took my mind a while to catch up with my heart. But it has, and I'm scared, too, Adele. I've never been in love before, but believe me, darlin', if love is what this is, I don't ever want it to end. Will you forget about a partnership and marry me?"

"I think marriage is a major partnership. Are you sure about this, Remy?"

"Very sure. We can be engaged for a year or ten years or ten days, but I want to know that at some point, we're going to be together forever. And besides, if you marry me, we can have that room we've been warming up, and the kids can all have their own rooms."

She dropped down on her knees in front of him, took her hand from his, and cupped his face in her hands. "This is the craziest thing I've ever done, but yes, I will marry you. How about on July Fourth? Both of our families will be here, and they're bringing food, and we'll have fireworks. We could surprise them all and get married in the morning and have a whole day for the reception."

He leaned forward at the same time she did, and they sealed the engagement with a long, hot kiss. They'd barely broken away when the sound of a truck coming down the lane made them both turn their heads in that direction.

"That looks like Walter's truck. If he's changed his mind, I'll shoot him, and you get the shovels," Adele said.

"We don't need to call a committee meeting for me to agree to that," Remy said as he stood and pulled her up beside him.

Walter got out of the truck. "Hey, y'all! Guess what

we did on the cruise?" He went around to help a gray-haired lady out of the passenger's side. "We done went and got married! Me and Vivien thought we wanted to get married, but we wanted to see if we could live together first. A cruise seemed like a perfect way to do it. And we've decided to buy an RV and travel around the whole United States for a year. We're hoping to find a retirement place as we travel. I ain't got the time to hear about the ranch or play a game of poker; my lawyers have the papers drawn up for one of you to sign tomorrow morning. So are you ready to draw straws? Vivien has them in her hand right now."

The gray-haired lady held out evenly matched straws. "Luck of the draw gets to buy this place."

Remy drew Adele close to his side. "This gorgeous redhead just now agreed to marry me, Walter. We'll both be at the lawyer's office tomorrow morning to sign the papers, and we're getting married on July Fourth. You and Miz Vivien are invited. But we'd like to keep it a surprise until that day, so don't tell anyone."

Walter whipped off his hat and slapped his thigh with it. "I knew you two was made for each other the minute I sat down with you at the table. I just knew it. Congratulations. Me and Vivien will be right honored to come around on the holiday. Hell, we might even have our RV by then and shove off from here on our retirement adventure. Well, ain't no use in goin' inside, and I don't have to watch either one of you whoop the other one or cuss a blue streak 'cause you didn't get the ranch. Me and Vivien is going to town to celebrate."

"See you tomorrow then. What time? And do you want money orders or checks?" Remy asked.

"I don't care which one you bring along with you. I've trusted you kids with my ranch, so I trust you to be good on your checks," Walter said.

He drove away in a cloud of dust, and Remy turned Adele around to face him, tipping her chin ever so slightly for another kiss. "I really do love you. We're going to make a wonderful life and an awesome family."

"I love you, Remy," she said simply.

"Think we should go tell the kids or surprise them on the Fourth?"

"We should tell them and swear them, especially your angel Jett, to secrecy. But not right now. For the next five minutes, I want you to hold me right here on our ranch—not mine, not yours, but ours."

"Yes, ma'am," he murmured softly into her ear.

---

*July Fourth*

The house was full of women talking about babies, cooking, running a ranch, and keeping their men happy.

The yard was full of kids—some on blankets, playing games, some running around trees, playing tag.

The porch was full of men talking about cattle, hay, and the weather, with a smidgen of politics thrown in for good measure.

Adele disappeared up the stairs to her bedroom and dressed in a blue-and-white-gingham sundress. She pulled her hair out of the ponytail and let the soft curls fall to her shoulders, drawing one side back behind her ear with a pearl clip that her grandmother gave her for her sixteen birthday. Digging around on the floor of her closet, she found her white cowboy boots with the heart cutout stitched in blue on the front and jammed her feet down into them.

She met Remy on the landing as he came out of his room. He'd dressed in a snowy-white pearl-snap shirt and a pair of tight, black Wranglers, and his boots were polished so well that she could see her reflection in them.

"Well, cowboy, are we ready to do this?" she asked.

"My God, but you are a stunning bride. I've been on pins and needles that you'd change your mind. Yes, darlin', I'm very much ready to do this." He took her hand in his and they walked out onto the porch.

He picked up a microphone, turned it on, and tapped it against the porch post. Women poured out of the house. Nick, Leo, Bella, and Jett came running up to the end of porch beside the wind chimes, where they stood beside a man with a Bible in his hands.

"Hey, everyone, we have a big Fourth of July surprise for you. No, we're not setting off fireworks right now, kids." He chuckled. "Miz Adele O'Donnell has agreed to marry me, and we're about to have the ceremony right now. So if y'all will gather 'round, it won't take long, and then I'm told that dinner will be served out under the shade trees."

"Oh. My. Lord!" Cassie gasped and grabbed Adele in a hug.

"Not yet, Sister. Wait until the ceremony is over, or you'll ruin my makeup. But you can catch the bouquet when I throw it!"

Remy handed the preacher the microphone, and he started the traditional ceremony. "Dearly beloved, we are gathered here..."

Adele looked right into Remy's eyes and said, "I love you, Remington Luckadeau. I want you to know that."

The preacher stopped in the middle of his sentence.

"I promise to love you forever. And let's both live to be at least a hundred years old because it will take that long to use up all the love in my heart today."

"I think our love is like a good, deep well that never runs dry. If we live to be the oldest people on earth, we'll still have another bucket of love to take care of us."

"Well." The preacher chuckled. "I think we've just heard the vows, and now it's time for the wedding rings." He held them up between his thumb and forefinger. "I understand that when Miz Adele was asked what size diamond she wanted, she said all she wanted was a gold band. This circle is a symbol of never-ending love and respect, and the gold signifies something precious. So if you will put them on each other's fingers to seal this marriage, I will bless them."

Every head bowed as he prayed.

Every hand clapped when he pronounced them man and wife and told Remy he could kiss the bride.

He bent her backward in true Hollywood fashion and laid a kiss on her that would do any cowboy proud. When he lifted her back upright, he turned to the family.

"I am the luckiest man on the face of this earth."

"And I'm in love with the luckiest," Adele said when she could catch her breath, "and the sexiest cowboy on the face of the earth."

He swept her off her feet and carried her off the porch and to the tables that had been set up for dinner, sat down in a chair with her in his lap, and whispered just for her ears, "I bought a new bed for our room. It was delivered this morning, and it's set up, waiting for us."

"How did you manage that?" she asked.

"I've got lots of secrets up my sleeves, Mrs. Luckadeau," he said. "But to answer your question, I did tell one person about the marriage today, and that was my mama. She and Daddy are taking all four kids down to Dallas tonight to some place called Great Wolf Lodge. They're going to check in to the hotel there and let them play all day tomorrow and then bring them home on Wednesday, on their way back to Goodnight. Mama is so tickled to have granddaughters that she wants to spend all the time she can with them. Do we need to talk about this, or is it okay?"

Adele brought Remy's lips to hers for another kiss. "I think that is a great idea, darlin'."

"When we're old, I'll tell our grandchildren this old cowboy's love story about the luck of a draw that never actually had to happen."

"Yes, we will," she said as she kissed him one more time.

Dear Readers,

A few years ago, three Luckadeau cousins appeared in my virtual world, hats in their hands, scuffed-up boots on their feet, with stories to tell. I told their stories in the Lucky series and loved every moment I got to spend with them.

A couple of years later, the O'Donnells came to visit and brought two friends with them. The Spikes & Spurs series started out to be a trilogy, but then one more story had to be told, and one more story after that, until it became a seven-book series.

After that, another group of cowboys appeared with stories to tell, but the O'Donnells still had three cowboys who really wanted their stories told, so what could I do? They showed up in Burnt Boot, Texas, right in the middle of a family feud between the Gallaghers and the Brennans, and we had so much fun all those months that they lived in my head.

I thought when that four-book series was finished that I'd told all the O'Donnell stories that there were to tell. Not so! Adele O'Donnell let me know that she had a story, and it involved a Luckadeau. That made me sit up and take notice. Then, when Remington Luckadeau started telling me his side of what happened when they both wanted the same ranch—well, there was nothing to do but tell the story.

Today, I give you the love story of a cowboy who was a playboy all his life until he met a feisty, red-haired O'Donnell woman who wasn't a bit impressed with his player skills. I truly hope you enjoy the blending of these two families.

As always, I want to thank Sourcebooks for taking me in and letting me tell those first three Luckadeau stories, and then working with me through four more cowboy series. Thanks to all the behind-the-scenes folks, with special thanks to Dawn for the amazing covers.

I have the best fans in the world. They came up with names for the animals in this book. So thank you to Judi Jensen for naming the old cow dog, Boss. She is my cousin, and my uncle Coy, her father, had a wonderful old turkey dog (he operated a huge turkey ranch in Northern California) named Boss. So thank you for the name and the memories! Thank you to my wonderful friend and fan Marge, for naming the cat for me. I loved the idea of naming her Blanche after one of the *Golden Girls* characters. Thank you to my amazing supporter and friend Kim Cornwell, for naming the rooster who never crowed in the morning but only at night. Jerry Lee thinks he should only perform after the sun goes down.

Also, I want to thank Kathleen O'Donnell (yes, that's really her name) for following my blog, *A Little Sweet Tea and Sass with Carolyn Brown*, and winning the right to name a secondary character in a contest. Cassandra Grace is Adele's younger sister in this story, and Kathleen named her without even knowing just how sassy Miss Cassie could be.

And as always, a big thank-you to my husband, Mr. B. It takes a special person to live with an author, and he does a wonderful job of it.

Happy reading,
Carolyn Brown

# About the Author

Carolyn Brown is a *New York Times* and *USA Today* bestselling author with more than eighty books published and credits her eclectic family for her humor and writing ideas. Her books include the cowboy trilogy *Lucky in Love*, *One Lucky Cowboy*, and *Getting Lucky*; the Honky Tonk series *I Love This Bar*, *Hell Yeah*, *Honky Tonk Christmas*, and *My Give a Damn's Busted*; and her bestselling Spikes & Spurs series *Love Drunk Cowboy*, *Red's Hot Cowboy*, *Darn Good Cowboy Christmas*, *One Hot Cowboy Wedding*, *Mistletoe Cowboy*, and *Just a Cowboy and His Baby*. She was born in Texas but grew up in southern Oklahoma, where she and her husband, Charles, a retired English teacher, make their home. They have three grown children and enough grandchildren to keep them young.

# Can't get enough cowboys?

© David Wagner

## *Neither can we.*

Read on to see what's being rounded up by
Sourcebooks Casablanca!

# RECKLESS
## *in* TEXAS

# Chapter 1

IT WAS LABOR DAY WEEKEND AND THE NIGHT WAS tailor-made for rodeo. Overhead the sky had darkened to blue velvet, and underfoot the West Texas dirt was groomed to perfection. Music pounded and the wooden bleachers were jammed with every live body within fifty miles, plus a decent number of tourists who'd been lured off the bleak stretch of Highway 20 between Odessa and El Paso by the promise of cold beer, hot barbecue, and a chance to get Western.

Violet Jacobs maneuvered her horse, Cadillac, into position, mirroring her cousin on the opposite end of the bucking chutes. She and Cole both wore the Jacobs Livestock pickup rider uniform—a royal blue shirt to match stiff, padded royal-blue-and-white chaps to protect against the banging around and occasional kick that came with the job. Tension prickled through Violet's muscles as they waited for the next cowboy to nod his head.

She and Cole were supposed to be emergency backup during the bull riding, charging in only if the bullfighters—the so-called cowboy lifesavers—failed to get the rider and themselves out of danger. Trouble was, the odds of failure got higher every day. For a bullfighter, speed was key, and if Red got any slower they'd have to set out stakes to tell if he was moving. He'd worn out his last legs two weeks back. What he had left was held together with athletic tape, titanium braces, and sheer stubbornness. At some point, it wasn't going to be enough.

Violet's gaze swung to the younger of the pair of bullfighters. Hank vibrated like a bowstring as the bull rider took his wrap and used his free hand to pound his fist shut around the flat-braided rope. The kid was quicksilver to Red's molasses, as green as Red was wily. If he would just listen, work with Red instead of trying to do it all…

The gate swung wide and the bull blasted out with long, lunging jumps. Red lumbered after him like the Tin Man with rusty hinges. The bull dropped its head and swapped ends, blowing the rider's feet back, flipping the cowboy straight off over his horns. He landed in a pile right under the bull's nose. Hank jumped in from the right, Red from the left, and the two of them got tangled up. When Red stumbled, the Brahma caught his shoulder with one blunt horn and tossed him in the air like he weighed nothing.

Cole already had his rope up and swinging. Violet was three strides behind. The instant Red hit the ground, the bull was on top of him, grinding him into the dirt. When Hank scrambled to his partner's rescue, the bull slung its head and caught the kid under the chin with his other horn, laying him out straight as a poker.

Cole's loop sailed through the air, whipped around the bull's horns, and came tight. He took two quick wraps around the saddle horn with the tail of the rope and spurred his horse, Dozer, into a bounding lope. The big sorrel jerked the bull around and away before it could inflict any more damage. Violet rode in behind shouting, "Hyah! Hyah!" and slapping the bull's hip with her rope. He caught sight of the catch pen gate and stopped fighting to trot out of the arena toward feed and water. Violet wheeled Cadillac around, heart in her throat as she counted bodies. The breath rushed out of her lungs when she saw everyone was mostly upright.

The bull rider leaned over Hank, a hand on his shoulder as a medic knelt in the dirt next to him, attempting to stanch the blood dripping from his chin. A second medic supervised while two cowboys hoisted Red to his feet. He tried a ginger, limping step. Then another. By the third, Violet knew it would take a lot more than a can of oil and a roll of duct tape to fix the Tin Man this time.

---

The Jacobs family gathered in the rodeo office after the show for an emergency staff meeting. The five of them filled the room—her father, Steve, was six-and-a-half feet of stereotypical Texas cowboy in a silver belly hat that matched his hair, and Cole, a younger, darker model cast from the same mold. Even Violet stood five ten in her socks, and none of them were what you'd call a beanpole. It was just as well she'd never set her heart on being the delicate, willowy type. She wasn't bred for it. Her five-year-old son, Beni, had tucked himself into the corner with his video game. Her mother, Iris, was a Shetland pony in a herd of Clydesdales, but could bring them all to heel with a few well-chosen words in that certain tone of voice.

Now she shook her head, *tsking* sadly. "Did y'all see that knee? Looks like five pounds of walnuts stuffed into a two-pound bag."

"He won't be back this year," Violet said.

Her dad *hmphed*, but no one argued. Even if Red wanted to try, they couldn't put him back out there for the three weeks that were left of the season. It wasn't safe for Red or for the cowboys he was supposed to protect. It was sad to lose one of the old campaigners, but he'd had a good, long run—clear back to the days when the guys who fought bulls were called rodeo clowns, wore face paint and baggy Wranglers, and were expected to tell jokes and put on comedy acts. Nowadays, bullfighters were all about the serious business of saving cowboys' necks. Leave the costumes and the stand-up comedy to the modern day clowns, pure entertainers who steered well clear of the bulls.

"Saves us havin' to tell Red it's time to hang up the cleats," Cole said, blunt as always. "Who we gonna get to replace him?"

Steve sighed, pulling off his hat to run a hand through his flattened hair. "Violet can make some calls. Maybe Donny can finish out the year."

Oh, come *on*. Donny was even older than Red, if slightly better preserved. Violet opened her mouth to argue, but her mother cut her off.

"It'll have to wait until morning." Iris began stacking paperwork and filing it in plastic boxes. "Y'all go get your stock put up. We've got a date for drinks with the committee president."

And Violet had a date with her smartphone. Fate and Red's bad knees had handed her an opportunity to breathe fresh life into Jacobs Livestock. She just had to persuade the rest of the family to go along.

———

Once the stock was settled for the night, Violet herded Beni to their trailer and got them both showered and into pajamas. She tucked him into his bunk with a stuffed penguin under one arm—a souvenir from a trip to the Calgary Zoo with his dad earlier in the summer.

"Can I call Daddy?" he asked.

She kissed his downy-soft forehead. Lord, he was a beautiful child—not that she could take any credit. The jet-black hair and tawny skin, eyes as dark as bittersweet chocolate…that was all his daddy. "Not tonight, bub. The time is two hours different in Washington, so he's not done riding yet."

"Oh. Yeah." Beni heaved a sigh that was equal parts yawn. "He's still coming home next week, right?"

"He'll meet us at the rodeo on Sunday."

He'd promised, and while Violet wouldn't recommend getting knocked up on a one-night stand, at least she'd had the sense to get drunk and stupid with a really good man. He would not let his son down, especially after he'd been on the road for almost a month in the Pacific Northwest at a run of rich fall rodeos. The rodeos that mattered.

She heaved a sigh of her own. Of course her rodeos mattered—to the small towns, the local folks, they were a chance to hoot and holler and shake off their troubles for a night. The contestants might be mostly weekend cowboys with jobs that kept them close to home, but they left just as big a piece of their heart in the arena as any of the top-level pros. Still, the yearning spiraled through Violet like barbed wire, coiling around her heart and digging in. It cut deep, that yearning. Nights like this were worst of all, in the quiet after the rodeo, when there was nothing left to do but think. Imagine.

At legendary rodeos like Ellensburg, Puyallup, and Lewiston, the best cowboys in North America were going head to head, world championships on the line. Meanwhile, Violet had successfully wrapped up the forty-third annual Puckett County Homesteader Days. Jacobs Livestock had been part of twenty-nine of them. If her dad had his way, they'd continue until the rodeo arena crumbled into the powder-dry West Texas dirt, her mother and Cole trailing contentedly along behind.

How could Violet be the only one who wanted more?

"Night, Mommy." Beni rolled over, tucked the penguin under his chin, and was instantly asleep.

Violet tugged the blanket up to his shoulders, then pulled shut the curtain that separated his bunk from the rest of the trailer. Finally time for dinner. She slicked her dark hair behind her ears, the damp ends brushing her shoulders as she built a sandwich of sliced ham on one of her mother's fat homemade rolls, a dollop of coleslaw on the plate alongside it. Before settling in at the table, she turned the radio on low. The singer's throaty twang vibrated clear down to her heartstrings, reminding her that the only man in her life had yet to hit kindergarten, but it muted the *tick-tick-tick* of another rodeo season winding down with Violet in the exact same place.

She prodded her coleslaw with a fork, brooding. Red had been operating on pure guts for weeks, so she'd made a point of researching every card-carrying professional bullfighter in their price range. Was her prime candidate still available? She opened the Internet browser on her phone and clicked a link to a Facebook page. *Shorty Edwards. Gunnison, Colorado.* His status hadn't changed since the last time she checked. *Good news! Doc says I can get back to work. Any of you out there needing a bullfighter for fall rodeos, give me a call.*

Shorty was exactly what they needed. Young enough to be the bullfighter of their future, but experienced enough to knock Hank into line. Good luck persuading her dad to bring in a complete stranger, though—and not even a Texan, Lord save her. She might as well suggest they hire the devil himself. Violet drummed agitated fingers on the table, staring at Shorty's action photo. Jacobs Livestock needed new blood, an infusion of energy. Fans and committees loved a good bullfighter.

Her dad *had* said she should make some calls. As business manager for Jacobs Livestock, she would write up the contract and sign the paycheck, so why not get a jump on the process? She could discuss it with her parents before making a commitment.

Her heart commenced a low bass beat that echoed in her ears as she dialed his number. He answered. Her voice squeaked when she introduced herself, and she had to clear her throat before explaining their situation.

"Three rodeos?" he asked. "Guaranteed?"

"Uh…yeah."

"And you can give me a firm commitment right now?"

"I…uh…"

"I've got an offer in Nevada for one rodeo. If you can give me three, I'll come to Texas, but I promised them an answer by morning."

Violet's mouth was so dry her lips stuck to her teeth.

She'd never hired anyone without her dad's approval. But it wasn't permanent. Just three rodeos. Sort of like a test-drive. If Shorty turned out to be a lemon, they could just send him back.

"Well?"

"Three rodeos, guaranteed," she blurted.

"Great. Sign me up."

She ironed out the details then hung up the phone, folded her arms on the table, and buried her face in them. When the first wave of panic subsided, she sat up, pressing her palms on the table when her head spun. *Chill, Violet.* She was twenty-eight years old and her dad was always saying the best way to get more responsibility was to show she could handle it. They had a problem. She'd solved it. Once the rest of them saw Shorty in action, they'd have to admit she'd made the right choice.

*Because you have such an excellent track record when it comes to picking men...*

Violet slapped that demon back into its hidey-hole. This was different. This was business. She was good at business. As long as Shorty Edwards was exactly as advertised, she was golden.

# Chapter 2

THE LAST BRAHMA TO BUCK AT THE PUYALLUP, Washington, rodeo was a huge red brindle named Cyberbully. Three jumps out of the chute he launched his rider into the clear blue sky. The cowboy thumped into the dirt like a hundred-and-forty-pound sack of mud and stayed there, motionless, while the bull whipped around, looking to add injury to insult.

Joe Cassidy stepped between them and tapped Cyberbully's fat nose. "Hey, Cy. This way."

The bull took the bait. Joe hauled ass, circling away from the fallen cowboy with the Brahma a scant inch behind. The big son of a bitch was fast. Caught out in the middle of the arena, Joe couldn't outrun him, so he opted to let Cy give him a boost. With a slight hesitation and a perfectly timed hop, he momentarily took a seat between the bull's stubby horns. Startled, Cy threw up his head and Joe pushed off. As he was thrown free, he saw a flash of neon yellow—his partner sprinting in from the opposite direction. "C'mere, Cy, you ugly bastard!"

The bull hesitated, then went after Wyatt. Joe landed on his feet and spun around to see Wyatt vault up and onto the fence next to the exit gate with a stride to spare. The bull feinted at him, then trotted out.

"Ladies and gentlemen, give a hand to our bullfighters, Joe Cassidy and Wyatt Darrington!" the rodeo announcer shouted. "That's why these two are the best team in professional rodeo."

The air vibrated, fans whistling and stomping their appreciation as Joe jogged over to check on the cowboy, who had rolled into a seated position.

"You okay, Rowdy?" Joe asked, extending a hand to help him up.

"Yep. Thanks, guys." Rowdy swiped at the dirt on his chaps and strolled to the chutes, unscathed and unfazed.

Wyatt folded his arms, glaring. "We should let the bulls have the ones that are too dumb to get up and run."

Joe snorted. That'd be the day. Wyatt was hard-wired to save the world—even the parts that didn't want saving.

"That wraps up our rodeo for this year, folks!" the announcer declared. "If you have a hankering for more top-of-the-line professional rodeo action, come on out to Pendleton, Oregon, next week for the world-famous Roundup…"

One more rodeo, then six weeks off. Seven days from now, after Pendleton, he was headed home. Fall was Joe's favorite time of year in the high desert of eastern Oregon, weaning this year's crop of colts and calves under the clear, crisp sky.

He twisted around, checking the spot where the bull had tagged his ribs. Not even a flesh wound thanks to his Kevlar vest, but the big bastard had ripped a hole in his long-sleeved jersey. "Damn. That's the third one this month."

Wyatt took off his cowboy hat and wiped sweat from his forehead with a shirtsleeve. "You're gettin' old and slow, pardner."

"Five years less old and slow than you."

"Yeah, but I take better care of myself."

"Says the guy with five shiny new screws in his ankle." Joe nodded toward Wyatt's right leg, supported by a rigid plastic Aircast. "How's it feel?"

"Like they drove the bottom two screws in with a hammer." Wyatt rotated the ankle, wincing. "Still works, though, so they must've got 'em in good and tight."

Joe rubbed the sting from the elbow Cyberbully had smacked with the top of his rock-hard skull. He ached from head to toe with the cumulative fatigue of six straight days of rodeo piled on top of all the other weeks and months of bruises and bodily insults. "What the hell is wrong with us?" he asked.

Wyatt started for the gate. "I'm in it for the women and free booze. Let's go make that stupid shit Rowdy buy us a beer."

"Just remember, you're driving," Joe said, yawning.

Wyatt sent him a sympathetic glance. "Long night, huh?"

"Yeah." Tension crawled up his back at the memory. Goddamn Lyle Browning. Someone should've castrated the bastard by now. His wife had plenty of reasons to cry, but why did she insist on using Joe's shoulder?

Wyatt shook his head. "I shouldn't have left you alone at the bar. You were already upset before the weepy woman."

"I wasn't upset." The tension slithered higher, toward the base of Joe's skull.

"Bullshit. Your old man lives fifteen miles from here and couldn't show up to watch you in action. That sucks."

"I'm thirty years old, not ten. It's not like he skipped

a little league game." But he'd missed plenty. Most of Joe's high school sports career, in fact.

But that was ancient history. Joe tipped off his cowboy hat, peeled the ruined jersey over his head, then balled it up and gave it a mighty heave. It landed three rows up, in the outstretched arms of a little girl in a pink cowboy hat, who squealed her excitement. Joe smiled and waved and kept moving. He wanted to be gone. Far, far away from Puyallup and any expectations he hadn't been able to stomp to death.

"I haven't seen Lyle's wife around today," Wyatt said.

"Probably still hugging the toilet."

Or maybe she'd finally smartened up and left. 'Bout time. Lyle Browning was a sniveling dog, dragging along on the coattails of his dad's successful rodeo company. They'd grown up in the same small town and Joe had started working summers on the Browning Ranch when he was fifteen, but he and Lyle had never been friends. Early on, Joe had had some sympathy. Had to suck for Lyle, his mom dying when he was so young, and his dad not exactly the nurturing type. At some point, though, a guy had to take responsibility for his own life.

As they stepped into the narrow alley behind the bucking chutes, a hand clamped on Joe's shoulder. "Hey, asshole. I need to talk to you."

The words were slurred, the voice a permanent whine. Joe turned and found himself face-to-face with the last person he wanted to see. He brushed off the hand. "Whaddaya want, Lyle?"

Lyle Browning tried to get in Joe's face, but came up short by a good six inches. Even at that distance, his breath was toxic. "You prick. How long you been sneaking around with my wife?"

"Don't be stupid."

Lyle rolled onto his toes, swaying. He smelled like he'd passed out in the bottom of a beer garden dumpster. Looked like it, too. "Everybody saw you leave the bar together, you son of a bitch, and she told me what happened when you got back to her room."

The *hell* she did. But Joe could think of a dozen reasons Lyle's wife would want her husband to think she'd gone out and gotten a piece. At the very least, it'd sure teach him to screw around every chance he got. Lyle had mastered the art of trading on his daddy's name with the sleaziest of the buckle bunnies who hung around looking for a cowboy-shaped notch for their bedpost. Too bad for them, they got Lyle instead.

"See?" Lyle crowed. "You can't deny it."

Joe ground his teeth. Hell. He couldn't. Not without humiliating her all over again in front of the gathering crowd. "You're drunk. Crawl back into your hole and sleep it off. We'll talk later."

"We'll talk now!"

Joe put a hand on Lyle's chest, making enough space to take a breath without gagging. "Back off, Lyle."

"Don't push me, asshole!" Lyle reared back and took a wild swing.

His right fist plowed into Joe's stomach. Even if Lyle wasn't a weenie-armed drunk, it would've bounced off Joe's Kevlar vest. His left fist grazed Joe's chin, though, and that was too damn much. Joe popped him square in the mouth. Lyle squealed, arms flailing, then toppled straight over backward, his skull smacking the hard-packed dirt. He jerked a couple of times before his eyes rolled back and the lights went out.

Joe barely had time to think *oh shit* before Dick Browning's voice sliced through the crowd. "What the hell is going on here?"

A whole section of the onlookers peeled away to clear a path. Dick crouched over his son and gave him a not-very-gentle tap on the cheek. "Lyle! You okay?"

Lyle moaned, his head lolling off to one side. Dick jumped up and spun around to face Joe. Where Lyle was scrawny, Dick was wiry, tough as a rawhide whip. He was only a hairbreadth taller than his son, but somehow, when Dick decided to get in your face, he made it work.

Joe took a step back and put up his hands. "He took a swing at me."

"What did you expect? You mess with a man's wife—"

Like Lyle was any kind of man, but Joe didn't dare say so. Sweat beaded on his forehead, part heat, part panic, as his gaze bounced off Dick's and around the curious crowd. This was not the time or place to set Dick straight. "Can we talk about this later, in private?"

"You disrespect my family, assault my son—there is no later," Dick snapped. "Consider yourself unemployed. And don't bother showing up at Pendleton, either."

Joe flinched, the words a verbal slap. "That's crazy. You know I wouldn't—"

"Then why would she say so?"

Joe opened his mouth, then clamped it shut. God*damn*it.

Wyatt yanked him backward and slid into the space between Joe and Dick, smooth as butter. "If that piece of shit you call a son could keep his dick in his pants, his wife wouldn't be out at the bar drinking herself into a coma."

"This is none of your business."

"If it's Joe's business, it's mine. We call that friendship—not that you'd know." Wyatt leaned in, got his eyes down on Dick's level. "Don't give me an excuse, Herod, or I'll lay you out in the dirt with your spawn."

Joe grabbed him, afraid Wyatt might actually punch the old man. "You can't—"

Wyatt yanked his arm out of Joe's grasp. "It'd be worth the bail money."

For a long, tense moment they remained locked eye to eye. Then Lyle groaned, rolled over, and puked. Dick jerked around, cursing. "Somebody give me a hand getting him over to my trailer."

Out of reflex, Joe took a step. Wyatt jabbed an elbow into his sternum. "Don't even *think* about it."

He hauled Joe away, around the back of the grandstand, over to the sports medicine trailer that also served as their locker room.

"Who is Herod?" Joe asked, unable to process the rest of the scene.

"The most evil tyrant in the Bible, but only because Matthew never met Dick Browning." Wyatt yanked open the door to the trailer and dragged Joe up the steps.

Matthew. Herod. Christ. "Who says that shit?"

"I'm a preacher's kid," Wyatt said. "I get my gospel up when I'm pissed."

Preacher. Hah. Try *Lord High Bishop of Something or Other*. Wyatt's family learned their gospel at Yale Divinity. He read big fat history books for the fun of it. For two guys who had nothing in common, Joe and

Wyatt had been a dream team from the first time they worked in the same arena, and hell on wheels outside those arenas. The mileage added up, though, and a thirty-year-old body didn't bounce back from hangovers the same way it used to. Joe sure didn't miss them, or waking up next to woman whose name was lost in his alcohol-numbed brain.

As they stepped into the trailer, one of the athletic trainers grabbed a gauze pad and slapped it on a split in Joe's knuckle. "You're dripping. Wipe it off, then I'll see if you need stitches."

Wyatt leaned against the counter and folded his arms. "What he needs is a rabies vaccination."

The trainer's head whipped around in alarm. "It's a dog bite?"

"No," Joe said.

"Close enough," Wyatt said. "He cut it on Lyle Browning's face."

The trainer smirked. "So, more like a rat. Better dissect Lyle's brain to see if he's rabid."

"Good luck finding one," Wyatt said. "But I volunteer to knock him over the head. And his little daddy, too."

"Not very Christian for a choir boy," Joe muttered.

Wyatt's grin was all teeth. "One of a long list of reasons the Big Guy and I are no longer on speaking terms."

Fifteen minutes later, the last of the cowboys had cleared out of the trailer and the trainers had gone to have a beer, leaving Joe and Wyatt stretched out on the padded treatment tables. Stripped down to a pair of black soccer shorts with his blond hair slicked back and a bottle of water dangling from long, manicured fingers,

Wyatt looked exactly like what he was—the product of generations-deep East Coast money. When asked how he'd ended up fighting bulls, he liked to say it was the best legal way to be sure his family never spoke to him again. The reporters thought he was joking.

Joe's knuckle was bandaged, but his whole hand throbbed in time with the pounding in his head. His initial shock had morphed into fury, churning like hot, black tar in his gut. He punched the pillow with his uninjured fist. "I *should* skip Pendleton. It'd serve Dick right."

"Don't be an idiot," Wyatt said. "Just because you're his chore boy on the ranch between rodeos doesn't mean Dick has shit to say about when and where you fight bulls."

Joe scowled, but couldn't argue. The mega-rodeos they worked were too much for any one stock contractor to handle. Cheyenne lasted two weeks. Denver had sixteen performances. Rodeos that big hired a main contractor to gather up at least a dozen others, each bringing only their best bulls and horses. The rodeo committee also hired the bullfighters. Down in the bush leagues, you worked for the contractor. At the elite level, they were freelancers. Joe and Wyatt were the most sought-after bullfighters in the country, stars in their own right, which meant they could pick and choose from the most prestigious rodeos.

It irritated Wyatt to no end that Joe chose to stick mostly to the rodeos where Dick Browning had been hired to provide bucking stock, and continued to work on Dick's ranch for what was chump change compared to his bullfighter pay. Wyatt blamed misplaced loyalty.

And yeah, Dick had given him his start, but Joe had paid that debt a long time ago. The ties that bound him were buried deep in the hills and valleys of the High Lonesome Ranch. He loved that land like nothing else except the stock that ran on it.

How could Wyatt understand? He wasn't a cowboy.

He cocked his head, his gaze sharpening. "You're really pissed."

"Wouldn't you be?" Joe shot back.

"Hell yeah, but I would've throat-punched both of them ten years ago. This isn't the first time Dick has blown up in your face. It isn't even the first time he fired you."

"I deserved it most of those other times." When Joe was a showboating twenty-year-old with more guts than common sense. The anger boiled up again. "I'm not a brain-dead kid anymore."

"So tell him to go screw himself."

Joe shook his head and Wyatt hissed in frustration. "Geezus, Joe. What's it going to take?"

Joe couldn't imagine. The High Lonesome had been the center of his world for too long. Solid ground when his home life was anything but. Dick's great-grandfather had veered south off the Oregon Trail to homestead there. He had given the ranch its name because the rugged miles of sagebrush desert were high in altitude, lonesome in the extreme, and spectacular in a wild, almost savage way that possessed a man's soul. Joe could cut off a limb easier than he could walk away.

"You were right before." Wyatt adjusted the ice pack on his ankle, then reached for his phone. "If Dick wants to shoot off his mouth, slander you in front of half of pro rodeo, you should call his bluff. Let him explain to the committee in Pendleton why you're not there."

Joe bolted upright. "I can't leave the Roundup short a bullfighter."

"You won't." Wyatt's fingers danced over his touch screen before he lifted it to his ear, holding up a palm for silence when Joe tried to speak. "Hey, Shorty! This is Wyatt. I heard you're looking to pick up a rodeo or two before the season ends. How does Pendleton sound?"

Joe opened his mouth, but Wyatt shushed him again.

"Yes, really. Would I joke about something that big?" A pause, then Wyatt grinned. "Oh yeah. I forgot. That was a good one. But I paid you back for the airfare, and I'm serious this time. Joe wants out. You want in?" Another pause, and a frown. "Where, and how much?" Wyatt listened, then grimaced. He covered the phone with his hand and said to Joe, "Shorty Edwards can come to Pendleton in your place, on one condition."

"What condition?" By which Joe meant to say, *Are you crazy?*

"How do you feel about Texas?" Wyatt asked. When Joe only gaped at him, he shrugged and said into the phone. "Guess that means yes. See you in Pendleton, Shorty."

He hung up and tossed the phone aside.

Joe stared at him, horrified. "You did not just do that."

"Bet your ass I did." Suddenly every line of Wyatt's body was as sharply etched as the ice in his blue eyes. "I will do whatever it takes to pry you away from that son of a bitch."

"Dick's not that bad." But there was no conviction in Joe's voice. He was tired and hurting and every time he replayed Dick's words, heard the contempt in his voice, his chest burned with humiliation and fury. How could he stroll into Pendleton and pretend it was all good?

"If you stay, you'll end up just like him—a shriveled up, rancid piece of coyote bait."

Joe stared at the ceiling, sick of arguing. Sick of it all. Silence reigned for a few moments. Then Wyatt sighed, and the pity in his voice cut deeper than Dick's lashing tongue.

"Have some pride, Joe. Go to Texas. Get a little perspective." Wyatt flashed a knife-edged smile. "At least give humanity a chance before you sign over your soul to the devil."

# Can you handle the heroes of Kari Lynn Dell's Texas Rodeo?

## *Reckless in Texas*

Rough and tumble, cocky and charming, Joe Cassidy's everything a rodeo superstar should be...and he's way out of Violet's league.

## *Tangled in Texas*

It took thirty-two seconds to end Delon's rodeo career, but when his path crosses with his all-too-perfect ex, Tori Patterson, it'll only take one to change his life.

## *Tougher in Texas*

With rodeo season kicking into high gear, Cole needs a hand, so he's relieved when his cousin offers to send a capable cowboy. Cole expects a grizzled Texas good ol' boy. He gets Shawnee Pickett.

# HOW TO WRANGLE
# A COWBOY

Fall in love with the Cowboys of Decker
Ranch from RITA finalist Joanne Kennedy.

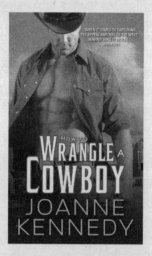

Ranch foreman Shane Lockhart fears his livelihood—and
his young son's security—are threatened when the ranch
is taken over by the late owner's granddaughter, the most
beautiful, exasperating woman Shane has ever met…

*"Kennedy's characters are sexy, smart, flawed—
real. If you are a fan of Western romances, Joanne
Kennedy should be at the top of your list."*

**—Fresh Fiction for *How to Kiss a Cowboy***

For more Joanne Kennedy, visit:
**www.sourcebooks.com**

# *BLAZING HOT TEXAS COWBOY*

Kim Redford reels you in with this Smokin'
Hot firefighting cowboy whose rekindled
love ignites flames of passion.

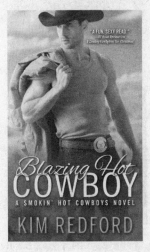

Lauren Sheridan's return to Wildcat Bluff after the death
of her husband is bittersweet. Thirteen years have passed
since she set foot in the place that holds her heart...and the
sizzling memories of her high school sweetheart.

Kent Duval last saw Lauren when she was sweet sixteen and
they were head over heels in love. Now she's back, spunky
daughter in tow. As the heat between them builds, Kent
can't help but wonder if past flames can be rekindled and
second chances really do exist.

For more Kim Redford, visit:

**www.sourcebooks.com**

# Carolyn Brown proves even love is bigger in Burnt Boot, Texas

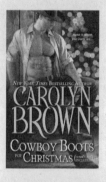

## Cowboy Boots for Christmas

Welcome to Burnt Boot, Texas; you won't want to leave! Spend the holidays feasting, frolicking, and feuding with the Brennans and the Gallaghers as Finn O'Donnell and Callie Brewster just try to find a little peace and quiet...

## The Trouble with Texas Cowboys

Can a girl ever have too many cowboys? Jill Cleary wonders when she finds herself being fought over by a Brennan and a Gallagher—and it's dark-eyed Sawyer O'Donnell who makes her blood boil.

### One Texas Cowboy Too Many

Leah Brennan has always been the good girl of her clan—until a tattooed, ponytailed bad boy saunters into her life in the form of Rhett O'Donnell.

### A Cowboy Christmas Miracle

It will take a miracle bigger than the state of Texas for these two feuding families to survive the holidays, especially when Declan Brennan falls hard for Betsy Gallagher!

# Dare to fall in love with Nicole Helm's Big Sky Cowboys

### Rebel Cowboy

Welcome to Big Sky Montana where you'll find a struggling ranch, a woman determined to save her family no matter the cost, and the NHL-star-turned-cowboy who makes it all possible.

### Outlaw Cowboy

Caleb Shaw's sworn to walk the straight and narrow, but when Delia comes to him for help outrunning the law, this cowboy will find just how easy it is to go from *hero* to *outlaw*.

### True-Blue Cowboy Christmas

Summer Shaw has never felt like she's belonged, but when she meets a widower cowboy and his young daughter over a snowy Montana Christmas, she realizes she may have finally found her way home.